A
SMALL
FIRE

GLADYS SCHMITT

A
SMALL
FIRE

DIAL PRESS   1957   **NEW YORK**

DESIGNED BY WILLIAM R. MEINHARDT

PRINTED IN THE UNITED STATES OF AMERICA

BY THE HADDON CRAFTSMEN, SCRANTON, PENNA.

For

Simon

"A small fire sufficeth for life."

SIR THOMAS BROWNE

A
SMALL
FIRE

Chapter 1

It TOOK A long time for me to build up any excitement about the new professor of piano. I had missed the stormy faculty meeting in spring when they hired him. I was sitting in a funeral parlor at the time, trying to get to the body of my grief through the smell of florists' flowers; I was coping with my little black hat, which everybody who tried to kiss me knocked halfway off my head; and I did not know and would not have cared that he refused with a maddeningly cool arrogance to play for the faculty, managing to get it across that his reputation and his recordings ought to be enough to qualify him for a place in a department like ours—the most undistinguished division of what he considered a second-rate College of Fine Arts. And later, in the wan, washed state that comes upon a person after a loss, I felt only the mildest interest in the stories that went the rounds of the faculty dining room. I knew, but I scarcely cared, that he had asked for vodka and tonic when the Dean was serving martinis; that he had spent most of the evening talking nuclear physics to Dr. Grüenberg, who was at the party only because he happened to be married to Emily Grüenberg, the 'cello teacher; and that he made no secret of his allergic reactions to the beautiful centerpiece of roses.

3

I was not prepared to give him my undivided attention either on that evening in September when Genevieve Willis came up to me outside the Music Building to offer the latest particulars. I almost never leave the building as late as half past six, and the lights were coming on all over the empty campus and I wanted to stand there at the top of the long flight of stone steps, I wanted to watch the lights come on alone. The round, frosted globes of those lights seemed in the clear twilight to be floating like a crowd of detached moons among the upper branches of the ginkgoes and the maples. It was as if the trappings of a carnival had been strung up over the summer-dried lawns for the students who would be arriving tomorrow and day after tomorrow. I had seen seven classes come like that to learn and fail to learn and search for friends and grope after love under these same lights and trees, and I wanted to feel the flow of continuity —I suppose it was a womanly want: I was thirty-six and I have no children of my own.

Anyway, I was standing on the steps in a kind of daze when Genevieve Willis, the harmony teacher, came back from an early dinner to force rigorous order upon her office. She was full of Mr. Sanes, she had eaten across from Mr. Sanes in the faculty dining room, and she was afraid the new professor was going to be even more difficult than everybody had anticipated. Exactly how he had made himself difficult during their dinner conversation, I didn't gather: Jenny Willis talks so much and so fast and in such a strident voice that I consider my Christian duty done if I listen to a third of what she says. But out of the welter of her talk I drew at least a vague image of him, which I placed not in the steamy dining room but out there among the thinned branches and the floating moons: a tall man of about forty, dark, a little stooped, with cropped hair. One thing I do remember: she said he was wearing a heathertone jacket, and from that day to this I have watched for that jacket in vain. No jacket I have ever seen on him could by the furthest stretch of the

4

color-sense be identified with heather; and I have often wondered whether he had such a jacket and did away with it in contempt—as he did away with so many other things— or whether the jacket was invented by Jenny Willis to give a circumstantial note to an otherwise confused description.

I was glad that she had had her dinner. I did not want to eat mine with her, that much was certain—for years I had been spending as little time with her as I decently could. It was not her compulsive talking alone that made me stay clear of her: she was ten years older than I, and, whenever I was depressed or tired, I took the very sight of her as a kind of threat of what I myself might some day be. Not that she was a typical teaching spinster. There was a certain dash about her—in her trim dark dresses and her harlequin spectacles and the straight dark bangs that covered half her forehead, masking the two long furrows there. Her presence would have been acceptable enough if she had not marred it by her manner—she meant to be forthright and gay, and all she succeeded in being was presumptuous and prurient. Her mouth was loose and looked the more so because the rest of her face was immobile, with fixed, peering eyes. She had an unusually striking pair of legs, and the students, by way of taking vengeance for the strictness of her discipline, used to stare at them and talk about them; and she herself never sat down without stretching them out in their sheer orange-tinted stockings, either for her own pleasure or for general approbation. Though she never gave a person a direct or giving look, she always insisted on being looked straight in the face whenever she was talking, and she broke off suddenly when she saw that I was staring over her shoulder, and said, somewhat sulkily, "I thought you'd be interested."

"Naturally I'm interested. It looks as if he were going to be pretty impossible."

"Impossible is too good a word for him. Now that I look back on it, I doubt he would have bothered to recognize me, though I'm sure he knew who I was—after all, he was

5

sitting right across the table from me at the Dean's that night. I asked him whether he'd found an apartment, and he said in his superior way, No, he hadn't, he couldn't understand how the people around here managed to live in those little boxes. Simply to be helpful, I suggested that maybe he ought to look at one of the older buildings like the one where the Colvins and the Gardiners live, and do you know what he said? He said he'd seen that place, and it struck him as bourgeois and depressing. Two of our associate professors have been living there for years—and he thinks it's bourgeois and depressing!"

"Maybe he was afraid it would be noisy. Most of the people there do have a lot of children—"

"It isn't quiet he's interested in—it's a fancy address, you can take it from me. He said he wasn't particular about being close to the school; he'd just as soon live in one of those new buildings downtown. Maybe he can afford a place like that—I wouldn't be surprised to hear he's making eight or ten thousand a year."

"I doubt it, Jenny. They stretched a point if they gave him seven. I'm an associate professor, and I'm not making anything like that myself."

"You can't put yourself in a class with Mr. Sanes. He's somebody very special. In a school like this, all you have to do is be a man and make a few recordings for some little fly-by-night company, and you can name your own price."

Her voice had shattered the magic. The lights were mere electric lights, and the buildings that bordered the burnt lawn—the Drama Building, the Architecture Building, and the Hall of Painting and Design—were black Victorian hulks against the washed-out west. It was cool, too, and I began to think about my sweaters: If it turned any cooler, I could put on my new sweaters tonight. They were a dull dark brown, exactly like my hair, dark enough to make my skin look pale, and bulky enough to show that I am still slight. I saw myself on the way to some high occa-

6

sion, dressed in them and a copper-colored skirt; though what high occasion could be in the offing for me, I did not know.

"I can see I'm holding you up. You probably have an appointment."

I had no appointment, and I disliked being reminded of that fact. There is always a time at the beginning of the term when the phone is silent and the September pages of the appointment book are bare and some primitive, self-destructive part of the mind keeps insinuating, against all reason, that nobody will get in touch, keeps invoking the white and faceless specter of total isolation. "I haven't got any appointment, but I haven't eaten dinner, and I've got to go home and straighten up my place," I said.

"I suppose it's going to be very lonely for you over there."

As yet it had not been lonely. Emily Grüenberg, the 'cello teacher—she would certainly get in touch—had come in with me after the funeral and helped me to lay all wounding things to rest in cartons and mothproof bags. I had spent the whole summer in Wisconsin, coaching at an Opera Workshop; and the clutter of my return lay over the barrenness: my dresses and underthings were on *her* bed, my books and my briefcase were piled up on the bare top of her dresser. "I haven't had time to be really lonely yet, but I'll be lonely later, I know."

In the embarrassing pause that came after that, I thought how Jenny Willis must also be wondering whether the telephone was ever going to ring. I did not want to think of her facing protracted solitude; if I allowed myself to imagine, even for a moment, the hard eyes going blurred and the loose mouth going tremulous, I would lose the firmness that was my only defense against her constant attacks on my time and my serenity.

"Well, go along about your business, Frieda. All I wanted to tell you is: he's impossible. I'm sorry for you. I wouldn't want to have an office next door to *him* for anything in the world."

I had quite forgotten about that closeness, and I pondered it as I walked across the campus. The big room that he would teach in, the one room with the really good Steinway in it, had belonged to Dr. Laurent, now savoring his retirement in Bordeaux. All Dr. Laurent's students had played with a kind of rigid precision, as if they were so many metronomes; it usually took a student of his a couple of years after graduation to relax and play like a human being again. But in every other respect, he had been an urbane and amiable old man, eager to tell stories about Debussy and Ravel and Fauré to anybody who wandered in between one lesson and another, and able to identify a fair number of the pigeons that came and sat on his windowsill—he and I had been feeding those pigeons for years on sunflower seeds out of a little hemp bag that he kept in his desk. One thing looked certain: I would not be feeding any pigeons on the windowsill with Mr. Sanes.

Chapter 2

MINE WAS A big old apartment house, not bourgeois but probably depressing. There were many things in its favor: large rooms, a reasonable rent, solid construction to keep out the heat, buckeye trees at the front windows, and a certain uninvolved friendliness on the part of the neighbors. All this considered, I did not follow my friends' advice: I did not move out to detach myself from the memories or to save myself the trouble of looking after an extra room.

Anyway, it amuses me to hear people talk about the business of additional work. My mother had been a partial paralytic for the last seven years, and I had been taking care of her, and my current problem was to find enough to do with myself. It is not that I am fussy or have more energy than most; it is only that to sit with folded hands, to accept the sitting position as the normal one, is something that long habit has made impossible for me. During the first week of mourning after my mother's death, when other people were doing everything for me, I was wild with frustration, I felt that gratefulness was keeping me tied to a chair; and, since I had to do something, I did further violence to my already deteriorated singing voice by smoking a couple of packs of cigarettes a day.

9

I had been back in town only since yesterday morning, but the kitchen, the bath, the little foyer, and the living room had already undergone my scrupulous and obsessive kind of cleaning. The faded green damask sofa and the antique chest had been cleared of their clutter; and the bunch of rhododendron leaves—I had bought them for the brass jar on the cherry wood coffee table this afternoon to relieve the emptiness—only emphasized the orderly barrenness and the flaws. One arm of the sofa was dented in; for seven years I had been sleeping on that sofa, and my head, pressing through the pillow into the upholstery of the arm, had hollowed out a place. Tonight, provided I could bring myself to put the bedroom to rights, I would sleep in the bed that had always been my mother's bed.

I had left the bedroom in a deplorable mess since the morning of my arrival. I knew that if I walked into it I would scarcely be able to see the bedspread for my opened suitcases and the clothes that had come out of them; my books, my briefcase, my music and papers were lying over the rose-colored marble top of the dresser; and my old coat and my two new sweaters were draped over the armchair. Since the confusion was on my conscience and since I had every reason to feel rested and ready to start in—I had sat for twenty minutes in the restaurant over a glass of brandy and a couple of cigarettes—I wondered why I did not walk into the bedroom and why, when I had turned on the lights in every other part of the apartment, I should have chosen to leave that particular room in the dark. I went to the front of the sitting room and looked across the piano at the buckeye trees in the light of the street lamp, their upper leaves yellow and translucent and riddled by the summer ravages of the caterpillars. I wondered whether I could be superstitiously afraid of my dead, and I deliberately called up an image of my mother's face. I saw that face, not as it had been against the puckered white satin of the coffin and not as it had been after the final stroke, but as I had seen it through

10

most of the time when she was forced to depend on me—peaked and lively, drawn up a little on the right side, twisted into a merry strangeness, as if her first bout with death had left her with a knowing and convivial look. No, certainly I was not afraid.

Well, then, could it be that I was reproaching myself with something? Hardly anybody remembers a still unsodded grave without some measure of guilt, some portion of regret. There were things that I had left—and not left willingly—in order to come back to look after my mother: there was my thriving class of private pupils in New York; there were the occasional but gratifying invitations to sing the soprano solo parts in choral works; there was what my friends used to call my "connection with Lewis," which—even marred as it was by difficulties and equivocations—still kept me crucially involved. I sat down on the cracked leather ottoman and tried to conjure up the characteristic savor of those days before I was called back home, and it was strange what things I could remember: not my own living room crowded with semi-notables, but a small lighted Christmas tree on somebody else's fire escape; not the time when my voice came out solitary and satisfactory in "Have Mercy on Me, Lord" in the *St. Matthew Passion*, but myself in the mirror before I stepped onto the stage in my black gown and my round white starched collar; not the strong embrace of reconciliation after any of our quarrels, but the fact that Lewis had once broken the crystal of his wristwatch by swinging it against my big turquoise bracelet. It is unhealthy, I suppose, to search consciously after the savor of a life. If we cannot find the savor, what we encounter in search of it is automatically rubbish. My existence back there looked to me like an empty metropolitan street in the first hours of a bright March morning—newspapers and crumpled cigarette packages and empty candy wrappers stirred by an erratic wind and exposed for what they are in the pitiless cleanness of a rising sun.

No, if I had felt cheated of that life in the first months, or even in the first year or two, the feeling had passed off a long time ago. My income from the college was less than what I used to get from my private pupils in New York, but it was secure and there was a pension attached to it. If I had once taken satisfaction in the purity with which I sang certain arias, I was old enough now to mock myself a little about the purity of my voice—and my intentions: my voice had been too light for richness, and I had fancied myself in the white collar and the black gown; and anyway, my voice had deteriorated and would have deteriorated just as quickly in New York. As for Lewis, it had taken only five or six return visits to show me that mere absence was an insurmountable handicap—somebody succeeded me almost as thoroughly as I had succeeded his wife, though he was as unwilling to lose me as he had been to divorce my predecessor. There are certain men—and Lewis was one of them—who are painfully aware of the thinness of the present and therefore stand in need of a many-stranded, contrapuntal past.

It was not self-reproach over any living resentment, then, that kept me from crossing the threshold and turning on the lights in there. Minor derelictions I had been guilty of in my dealings with my mother: there were the times, maybe as many as two out of every week, when I had gone out and left her to a dull and solitary evening after a dull and solitary day; there had been occasions when the click of my heels coming in answer to a request of hers had been so brisk that it must have implied more anger than readiness; probably I had often indicated in a look—through I had never put it into words—that I wished I could read a book or listen to a record in uninterrupted and unthreatened peace. But my mother had never suggested that she wanted self-obliterating devotion. She had told me to go out oftener than I had gone; she had omitted those long apologies and excessive thanks that accuse the giver of unwillingness; and

12

she had always smiled at me with so much candor when I pulled up her comfort and turned out her lamp that I could not think she begrudged me my little allowance of solitude.

Pull up the comfort, turn out the lamp . . . These and a hundred other things I would not be doing anymore. I would not be bringing our ten o'clock pot of tea into the bedroom. I would not be washing her nightgowns or her housecoat. I would not be carrying the damp washcloth in from the bathroom so that she could freshen up before she went to sleep . . . I knew than that it was not superstitious fear or self-recrimination that kept me sitting on the ottoman in the not-to-be-interrupted stillness. It was something that she would have been grateful for, something I wished she could know about: it was sheer simple regret over losing the kind of life that the two of us had made in this place. A limited life, of course—riddled like those leaves out there in the light of the street lamp, dried and marred and with the imminence of the end scrawled all over it—yet it had been the only life, the only real involvement I had known for several years. And the realization that it was over was bleak and appalling. With that realization before me, I knew I could not sit the evening out by myself—I would have to get in touch with somebody, anybody, on the telephone.

The person I wanted to call was Emily Grüenberg. But, stupid as it may seem, I am always hesitant about calling up at the house of a married couple in the middle of the evening. There may be voices talking and laughing in the background, and the hostess may feel ashamed that there should be a party to which the caller has not been invited, though it is natural enough that married people should want to get together and talk about their children and their furniture and their marketing without the unmarried standing critically by. Still, after I have phoned myself into such a situation, I am embarrassed and haven't much to say, and after I hang up I feel more than ever alone.

So, since I felt a little too raw to risk a call to Emily, I

13

thought of having some students in, though any last-minute student party was bound to be small: most of the ones who lived in town would already be busy for the evening, and a good half of the out-of-town people wouldn't yet have come in. Of my own crowd, the ones that studied voice with me, the only person who was careful never to turn me down was my bellowing baritone, Frederick Wade; but he considered it his duty as a male to paw every woman he talked to, without consideration for her age, her station, her appearance, or her inclination, and tonight I did not feel quite up to his clichés and his masculinity. So it seemed best for me to round up a few of the instrumentalists, and Cathie Dugan, the star senior pianist, was the first one I called.

She is a strange one, Cathie Dugan, though I have always liked her. If you happen to see her coming across the campus at a distance, you think of her as free and boyish: she walks with a stride, and her yellow-brown hair is so thick and curly that she has to keep it clipped—old Dr. Laurent used to say that her hair seemed to be fitting on her head like a cap made out of Russian broadtail. But if you see her at close range as I have often seen her when she plays accompaniments for my vocal students, you know that the impression of freedom is actually an illusion. Her eyes, which are a fine greenish blue, get blank and pained if they have to sustain a look; her nose is narrow and aristocratic, but it quivers at the end like the nose of an unhappy animal; and, though her mouth is soft and generous in repose, it gets a stretched, dry look whenever she smiles. There is tension in her hands too—more tension than her old teacher's discipline can justly be blamed for. Cathie Dugan makes herself touch people, and, when she does it, only her palms accept the contact. Her fingers shoot up and away, her fingers are always curled back like the fingers of a Geisha girl.

She was at home, and her mother, who answered the phone, said she would be so glad to hear from me—which

14

she was. "Oh, Miss Hartmann, how nice, what a good way to start the year!" she said.

"I'm here by myself, and I thought maybe you'd like to come over."

"I'd love to. I could get dressed in a minute. Tell me, how did it go in Wisconsin?"

"I guess it went pretty well—they want me to come again next summer."

"I knew they would. Only, I'd rather they didn't—I mean, I'd rather you'd stay in town. It was lonely here all summer without you. There must have been ten times when I was dying to come over and talk to you."

"I missed you, too, Cathie." It wasn't a fabrication. There are certain students who, for no particular reason, attain a kind of permanence in recollection. I had thought of Cathie Dugan several times in Wisconsin. I had wanted to see her, not with anything that could be described as yearning, but as we sometimes feel a mild wish to buy a potted primrose or have a cup of Chinese tea.

"Are you well, Miss Hartmann? How's your—"

There was a long pause. The poor little thing had been on the point of asking "How's your mother?" She had completely forgotten, and now she was cataclysmically remembering, that my mother was dead. I could not help her, and she came out of it better than I would have expected: she changed the question to "How's your laryngitis?" and I did what I could to make it easy for her to finish off the call. But she kept on talking with a persistence that puzzled me, considering how soon we would be in the same room. There was something on her mind, and it suddenly occurred to me that she might want me to ask Vincent Booth to come too. Last spring they had been friendly or a little more than friendly, though both of them were so reserved that their status with each other had not been mentioned, was only something to conjecture about.

15

"I thought I might ask a couple of others. Would you like to bring Vincent?"

There was another pause, even longer and more uneasy than the one that had sidetracked our conversation onto my minor afflictions. "I don't know whether you'd better ask him," she said.

"Are you two having a squabble or something, Cathie?"

"No, not exactly. In a way, I suppose we are. To tell the truth, Miss Hartmann, I haven't seen Vincent, he hasn't called me since day before yesterday, and *I'm* not calling him. . . ."

"Anything serious?"

"I don't suppose you'd call it terribly serious. The fact is, it was about Mr. Sanes."

The air of contention that clung around that gentleman was recurrent and marked enough to make me curious. "How could you quarrel about him?" I asked, advancing a good deal further than I usually did—at least without a direct invitation—toward the private business of a student. "You havn't even had a lesson with him. What would there be to squabble about?"

"That record of his—you know, the one with the Brahms intermezzi and capriccios. You've heard it, haven't you, Miss Hartmann?"

"No, Cathie, I haven't." I had seen it in the hands of Dr. Boyd and Jenny Willis and other members of the faculty last spring, when a pitched battle was going on over the merits of the performance, though, out of consideration for my troubles, nobody had insisted that I listen to it, nobody had tried to drag me in.

"Well, you ought to. I've got it, and I'd love to bring it over and play it for you and see what you think. Would you let me bring it over tonight?"

"Certainly, if you'd like to." I was a little pained that she should want to fill up the evening with anybody's music, even the music of a prospective teacher whom she was

16

plainly excited about. I had wanted talk: music—especially recorded music played on my limited little player—could not break the hard arc of loneliness that seemed to be bending over me tonight.

"Good, then, I'll bring it. And I tell you something else, Miss Hartmann: now that I think of it, it would be a good idea if you would call Vincent and ask him to come."

I found myself unwilling to oblige her, even though I always enjoyed his company. I was no more in a mood for supervising a lovers' spat than I was for listening to records; and I was certain from the charged, hard tone of her voice that she meant to quarrel with him in front of me. Yet, now that she had exposed herself—and at some cost—to make a direct request, what could I tell her? "All right, that's easy. I'd like to see him. I always like to see him," I said.

My telephone conversation with Vincent consisted mostly of my asking him direct questions and his saying "Oh!" and "Yes" and "Yes, thank you" and "Yes, indeed!" He is a white rabbit of a boy, and there is something startled and apologetic about the way he talks, though what he conveys is not self-mistrust but acute sensibility. He is small—it was my impression that he must be about an inch shorter than Cathie Dugan. He is delicately made, with a small, meditative, pale face and with two childish bumps on his forehead, one of them usually hidden by a thatch of straight light-brown hair. I have heard Dr. Boyd, the conductor of the college orchestra, admit that Vincent Booth plays better violin than the current concertmeister; but he invariably adds that Vincent is too ineffectual to inherit the first desk, that he lacks the necessary authority. Myself, I don't know that I would agree: I like his playing and I always find it pleasant to watch him. When he stands up to play, for all his smallness and paleness, he has a certain sturdiness.

Now that I had lined up some sort of evening for myself, it was possible for me to go into the dark bedroom and turn on the milky Victorian dresser lamps that I had bought

17

for her and she had loved. It had been futile for me to try to bury my loss under such a mound of confusion. I closed my suitcases, I hung up my coat and my dresses in the barren cupboard, I pulled the crumpled bedspread straight and let the bed be honestly and nakedly an empty bed. And when I had taken away my music from the dresser, I found that I could contemplate with tenderness the one trace of her that had not been folded or scoured away—the ring in the rose-colored marble where her perfume bottle had always stood.

I went into the kitchen then and broke up some canned tuna and chopped up some ripe olives for a salad; I got a package of those half-baked rolls out of the refrigerator—they taste less synthetic if you let them warm up to room temperature before you put them in the oven; and I measured the coffee into the coffee pot, half again as much as I would have used to suit my own taste. The students like their coffee black and thick and poisonous, probably because they don't really care at all for coffee, but take it as a kind of sophisticated ritual, and the harsher it is the more they are convinced they are living a life of urgency and desperation. With all that done, I went back into the bedroom and changed into my new sweaters, which were as kind to me as I had expected. Since I still had ten or fifteen minutes to wait, I sat down in the corner of the sofa with *The Sane Society,* going at it as if it were the family washing; and I managed to finish off twelve pages before the buzzer told me that one or the other of the students was waiting downstairs.

Chapter 3

ANYBODY WHO HAS taught for more than a couple of years knows that there is seldom anything to be gotten out of a social evening with students. Friendship—the free exchange between equals—is the last thing they would want from any member of the faculty, and outside the classroom the teacher is forced to resign himself to serving one of the only two purposes that they can conceive for him: either he must be a quaveringly responsive audience before whom they can put on a performance of their current concept of themselves or a monumental authority massive enough to relieve them, at least for a little while, of their own insecurity.

With this alternative in mind, it would be better to take one's students one at a time, or to assign one evening to the histrionic ones and another evening to the deferential ones. The histrionic class calls for sensibility and volatility—the shrill and ready laugh, the epigram so brief that it will not hamper the flow of the performance, the appreciative nod and the understanding sigh. The deferential class, on the other hand, calls for detachment and steadiness of purpose —patient circling around a subject before settling upon it, sentences carefully planned to elicit an answer, and unruffled ease and relaxation when no answer is forthcoming at all.

19

The histrionic and the deferential can be combined if each of the two groups is large enough, but when the teacher finds herself—as I found myself that evening with Cathie and Vincent—fixed immovably between one histrionic character and one deferential one, she is in an insoluble dilemma. Whatever she offers to one is bound to be unacceptable to the other, and—the claims being equal—she is likely to grow dull and stupid under the certainty that she is defeated from the start.

On that particular evening Cathie Dugan was performing with a heady zest. She had settled herself in the proper place for a protagonist: she sat in the corner of the sofa under the standing lamp, with the circle of white light coming straight down on her newly washed, yellow-brown, Russian broadtail hair. She had dressed herself for the part in new fall clothes, and she was acutely and nervously aware of them; not only did she solicit our praise for the dark green corduroy skirt and the matching monkey-jacket as soon as she walked in, but she also kept calling our attention to them by plucking and stroking the cloth for the better part of the evening. She wanted a sprightly, intimate responsiveness from me that Vincent's expression made it impossible for me to give; she touched me whenever she had a point to make and sometimes when she hadn't—she touched my forearm and my knee and my shoulder with the palm of her Geisha girl hand. And, although she was making something of a strident nuisance of herself as she kept looking at the record—she had laid it in an obvious spot on top of the antique chest in the expectation that Vincent would say something about it, which he wouldn't—it was hard to be exasperated with her because she was so plainly suffering from her own tension. Her voice, reeling off a whole summer's supply of anecdotes, was without conviction, and her face, on the few occasions when she stopped trying, looked harassed and tired.

Vincent was passive, but his passivity was tinged with

disapproval. His face had taken on the stubborn look that is characteristic of gentle people who are unwilling to endure and unable to protest. He had nothing to add to the conversation but monosyllabic answers to direct questions, and he did not share the sofa with us but sat instead in comparative shadow, straining his eyes and puckering his pale eyebrows over old copies of *The Musical Quarterly*. I could not tell whether his annoyance sprang from their recent squabble or from the performance his friend was putting on in front of me. He had brought a bottle of Tokay for the evening, and whenever our glasses were empty he came over and filled them, wiping the bottoms of them meticulously with a paper napkin before he set them down on my cherry-wood table top. There was something mournful in this careful, systematic, joyless dispensing of his gift. I felt that the party was not worthy of what he had brought to grace it, and I was sure that of the two of them he was the one who was suffering more from my sluggishness and insufficiency.

Sluggish I was—so sluggish that I did not even want to bestir myself to put on the coffee and get out the buns and the salad. The inability to find any suitable pattern of behavior had made me miserably self-conscious. I sat in a rigid position, aware of an intensifying stiffness at the nape of my neck, and twice I caught myself looking at my watch and thinking that it had stopped: every fifteen minutes seemed like the better part of an hour.

I had given up any attempt to direct the party. If I had any aim in the course of that evening, it was a negative one: I did not want to listen to Mr. Sanes' recording, and I did not want to be called on to make a definitive statement on the flaws or merits thereof. The affair of the record, merely annoying at first, had begun to look downright dangerous to me as my weariness increased. Mr. Sanes' performance was plainly a charged issue between Vincent and Cathie, and anything I might say about it would very likely be repeated to my colleagues. So, whenever Cathie turned her pointed little chin toward the record on top of the chest, I started to talk about something else; and this strategem, crude and inane as it was, had served me very well until half past ten, when I tried to divert her by asking her whether she'd seen anything of Frederick Wade.

"Oh, no, he's been immersed in Civic Light Opera—positively immersed all summer long," she said, describing an arabesque in the air, though whether it was intended to represent Fred Wade's immersion or her own loathing for Civic Light Opera I did not know. "Have *you* heard from him, Miss Hartmann? Well, I can tell you, that's only because he doesn't know you're back. He's mad for you—he'll be certain to call you the minute he hears."

Fred Wade's devotion—or what Cathie took for such—was nothing to stir me out of my torpor. Another long, disquieting silence—there had been half a dozen of them this evening—settled down on the three of us. I said for lack of anything else to say that I had better be thinking about what Fred would sing for his graduation recital; and that, too, was a dreary thought: whatever I would care to concentrate on for months with him was sure to be something I could not bear to hear him vulgarize. "Do either of you have any ideas?" I said. "Not German lieder—we'll have to have some, of course, but I guess we'd better keep them down to a minimum."

Vincent closed *The Musical Quarterly* to indicate that he was eager to give any problem of mine his undivided attention. "How about some opera arias?" he asked in his tentative, quiet voice. "Not Mozart—I don't think he has the finesse for that—but some of the Italian things might stand up pretty well."

"That's not a bad idea, except that they never sound very good without orchestra," I said. "It's a thankless job for the pianist, too, playing arrangements. What do you think, Cathie? Would you mind playing a little Verdi for a change?"

22

Her eyes, meeting mine, suddenly took on the pained and shifting look. "Well, I don't know, Miss Hartmann, you see, I've been thinking over the whole business of playing accompaniments—I've been thinking about it a lot this summer, and to tell the truth—to be perfectly frank, I mean—I guess I'm not going to play any accompaniments at all this year."

Her manner had implied that my feelings were going to be hurt, and they were, though they would probably not have been if she had not expected them to be. I gave her a synthetic smile, and the fact that I was at loss for an answer made it necessary for her to go on.

"It isn't that I don't enjoy playing accompaniments for your students—I've always loved it, and I'm sure it's been very good discipline for me. It's just that I've only got one year left, and I want to concentrate—I want to get everything I can in this one year out of Mr. Sanes."

"Well, *that* shouldn't be too terribly hard for you to do," said Vincent. It was the first thing he had said with any conviction during the entire evening, and it was utterly unlike him. He was appalled at his own utterance, that much was certain: he sat stiffly, still leaning forward and staring down in a deprecatory way at his hands, which were clutching the folds of grey flannel around his knees.

"That's a hateful thing to say!" There was so much venom in her voice that I knew they had not had a difference and said a cool good-bye; they had parted on a white-hot flash of rage; and they would never have risked coming together in the same room if they had not considered me a better mediator than I could be tonight.

"Oh, let's take it easy," I said, but my spiritless voice betrayed me and implied what I did not intend: that no quarrel between adolescent lovers was anything to be taken to heart.

"It's a serious business, Miss Hartmann," said Cathie. "When a person disparages the teacher who is going to be

23

the most important person in your life, the most important person in your art and your career, then that person is doing you a serious injury." She set her wine glass on the table with a little thud as if to indicate that she would rather not be seen drinking such a person's wine.

"I didn't disparage him. All I said was: he wasn't anything to get so excited about."

"And whom," she said, emphasizing the incorrect objective with an elegant flourish of her hand, "just whom do you think is somebody to get excited about?"

"I don't know—all I can say is: *he* isn't."

He pointed to the record where it lay, and for the first time all three of us were obliged to look at it at once.

"You're not being fair, Vincent. You're just saying things to destroy my confidence, and it isn't fair to do that to anybody, do you think, Miss Hartmann?"

"I couldn't say, Cathie. After all, I don't know exactly what he said."

"Well, I'd like to play that record for somebody who isn't prejudiced, somebody like you who hasn't got her mind made up beforehand."

"Miss Hartmann probably heard it long before you did."

"It just so happens you're wrong about that. She never heard it at all."

"All right, then, let's play it," he said, getting up. "I'm game, I can take it, if it's all right with Miss Hartmann."

I nodded—anything seemed preferable to a continuation of what was going on between them. He went with an expressionless face and with quick, quiet, animal steps— the only sort of walk that can properly be called a tread— and picked up the record from the top of the chest.

"And may I request," said Cathie, "that there won't be any comments before the playing."

"I wasn't going to make any comments. Here, Miss Hartmann, you can have the honor of holding the envelope and reading all about the great man."

But I never got around to reading any of the notes. There was a photograph in the upper lefthand corner of the envelope—the performer at the piano in a white shirt and a somber mood—and one look at it was enough to edge me over onto Vincent's side of the argument. Arthur Sanes was old enough to know better than that—nobody at his age ought to put that kind of dramatic profile into general circulation. No matter how good-looking you are at forty—and he *was* good-looking in a wry, supercilious, sun-dried way—you are a fool if you try to make an astringent twentieth-century version of Byron out of yourself. I suspected that somebody had dabbed his face with oil before training the flash-bulbs on it: there were glistening highlights on the high slope of his forehead and the aquiline curve of his nose and the blunt wedge of his chin. Somebody had probably suggested, too, that he would be at his most effective if he could assume an austere and uncompromising expression: his thin mouth was folded in against itself in a straight and scornful line, and his eyes stared with brooding contempt at the aggressively long and sensitive fingers laid out dark and stiff and totally without conviction on the blinding whiteness of the keys.

"That's exactly what he looks like," said Cathie.

I thought: The more's the pity. If he looked like that, ten chances to one he would play like that. Both of them—she from her circle of light under the lamp and he from his patch of relative shadow near the record player—were watching me, and I could only hope that my face was too torpid to register much of anything. Yet I abandoned my impassivity after the first few bars: I straightened up and laid the envelope face down on the coffee table, wanting to detach the picture from the entirely unexceptionable sounds that were issuing from my little phonograph. Whether he looked like a fraud or not, Mr. Sanes' playing turned out to be the exact opposite of flashy—it was scrupulously correct, completely restrained, and undeniably intelligent.

I had been hoping that I would find something to tell

25

his future student in praise of his performance, and now it seemed to me that there was much that was affirmative to be said. Mr. Sanes respected the composer—I had to admit that I had never heard anybody take fewer liberties with the printed score. He used his pedal very discreetly, and the contrapuntal texture was allowed to come through without blurring; the massive chords were full-bodied without obscuring the melodic lines, and every now and then I found myself hearing inner voices and fragmentary motives that I had never been aware of before. Certain of the intermezzi, like the one in E major, that I had never considered anything more than mood pieces in the past, took on more meaning under this kind of treatment, and, if it had not been for the embarrassment that invariably comes over me when I give myself up to music in other peoples' presence, I would have offered Cathie the assurance of a look or a smile.

But after the break—we were silent and nobody met anybody's glance in the time that it took to turn the record over—after the break I was glad I had waited to commit myself. My enthusiasm, if it deserved so strong a word, seemed to drain away as my surprise decreased. The Brahms intermezzi and capriccios are static enough as it is, and he took them at a draggingly slow tempo without a hint of rubato: I began to wonder whether I wouldn't have found it unbearably monotonous if it hadn't been for the charged atmosphere in which I was listening. Clarity was all very well, but was clarity enough? Didn't these pieces call for something more—a singing tone and soaring climaxes and casual grace? And some of the capriccios, like the one in C major, he played at such a plodding pace that I began to wonder how much he could have in the way of sheer technique. Could he, for instance, even come to grips with such war-horses as the *Appassionata* and the *Waldstein*?

Vincent lifted the lid of the phonograph as the music stopped and the needle drew a muted grinding from the inner grooves. Cathie stretched her long legs and gave me a

26

triumphal look that I could neither respond to nor utterly reject without injustice, and I picked up my glass and drank a little of my wine to sustain me in my unpreparedness. Out of the corner of my eye I could see Vincent, deferential and waiting. I sipped and remained silent until he brought himself to voice the unnecessary question. "Well, Miss Hartmann," he said, thrusting his uneasy hands into his pockets, "what do *you* think?"

"Certainly it's a very *intelligent* performance." The vigor of my statement was somehow compromised by my having waited to be asked and by my strangely complaining tone when I intended merely emphasis. "The approach is unusual—I'll want to hear the record again—but I can honestly say he made me hear certain things I just wasn't conscious of before."

Cathie—when she is keyed up she moves with a jerky and graceless speed—Cathie startled me by reaching across me and snatching up the record envelope. "Here," she said, following the print with the tip of her stretched index finger and making up for any faltering in my voice by the authoritative force of her own, "I know what you mean, and there's something here that gets it across perfectly. 'Mr. Sanes' playing stresses the architectonic aspects of the music—' "

"Oh!" said Vincent softly, looking down and jingling the loose change in his pocket. "The architectonic aspects? At the risk of showing how ignorant I am, I'd like to ask you what that means."

She reddened. "Anybody knows what it means—proportion, form—as in buildings, as in architecture. Isn't that right, Miss Hartmann?" She jerked her monkey jacket into place and gave me one of her forced, unsteady looks.

"Well, I guess it means that he has a great deal of respect for the structural aspects of the music." The word "aspects" is one that I never use, and the realization that I had borrowed it from the back of the envelope was embarrassing to me. "And he *does* have that," I said, bending forward

27

to aim the assertion at Vincent. "I was perfectly sincere when I said I heard things that usually get lost."

"Oh, I'm sure you were," he said, drawn out of the shadow by his need to show me a face innocent of any doubt concerning my sincerity. "And I agree on that—I'll freely admit that he does have that. Only, isn't it pretty easy for a person to have that if he doesn't have anything else?"

"Doesn't have anything else!" The shrillness with which she uttered it startled us both. "Next thing you'll be saying that the man isn't even qualified to be a teacher—"

"Look, now, let's not get into his qualifications as a teacher," I said. "You can't do that, not in my presence, anyway." It was a cowardly thing to resort to, but, matters being as they were, I felt justified. "All of us take it for granted that you students get together in private and tear us to bits. But Mr. Sanes is a colleague of mine, and it just isn't protocol for me to stand by and let you go at him like that."

"No, of course not," said Vincent. "I'm awfully sorry." He sat down on one of the ladder-back chairs on the other side of the bunch of rhododendron leaves and turned his stubborn look on Cathie, who was balancing the record on her knee and staring at the photograph. "All I was trying to say was—"

"Do we have to listen to it over again? I'm sure both of us know exactly what you said."

"And what *I've* been wanting to say—" I could catch a certain spinsterly and pedagogical note in my voice, and I did not like it—"what I've been wanting to say is that there are a lot of things I like about Mr. Sanes' playing. It's clear, it's controlled, it's very scholarly, and it's certainly unaffected."

"But I'm afraid I've got to disagree with you there, Miss Hartmann," he said, looking at me over the greens with a scared earnestness. "Everything he does on that

28

record seems affected to me, though it's not what a person usually thinks of as affectation. It isn't corny or showy or anything like that—it isn't that obvious, and it isn't that innocent. It's hard to put your finger on it, but it's affectation just the same: it's pretending to be more detached and exalted than anybody could really be. I know it's going to sound like a contradiction, but it's the only way I know to get it across: what looks like unaffectedness to you looks to me like a very special and involved kind of affectation."

My glance, withdrawing from Vincent in order to relieve him of unnecessary embarrassment, had lighted again on the contemptuous photograph; and I found myself thinking that if the style of the playing were added to the picture the sum might check off with what had just been said. But such mathematics I knew to be spurious, and I deplored them, even though they were unsettling enough to leave me for the moment with nothing to bring up in Mr. Sanes' defense.

It was Cathie who defended him, and a Cathie that I could not love. She sat on the edge of the sofa with her elbows on her knees and her sharp little chin grinding into her tight little fists; and there was an unbecoming look, a knowing and jeering look, in her greenish eyes. "Naturally you have to disparage his poise and detachment," she said. "Naturally you have to attack his self-possession—since you haven't got any yourself. And how else could you attack it if you didn't call it affectation? It's a very neat trick, but it's only a trick, and if you think it has any effect on me you're making a big mistake. We're very different—let's face it, Vincent. What you hate about Arthur Sanes is exactly what I want, exactly the sort of thing I like and trust. I don't need anybody to get sugary pleasant and play up to me because he's unsure of himself and worried about what I'm going to think. Somebody who knows his own value and doesn't have to give a damn about anybody else—maybe a person like that is hard on your ego, but *I* get

29

a tremendous feeling of confidence out of that kind of authority."

Authority . . . The word had a familiar ring, and I searched my mind, trying in the meantime to keep my eyes from his suddenly flushed and vulnerable face. Authority . . . Surely she couldn't be as cruel as that: surely she couldn't know that Dr. Boyd had doomed this gentle friend of hers to the second desk for all time on the grounds that he had no authority. . . .

"You *are* prejudiced, you know," she said, but she said it without the former antagonism, as though she hoped the statement of a just reason for her anger might carry an implicit apology for the anger itself.

"I'll admit it, I *am* prejudiced." He reached around the greens, picked up the wine bottle, and filled our glasses, leaving the last short measure with the sediment for himself. "I only saw Mr. Sanes once, that time he was here last spring," he said, "but that one time was enough for me."

I waited, thinking it was Cathie's place, not mine, to urge him out of his reticence; but when I looked at her out of the corner of my eye, I knew she was not going to ask him anything: her eyebrows were up and her lips had fallen apart. It was obvious that this was the first news she had heard of any such encounter, and she was a little dashed and not over-eager to hear any more of it.

"Well, aren't you going to tell us what went on?" I said.

"Yes, I suppose so—that is, if you want me to." He leaned forward slightly, not looking at us, his eyes fixed on his knees and his hands closed tight on the arms of his chair. "Both of you know the Bruch Concerto, that thing I was playing at the end of last semester."

We nodded, but he went on to explain that it was full of a soggy kind of feeling—one of the standard things for violinists, yes, but scarcely a genuine work of art. He wanted to point out to us too that, though Mr. Cusick, his violin

30

teacher, had been the first to suggest it, he, Vincent, had raised no objections to the thing, partly because he had wanted to please Mr. Cusick, of whom he was very fond, and partly because it would be a new experience: he had never played "anything drippy and melty like that before."

"Drippy and melty . . ." Protected by the screen of rhododendron leaves and loosened somewhat by his scant share in the bottle of Tokay, he told us how he was going through the first movement of the Bruch—all those passionate thirds and sixths, all those inflated heroics—playing it up there in Mr. Cusick's drab and dusty corner room, in the sultry heat, with the windows open and the smell of dug-up earth and new-cut grass coming in. Something—maybe the dissolving warmth of the May weather or the end-of-the-semester feeling of things drawing to a close—something had betrayed him, had made him powerless before that questionable music: all of a sudden he had found himself immersed in the warm surge and lap of it, had felt as if he had lost himself in it and had enjoyed being lost. And while he was playing he had done something that he didn't usually do, he had kept looking at Mr. Cusick; he and Mr. Cusick had "somehow gotten into a conspiracy of corn together"; he wouldn't say that he had been "egged on or anything like that," yet he might have censored himself, he might have "pulled himself together and cut it out" if it hadn't been for the nod and the smile and the gleam of gratification in Mr. Cusick's kind and faded grey eye. Anyhow, that was the way it had been, he had been playing the first movement of the Bruch like that, he had finished and Mr. Cusick was still in a state that couldn't exactly be described when the door swung open and Dr. Holland and Mr. Sanes walked in.

Now Dr. Holland by himself was bad enough under the circumstances, since he was a dry man and a cool one and the head of the department to boot. He had always thought of Dr. Holland as being distinguished and a bit

31

forbidding, but Holland looked downright human and even a little seedy beside Mr. Sanes. Mr. Sanes, dressed in a way that wasn't at all the usual thing on campus—"a grey sharkskin suit so light it was almost white, and a black linen shirt, and an oyster white tie, and everything perfect from his black Ivy League crew-cut to his charcoal-grey suede shoes" —seemed by his appearance and his erect and supercilious bearing to be asserting his superiority over the old violin teacher in a creased coat and baggy trousers. Before he made the rounds to be introduced to his future colleagues, who had all of them been teaching for four or five hours in the unseasonable heat, "couldn't he have taken off his coat, couldn't he have shown that he was bothered by the weather like anybody else?"

Still, since Dr. Holland had the necessary poise for handling ticklish situations, the whole business would probably have passed off decently enough if Mr. Cusick hadn't tried to make up for a slight or an imaginary slight, hadn't suddenly noticed that his student was standing on the outskirts of the circle, hadn't felt it was his obligation to drag his student in. "So he introduced me, and Mr. Sanes made it very obvious that he didn't exactly care to be introduced to a student, but that didn't throw Mr. Cusick, he didn't notice at all. He went right on, telling him all the things I had played and saying how well he thought I played them. He said too much—to tell the truth, he often says too much. . . ."

I believe I blushed: I could see the little old violinist— marked by his status as an immigrant and an object of administrative benevolence, so timorous, so eager to please that his talk and his manner had become over-ingratiating —I could see the poor old Pole in his creaseless trousers and his limp coat, with his shock of unkempt white hair and his yellowish-white moustache, bowing and gesturing and smiling foolishly into the contemptuous face on the record envelope, going on interminably, too carried away by his need for a sustaining trust in the indulgence of mankind to see the growing scorn and disgust in that face. And, seeing all that, I could not look at Vincent, who had learned much from Matt Cusick, and who, if he could not honor him, still loved him. "Maybe Mr. Cusick didn't even notice. Maybe he thought Mr. Sanes was being perfectly friendly," I said.

"Oh, I'm sure he didn't notice, he kept right on harping on my musical feeling, whatever that is. He kept patting me on the shoulder and saying I had real musical feeling, great musical feeling—he was going on like that when Mr. Sanes broke in. 'Yes, I gathered that,' he said to Mr. Cusick, and then he turned around and talked to me, not looking at me—he's tall, you know, he stared right over the top of my head. 'We were waiting out there in the hall for you to finish,' he said, and his face was like a piece of wood, he never cracked a smile. 'I could hear you were really carried away with yourself.' "

I believed the story, it had the undeniable shape and color of truth. I believed it, and I deplored it: I also was fond of Matt Cusick—fond, too, of this gentle and generally reasonable boy whose one springtime lapse had come through a door to a mocking ear, who had been exposed and commented upon in all his vulnerability. But some obscure obligation—perhaps to my position as a teacher and perhaps to a prejudged and undefended stranger—forced me to fill up the silence left open by a plainly disturbed and stymied Cathie. "But listen," I said, seeking his glance again over the greens, "we've got to look at it from Mr. Sanes' point of view. After all, Mr. Cusick put him in a spot—it's hard to imagine what he could have said in that kind of situation. Maybe it wasn't calculated at all—maybe he just said the first thing that came into his head."

"Oh, it was calculated, I'm sure of that, Miss Hartmann. There isn't a thing about him that isn't calculated—you wait and see."

If I had expected Cathie to take up my line of defense

33

of Mr. Sanes, I was disappointed. She asked Vincent to give her a cigarette, though the pack of mine from which she had been smoking all evening still lay close to her on the coffee table. When he stood up to offer her one, she looked remorsefully and beseechingly into his eyes, and before he sat down again she saw to it that she touched his hand. She was responsible for the fact that our conversation moved for the rest of the evening at a crazy, veering pace; possibly she was searching for ways to get around to some subject which would allow her to express or imply her affection for Vincent. The loyalty that made her feel a need to salve an old wound of his, and to salve it quickly and publicly, was touching to me; but it left us all unmoored and embarrassed—half a dozen things were tried, but nothing got itself said. When I went into the kitchen to take out the salad and put the half-baked rolls into the oven she did not make her usual offer to come and help me; and when I came back into the living room to say that everything, coffee and all, would be ready in a few minutes, I found him still sitting pretty much as he had been sitting, though she had gotten up and come to him—she was standing behind him with her hands on his shoulders and her chin resting on top of his head.

Why that little pantomime of intimacy should have disturbed me, I do not know. It was the mildest, most innocent kind of intimacy, and I have never been able to work up the proper show of concern when Jenny Willis tells me that common decency is being flouted in the corridors because such-and-such a he-student is lying on a marble bench with his head in a she-student's lap: lust does not seem to me by any means the worst of all evils, and I have what is probably an inordinate respect for love. Yet the sight of Cathie Dugan forcing her Geisha girl hands down onto his slight shoulders and pressing her pointy little chin onto his childish head was somehow very disquieting. Possibly I was disturbed because there was something unspontaneous, something assumed about the whole business: he was awkward, he was submitting rather than participating, and his fingers looked aimless and pathetic lying there loose on the arms of my chair.

No, I should have known better than to look forward to an evening with students. They are not "friends," though they imagine they would like to be; the coffee and the conversation have to be brewed too strong if they are to be pleased and served; and the only advantage to be gained from an evening with them is a negative one: their tirelessness makes the watcher willing to settle for the mere act of going to bed. So when they thanked me at the door for a very profitable evening, I could say without dishonesty that I had profited too: I was ungodly tired, and it took me only fifteen minutes to fall asleep.

Chapter 4

For the last four years I have been eating lunch on Wednesdays and Fridays in the faculty dining room with Harrison Frye. No loyalty binds me either to the man or the place: lunching with him is a tiresome ritual performed in an atmosphere saturated with steam and stale gossip and the smell of creamed onions; if I could arrange more than an hour's interval between my lessons, I would never eat on campus, and I would probably have remained on the most superficial terms of acquaintance with him if someone hadn't started the story that he was having an affair with me.

I can still feel the white current of fury that circulated through my body the first time I heard that story from Jenny Willis. It was beyond her, she said, why I should have been so put out. Wasn't he young, a well-preserved forty-five? Wasn't he impressive, with those fine white teeth and those broad shoulders and that wonderful resonant baritone? He was—but, whatever he was, he was not for me. "Well-preserved" is a term that makes me think of specimens in jars in a biology lab, and the teeth were so perfect that there didn't seem much merit in their not being false. As for his baritone, it was bound to be a drawback to him

36

under normal circumstances, since it was disheartening to hear obviosities uttered in a ministerial voice that should have been sending forth spiritual certainties from behind a pulpit.

It was because of the stories, then, that I went on meeting him at twelve-thirty on Wednesdays and Fridays. To stop would have been to lend credibility to the rumors by taking notice of them; and by the time the gossip had subsided, nothing but an act of rudeness could have broken our customary get-togethers. Harrison was always there ahead of me in the faculty dining room, saving our table, filling our water glasses at the fountain, and, what with his "unfortunate domestic situation," as it was politely referred to by the faculty—he lived with an unmarried sister who was an alcoholic—I did not like to wound his sensibilities. Besides, since he taught English to all the freshmen in the Music department, something he would tell me at lunch would often turn out to be very useful to me in my dealings with students of my own. It was not unusual for his freshmen to pour out their hearts to him in their weekly themes, and on a good many occasions it was a remark of Harrison's that kept me from mistaking fear for arrogance or grief for sulkiness or thwarted affection for hostility.

So Harrison and I were together eating a couple of peach and cottage cheese salads that first Wednesday of the term when I came face to face with Arthur Sanes. The dining room, with newly refurbished tile and aluminum and leatherette, was filled to capacity, and everybody was asking everybody else, with forced cordiality and without the slightest interest in the answer, "And how did you spend *your* summer?" Harrison knew better than to kill off a conversation with anything as inane as that; but I wasn't exactly fascinated when he favored me with a circumstantial description of what the Japanese beetles had done to some roses he had planted for Corinne. I found myself watching a jam-up at the steam-table on the other side of

37

the long room, and all of a sudden I was aware of a new back at the edge of the little crowd—black Ivy League crew-cut, tanned neck, cream-colored shirt-collar turned back over the collar of a fine camel's hair jacket, shoulders a little stooped, so that the pleat at the back of the jacket spread a bit. "Oh, look," I said, breaking in on Harrison, strangely callous to him and his Corinne and his devoured roses. "I bet that's Mr. Sanes."

"Sanes?" he said, turning the monumental upper part of his body all the way around to look. "Oh, yes, that's Sanes." It was either a habit or a conscious assertion of masculinity with him to call all males, whether they were faculty members or students, exclusively by their last names. "I suppose you've met him?"

"No, Harrison, I haven't."

"Neither have I. They say he has a distinguished reputation."

"He's made some good recordings." Now that Harrison had swung back and was facing me again, I was not so afraid that the presence might suddenly turn and catch us obviously staring, and I allowed myself to complete my contemplation of the back view. There were brown trousers with meticulous creases in them, and there were crepe-soled reddish brown leather shoes—the general effect was quite in harmony with Vincent's observation: conscious, even calculated, and certainly not the sort of thing usually worn around here.

"There's just one thing that hasn't been cleared up for me," said Harrison, annoyed at my preoccupation—I was holding him suspended at the climax of the tragedy of the roses. "If he's so distinguished, then what's he doing here? Why isn't he at Curtis or Juilliard or some place like that?"

It was a good question, but I was not given time to consider it. Mr. Sanes, probably not accustomed to waiting in such a crowd for his food, had plainly given up. He turned away from the steam-table with an empty tray in his hands and a disappointed look on his face, and I stared at him shamelessly, put off my guard by seeing a scornful photograph changing into a baffled man. He did *not* look like his picture, but then scarcely anybody could make a face like that for fourteen hours a day. The presence of color also confused me: the skin of his face was pitilessly sunburned; the straight mouth looked pale by comparison; and the eyes were hazel—light brown irises startlingly translucent since he had turned around into a slant of sun. I continued to stare until my scrutiny ended in a shock: those light and somewhat faded eyes were looking straight into mine.

He bowed, and, although there was a certain constriction that might have been mockery at the corners of his thin lips, I thought it was gracious of him to extend himself to a gaping stranger, and I bowed too.

Harrison turned ponderously around to see who had captured my attention. "I thought you said you didn't know him," he said.

"I don't."

"He probably knows who you are."

"I doubt it. Why should he?"

It was one of those leading questions I had always been very careful not to hand to Harrison. The answer was fulsome, but I did not hear all of it since I was covertly following the enigmatic moves of Mr. Sanes at the other end of the dining room. He was putting down his empty tray— his hands were thin and brown with long square-ended fingers; he was walking, disburdened, in our general direction; good God, he was making straight for me. When he got there, he stationed himself directly in back of Harrison, looking down with a face that I would never have suspected of an unusual capacity for contempt, favoring me with a very dry but certainly not unfriendly smile.

"You're Miss Hartmann, in Voice, aren't you?" he said. "Dr. Holland pointed you out to me yesterday—I thought I was going to meet you then. But you were clicking down the hall at such an efficient rate I knew I'd never catch up with you. Well, anyhow, let's do it now. I'm the new man in Piano—Arthur Sanes."

Yet the words themselves—especially when they have to stand in the light of the photograph and Vincent's evaluation of the man—the words themselves by no means carry the tone of that little speech. If there was a jab at me in the remark about my efficient clicking—I *do* click, I freely admit—it did not carry any hint of censure; it suggested rather that he had been paternally amused. If the "Well, anyhow, let's do it now" suggested that the introduction was a tiresome business to be gotten over with as soon as possible, he managed to convey by lifting his right arm that he was willing at least to offer touch: his right hand, a very fine one with the tendons showing strong through the sunburned skin, swung outward a little to let me know he would gladly have shaken hands with me if he had not been impeded by Harrison's head.

"Mr. Sanes, let me introduce Mr. Frye. He's in English," I said.

He certainly didn't put himself out for Harrison's benefit. With the completely ungiving look he must have trained upon poor Mr. Cusick, he stayed precisely where he was, so that Harrison's head had to come up and around uncomfortably and unbecomingly; and, though there was nothing in his way this time, he made no offer to shake hands. "English?" he said in a clipped, clear voice that might have been calculated to do away with overtones and implications, yet, by its very bareness, somehow gave the impression that, to him, the English department was no department at all. "Then you're not in Music, Mr. Frye?"

Harrison, piqued to have it pointed out that there was anything he was not in, went to some lengths to explain in his rolling voice that he had a close if unofficial connection with that department: the students he taught were exclusively musicians.

40

"Really?" He was looking—and I thought again of Matt Cusick, I saw the yellowish-white moustache going up and down—he was looking, with an expression not totally innocent of contempt, at the perfect part in Harrison's damp black hair. "How many hours a week do *you* teach, Miss Hartmann?" he asked, and I could not doubt that he had put the emphasis on the word for one purpose only: to remind me that he had crossed the faculty dining room to communicate with me, and not with anybody else.

"Twenty-three. Four of them on Saturdays, unfortunately."

I said it coldly, and the coldness registered. He sought my look, and there was an unexpected and disarming gentleness in his hazel stare; the starkness of his face adjusted itself—and this was strangely touching—to what was evidently a rare and certainly an appealing smile. "That's a killing schedule. How do you manage it?"

"You get used to it," I said, unable to sustain the look, transferring my attention to my salad. "I've been doing it for years. Anyway, you must have almost as many hours as that yourself."

"Yes." He was apparently unused to having his glance rejected—his voice, which had been simply cool until now, took on an edge of real asperity. "However, I also have the conviction that I'm not going to be able to put up with it for very long."

"It *is* an atrocious schedule," said Harrison, abandoning his attempt to look at Mr. Sanes and offering his moral indignation to me.

"In a way, Harrison, yours is just as bad. Mr. Frye marks ninety themes a week, you know."

It was not an uncomplicated need to be charitable to Harrison, to force the presence behind him to give just recognition to his Herculean labors with at least a cluck of the tongue or a shake of the head, which had activated me. During the brief time we had been able to look at each

41

other, I had sighted something quite different from the mocker in the publicity picture on the record envelope, something appealing enough that I did not want to consider it lost, something that I wanted to conjure back again, particularly because I had been the one who had driven it into retreat. And he responded—he even brought himself to the point of addressing a direct question. If it was an unfortunate question, that was no fault of his: how could he know that Harrison's "domestic troubles" had brought his scholarship to a standstill, how could he guess that Harrison had not turned up on the promotion list last year because it was pretty plain he would never get around to taking his Ph.D.? "What's your field, Mr. Frye. I mean, what did you take your Doctor's in?" he said.

"My field is the seventeenth century, with emphasis on the metaphysical poets."

I virtually blushed for him. If he could lay claim to any "field," it was eighteenth century prose, the field in which he had taken his Master's. Since the metaphysical poets had come into fashion, he had done some reading in them, naturally; but he would never have presented himself as an authority on them to any member of his own department or even to me; and I was convinced that ignorance about such matters in Mr. Sanes was nothing to be safely depended upon.

"Really? That's fascinating stuff." It was strange that the word "fascinating," worked threadbare as it was by female students describing fraternity men, should have taken on as he uttered it the glint of sophistication which had been worn out of it long ago. I thought that he must have gone to tea-dances and speakeasies in the twenties. "Those seventeenth century boys are getting top billing these days. I can see why your classes would be stampeded," he said.

I explained as well as I could that specialized studies were more or less useless impedimenta here in the College of Fine Arts. I stressed the fact that the primary interest of the students—and usually their only interest—was in their

42

major subject: Painting, Drama, Architecture, Music; and while I uselessly named those obvious categories, my look again got tangled up with his, this time most disturbingly. I went on to say that if T. S. Eliot himself were to come here offering a class in the metaphysical poets, he would probably go begging, and poor Mr. Frye—I should have deleted the "poor", and I knew it—Mr. Frye, for all his scholarship, was probably doomed to teach freshman English for the rest of his days.

But I was by no means a brilliant advocate. A smile that could be labeled nothing but supercilious stretched the corners of his pale mouth; his hazel eyes hardened and narrowed and would not release my glance. "Yes, I can well believe that," he said when I trailed off; and I remembered myself saying just those words in a not too different tone when Frederick Wade, my bellowing baritone, gave me an excuse for lateness which I knew to be a lie.

I would have been willing now to see him leave and try his luck again at the steam-table, but the constraining little stretch of silence did not send him about his business. He flicked an invisible something from the lapel of his camel's hair jacket, and said, looking up with the dry smile he had given me in the beginning, that, since we were next door neighbors, we'd probably be seeing each other every now and then.

"I certainly hope so." I couldn't have offered less, and I had been careful to keep my voice polite rather than enthusiastic for Harrison's sake; but Harrison was beyond appeasement—his large face was sour with irritation.

"We get pretty noisy on the Steinway in there every once in a while, Miss Hartmann. I hope we haven't been disturbing you too much."

"No," I said, smiling at him—since Harrison was miffed beyond repair, it seemed useless to offend Mr. Sanes as well—"no, really I'm so used to the students in that room I don't even hear them anymore."

"*I* heard you," said Harrison. I started, because it was

as aggressive as it was unexpected. It fairly boomed out of him, and two or three of our neighbors turned around to look.

"Really?" The hazel eyes were veiled. The voice was low, tense, and staccato.

"Yes, I heard you the other night."

"What night was that?"

"Why, night before last, some time around ten o'clock." He did not turn, he addressed it sullenly to his salad. "I heard you all the way up at the other end of the building—I'm in 309 on the top floor, you know."

"You heard me practising?"

It came out of him in a low voice, but with terrifying intensity. Affront, hate, and something close to fear agitated every word of it, so that is was—quite crazily, for no reason at all that I could see—an accusation and a confession. It certainly should have shaken Harrison out of his phlegmatic despondency—it upset me so much that I could not continue to look at Mr. Sanes' changed and vulnerable face.

"Yes," said Harrison. "That was you—wasn't it?—playing a Bach fugue or something. You kept going back to the beginning—"

"How did you know it was me?"

It was such a queer question that even Harrison paused and pulled down the lobe of his ear before he answered it. "Why, I was marking themes up there in my office, and I got thirsty, and the fountain on our floor was out of order, so I had to come down and use yours," he said. "The lights in your room were the only ones on, so I knew it was you. That's all there was to it, you know."

The last sentence had implied—and there is never much subtlety in Harrison's implications—that there wasn't anything in the business for anybody to get excited about. Yet all three of us were excited, so excited that we were bound to attract attention from the people around us; and, since I had caught a glimpse of Arthur Sanes before lowering my eyes, I did not want to have him exposed to anybody

44

else. Even if, by this time, his face had managed to assume the scornful mask he presented to the world in his publicity photograph, his skin would betray him: his skin had taken on the uneven, greenish cast that spreads over sunburn in an attack of pallor. Sick and unmanned—that was how he looked—sick in the spirit, sick at heart.

"Harrison can't get much work done at home—Harrison usually *does* work in his office a couple of nights a week," I said.

"Really? I didn't know that." His tone was icy now, icy and venomous. "There's one thing, though: the agony won't be going on too much longer. As soon as I find myself a place that's fit to live in, I'll have my own piano shipped down from New York. In a couple of weeks I won't be inconveniencing anybody anymore."

"Oh, I didn't mean that you were inconveniencing me," said Harrison, too dull as yet with perplexity to feel the sting of the affront. "I've been in that building too long to let myself be put out by that sort of thing. Fact is, I enjoy it —everything, that is, except the brasses."

"That's reassuring."

Another charged silence hung over us. Harrison picked up his fork—ponderously, deliberately—and held it suspended over his mound of cottage cheese.

"Well," said Mr. Sanes, "if you'll excuse me, Miss Hartmann, I'll be going. It begins to look as if a person might get something hot to eat without exposing himself to a wrestling match." He bowed and stepped backward, and there was mockery in the curt downward jerk of his chin. He thrust his hands into his pockets and sauntered away with his head a little on one side, and a disproportionate melancholy came down on me—there was such a disparity between his approach and his retreat. Harrison indulged himself in a crass pantomime of relief.

"Well," he said, "I've seen some weird characters around here in my day, but this one beats everything."

"Weird?" There was nothing I wanted less than an

45

exchange of misgivings. "I wouldn't say there was anything weird about him."

"Wouldn't you? Then all I can say is: *I* must be crazy. That stuff about my hearing him practise sounded absolutely paranoid to me."

I teased him—not too adeptly—about his amateur psychoanalysis, and dragged him from there to conversation about Mr. Baird, who counseled our problem students, of which we had more than our share. He eluded me and edged back to the original subject only once: I called his attention to the improvement in Mr. Baird's color—the poor man had been suffering from jaundice—and he said that, speaking of complexions, it was a pretty expensive-looking sunburn that our new genius had gotten for himself. I had not thought of it as being expensive: all the while I had been staring at it, I had taken for granted that Mr. Sanes had gotten it under a sun-lamp, and now I wondered why I should have felt certain of any such thing. Had there been any particular quality about his sunburn? Was I really able to distinguish between the kind you get in solitude under a sun-lamp and the kind you get in company out on the sand? For the rest of the lunch hour—and there wasn't too much of it left—I kept testing my capacity to tell the one from the other, I kept looking at the peeling arms and faded faces on our side of the faculty dining room. But I could not make a complete survey—my range was circumscribed: I did not dare to look in any direction where I might find myself encountering the hazel stare of Arthur Sanes.

Chapter 5

IT WAS NOT because I wanted to talk to him again that I walked over to the college library that afternoon in October. In the two weeks gone by since our introduction in the faculty dining room, whatever confused and nameless thing I had felt for him had thinned and faded. I suspected him of avoiding me—he bowed elaborately when he saw me at a distance, but when he passed me and might have stopped to speak he hurried on with a look of preoccupation on his face; and besides, I was growing more and more disturbed by the sort of talk I kept hearing through our mutual wall. I am by no means above taking sarcastic little digs at the students, particularly if nothing but digs will stir them out of their complacency; but from what I could hear through the wall—I confess to eavesdropping, I heard much more than I would have heard if I hadn't listened—the icy taunt was Mr. Sanes' primary, if not his exclusive pedagogic device. Maybe his students were stimulated—Cathie, at any rate, announced herself marvelously stimulated—but most of the others could scarcely have been described as happy: after the lessons the boys usually went down to the lobby in a sullen or quarrelsome state of mind, and the girls retreated to the washroom, some of them to smear on

47

a defiant extra layer of lipstick and some of them to weep.

My reason, then, for walking over to the library in the Hall of Painting and Design was at best a negative reason. My day had been crowded and harried: I had been harsh and nasty with Virginia Caputo who had done serious damage to her voice by singing torch songs in a night club; I had shown that I was out of patience with my gentle Negro tenor Claude Harbison, who was always coming late from his waiter's job; and I was too rattled to subside as a weary person should subside at the end of the day, too raw and self-recriminatory to want to be alone.

In certain small libraries—and ours is such a one—there is the possibility of peace without total silence, community without responsibility. You can be surrounded by people you know or partly know without incurring the obligation to talk or to listen; a mild accompaniment of muted voices mitigates the bleakness of your private meditations; if you look up for relief from reading, you can be almost certain of encountering a fleeting glance or an unasking smile. It was this duty-free companionship I was looking for in the library—that and the essential charm of the place. It is a spacious room, carpeted in moss-green broadloom by the grace of some unremembered donor; and it is lined—walls and ceiling and bookcases all alike—in pale, curiously carved, yellowish wood. The mellow five o'clock sun was streaming through the leaded windows when I walked in, and I let myself down into a square of it at a bright, deserted table. In front of me were three or four books on Flemish Art which one of the students had taken down from the stacks, and I pulled the closest of them toward me and began to turn the pages. There were dozens of illustrations, many of them in color, and I went through them slowly, looking at the canny saints and the thick and pious burghers, and pausing over the good women, all of them as real as a person's neighbors and none of them particularly beautiful, whom the painters had used as models for the Mother of God.

48

One of these women, a Weeping Madonna by a certain Dirk Bouts whom I had never heard of, kept drawing me back. She was in the middle of the book, and whatever I saw beyond her—all the naked infants and sturdy young men and bluish hills and feathery trees—seemed, beside the immediacy of her raw-eyed grieving, like the unreal images we remember from our dreams. After three or four attempts to go beyond her, I gave myself up to her utterly; I put my elbows on either side of the book and rested my cheeks in my hands and stared into her face. It was a broad face and a young one—no mother of a man in his thirties could have come with a face as young as that to the foot of his cross. The chin, the mouth, the flesh of the cheeks were all firm and pliant; if there were furrows in the forehead or creases in the neck, they were hidden by the drooping folds and gathers of the wimple; the only visible wrinkles were the dark and swollen crows' feet showing like bruises just below the eyes. The eyes themselves—it was almost impossible to look away from them—were bloodshot, suffused with tears, red-blind with weeping. They gazed unseeing from under the fringes of sparse, drenched lashes on the puffed upper eyelids; without feeling it, without knowing it, they spilled their transparent, elongated drops over the cheeks, toward the nose, down almost as far as the corners of the lips. The lips, too, were swollen and so tightly pressed together that I knew they must be sealed with the dried scum of sorrow. To open them would be a bursting violence; it would be long before they could learn again to utter an articulate word, long before they would be capable of anything but a broken murmur or a shaken sigh.

And now as I stared at her, barely conscious of the discreet voices moving around me, I knew why it was that I was drawn to her and to her only: strange as it may seem, I envied her grief, I was jealous of the depth and intensity of her pain. When had I wept like that? Not since my childhood. That girl in the pale blue sweater over there—had she ever wept like that? Old Dr. Daniels, taking off

49

his bifocals to read the titles of the books on the shelves —would he ever weep like that, even once, before he went into his grave? Not very likely: such mourning—yes, and with it the fierce exultation that can be known only by such mourners—had fallen out of fashion. We lived, as it were, toward the back of the book, with the naked infants and the sturdy young men; numbly, in a monotonous dream, we wandered among the feathery trees and the bluish hills. I turned back to them once more, those hills and trees, as if to acclimatize myself, as if to adjust and resign myself to my proper spiritual habitat. But I wanted the eyes, and I would go on wanting them as long as my heart persisted in beating; I could teach myself to relinquish much, but I would never learn to renounce the bloodshot eyes.

The girl in the blue sweater put on her trenchcoat, gathered up her books, and went away, leaving an unpeopled, sunlit stretch in front of me. It was growing late and many were going: there was nobody now at the table directly opposite mine, but at the one on the other side of that there was a solitary man, intently reading. Though most of his face was hidden from me—his dark, blunt-ended fingers were spread across the top of it either to support the forehead or to shut out the brilliance of the light—I knew that it was Arthur Sanes, and I did not want to be caught a second time in the act of staring. I turned a page or so of my book and looked distractedly at the print, seeing only the proper names: the Emperor Otto, Hugo van der Goes, Brabant, Louvain. . . .

Yet what I had seen in that one agitated glance persisted in my inner vision. I read that Dirk Bouts had marched yearly in the town procession of the Holy Sacrament, and I thought how wearily the stooped shoulders slanted toward the table. I read how this same Bouts, in payment for his services in the processional, was granted an allotment of Rhine wine, and I thought of the lips, still pale against the unfaded sunburn, laid against each other in a line of intense concentration that was not unrelated to pain. It was strange, too, that the sight of him, more than the sight of anybody else I could think of, seemed acceptable to me after my long staring at the Weeping Madonna. If there was a certain daemoniac quality about him—where Harrison fancied he saw paranoia—at least he refused to recede into the general inspidity.

I do not know what I would have done—I might have tried to slip out unseen or I might have waited for him to go away without noticing me—if Mrs. McCausland, the librarian at the main desk, hadn't started to lecture a drama student who had just confessed to losing the second volume of Strindberg. Probably because he didn't object to being viewed in a becoming display of masculine defiance, he was cocky about the matter: "It's lost, I lost it, I told you I'd pay for it, and that's all there is to it," he said. Whereupon Mrs. McCausland had to show her authority to the small audience, had to shatter the peace of the library with a high-minded oration. Books were valuable, she would have the young man understand; the property of the library was as important to the library as the property of the individual was to the individual; anybody old enough to be in college ought to have more of a sense of responsibility. . . .

Everybody looks at somebody when that sort of scene breaks out, and there was nobody for me to look at but Arthur Sanes. He took his hand away from his face and came up out of what was plainly total immersion: his book had undone him as completely as the melting passages of the Bruch concerto had undone poor Vincent that afternoon last spring. I saw him sigh and make a nervous movement with his shoulders. His eyes blinked against the sunlight, turned briefly toward the main desk, and settled on me. He nodded and formed the syllables of my name without actually uttering them; and then, as if the sight of me

51

were acceptable or even mildly welcome to him, he gave me a wan and limited kind of smile.

"You may not use your library card until the fine is paid in full," said Mrs. McCausland.

"I don't have to use this library at all. I'm a resident. I can always get my books at the public library where they don't make you feel like a convict."

"Nobody's making anybody feel like a convict. You're simply expected to show a decent respect for the books."

In the silence that followed, Mr. Sanes got up, still weakly smiling, came over, and stopped at the end of my table. "What do you say we get out of here?" he said.

I nodded and stood up, though I have never been quite certain why I did it. Maybe I had somehow wept without tears along with the Weeping Madonna—maybe my willingness was the sort of shaken docility that comes over a child at the end of a spell of crying. At any rate, I walked beside him out of the library, into the resounding marble hall that lies beyond it, through the somber doors with their heavy wrought-iron grillework, into the strange warmthlessness of the clear sun. I was not in the proper frame of mind for making the easy chatter expected on such occasions, and I was relieved when he took over. "When you think of all the irreplaceable manuscripts that went up in smoke at the burning of Alexandria, that librarian seems to have been making an ungodly fuss about the loss of one volume of Strindberg," he said.

"It was so peaceful and quiet in there before they started."

"Yes, it's very quiet, that's the best thing about it. A person is grateful enough for the quiet to be willing to overlook some of the monstrosities."

"What monstrosities?"

"Oh, I don't know—that crazy carving—those bulbous angels up to their necks in grapes and pears."

"Are they angels? I never noticed."

52

"Cupids or seraphim or something like that."

"Well, don't expect me to abuse them. I like the library, I guess."

"Do you? I wouldn't have thought it."

"Why not, Mr. Sanes? Because you gave me credit for better taste than I've got?"

"Oh, no, not at all. The place isn't as bad as *that,* you know." He laughed an uncomfortable laugh and turned to me without looking into my eyes. "I've been there pretty often, and I've never seen you there before. That was the only thing I meant to imply," he said.

We had been walking until now under an interlacing of dark branches, some of them still holding a few dry, metallic-looking leaves, some of them silkily black and bare. Now we stepped out under the open, dappled sky, and I was startled and silenced by a double revelation: I saw the orange mackerel clouds ranged against a vast yellow glowing, and I knew that he was not unmindful of me. Sometimes—and the thought took unto itself the cool radiance of the evening—sometimes when he had been sitting in the library with his forehead resting on his hand, he had looked up, and looked for me.

"Well, the campus is handsome, anyhow."

I knew it was a peace-offering intended to make up for the disparagement of the wooden angels, but I could not answer it with anything more than a nod—my mind was on something else. I was thinking with disproportionate concern that in a few minutes we would be coming to a point of decision: not fifty feet away stood the two big sandstone pylons that marked the place where the path across the campus came out onto the public street. And what was going to happen when we got there? Very likely, nothing: very likely, he would go to his place—wherever that might be—and I would go to mine. Maybe we would stand and chat a little in the shadow of those pylons; but, since my bus stop was a good two blocks away—one of them across a bridge—there was small possibility of his offering to walk the rest of the way with me.

"You seemed to be pretty absorbed up there in the library. What were you reading?" he said.

I started: it was as if I were seeing his eyes looking covertly out at me through the spaces between his spread fingers. I stared down at the clumps of barberry bushes that lined the path, almost leafless now but with their tear-shaped scarlet fruit still clinging to their thorny twigs, and I thought of all the glances that had passed between us: he and I were connected by a transitory weaving of glances, if by nothing else. "Actually I wasn't reading," I said after a silence that must have seemed unaccountably protracted. "I picked up an art book—it was lying on the table. I was looking at a painting by Dirk Bouts—a Flemish medieval thing—"

"Maybe you wanted to take it home with you. I bet I hurried you off before you got a chance to check it out at the desk."

"No—"

He stopped and I stopped with him some twenty paces from the pylons. He looked at me and I looked at him, and his hazel eyes showed drained, weak, and gentle in the oblique light of the sun. "You probably *did* want to take it with you. Let me go back and get it for you," he said.

"Oh, no, thanks very much, but really I don't want it." As soon as the words were out of my mouth, I regretted them: they were calculated to make me seem irrational and capricious, and, considering the simple earnestness of his offer, they constituted an inexcusable ungraciousness. "What I mean is: it's a very painful kind of picture—it's a Weeping Madonna at the cross. It's the wrong sort of thing to take home with you. If I had it at home, I'd look at it too much."

"I know what you mean," he said, walking slowly on toward the end of the pathway. "Somewhere at my place at the bottom of some drawer I've got an original George Grosz—*Keine Augen—No Eyes*. It's one of his pacifist things, a blind war veteran begging in the street with a cup and a dog. After I had it around for a couple of days I put it away in a drawer—I just couldn't bear to look at it anymore."

I stopped and stood with my back against one of the pylons, partly because he had shown some inclination to halt there and partly in surprise: I would never have dreamed he could give a comparative stranger so intimate an insight into himself. I looked at our shadows, long and bluish, on the pavement, and I wondered what besides the Grosz original was in that drawer of his.

"Where do you go from here, Miss Hartmann?"

"Across the bridge." I wished he had not called me "Miss Hartmann"—I had liked it better when he called me nothing. "Over to the bus stop in front of the Board of Education."

"If it's all right with you, I'll walk over there too."

"Of course it's all right with me."

Yet there were other places where I would have preferred to go for a stroll with him. I am afraid of heights, and I have never gone across that bridge without suffering, at the very least, acute uneasiness. I can usually avoid a real attack of dizziness by walking as far as possible from the railing and by keeping my eyes fixed straight ahead; but the thought of the crossing still falls like a sickly stain across my mind every morning when I am brushing my hair and every afternoon when I am locking my classroom door behind me; and I have dreamed several times of finding myself in the middle of the span, so overcome with dizziness that I have to get down and crawl the rest of the way on my hands and knees. There is a gorge under the bridge, a raw piece of countryside, a strange, wild thing to come upon in the middle of a city—maybe the rawness and the incongruity have added something to my fright.

55

Nothing but a few dilapidated houses have encroached on the rank tangle of sumac and ailanthus down there in the gorge, and even these are obvious only in the wintertime when all the weeds are gone and all the boughs are bare. But my companion—he had insisted with a wry kind of gallantry that I walk on the inside, closer to the railing than I had ever been before—my companion caught sight of those houses and pointed them out to me, and I could scarcely refuse to look. "Yes, I know, they're our own particular brand of slum," I said, trying to convince myself that what I was feeling was only the *fear* of dizziness. "It's a disgrace that anything as bad as that should be allowed to stand."

"In New York there are blocks and blocks that are a good deal worse than those."

"Yes, I know. Do you miss New York much?"

"No, I can't say I miss it." He had stopped toward the middle of the span, near the sickening scene of my nightmares. He was propping his elbows on the railing and looking down on the scarlet sumac and the yellow ailanthus, and he plainly expected me to take the same position. "How about you?" he said. "Do you ever get homesick for the place?"

"Not as homesick as I thought I'd be." I was surprised that I had been able to answer him in such a casual voice. It was not only that, as soon as I leaned against the railing, sumac and ailanthus and ironweed and tattered goldenrod shifted and merged on a surge of giddiness; I was strangely moved also by the realization that he had troubled himself to find out where I had come from, had gone to the lengths of asking somebody or at least had listened while somebody was talking about me.

"Actually, you know, that city is a monstrous fraud." Either his voice had undergone a startling change or my state had made me suddenly vulnerable to a jarring harshness in it. "Theater, for instance—what have you got, aside

56

from the usual Broadway kitsch? Two or three things a year at best. What they play at the concerts always turns out to be the same old stuff—there's a lot more music to be gotten out of records now. If I want to let myself go, I prefer to do it in private—I don't want to do it in a public concert hall with somebody breathing on my neck and somebody else staring into my face. As for the 'spots,' you can have them if you want them—I'm too old to get anything out of that sort of nonsense anymore."

I looked at him and did not want to look at him long. One of his disturbing changes had come upon him: his eyes were narrowed to glinting slits and his pale mouth was twisted in an ugly smile. Even in my confusion and my dizziness it struck me that he spoke of the city with a peculiarly personal malice, as if it were a human being and had intentionally done him some irrevocable affront, some intolerable injury. Though I never thought of going back to live there anymore, I bore the place no grudge: it called up in me nothing more intense than a melancholy regret. Yet it was a hard city, and I had known many people who had suffered in it from poverty, from loneliness, from unforgettable wounds to their pride . . . "Unless you're happy in it, it can be pretty grim," I said.

"Happy in it!" He made a wide gesture that swept my look with it over the railing and into the void. "What civilized human being could be happy in it, I'd like to know. London, Paris, Rome, even San Francisco—there a person can live like a member of the human race. But New York—"

"Still," I said, grinding my elbows against the railing and trying to anchor my veering vision on a crumbling black chimney, "you'll have to give it credit for one thing: the food is good."

"They can keep their food, too. There are worse things in this world than having to eat in mediocre restaurants."

"Yes, I suppose so." A slight wind was rippling the

tops of the trees, and I had to step back and put my hands up to my eyes—the yellow and scarlet quaking and swaying had proved too much for me.

"What's the matter, Miss Hartmann? Aren't you feeling well?" The voice was reserved, but an unquestionable ring of concern sounded in it, and—what was more—he linked his arm through mine.

"No, I'm all right, it's just that I'm afraid of heights."

"Are you? Why the devil didn't you tell me? Come on, we'd better get off this thing." He led me on, and his arm, thin and vigorous and trembling a little with the effort of holding me steady, pressed hard against the length of mine. "Of course, it's nothing to be alarmed about, but it must be very unpleasant. I wouldn't know from experience —I never had anything like it myself."

And then, as if he took it for granted that I must be embarrassed or even humiliated at having been forced to reveal such a weakness, though he continued to give me his support, he deliberately turned his eyes away from me and made a point of giving the conversation a superficial twist. American restaurant food in general was, he assured me, highly overrated, and the food in New York wasn't anything as good as it was cracked up to be. The best food to be gotten in restaurants on this side of the Atlantic was nothing beside what you could put together in your own house, provided you could draw on some European experience and a bit of imagination. "Myself, I won't hesitate to tell you I'm an excellent cook," he said, releasing my arm as we stepped off the bridge, releasing it with a promptness that was almost insulting. "I can turn out a better *coq au vin* than you can get in any French restaurant in New York, and all it takes is a little time and an open mind—a person has to be willing to experiment."

He went on like that for the remainder of our walk to the bus stop, describing one complicated dish after another, disparaging American bread and pastry, telling me

58

what wines and herbs he always kept on hand. In fact, before we reached the Board of Education building he had gone on so long and in so much detail that I wondered whether he meant to invite me to come over to his place and sample the marvels of his cuisine, an invitation which, if it materialized, I would have to refuse: I was eating dinner at the Grüenbergs' that night. Since I was no cook to speak of, I had nothing to add to his monologue; I was as silent at the end of our walk as I had been at the beginning of it, and I fell again to staring at the mackerel sky. Though it had faded—the sky itself was a pale, dull rose and the clouds dappled out across it were a purplish grey —it had the charm that settles by chance on whatever catches our eye after a crisis: I wasn't dizzy, and the air seemed light and delicate and delicious to breathe, and the quieted colors were subtle and grateful to my tired eyes.

"Where are you bound for, Miss Hartmann? I mean, are you all right, are you sure you can get there all right alone?" he said.

"Oh, yes, I'm fine. I'm going home and wash up a bit, and then I'm going over to the Grüenbergs' for dinner." I would not have explained I was otherwise engaged if I had not been afraid that some happy anticipation of being asked to join him had leaped into my look at his first question, forcing him to spell out exactly what he *did* mean.

"Who are the Grüenbergs?"

That was very annoying. If he actually did not know one of his own departmental colleagues by this time, it was a pity; and if he did know her and was pretending that he didn't, then it was an irritating piece of affectation.

"You know Emily Grüenberg. She teaches 'cello. You must have seen her a dozen times by now," I said.

"Oh, yes, the one that's married to the melancholy nuclear physicist with the caved-in cheeks. Yes, I remember now—she's the imposing Germanic type, a regular Brünnhilde. I suppose you like her?"

I said, with some show of being nettled, that I liked her very much. I even went so far as to add that I didn't have dinner with anybody I didn't consider a friend.

"Am I to take it the same thing goes for lunch?" he asked. The twitch at the corners of his mouth, though it was certainly not innocent of malice, had more merriment than mockery in it, and I had to smile at him in spite of myself.

"About lunch," I said, "one is forced to be a little more liberal. One usually eats lunch with any colleague who happens to be around."

"Does one, indeed?" he said, really smiling now—and I knew I had been cornered into making a belittling comment on poor Harrison Frye.

I was exasperated enough to keep silent for the rest of the wait. He also said nothing, but stood beside me and stared down at the cracks in the pavement until my bus came up the street, whereupon he offered me the dry, brief pressure of his hand. "I tell you what," he said as the door of the bus wheezed open to admit me, "you've got to come up and see whether I'm as good a chef as I make myself out to be. Let me get in touch with you—I'll let you know the first of the week, Miss Hartmann. What do you like— a steak bordelaise?"

I nodded from the steps while the irate driver waited.

"All right, good, I'll make you a beauty one of these days."

Chapter 6

I NEVER TOLD ANYBODY he had given me a kind of invitation to his place for dinner. Maybe I suspected from the beginning that the said invitation would never materialize, since I suppressed an impulse to mention it at the Grüenbergs' supper table and I was careful to delete it when I summarized the encounter for Emily, talking about it in the most offhand way when she and I were in the kitchen doing the dishes by ourselves. And, as things turned out, I had plenty of reason to congratulate myself for keeping it quiet in the weeks that followed: nobody likes to do his waiting in public, nobody wants even his closest friends to stand by and cluck their tongues in sympathy while his well-grounded expectations are being turned into unwarranted assumptions. This much at least I learned from the experience: there was no telling how the exotic spiritual chemistry of Arthur Sanes was likely to react to anything. What might have been expected to catalyze the usual human being into some sort of amiable activity had brought on in his case nothing but a deterioration of the whole relationship. Since that afternoon when we had talked of *Keine Augen* and the Weeping Madonna he had been going to insulting lengths to keep himself as clear as possible of me.

He stayed out of the corridor when I was in it. To avoid meeting me in the faculty dining room he ate his lunch very late or did not eat it at all—I could draw no other conclusion from his total absence when I was in the place. When he saw me at a distance, he turned off at a fountain or a bulletin board in order not to run into me. If we were forced into proximity by the crowds at the end of classes, he pretended not to see me until I was under his nose, and then he nodded absent-mindedly as we passed. During this period of detachment, my mind kept veering in the most baffling and exhausting manner—I was eaten up by indecision and curiosity. There were times when the only possible explanation seemed to be that he despised me, that a single advance, one small taste of my company, one minor revelation of myself had been enough to repel him, to make him want to avoid me for the rest of his days. And then again—it might depend on some temporary break in the chill and somber weather, or on some kind comment that somebody else had made concerning me, or on how much sleep I had managed to get on the preceding night —I would think that such an elaborate system of evasion, such scrupulous avoidance would not have been necessary to get rid of a nonentity. Somehow I had acquired—or so I liked to tell myself—an unquestionable, if unaccountable importance in the mind of Arthur Sanes.

It was during those weeks that I abandoned my earlier attempts to control my eavesdropping. Before our strange walk on the bridge—it had taken on an unearthly cast partly because I had been dizzy at the time and partly because it had been isolated afterwards from any succeeding experience—I had spent a comparatively small amount of time in my stuffy little office. In the intervals between lessons I had stayed in the big rehearsal room where I did my teaching, leafing through music or chatting with anybody who dropped in; and, if I had remained a little longer than necessary within the range of his voice once I got into my office, I could always excuse myself on the grounds that I never came there without good cause. But now it was as if I had turned my back on my own students to fix my attention on his: his lessons were my real concern—my own were workaday matters to be gotten through with speed and mere efficiency. I heard him tell George Bauer that he needn't improve on Bach by using the pedal: Bach had somehow managed to survive for two hundred and fifty years and ran a fair chance of surviving somewhat longer without his assistance. I listened while he told Isabelle Seifert, after a humdrum performance of the Scherzo of the Chopin B flat Sonata, that it was lucky the funeral march came next—considering his state of mind, he couldn't imagine feeling up to anything else. And my involvement in what was going on in his room was so intense that I felt wildly confined because I could not participate, could not, for instance, tell Cathie Dugan that she'd better not ask him to let her work on the Schumann Fantasia.

My worry had nothing to do with the fact that the Schumann C Major Fantasia makes great demands upon even the most accomplished technique. That Cathie was capable of mastering it, I was certain: I had heard her rattle it off with mechanical brilliance when she had started to work on it for old Dr. Laurent: those Geisha hands of hers had agility and a hard, brittle sort of power. No lack of dexterity on Cathie's part would serve to set off one of those characteristic diatribes of his, punctuated with long and eloquent pauses which the listener could only ascribe to his being too sick at heart or affronted or disgusted to speak. If he was on the point of delivering himself of one of these—and recently during Cathie's lessons there had been a twang of impatience in his voice—it would have to be about the interpretation; and there, I knew, he would find more than enough material for the exercise of his humorless wit. If Cathie's interpretation of the Schumann Fantasia was going to be anything like it had been last May,

63

it was going to be thoroughly pedestrian and peculiarly fragmented: she walked where she should have soared, contemplated where she should have brooded, and succeeded in turning a passionate entirety into a series of neatly constructed sections, no one of which seemed to have much to do with any of the others. And, since she had not had much time for me of late—she was practising five hours a day and growing lean and angular in the service of her new sardonic god—I could not tell her, without revealing my status as an eavesdropper, any of the things I thought she ought to know before she exposed herself to his devastating comment.

Yet I must say that Mr. Sanes conducted himself with commendable control when she ran through the opening movement for him for the first time. I remember wondering whether his forbearance in regard to her insufficiencies might have its roots in his own past. Anybody who played as he played in the recording of the Brahms capriccios and intermezzi might, in his student days, have played Schumann with Cathie's rigid musical conscience. At any rate, he did not interrupt her, and it was his custom to interrupt, sometimes by knocking something against something, sometimes by emitting a little laugh that sounded like a snort, sometimes by fetching up a loud sigh. She played through the first movement—with a shade more brilliance but with all the old want of ardor and cohesiveness—before he offered any comment, either uttered or implied. Apparently he had some consideration either for the ghosts of his own past failings or for the raw nerves of his star student: all he said was that he could wish for a little more involvement, a little more sweep, a bit more *feeling* in the thing. . . .

Because I was called in by Dr. Holland to interview a foreign exchange student—an Israeli tenor who was registering very late—I almost missed the second installment of the Sanes-Dugan drama; but even from the main Music office, seven doors down the hall, I could hear with a degree of apprehension that must have puzzled both the Palestinian and the department head what Cathie was doing to the Fantasia. While I planned Mr. Perlstein's schedule and arranged for three make-up lessons to be taken before the end of November, I realized that her eagerness to please her teacher had betrayed her into something far more deplorable than her arid performance of a week ago: she was forcing an excess of "feeling," and all of it was embarrassingly false—I had been hearing her play for three years and more, but I would never have dreamed she could play in such execrable taste. I rounded off my interview as quickly as I could, sensing all the while that I was being cavalier to my superior and cool and inhospitable to an eager young stranger; but I could do no more if I wanted to get back into my office in time for the commentary, and the commentary I simply could not bring myself to miss. I went down the corridor—not clicking, walking on the balls of my feet—and shut my office door without a sound behind me. Through the last few bars of Cathie's performance I pretended to be filling out an official schedule for the boy from Israel, but that was futile labor: I kept writing things in the wrong places, and in the silence that came after the last chord I could only stand up close to the wall and chew on the end of my pencil. It was a long silence—I could imagine her bony little face, flushed with labor and turned up to his in expectation of his praise.

"Oh, God, I never should have done it," he said at last in a voice of desperate weariness and disgust. "Forget it, abandon it, let it alone. Last week it was nothing—just dull, inoffensive nothing. This week—well, never mind, never mind—*I* did it, I should have known better, I've got nobody but myself to blame."

"Why, what's the matter with it?" she asked in a voice so scared and muffled I could barely make out the words through the wall.

"What's the matter with it? What's the point of asking?"

65

"I want to know, I've got to know."

"But when you ask a question like that, Miss Dugan, it's like asking somebody 'Why don't you love me?' When you ask a thing like that, you stick out your neck, as you very well know."

"Still, I think you owe it to me to tell me what's the matter."

I admired her courage and deplored her lack of tact. To face him out, to demand the full force of the verbal slap in the face—that was all of a piece with her usual jerky frontal attack on life. But to use the word "owe," to remind him that she had paid for his services and expected him to do what he was hired for—that was scarcely wise.

"All right, Miss Dugan." Now the voice was low and incisive. "You want to know, and apparently it's written down somewhere in the catalogue that I'm supposed to tell you, that's what they're paying me for. When I suggested you play it with feeling, I didn't mean for you to turn it into a caricature—I meant something else which it's obviously useless to try to get across to you. Let's just say that your performance suffers from the grossest type of sentimentality. I freely admit to being at fault as a teacher—I confess, in this particular instance, you didn't get your money's worth out of me. I should have guessed what you would do with it beforehand, I should have seen your limitations and kept you where you belonged. Well, it was a mistake, and you've wasted a certain amount of money and a certain number of hours. All I can do at this point is assure you that nothing of the sort is ever going to happen again."

"Mr. Sanes, I didn't mean anything at all like that—"

"No? Then why don't we skip it?"

"Skip what?"

"This unfortunate incident, this particular piece of music, the whole thing."

66

"And if I don't want to skip it—if I want to try again—"

"That would be pretty stubborn of you, Miss Dugan— stubborn and useless. It would only entail an inexcusable waste of your time—and mine."

"But surely there's something else that I could do with it. Surely there's some other way I could approach it—"

"There's no other way you can approach it. Unless—" he emitted one of those short, snorting laughs that seemed to me appallingly out of place at the moment—"unless you can arrange to go back and be born all over again."

"Last spring when I played it for Dr. Laurent he told me—"

"You must excuse me, Miss Dugan, if I'm not in- terested in what he told you. There are some of us—and apparently Dr. Laurent must be one of them—there are some of us who simply don't have the emotional capacity for this sort of thing. I think I've told you on other occasions that you have a very creditable technique. I'll add that your musical understanding, if it's applied within the proper limits, is quite satisfactory. But your capacity for emotional experience is obviously narrow—tame and narrow—and it shows itself pitifully incapable when you work with anything like this."

"I could try, Mr. Sanes. I might learn—"

"I doubt it, Miss Dugan. What I'm talking about is something nobody learns—it's a thing you live."

"Couldn't I just work on it a little bit longer? I think I deserve at least another chance."

"Work on it if you want to—*I* can't stop you. But I can't see what sort of satisfaction you'd get out of making a travesty out of Schumann and an embarrassing spectacle out of yourself."

"Was it as bad as that?"

"Every bit as bad as that, Miss Dugan. Why should I exaggerate? Now, maybe you'd like to step out and have a cigarette or a drink of water before you tackle the Bach Partita."

She did then what I expected her to do: she waived the remainder of her lesson. There were ten minutes of it left, according to my wristwatch; and, though she was probably shattered beyond all thought of playing, she salved her poor pride by making a tight little speech to the effect that *she* was not one to watch the clock at lessons, no matter what anybody might think. I heard her close the door behind her as she left him. I did not hear what direction she walked in—probably she was wearing a pair of those flat-heeled, crepe-soled shoes. I did not expect that he was going to leave so soon: I had just time to get back into my chair and bend over the schedule when his heavier tread went by. I was somehow sure that he looked in through the clear glass panes in my door and saw me sitting there, and my face flushed with a hot, strong exultation. I was glad that he saw me, I was glad he should know I had heard him in his hatefulness. If I was shamed because he had drawn me on and thrust me off, it was good that he also had a cause for shame. I picked up the pencil and made hard, incisive marks on Mr. Perlstein's schedule. The wave of heat that had passed over me gave way now to a creeping cold that made me shiver and chafe my hands. I was still shivering and I was smiling a totally inappropriate smile when my door was pushed open and Cathie came in.

Her feet—I stared at them first—were bare in their green suede oxfords and seemed pitiful because they looked cold. The veins branched in a blue network over the tops of them and showed along the straight bones of her shins. She was wearing the same green corduroy skirt that she had worn at my place the evening when we had listened to the recording, but the cloth had gone raw and shabby-looking as corduroy will in no time at all, and she was without the monkey-jacket—she had on a thin white cotten sweater instead. The sweater was eloquent of her recent suffering:

68

the front of it was stretched and wrinkled where she had been pulling it and twisting it in her nervousness, and under her armpits were two big rings of sweat, giving a greyish cast to the sleazy cloth. Her face—I scarcely dared to look at it—was shiny and bloodless. Her hair was plastered to her forehead in bizarre curlecues, and I can find no word except "crazy" to describe the fixed, empty brightness of her large green eyes.

"Good heavens, Cathie, where's your jacket? You'll catch pneumonia if you run around in a sweat like that," I said.

"Am I sweating?" Staring straight in front of her, she raised her hand slowly and touched the drenched side of her sweater. "I certainly am. I must look awful. Is there a window open? I guess I *do* feel cold."

I got up and closed the chink, grateful for any activity that would delay my choosing either to admit I had been eavesdropping or to pretend I hadn't heard a word. "Maybe you're catching a virus," I said, thereby edging myself into a better position for pleading total ignorance. "Maybe you ought to go over to the cafeteria and get yourself a good hot cup of tea."

She gave me the sort of look of scornful forbearance which only an adolescent can turn upon an adult. "Tea wouldn't do me any good," she said. "You wouldn't think so either if you knew what just went on in there." Without turning, without looking around, she made a backward gesture toward the wall with her open hand.

And, since it was plain that she credited the wall with much more solidity than it had, since she concluded that I had no idea what had been going on in there, there was no longer any question of choice for me. I could only settle back into my chair and ask her with a falseness which she was far too rattled to detect whether she had had some sort of run-in with Mr. Sanes.

"Run-in?" she said, her rigidity suddenly broken up

69

into pointless movements—her tongue coming out and moving across her lower lip, her eyes blinking, her hands going back to the squeezed front of her sweater. "It wasn't a run-in. It was more like murder. I played the Schumann Fantasia for him—"

"Yes, I know." I took a groundless moral satisfaction out of putting at least that much of my eavesdropping on record. "I heard you playing—"

"He hated it—he annihilated me."

"Why don't you sit down, Cathie?" I nodded toward the chair on the other side of my desk and held out my pack of cigarettes.

She came and took one and bent toward me across the desk while I gave her a light. She was always a scrupulously scrubbed little thing, but now the acrid smell of her trouble clung around her, and I wondered whether he had caught it and knew that it would have filled him with disgust. She let herself down into the chair with a shaking sigh, and I was glad to have her sitting, glad to have the naked coldness of her legs out of sight. "I've got to talk to you about it, Miss Hartmann," she said. "I know it's late, but I've got to tell somebody, and I can't go home and tell my mother."

I could not say I had already heard the whole of it: the time for that was past. It was equally impossible, given the wild green look of exigency, to plead my status as a teacher, to say I had no right to interfere between her and Mr. Sanes. I thought of asking her, "Where's Vincent? How about Vincent?" It seemed to me at the moment that he would be the proper comforter, but I knew she must have played that Fantasia for him before she played it for her teacher—doubtless he had made a futile effort to tell her what was coming—and it would seem like rubbing a burn even to mention his name. "All right, Cathie, go ahead and tell me," I said, prepared to hear in narrative what I had heard in action, never suspecting that there would be a difference.

70

But it was precisely in the difference that the bite of my eavesdropper's conscience made itself felt: what he had said to her and what she had thought he said were distressingly at variance, and I was in no position to point out the inconsistencies. That trait of hers of flying out, of darting with rigid passion beyond the point where anybody else would go, had been at work in her again: she had taken certain of his implications—doubtless those implications had been there, but she had twisted them into monstrous and unshakable conclusions. Mr. Sanes had let her know that she was a poor, limited creature—spinsterish, dull, all tied up in herself, incapable of ardor; and, since Mr. Sanes was the ultimate source of authority for her, every judgment he had passed on her she accepted as true. There was not the slightest use in my gainsaying him—she simply would not allow it. Remembrances had kept crowding in on her while he talked to her in there: from her childhood on she had been building the walls of a prison around herself, and now she was closed in with her own emotional poverty. Unless she could break those walls—she clenched her hands to break them, she beat on my desk with her poor, strong, bony fists —unless she could break those walls and get herself free, she would go mad. She would have nothing to do with the life he considered her fit for—she might as well be dead.

That depressing life as she sketched it out for me in the hard black lines of her bitterness was essentially not very different from my own: teaching—she said it with contempt —teaching one generation of morons after another; performing at weddings and church affairs and little gatherings of friends and relatives; saying of every work in which the human spirit has passed into ecstasy or passion, "I am too tame and limited for this, this is beyond my reach." She did not realize how closely her nightmare conformed to my reality, and I do not think I blamed her: while I watched the tears running in quick succession over her shiny cheeks, I caught a glimpse of the way my own present would have looked to me if I had foreseen it with the eyes of my youth, and I was sorry for her without being sorry that I was resigned. I knew that nothing could be gained by interrupting her—there was something salutary for her in this wild dashing into the face of things; and I merely waited until she subsided, beaten, after her attack on her projected fate, and wiped her eyes fiercely with the back of her hand, and looked at me. "My God, Miss Hartmann, how am I ever going to stand it? What am I going to do?" she said.

"In the first place, I don't think it could have been as bad as you think it was—what Mr. Sanes said to you, I mean."

"You think I'm exaggerating, but honestly I'm not. It was probably worse than I'm telling you. There were probably some things that were so terrible I had to put them out of my head."

"I doubt it, Cathie. Really, I doubt it."

"Don't try to make it any better—I know how it was. It was the worst thing that ever happened to me."

"If you want to think it was the worst thing that ever happened to you, there's not much good in my going into it with you, is there? You'll only get furious with me if I try to offer you any suggestions."

"Oh, no, I won't, Miss Hartmann, honestly I won't." She looked at me with a spurious reasonableness in her marred face. "I know I've got to start picking up the pieces. I've got to have something to work on, I've got to do something, I know I do."

"Well, then, the trouble between you and Mr. Sanes came up over one particular piece—didn't it? You never had that kind of difficulty—did you?—over the Bach Partita."

She nodded and shook her head successively, taking on the air of a child who is paying attention in good faith, but I did not trust her. There was a disturbing shallowness, a frightening impenetrability in the green look she forced to answer mine.

"Then the first thing to do would be to remove the source of the agony—wouldn't it? If you gave up the Schumann Fantasia and started fresh on something else—"

"I won't do it!" I hoped that Dr. Holland had taken himself out of the building by this time: she could have been heard from end to end of the hall. "Don't tell me that, I won't listen to that!" she said, banging her fists on the edge of the desk. "Nobody's going to talk me out of doing what I've got to do."

"Control yourself, Cathie, for heaven's sake."

"Don't kid yourself, Miss Hartmann—maybe I won't play it for him next week or the week after that, but don't kid yourself. I'll play it for him, and I'll play it the way he wants me to, before I get out of here next spring."

"All right, Cathie, all right," I said, letting myself sag a little against the back of my chair. I was surprised and relieved to find that she could stretch the matter out so far in time: there was no telling what might come up to dilute the desire and blunt the pain between now and next May. "Only, play it on the side, if you know what I mean—get it ready for him without letting him know. Just don't go telling him what you're going to do. That'd be like waving a red flag in front of his face."

"Don't worry, I won't say anything about it, not to him and not to anybody else. I've got to make some basic changes—"

"What changes?" I said with a shallow kind of sprightliness. It had occurred to me that what she needed most was some idea of what she could begin doing with the Schumann Fantasia. If she could go home now and sit down to work at the piano, she would propel herself over the black void of inactivity that always lies on the other side of a defeat. Any musical advice I could give her would serve that purpose; and whether it was sound advice or not scarcely made much difference, considering everything that might come about between now and the end of the year.

73

"What changes do *you* think I ought to make, Miss Hartmann?"

"Well, from what I heard in here, I'd say the first movement—"

Scorn leaped into her face again, scorn of my limited objectives, scorn of the pedestrian nature of my sensibilities. She stood up and made a wide, deprecatory movement with her hands. "I don't mean changes in the music," she said with the curbed anger of one whose patience has been tried by impervious dullness. "I'm talking about myself. I'm talking about the way I am, the way I live."

The way she was, the way she lived—on anything as vast and vague as that I was in no condition to commit myself. I was incapable, I was sick-hearted; and for the moment at least her white, contemptuous face was a stranger's face to me. "I suppose I'd be sorry if you made any radical changes of that sort, Cathie," I said, and I could not keep my weariness out of my voice. "The way you were was always good enough for me, you know."

"I hate the way I am! I loathe the way I am, and so does he! I refuse to be the kind of person he thinks I'm going to be!"

Petty as it probably was, I admit I was pained by the rejection. Mr. Sanes and Cathie Dugan as she meant herself to become—they were the aristocrats, and I was the workaday mediocrity at whose feet she flung the cast-off version of herself. I had thought of coming to her side of the desk and putting my arm around her shoulders: it had occurred to me when she got up and stepped out of my reach that I had at no point touched her; and communication, especially if there is pain in it, always seems incomplete to me if total separation is maintained—the tenderest speech still calls for the authentication of touch. But now I did not dare or even want to come near her. I gave her a level look and shrugged; and, since I almost never shrug, I felt the gesture to be artificial, cold, and out of place.

74

"Of course you'll do whatever you like, Cathie."

"It isn't what I like." She said it remorsefully, suddenly aware that she had accidentally wounded me in the course of her own struggle. "It's what I've got to do—I've got to change myself."

"But that isn't as easy as you think it is, making yourself over. When you try consciously to do something like that to yourself, it seldom comes off, it almost never takes, if you know what I mean. A human being is a very delicate, complicated kind of thing to play with. Once you take it apart, you're likely to get it together again all wrong—you might even drop it and smash it to bits." I gave her a wan and singularly inappropriate smile.

"But I've got to take that risk—I really do, Miss Hartmann."

"Yes, I know. Only, it's a pity that the times we're all beat up and our minds are scarcely working should have to be the times when we think we know exactly what we ought to do."

Both of us knew then that the talk was over. Something —maybe regret for having hurt me and maybe nothing more than the need to test the existence of human companionship after she had felt herself a pariah—something prompted her to lay her moist and icy fingers on the back of my hand. To this day I regret that I offered her nothing in answer. If I had caught those fingers and kissed them, she might have cried and I might have embraced her; it would not have been good pedagogy, but it might have brought her home to me much sooner than she came. She thanked me and told me that I had been good to her and she would always remember and be grateful; and the last thing I saw of her that afternoon was her bare legs—*they*, at least, looked a little warmer—going over the threshold and into the empty hall.

When she was gone, I found myself still incongruously smiling. My mind had been almost immediately closed to

75

her and had opened again, as certain books will always open to certain pages, on Mr. Sanes. I chewed the end of my pencil and thought what a great god he had turned out to be with his supercilious air and his fine jackets, and I knew that my smile was turning into a hateful smile. I had been listening more willingly of late to Jenny Willis and Harrison Frye and any of the others who were collecting information about him, and the record of his concertizing had certainly not been impressive: four New York recitals in the past six years—the ones given at eastern girls' schools and in some of the New England colleges were scarcely anything to crow about. As for his reputation with the critics, only Hansford Lindsay in the *Twentieth Century Review* had given him anything more than a routine notice so far as anybody at school had been able to find out. And Lindsay had praised him so inordinately, had compared him so fulsomely to the great dead Schnabel that the reviews had done his reputation more harm than good.

It was intolerably warm and smoky in the office, and I went to open the window. The air came in to me on a dank stream, and the campus, dun and muddy under the glare of a muffled sunset, looked like the grounds of a penitentiary. I wondered where the boy from Israel would be living and whether a day like this would be very disheartening to him after the Palestinian sun. I tried to picture him, and I knew with bitter self-reproach that I had scarcely looked at him in my nervous haste: he was to study with me, he had come a long, long way to sing with me, and I had not even looked him in the face. Well, tomorrow I would do better. Tomorrow I would pull myself together and do better with the Israeli and with everybody else. But the resolution failed to sustain me, and on the way out I said nothing but a curt good night to the charwoman. A fine drizzle had begun to fall, and I had no hat or kerchief, and I dreaded the long, wet walk across the bridge alone.

76

Chapter 7

For six years—long enough, unfortunately, for it to have become a custom—I had been giving a party for all the full time members of my department on Halloween. I use the word "unfortunately" not because the occasion had become routine or half-hearted or a burden to me. I looked forward to it, and so did everybody else: the date itself was a happy choice; people had been around the campus long enough to collect a great many things to say, and it was still too early in the term for them to be tired of each other. I had gotten into the habit of making extensive preparations for that party, concocting a new and exotic casserole dish every year, furbishing up my brass and crystal, and putting autumn leaves and sheaves of dried ornamental grass into the vases around my living room. It was an expensive evening—the liquor especially—but I never minded that: I liked the thought that people drank a little more and talked more loudly and loosely at my house on Halloween than they did at other school affairs.

It was, of course, the Sanes business that drained the pleasure out of the Halloween get-together. While he was working so assiduously at keeping himself out of my way, I scarcely felt inclined to ask him to my apartment for a social evening, yet it was unthinkable to exclude him: to exclude him would have been to do him a not completely deserved rudeness and to make a public concern of whatever private differences there were between him and me. So I was more than a week late in getting down to what used to be the amiable task of writing the little cards of invitation I had been dropping into the mail at this season for the last six years—I delayed in the vain hope that there might be some amelioration in the atmosphere between us; and when I wrote the invitations—I wrote them in a hurry on a bleakly sunny and empty Sunday afternoon—the usual aura of happy expectation simply was not there. More out of anger and arrogance than out of any suspicion that he would fail to answer, I drew a dark double line on his card under the R.S.V.P. And the preposterous fact that he could ignore me became a recurrent stab, sharpening rather than lessening as the week went by. I started my day in a fury at the school mailbox, collecting my notes of acceptance from Matt Cusick and the Grüenbergs and Dr. Boyd and Dr. Holland—but not a word from Mr. Sanes.

I invented an equivocal answer for anybody who might ask me, "Who's coming?." No matter who put the question —Jenny Willis or the guileless Matt or the gentle Emily— I suspected I was being pumped and prodded. My face tightened with resentment; I felt sensations I had not felt since I was a skinny, self-mistrustful twelve-year-old; I disliked the inquirer and detested myself. "Everybody—the usual crowd," I said, never daring to look at the person I was addressing. "It'll be about the way it always is, I guess." I was certain somebody was going to ask me outright whether *he* was going to be there, and, by the day before the party, the general failure to pose that question looked like the result of a conspiracy. I felt that they must know more than I did, that he must have made some taunting remark about me and my Halloween parties in front of one or several of them, that they must have gotten together behind my back and decided to save me the pain of his contempt.

The thirty-first was itself a series of minor crises. A certain paisley blouse I had meant to wear that evening—I had bought it at a bargain, and it was too big for me—was supposed to have come back from the dressmaker's the day before; and it occurred to me in the middle of one of my lessons that it had not arrived and that, unless I could get it before eight this evening, I would be reduced to wearing a weary brown velvet thing in which I had appeared twice this season and a depressing number of times last year. I telephoned the woman, who said with the most maddening unconcern that she just hadn't been able to get around to it; I lost my temper and gave her an exaggerated account of my social obligations for the day; and I was not entirely appeased when she told me she would finish it somehow and drop it off at my place late in the afternoon.

And then, before lunch, Jenny Willis dropped in, sleek and smooth, to tamper with my guest list. It had been the custom, and I'm afraid I told her so, to make up the party of *full time* members of our department. If I had invited the part-timers too, the men from the city symphony who rounded out their incomes by giving a few lessons at the College, no apartment the size of mine could have accommodated the crowd and the cost of the liquor would have been exorbitant. But Hughie Saunders—a recent Symphony import, an aggressively good-looking, red-headed, rosy clarinetist—had attached himself to Jenny Willis in his eagerness to get along in the world and couldn't bear the notion that anything should go on without his being on the scene. Jenny wasn't content with announcing pretty blatantly that she was going to bring him; she tried to get me to agree that Hughie was exactly what I needed to liven up my evening. But I only told her gracelessly that she could bring him along if she insisted, thereby losing everything, not only the right to exclude him if I wanted to but also any credit that would have accrued to me if I had given him a courteous invitation. Jenny walked out in something of a pique, and it was only by an effort of will that I taught my next two lessons well, restraining my annoyance at the feeble way in which Marge Eberley chirped *My Mother Bids Me Bind My Hair* and the vulgarities that Fred Wade perpetrated on Schubert's *The Wanderer*.

And then, when I was ready to leave—I was leaving late, it was past four-thirty, and my mind was unnecessarily urgent over an assortment of last-minute purchases I kept telling myself not to forget—when I was standing at the coat rack, taking down my coat, Vincent Booth put in an appearance. My impulse to excuse myself and go about my business was checked by his unusual pallor: he was always pale, but today his skin had a bluish kind of milkiness; and instead of getting into my coat I put it back on the hanger and turned around to take him on, even managing to suppress a sigh. But nothing about him—not the washed-out look nor the purplish circles under his eyes nor his hangdog manner of standing with his head down and his hands in his pockets—could make me overlook the desultory and purposeless way in which he seemed to be willing to consume my time by talking a lot of halting, disjointed drivel; I suspected him of putting in an aimless interval with me while he was waiting for a more significant appointment; and, especially since neither he nor his young woman had troubled themselves to drop in for more days than I cared to count, I was annoyed, and I opened my purse and took out my compact and began to powder my face. At one point in the futile interchange he asked me in a perfectly casual voice if I'd seen anything of Cathie lately. I shook my head and smoothed down my eyebrows; only, I told him, through the door. Now that I called it to mind, I was even more pained at her than I was at him. Earlier in the day, while I had been listening to the mutilation of *The Wanderer*, I had seen her face pressed against the glass pane and fancied she was looking for me, only to discover afterward that she was waiting for the release of Fred Wade, with whom she carried on a particularly shrill and affected little conversa-

80

tion in the hall. Loudness, shrillness, a tendency to paint her mouth a brownish orange and to do her fingernails in the same shade—these, so far as I could see, constituted the "basic changes" she had made to date. "Oh," he said, "I thought maybe you'd seen her." The sentence had the sound of an introduction, but it was followed by nothing; and after a long silence, during which I closed up my purse with a loud, conclusive snap, he stepped backward toward the door. "Aren't you feeling very well?" I asked, more charitable now that I was about to be let off. "You look a bit white around the gills to me." He put his small hand up to the underpart of his neck, the place where he might have expected to find a gill, and gave me a feeble smile. He said he was having a little sinus trouble and looked down at the floor as if he were ashamed of his sinuses, and I told him to take emperin, and he said good night. Yet strangely, for there was absolutely nothing in it, that halting and bodiless conversation left a clinging impression with me. It somehow transformed exasperation into melancholy: I was sad rather than furious when I took a final look into the school mailbox and found nothing there—it seemed to me then that I would have settled at this point for a last-minute refusal provided it had been worded with courtesy. I was sad while I bought the leaf lettuce and the French bread and the two additional bottles of soda: I meditated over the grocery counter on how much time can be spent in preparation for occasions which can survive, at best, only four or five hours. And, when I learned from the janitor that no package had come for me from the dressmaker's, I was neither surprised nor put out: I merely told myself that such is the way of the world.

I wish this philosophic sadness had remained with me for the whole of the evening. It was there at the beginning of the party: Hughie had not yet taken over the bar as he later took over everything, and I had too many duties to allow myself to be involved with any of the three little groups of four or five people that stood in my living room, talking

81

so loudly and vigorously that nobody but Mrs. Holland had found time or detachment to subside into a chair. I might even say I enjoyed the first stage of my party in a mild, remote way, taking it as a kind of spectacle through which I occasionally passed with drinks and dishes of peanuts in my hands. Everything was humming, nobody was lost— not even Matt Cusick. Dr. Boyd, probably eager to discharge his charitable duties early so that he could enjoy himself later, had engaged the Polish violin teacher in a conversation about the Czech Philharmonic—Matt had played in it before the war; and the talk was going so well that a few of the others had come over to hear. On the opposite side of the room, close to the piano, Michael Sokolov, who taught advanced composition and had a sour, fascinating face and an acid wit, was giving an account of his futile attempts to find out exactly how much he would get from the pension plan when he retired: on the basis of the explanatory leaflets distributed at regular intervals by the insurance company, he had arrived at two possible figures, one of them eleven dollars and sixty cents and the other one one hundred and sixty dollars a month; and nobody in the comptroller's office at the college or at the local headquarters of the company had been able to dispel his confusion. Julius Grüenberg volunteered his services as a mathematical consultant, but Emily and a couple of the others raised their voices to dissuade him. It was better to settle on the higher figure and dream about it in the interim, they said; in that case, anybody who died before he retired could die with his illusions.

Hughie, and Jenny Willis with him, had taken an advantageous position close to Dr. Holland, the department head. He was talking about his place at Penny's Run, which none of us had ever seen, and they were listening with all the avid attention that their academic situation seemed to them to require. I thought as I emptied the ashtrays that it had been a wise Dean who had set Dr. Holland—the incarnation of all things American—at the peak of the poly-

82

glot, semi-bohemian Music faculty. His person and his manner had a New England angularity; he seemed to disparage his impeccable English by the folksy twang in his voice; if he was respected among musicologists for his exhaustive two-volume work on secular music in the medieval world, he was also a great fisherman—his wife was always complaining that he kept their living room cluttered with feathers and bits of yarn and lengths of wire all winter, tying his own ingenious fishing flies by the dozen in preparation for spring. He was at once as informal and as remote as an eighteenth century weather vane. Everybody was at ease with him, and nobody had ever tried to get over the effective stockade he had constructed around his privacy. Everybody liked him, and nobody visited him: the only time the Hollands "mixed with the department" was at such traditionally established affairs as the one I was giving tonight. As I handed him his bourbon on the rocks I thought what I always thought when he gave me one of his rare smiles. If I were broke, he would do everything in his power to raise my salary; if I were sick in the hospital, he would stand at the foot of my bed for fifteen minutes, saying appropriate things; and if I were dead he would send an impressive floral piece, sit through the services, and leave quietly before the funeral.

I had to go to the kitchen to put the casserole into the oven, and I was sorry that Mrs. Boyd should come out to offer me help—there wasn't a thing to do out there, and she and I had nothing whatever to say to each other. She was a weary blond whose pedigree outstripped her intelligence; she was too vain to wear glasses, and her forehead was permanently furrowed by her rigorous efforts to see; whatever energy she had retained through the early years of what her parents considered a compromising marriage had been drained away in the anxious nourishing of a late-born, delicate only child; and it seemed downright cruel to introduce any subject that might tax her limited powers. She sniffed the casserole and said she was sure it was going to be delicious, though actually the ingredients, cold like that —eggplant and raw lamb and tomato and grated Romano cheese—were enough to make anybody sick. We exchanged a few recipes, and I was about to shepherd her back into the living room when she said, picking up my cheese knife and testing the edge of it, "Isn't there somebody missing? Oh, yes, I know—the new one, the pianist—Mr. Payne."

"It looks as if Mr. Sanes isn't coming," I told her with more chill than she deserved. If I suspected her of being a member of any conspiracy, *I* was paranoid: she moved in a pale cloud of distraction from measles to whooping cough and thence through a variety of allergies; she knew nothing about the affairs of the department—she was, in fact, incapable of distinguishing between Julius Grüenberg and Michael Sokolov though she had had at least five years in which to get the matter straight. "That's right, Mr. Sanes. It's one of those names that's so simple a person can't remember it. Is he playing a concert or something?" she said.

"Not that I know of."

I started for the arch between the kitchen and the living room, and almost collided with Emily, who was coming from the opposite direction—erect in posture, warm in color, and ample in size. She had dressed for the evening with a care and elaborateness that was European: her black hair was wound in a heavy braided coronet, her imposing figure was draped in moss green crepe, and there were Florentine silver chains with little pieces of turquoise dangling from them around her full throat and her round wrists. She had come out to give me a hand with the cooking and with Mrs. Boyd. "What is it you don't know of?" she said.

"We were talking about Mr. Sanes," said Mrs. Boyd, laying aside the cheese knife with a sigh, as if she parted from it with regret. "He isn't here."

"That I see already," said Emily in her husky German accent. She stepped up to the work table to open a new bottle of soda, and, as the top fizzed off, she flashed me a meaningful look which signified what I would have thought without prompting if I had been in more complete possession of myself. Whatever Mrs. Boyd heard out here, she would probably repeat in the living room—not out of malice, only for lack of anything much to say—and probably the first person to whom she would repeat it would be Mrs. Holland, who invariably took her aside at parties and drew her out about the afflictions of the hapless child.

What is it smells so funny?" said Emily, looking around.

"That's the cheese in the casserole. It's Romano."

"No, but I think it's terribly rude of him," said Mrs. Boyd. "Since it's his first year, I should think turning up at a party is the least he could do."

"Well, who knows what is going to be?" said Emily with sturdy cheerfulness. "It's early yet in the evening. Maybe he is going some other place and later he will drop in." She picked up the casserole and held it out to me.

"Did he say he was coming, Miss Hartmann?"

I felt cornered and assailed. I didn't care what Mrs. Boyd might tell Mrs. Holland, or what the latter might pass along to her husband in the privacy of their bedroom tonight. I snatched the casserole out of Emily's hands, thrust it into the oven with a grating sound, and banged the oven door. "No, he didn't," I said. "He didn't let me know one way or another."

"You don't mean to tell me, Miss Hartmann, that you wrote him an invitation and he didn't even have the courtesy to R.S.V.P.?"

"Yes, that's what I mean."

"Why, how rude of him! How horribly rude! And how inconsiderate of you!"

To have it handed out like that, wrapped up in a swath of well-bred sympathy, was galling, and all the more galling since I had brought it on myself. I had nothing to answer—no grounds for protest and no heart to agree.

85

"We don't know whether we should call it rudeness or not," said Emily. Her eyes fixed themselves on my unwitting tormentor with mellow reasonableness. "It could be there is something else."

"But what else could it be, Mrs. Grüenberg? It takes so little time and trouble to write a note—"

"With men it is always like this. Julius doesn't answer a letter two or three weeks. Where is your liquor, Frieda? The Bourbon is all used."

When we came back into the living room, it seemed to me that either I or my party had caught a fever. Everything had been accelerated in my brief absence from the scene: the coagulation of groups, the consumption of liquor, the production of smoke and noise. Instead of three knots of people there were only two—a small one dominated by the little sharp-faced Mrs. Holland, who was arguing for more aid to India, and a much larger one serving as an audience for Hughie Saunders, who was actually sitting on top of the back of my upholstered chair, with his feet on the overstuffed pillow—narrow feet, shapely in black lisle socks: Jenny Willis confided to me that Hughie was a scream, he'd just announced he couldn't enjoy himself unless he took off his shoes. He had, it must be admitted, a larger fund of amusing stories than anybody else: since he was a clarinetist, and a very able one, he got more outside engagements than any of us at school and almost anybody in the Symphony—he had played twice for the New York New Friends of Music last year. And whatever bits of information he picked up in his wandering he poured out for everybody's benefit, casually dropping names, willing to sing in a clouded tenor if musical annotation was called for, ready to adorn his tale with sound effects, imitations of a bird or a chugging train or a wailing child. It would probably not occur to him until late in his forties that he could be objectionable: his fine clear complexion, his flaming red hair, and his look of boyish candor—all of which I am sure

86

he often contemplated in solitude—gave him the conviction that he need proceed with only a minimum of caution. If, for instance, he had come tonight with a determination to watch himself in front of Dr. Holland, that determination had proved itself ridiculous in less than an hour. Who, with those hearty manners, would expect a fellow to keep his voice down? Who, with a homespun, farmerish twang like that, would have any objection to a fellow's taking off his shoes?

I had intended, once I had finished dispensing another round of drinks, to attach myself to the group around Mrs. Holland. To do so would have been a piece of self-discipline, since Hughie was bubbling on toward a territory all too interesting to me: he was talking about some of the fabulous New York music parties he had been in on, and I was pretty certain somebody was going to ask whether he had ever run into Arthur Sanes. But I had barely disburdened myself of all the glasses except my own—my first for the evening— when he sighted me, and after that there was no possibility of escape. "Why, Frieda Hartmann, look at you running around like a barmaid passing out drinks! You're white in the face, you're absolutely exhausted, you poor little thing!" he said, leaping down soundlessly on his stockinged soles from the top of my chair. Whereupon he announced that *he* was going to tend bar for the rest of the evening, and grabbed me by the arm with a merry forcefulness, and positively arranged me in the chair he had just abandoned, thereby making me the target of all assembled eyes. Not that he meant to let me inhabit that spot alone. After having acted on the decision that it would be more sensible to do the serving from the coffee table—within less than three minutes he had everything set up in a compact confusion on my newly-polished cherry wood—he came and perched himself much as he had been before, above and behind me, his feet on one arm of the chair this time, his knees close to my face, his toes wiggling under the loose mesh of the black lisle.

While he went on about some of the stunning studio apartments in Sutton Place, I sipped my drink and tried to avoid the consciously blank look of Dr. Holland, who stood as imperturbable as a wooden Indian on the edge of the little crowd. The drink—I noted the fact and regretted it, but I did not think of stopping—the drink was unusually powerful with me. As it tingled in my elbows and dulled the sensation in my fingertips, I remembered that I had been too sick-hearted to eat much of my lunch and too rushed to have anything for dinner but a few crackers and a glass of milk.

"But if you want to see a honey of a place," said Hughie, "the place you ought to have seen is the one that Arthur used to have on 57th Street."

"What Arthur?" said Michael Sokolov.

"What Arthur? Why, my good man, there is only one Arthur—by the way, it begins to look as if he weren't going to do us the honor, doesn't it?—the one and only Arthur Sanes. *That's* a studio for you—absolutely tremendous— they knocked out a wall to give him the space he wanted— really, Frieda, it was a good three times the size of this. Everything was all done up in white and mauve and olive green—subtle but striking. Even the wrought iron stuff— and there was plenty of that, let me tell you—was painted oyster white. He got a kind of a Baroque effect, if you know what I mean—things going places, lots of motion—draperies swishing across the windows and wrought iron curling all over the place—" The curling and the swishing called for gestures which I did not have to witness: all I got was the bumping, violent enough to make me wonder if my chair was going to survive the evening. "Treasures, too, and when I say treasures I mean treasures, for instance a Bronzini drawing—you can imagine what a thing like that would cost. And, speaking of costs, the rent must have been outrageous. I swear you couldn't get a place like that for less than four thousand a year."

"What I always say to Hughie is: Where did he get it?" said Jenny Willis.

"Oh, that's the sixty-four thousand dollar question—Where did he get it? Not out of the kind of concertizing he's been doing, that's for sure. And not out of private teaching either, if you're asking me. Even if you charge twenty dollars a lesson, you simply don't drag in *that* much."

Emily, who had attached herself to the political clique, turned her solid figure vigorously around and addressed us from a distance of several feet. "Who knows where this money comes from?" she asked in her gutteral voice over the intervening heads. "That man—how do you call him?—that one who teaches in Architecture here, it is said his father is vice president of a glass company. A man could be rich and also be a pianist and also teach in a college. It has been heard of, especially in Europe, before."

"Definitely, definitely," said Dr. Holland, and he turned on his heel and walked over to join his wife.

A faint and gentle smile, a smile of gratification at the essential decency of his superior, transformed the face of Michael Sokolov.

But this marked desertion did not present itself as a reproof to Hughie Saunders. If he felt anything, he felt released. "It's possible, but actually it isn't very probable," he said, taking the lot of us into his spacious confidence. "There are rumors, scads of rumors—of course, he's the sort that's bound to get them going—but where there's smoke there's usually a teeny-weeny bonfire, you know."

"What are you giving us, Hughie? What sort of rumors?" said Dr. Boyd, looking down iron-grey and scornful from all the easy superiority of his six-foot-two. Through the blur that was settling around me, I thought it was a singularly Boydian speech: it not only branded Hughie as a scandalmonger but also gave him the necessary encouragement to get on with his scandalous tale.

"Oh, it's general talk that he's got a female patron—

89

though he *is* a bit old for that sort of thing, don't you people think? It's general talk that the rent for the apartment comes out of a patron, though 'a patron' could mean any number of things."

"Yes, any number of things," said Michael, humming his m's and n's and rolling his r's, "so there is no need to give it a compromising definition even by implication. There is nothing peculiar if well-to-do people give assistance to artists. I am not at all disturbed to announce to you that a few years ago a friend of mine—a distinguished man of all your acquaintance—had such benefits from a lady. To say nothing of the fact that many of us are often filling in applications to foundations—"

"But this particular patron is no foundation," said Hughie. "This particular patron takes a great deal of trouble to keep in the dark—"

"This, again, is only natural, Mr. Saunders. Some generous people consider it an embarrassment to have such publicity—"

My glass was empty and freezing cold between my hands. I was numb with the Scotch and with a disproportionate wretchedness. What sort of apartment Arthur Sanes had, what kind of relationship he had with his "patron," all these things—so I told myself, hating Hughie's knees and feet—were nothing to me. My immediate problem was noise and a conviction of urgency about it: everybody was talking at once and something was ringing, probably something in my head.   :

"Hey, Frieda," said Hughie.

I loathed him and I could not answer him.

"Frieda," said Matt Cusick from the group around the Hollands, "did you know your house phone is ringing?"

"Oh, is it? I'll answer it," I said, and wondered at my audacity—there was such a silence as I went and such a stretch of wavering, precarious floor under my distant feet.

They were waiting, all of them, to see whether it was

90

Arthur Sanes, phoning on his way up. So was I, but when I lifted the receiver and found it was only the janitor, the denouement seemed uproarious, I wanted to laugh in everybody's face. "What did you want, Mr. Barry? Are we making too much noise up here?" I asked in a voice that was not exactly my own.

"No, nothing like that—so far, nobody's put in any complaints. All I wanted to tell you was: there's a box down here for you."

The box, with my tardy bargain blouse in it, seemed an even more hilarious comedown than the one that had preceded it; but I repressed an impulse to tell him to toss it into the incinerator and said I would drop down to pick it up some time later tonight.

"And *that*," said Hughie, flinging out his arms, "is the story of Arthur Sanes and his patron. Do you know what *I* need? I need something to wet my whistle." He let himself back down onto the floor and stalked over to the coffee table. He stood behind the confusion of bottles, looked around the room, and began to count the empty glasses, turning one of his fingers down for every empty glass in sight. "Come on, Julius, old boy," he said, though he had met that gentleman for the first time only a couple of hours ago. "There are too many alcoholics here for one bartender to cope with. How about giving me a hand?"

It was Julius who brought me my second Scotch, and I took it without protest. The fact is, I did not even think to protest: the sight of Julius' good long face with its shining spectacles and its deep downward lines from the corners of the nose to the corners of the lips filled me with a nostalgia as for a time long gone and a place long lost. Actually, what I was remembering with disproportionate yearning was the evening I had eaten dinner at the Grüenbergs'—the place was less than a mile away and the time was a few weeks ago. But a glowing quality, only warmed and intensified by the sips of liquor I kept taking, hung over the recalled event, doubtless cast forward upon it by the meeting in the library and the walk on the bridge; and I mourned my former innocence while I mocked it: imagine believing he was going to invite me to his place for a steak bordelaise, imagine being stirred up about *Keine Augen* and the Weeping Madonna and all that stuff! There was a smell of scorching Romano in the air, and I tried unsteadily to rise to the danger; but before I was halfway up I saw that Emily and Mrs. Holland were in the kitchen, dealing with the crisis efficiently. Somebody had put a progressive jazz record on my phonograph, and Hughie was holding forth about it. Mrs. Boyd excused herself to phone home and see whether the sitter had given her offspring the eleven o'clock medicine for hives. Michael and Dr. Boyd were engaged in a rather edgy argument about how much Bartok had been influenced by the twelve-tone system, and Matt Cusick was making a nuisance of himself by listening to them with a knowing smile which belied the pale confusion in his eyes. Mrs. Holland came out of the kitchen and announced that the burning smell was only the cheese dripping out onto the bottom of the oven; she and Emily had tested the casserole with a broom-corn, and it wouldn't be done through for another half hour.

I had timed myself correctly—I had expected to get the food on at exactly half-past eleven—but I was appalled that there should be so much of the evening left, and I concluded that what remained was going to be a misery. I kept on drinking because I was cold and nervous and hungry. Most of the others kept on drinking because the bar was on the coffee table: with everything right there, it seemed so easy to have another. There were moments of relative clarity for me, and in the course of them I did my duty: I disengaged Matt Cusick from the twelve-tone system and talked to him until I couldn't stand it anymore, and then went into the bedroom and combed my hair with numb and awkward fingers; I filled the ice-bucket—Hughie couldn't bother with it—and exhumed a dusty bottle of soda from the bottom of a cupboard; I looked for an earring that Jenny Willis had lost and found it on the floor beside the sofa, stepped flat, with one of the imitation sapphires gone. With Emily's expert assistance, I even managed to carry on a coherent conversation with the head of the department about the Mozart Memorial Program we were planning for next January, though all through the precariously maintained conversation I kept seeing myself as one of those circus dancers who go through their paces on a tightrope. The influence that emanated from Dr. Holland was, as always, reassuring, and I might even have pulled myself together if Jenny hadn't followed me into the kitchen when it was time to take out the casserole and put things on.

"Isn't that a business now—what Hughie was telling us about Sanes and his female patron?" she said, sitting down on a breakfast stool and giving me an excited and confidential look.

I rejected the look, opened the oven door, and sniffed the casserole. There was more heat than fragrance: I felt as if my head were being borne away from me on a wave of hot, expanding air. I had had too many, and I permitted myself the license of the intoxicated. "Do you want to know something, Jenny?" I said. "I could live without Hughie."

"I don't know what you've got against him. Usually people take to him, you know."

With the help of two pot-lifters and a great deal of self-discipline, I managed to get the bubbling casserole from the stove to the kitchen table, where it would have to stay until it was consumed. I had meant to serve my late supper from my coffee table, but dear Hughie had submerged my coffee table under a welter of bottles, glasses and spilled ashtrays. "He's too damned forward for his own good. He takes too much upon himself," I said.

"Oh, well, if you didn't want him to tend bar, you didn't need to let him. He only offered to do it out of the kindness of his heart."

93

"Oh, yes, the kindness of his heart!" I said with an exasperation intensified by my discovering I had forgotten all about toasting the French loaves. I would have to serve them cold, without the melted butter and garlic, and I had promised garlic bread to Michael Sokolov. "The poisonous gossip he's been spreading around here—the way he's been going on about this one and that one—"

"This one and that one?" There was a false perplexity in her voice. "As far as I can recall, the only person he talked about was Arthur Sanes."

"Well, God knows, he did a thorough job on *that*—" I stopped because I felt her eyes staring at me through the lenses of her Harlequin glasses.

"Do you mind?" she said.

"Not particularly." I flung it out with a liar's quick assertiveness. "I just don't think it's a decent thing to do."

"Actually, Frieda, he was very decent about it. He didn't tell the half of what he knows."

"I hope he'll keep the other half for a less public occasion. Dr. Holland was in the room—Mr. Sanes' superior, with the right to hire and fire. Dr. Holland heard everything he said—" I stopped again, remembering that Arthur Sanes had drawn me on and shoved me off, that he had avoided me for weeks, that he had cut my party without writing me so much as a formal R.S.V.P., and that anybody who would come to his defense after all that was simply a fool.

"Oh, if I were you, I wouldn't waste any worry on what Dr. Holland might think," said Jenny. "One thing's for certain: Mr. Sanes never gives a thought to anything Dr. Holland might think. Mr. Sanes is of the opinion that he's doing Dr. Holland a favor to teach in his department—"

She broke off, because Michael Sokolov had just stepped briskly into the kitchen. He lifted one of the French loaves and looked at it ruefully. "The bread is not yet toasted?" he said.

"I guess it's not going to be toasted. I forgot it."

94

"Ah, well, do not be upset. If we are fortunate enough to have a still heated oven, it can be done. Here—where is your garlic salt?—you will see, it is nothing. I myself will gladly make this little preparation for you."

While he was doing the slicing, the buttering, and the shaking of the garlic salt, I set up the buffet—the coffee, the salad, the plates and cups—and Jenny bestirred herself to the extent of laying out the silverware. "We must take them with a little salt, these stories which Hughie tells us about Mr. Sanes and his patron," said Michael without looking up from the work in hand. "It so happens I also know these matters, I also have been sometimes to musical parties in New York, and I think the rent of Mr. Sanes' studio, if it was paid by anybody, it was paid by a respected married woman, very rich and very well considered in musical circles—she has helped many as she is helping him. She is on the Board of the Philharmonic, and it is commonly said she is making some effort to get for him an appearance with the symphony."

But this balm of Michael's was not altogether soothing to my irritation. The respected married woman, very rich and well considered in musical circles, added the itch of curiosity to the pain. Though I knew I was under Jenny's scrutiny, I could not let the matter rest. While the garlic bread toasted in the oven and Michael helped me fold the napkins, I got around to her age—she was like around fifty—and her name—her name was Irish, McBride, McSomething, yes, McIvor. In spite of my drunkenness, I knew I was following a dangerous conversational route, but because of my drunkenness I was convinced nobody was noticing much; and I was shamed into a fierce blush when Jenny remarked from the stove that the bread was done and that we'd better forget about Mr. Sanes and call the others in.

Possibly because the kitchen was so hot with cooking and with milling, chattering people, what I had been drinking made a sudden fresh assault on me. I remember being crowded back into the vicinity of the oven, and thereafter I remember nothing until everybody had served himself and was seated in the living room—I suppose it was as good a time as any to lose track of: if I had said anything questionable, nobody could have heard me, there had been too much interest in the food and too much noise. I soothed myself with these considerations as I let myself carefully down into the corner of the sofa and accepted, with amazingly coherent thanks, the plate that Michael Sokolov had filled for me. I guessed that he had been leading me around in the blank interim and that now he would consign me to somebody else's mercy; but he settled beside me on the arm of the sofa instead.

"You are all right, Frieda? You are not feeling you will be ill or anything?" he asked me, looking down at me with a wry smile on his mouth and real concern in his eyes.

"Oh, no, I'm perfectly all right." I was amazed at the extent of my recovery. The room stretched out before me, steady and cleanly defined; and I sighed profoundly and said I hoped I'd been behaving myself.

"Oh, like a perfect lady."

"Did I say anything that was out of the way?"

"Not at all, as I can remember. In the kitchen you were giving a little talking-to to Miss Willis. It was about the things that Hughie said about Mr. Sanes."

I sighed again. Something—perhaps it was the almost painful sharpness of the faces and the objects before my clearing eyes—something made me long to remove all equivocations, to strip away all veilings of the mind and heart. "But I want you to understand one thing, Michael," I said, laying my hand on his sleeve. "I want you to understand that when I'm disapproving of Hughie I am not approving of Mr. Sanes—and I'm not basing my conclusions on anything Hughie said. Mr. Sanes has his own way of being perfectly hateful. He's been hateful to Matt Cusick,

96

and he's been hateful to me—he didn't even answer my invitation. For some crazy reason he's positively paranoid about having anybody hear him practising—you should have heard how hateful he was about *that* to poor Harrison Frye. And if his relations with his colleagues are bad, I wouldn't know what you'd call his relations with his students—he torments them and sneers at them and makes them feel ridiculous. Everybody he teaches is in some sort of nervous state, and poor Cathie Dugan looks to me as if—"

I fell silent because a pair of bright blue eyes were looking at me keenly: Hughie's eyes, in Hughie's boyish face, under Hughie's innocent looking brow. He had heard every word of it, and on the way home tonight he would repeat it, with embellishment, to Jenny. My remorse, coming up into my mouth with the taste of bile, was enough to turn my illusion of soberness into the real, the cold, the naked, shaming thing. "Oh, my God, Michael, why did I drink so much?" I asked.

"Let me get you some coffee. It will make you feel better."

"No, it won't—I wouldn't dare—excuse me, I've got to go and lie down for a minute," I said.

But, even though I could lock the bedroom door securely behind me, I could not lie down: coats, hats, purses completely covered the spread—the confusion on top of the bed harked me back, in my raw new soberness, to the evening when my clothes, wrinkled from being crammed into my luggage, had been heaped and scattered there. I did not ask myself why I should regret that evening with its hard conviction of loss and isolation. I knew I had possessed a cleanness, a decency, a capacity for sane compassion back there which I had betrayed in many small ways since and had outrageously betrayed tonight. Unreasonable as it may seem, it was inescapably borne in upon me that I had lost much in the weeks between, had loosened whatever well-intentioned hold I had, not only upon this

97

maddening but obviously tormented stranger, but also on my students, my friends, even my dead. It was a great deal that I grieved for in the five minutes I permitted myself to stay behind the locked door, with the muted noises of the tired party almost shut out; and, before I went back to wait for the end of the evening among the rest of them, I walked over to the dresser and touched the ring on the marble where my mother's perfume bottle had stood.

It seemed to me, when I came back into the living room with a properly powdered if chastened face, that some of them—particularly the Hollands and Emily and Matt Cusick—were trying to give this party in its last stages some ghostly likeness to its predecessors. The talk that went on while we finished off the supper was the sort of talk we had always had on Halloween, though it lacked the old conviction. Departures were unhurried and desultory: Hughie and Jenny made themselves responsible for emptying ashtrays and cleaning up the coffee table; and when I was left alone there was nothing for me to do but air the place and wash the coffee pot and clear a corner of the kitchen table for breakfast, since I had made up my mind to set the clock for seven and do the dishes before I went to school.

Airing the place was a desolate procedure. As soon as I pulled up the windows a dank wind streamed in, stirring the drapes, rustling the yellow leaves on the branches that I had bought for the party, making me shiver in spite of the thickness of my old velvet dress; and it occurred to me that, since the night watchman would be on duty, I might as well leave the wind behind me to do its dreary work while I went down to the lobby to get my paisley blouse, which had deteriorated so much in my imagination that I wanted to see whether it would be fit to wear. The corridors and stairways of all apartment houses take on an institutional air when the main lights are turned out: it was like walking around in a hospital in the middle of the night; I went

98

down warily, without clicking, and asked the night watch-man in a very low voice whether he could lay his hands on the package that had come for me. "There it is, over on the bench," he said, loudly enough to rouse echoes. But it was not the flat brown box my paisley blouse had come in: it heightened the hospital atmosphere by being a long white thing, the sort of box that can contain nothing but flowers.

I thought it had probably come from some of my students. To explain my brusqueness, I had mentioned to two of them that I was entertaining tonight; and I was sure, with the attendant remorse, that they had sent me something for my party, something I had not even used. I thanked the night watchman and started up the stairs with the package in my arms, but on the first landing I knew I was too curious to wait, and I balanced the box on the banister and broke the string. In the light of the dim little bulb I could see that they were white snapdragons, gratifyingly sturdy spikes, not any the worse for their long neglect. There were so many of them that I was sure a collection must have been made, and I put the box down on the landing and opened the envelope to see who had con-tributed. But there was no list of names—there was only a single sentence in an unfamiliar hand: "It wasn't that I didn't want to come—I couldn't come. Arthur Sanes."

In the strange and unnerving combination of emotions that assailed me then, surprise was the least of the ingre-dients. How could I be very much surprised, considering that he had singled me out and come over to me in the faculty dining room, had asked me to walk out of the Fine Arts library with him and talked to me about *Keine Augen,* had looked steadily at me with his faded hazel eyes and given me his dry smile? All these things were cleansed of the nightmare welter of rubbish that had accumulated around them in the intervening weeks; all these things were somehow authenticated by the very physical actuality of the snapdragons—their juicy stems, their crisp and delicate leaves, their tight green-tinged buds. I looked down at them in their tissue wrappings, and they justified me: I had not dreamed, I had not been presumptuous—the proof of that was in the flowers. Yet there was a sting in the exultation: if, in spite of all the arguments to the contrary, he was still weaving some thread between us, I had done whatever I could tonight to cut that thread. I had called him hateful and paranoid, I had told what I should not even have known about his dealings with his students, and Hughie had heard me. It was bitter regret for that betrayal, more than anything else, which made me snatch up the box and put my face against the flowers.

Chapter 8

I WROTE HIM A note to thank him for the flowers, a short note, casually worded and just this side of formality, saying only that I was grateful and that we had missed him and hoped he would come next year. But brief and ordinary as it was, that note cost me a great deal of trouble; no way of wording it seemed quite satisfactory, and I could not make up my mind what sort of paper I should write it on. School letterhead seemed pointedly cold, and ordinary typing paper seemed scarcely better, and after I had sent it off on a deckle-edged grey sheet in a grey envelope lined in striped tissue, I felt I had been too sociable, too intimate, and consoled myself with the conclusion that the paper manufacturers had simply not provided anything suitable for an occasion like this. No reply was forthcoming, and in all honesty I did not expect one; yet there was a change—a change that would have been perceptible to nobody but myself. He still kept his distance, but from his distance he often stared and smiled at me. At faculty meetings and at such public occasions as assemblies and lectures, he placed himself either intentionally or by chance somewhat behind and across from me; and I could not rid myself of the belief that, whenever my eyes were on somebody else, his eyes were on me.

101

I knew now by way of Harrison that he *did* eat his lunch on campus but ate it very late, sometimes not coming into the faculty dining room until a quarter of two, just fifteen minutes before the steam table and the counters were cleaned out. I would never have thought of going near the place at that time voluntarily, but when Dr. Holland proposed that he and I should eat there at one o'clock on a Tuesday to talk about the Mozart Memorial Concert in relative peace and quiet, I could hardly refuse. I remember being glad I had worn my new brown sweaters that day, not only because it was suddenly cold—though we had more than a week to go before the Thanksgiving break, the stretch beyond the big expanse of plate glass was powdered with a flour-like dusting of snow—but also because I was reasonably sure that *he* would wander in and stare at me; and the first thing I did after settling myself at the table across from my superior was to take out my mirror and restore the smoothness of my hair.

Dr. Holland was in the relaxed and expansive state of mind that would have prompted him to order cocktails if cocktails had been available, and the ease and warmth he exhibited over the grilled cheese sandwiches and the bowls of cream of tomato soup constituted a happy omen from my point of view. I had been meaning to ask him if I could take an extra day off at the end of the holiday, since I wanted to hear a little cluster of concerts in New York; and, though he had never denied me a single one of my few reasonable requests, he had granted each of them only after a stretched minute of deliberation—a wise system, which made it difficult, though not impossible, to ask for something else. And, though he worked around to the Mozart program more quickly than I had thought he would, I was not discouraged: sooner or later in the course of our talk we were bound to come naturally up against the subject of the Thanksgiving break; and, since I had no intention of looking up my past, no reasons except the most unessen-

102

tial ones for wanting to take the trip, I felt no urgency and was perfectly willing to bide my time. Nor could I suffer from boredom in the interim. Dr. Holland's talk, always keen and lively, was more than usually so this afternoon; he was peppering it with "damn it, Frieda," every here and there—a sign that he was feeling extraordinarily high-spirited. Though he never dealt in personalities, he rendered them pretty thoroughly in the process of passing on to the main point; and before we were well into our cream of tomato soup I had the gratifying conviction that I was being taken into administrative councils.

"I want to have two programs, one by the students and the other by the faculty," he said. "And would you believe it?—I've already run into trouble on both those programs. We're a temperamental bunch—damn it, Frieda, we're a very temperamental bunch around here. I was taking it for granted that Dugan and Booth would do the B flat sonata—they worked on it last year, you know— and I got an outright 'No' on that one, though what could be up in that area, I don't pretend to understand."

"I imagine it's just that Cathie has the idea she ought to spend her last year working on certain big, specific things . . ." I trailed off and looked down and cut my grilled cheese sandwich carefully into quarters, feeling that no undue attention should be brought to bear at the moment on the Schumann Fantasia.

"Oh, but the way I got it from Matt, the difficulty isn't with Miss Dugan. I don't believe it ever even got as far as Miss Dugan—it was Booth who threw in the monkey wrench. According to Matt, the little fellow stated point blank that he wouldn't play the B flat or anything else with the lady in question, which looks a little on the queer side to me, considering how thick the two of them were last year."

"Maybe they're spatting at the moment. They always did spat a lot." Actually, without having given the matter any conscious thought, I had concluded somewhere in the

103

dimmer reaches of my mind that there had been a break between Vincent and Cathie: looking back over the recent weeks, I knew I had not once seen them together since the afternoon when he had come into my office and tried to say something to me—I was certain now that he had been desperately trying—and gone away without being able to deliver one significant or revealing word.

"As for the faculty," he said, lowering his voice and looking around him—but the place was almost empty, a wide vacancy of unoccupied tables lay around us in the snow-foreboding light—"I'm at the end of my wits about the faculty. Not you, you'll give us a group of songs, I know—and Hughie's no problem, not in anything like this: he's already lined up Matt and Emily and the others to play the Clarinet Quintet with him. But I can't exactly imagine doing a concert to celebrate the Mozart Bicentennial without including the professor of piano, and only God in heaven knows what kind of idiotic nonsense has gotten into Sanes."

"Why, what's the matter with Mr. Sanes?" I said, not at all certain that I wasn't overdoing my attempt at off-handedness.

"That's a question I wouldn't presume to answer. *I* don't know him, and neither does anybody else—unless *you're* in his confidence—I've noticed he doesn't look bored or afflicted every time you open your mouth in a faculty meeting, and I can assure you, Frieda, *that's* a distinction."

"I'm not in his confidence."

"No? Well, I'm sorry to hear it. I thought maybe you'd be able to cast a little light on the subject. We're in the dark, we're all of us in the dark. Really, Frieda, let me tell you—it was the damndest thing. The end of the week—I think it was last Thursday—I ran into him in the hall and I asked him what he thought he'd play—you remember, I sent a memo about it around to everybody a couple of weeks ago. And, believe me, I never saw anything like it.

104

Damn it, Frieda, it was downright upsetting—I must have made him terribly angry just by bringing the matter up. He started to tremble—I mean it literally—he started to tremble, and sunburned as he is he went grey and spotty in the face. I thought at first maybe he was upset because he hadn't bothered to read my memo, so I explained the whole business from the start, and when I finished—he let me go on in some detail about it—he said in his sardonic way, 'Oh, yes, I know.' And then he told me he'd given the matter considerable thought and had been intending to drop me a note to the effect that when he was hired he hadn't understood he'd be expected to make public appearances, otherwise he never would have signed up for the job. Now, what can you make of a thing like that? Is he outdoing himself to be insolent, or is he just plain out of his head?"

I was imagining the scornful face turning livid under Dr. Holland's scrutiny, and I think I went a little pale myself. "I just don't know. I can't make him out," I said.

"Well, I'm not going to let it spoil my soup, that's for certain." He shook back his crest of snow-white hair and flashed me one of his rare smiles. I often thought that his sensibilities were more delicate than his angular person and his darting talk would lead anybody to believe, and it seemed to me that he was aware of having somehow ruffled me and that he wanted to re-establish the cheerful and comfortable mood in which we had begun. For something like half an hour—while the last wilted salads disappeared from the counters and the dining room was deserted by everybody but the two of us and three of the girls from the clerical staff—we made ourselves very merry; and it was his headlong exhilaration rather than any lingering diffidence in me that kept me from putting in my request for an extra day at the end of the Thanksgiving vacation.

I made up my mind to get it over with as soon as he came back from picking up our desserts at the almost denuded counter, but when I saw him crossing the dining room with the coffee and the angel food cake on a tray, I knew from the briskness in his step that he was going to snatch the initiative. "Do you know who's out in the vestibule?" he said, pouring the spilled coffee out of my saucer into my cup and sopping up the residue with a paper napkin. "Sanes is hanging up his coat out there, and I've got an idea, a real inspiration—I've just thought up the neatest way of taking care of Sanes."

"What's that?"

"Wait a few minutes, and I'll show you. Just wait until he's picked up his lunch, and you'll see."

I kept my eyes on my dry and weary angel food cake and took long gulps of coffee as an antidote against apprehension. I heard *his* voice—though it was speaking alone, I knew I could have distinguished it in a multitude of voices —making some remark to the woman behind the counter; I heard his step—the girls from the clerical staff had fallen suddenly silent—coming in our direction, then halting; and I knew that he had sighted us and was caught, exposed and embarrassed, in the middle of the almost empty room. Dr. Holland winked at me and wheeled around in his chair. "Hello, Sanes. How about coming over and joining us— we're just starting our dessert," he said, and, jumping up to move another chair over to our table, he indicated with a nod of his impressive white head the empty place that was on my left.

He came—what could he do but come?—and stood a few paces away from us, a little to one side of Dr. Holland, much as he had stood on that other day when I had been eating with Harrison, but this time he did not look at me. My first thought was no thought at all, was only an image of the snapdragons in their tissue wrappings: it seemed as if the white spikes of the flowers were there between us, palpably, painfully, an intolerable complication forbidding the exchange of a glance. Then I thought that he had

106

changed, that he was paler and thinner: the sunburn was going at last, the declivities in his cheeks had deepened, and there were greyish shadows around his eyes.

"Sit down, sit down," said Dr. Holland, with the broad geniality of a host urging a late-comer to take his seat at a banquet table; and all the time he kept flashing his merry, conspiratorial blue look at me. "I hope you haven't arranged your schedule so that you always have to eat your lunch at this ungodly hour. Nothing but the pleasure of having a talk with Frieda here could keep me waiting until after one—I begin to feel the pangs at half past eleven."

I did not dare to look at the presence that edged in beside me. I stared instead at the corner of the neighboring table, and saw it grasped by a narrow hand, and wondered whether the fingers clung with so much force in order to keep themselves from trembling. He was as close to me now as he had been when we stood on the bridge, and I felt that there was some impropriety in the fact that I could catch the tweedy smell of his suit and hear his breath.

"I always eat late. It makes the afternoon seem shorter," he said.

"Oh, so that's the reason, is it? I'll have to tell that to your colleagues. Some of your colleagues are under the impression that you get over here so late because you don't particularly care for company."

Even though the twang and the undercurrent of hilarity blunted the barb in that, I found it very disquieting. My heart was beating so fast and hard that I imagined the pounding must be visible through my sweater. I glanced covertly and briefly to the left, and thought I saw the ghost of a conciliatory smile. "Why did you get meat loaf? The meat loaf is terrible," I said, hoping to channel the current of Dr. Holland's high spirits and trying not to watch the unsteady hands as they took the plate and the roll and the cup of black coffee from the tray.

"You're right, Miss Hartmann, the meat loaf is terrible.

But that's my punishment, that's what I get for eating at this eccentric time of day. I have to eat meat loaf—there isn't anything else."

But the head of the department was not to be put off by any chitchat about food. With quick movements, he set the salt and pepper and the little glass jar of mustard over on Mr. Sanes' side of the table. "Here, spice it up a bit, and it'll be perfectly edible," he said. "I've just been selling Frieda a bill of goods. I've got her convinced—she's a good girl, she doesn't take too much convincing—I've got her convinced that she's going to sing four or five songs on the Mozart program. There's only one difficulty—she needs a good accompanist."

I was on the point of saying that Anna Webb, the secondary piano teacher, would be willing to accompany me; I had already told him so in the note I had written in answer to his memo; but I had scarcely opened my mouth when he flashed me a warning glance. "I tell you what," he said, resting his arm along the table and slanting the upper part of his body, so that he could look straight into Mr. Sanes' face, "suppose *you* do it. If you don't want to take the time and trouble to work up a sonata, all right. But surely you won't mind accompanying Miss Hartmann."

I was appalled beyond blushing. I stared at the dark and tendonous hand—it was spreading on mustard with a little scarlet plastic shovel—I looked at the hand and waited for the trembling to begin. But, strangely, there was no trembling: the spreading motions became more broad, more masterful; if he felt anything, what he was feeling was—unaccountably—relief. "I'd be glad to," he said with a readiness that certainly constituted a letdown for Dr. Holland and made it possible for me to raise my eyes. There was nothing questionable in my neighbor's face—no repressed anger, no mockery to belie the cordial note of his voice, nothing but an obliging and uncomplicated smile.

108

I could have believed—God knows, by this time I wished to believe—that he had reversed his position on the Mozart program because he wanted a closer connection with me, even if he had to get it at the cost of a humiliating turnabout. But something—it must have been the inexplicable relaxation of his hands, since there was nothing but a formal kind of friendliness in his face—something warned me not to take it for granted that a desire for my company was the sole explanation. While we discussed which of the songs I was going to sing, he showed none of the shame-faced pleasure of the male who has managed to arrange a private encounter with a female without committing himself. In fact I could not rid my mind of the conviction that he was vastly relieved over something, though I hadn't the slightest idea what he could be relieved about: his tone, his few spare gestures, and his smile whenever I dared to look at it, all conveyed a tremulous kind of hard-won quietude.

For the next fifteen or twenty minutes, while he was getting down his coffee and meat loaf, the burden of our talk lay for the most part on me. Though his replies were long and cordial, he did not seem to have the self-possession for initiating anything; and Dr. Holland had not yet adjusted himself to the collapse of the expected fun: he kept looking my way as if to assure me that he *had* been given a flat negative less than a week ago. But I doubt I provided him with any convincing pantomime of confidence: I was having troubles enough of my own. When two people are sitting close at a small table and trying to keep clear of touch, they are almost certain to blunder into it: Mr. Sanes dropped his paper napkin and grazed my knee with his sleeve when he was trying to retrieve it; I could not avoid his fingers—they were extraordinarily cold—when I handed him the sugar bowl; and once when he was making a rather forced gesture to indicate to Dr. Holland that none of Mozart's songs were trivial in his opinion,

109

his elbow bumped hard against mine. All this was painful to him—I gathered as much by the fact that he finally took refuge in facial and bodily rigidity—and certainly it was painful to me. I began to wonder how long it would be before Dr. Holland broke up the party; and I knew that I had not been as conscious of my person or as dissatisfied with my behavior since I attended a dance in my first evening dress when I was fifteen years old.

"When would you like to start rehearsing, Miss Hartmann?"

"Any time at all. Any time that's convenient for you."

"I suppose we ought to get together as early as we can. What I mean to say is: I don't want to touch the things until I see what you're intending to do with them. How about some afternoon next week?"

Though he had given no particular stress to the word "afternoon," I found it unpleasantly, even offensively pointed. By specifying an afternoon, he had forestalled any presumptions about coming to his place for a steak bordelaise. "I have no free afternoons this coming week," I said. "I teach every afternoon Monday through Friday, and there wouldn't be any point in my doing it then—I'm much too tired. As for Saturday and Sunday—both of them happen to be taken up. I've got a couple of engagements that I wouldn't want to miss."

"Then how about making it some day during the Thanksgiving holiday?" he asked, looking at me over the napkin with which he was fastidiously wiping the corners of his thin lips. "On second thought, it'd be better then. If we made it then, I could cook a steak for you. I've been meaning to put together a dinner for the two of us for a long time, you know."

If he had said it casually, if he had not demanded and held my glance while he was saying it, I would have let him understand that I had more intriguing things to do with my vacation. I might even have taken the occasion—

it was such a natural one—to ask Dr. Holland for the extra day at the end of the break, knowing that the presence of one of my colleagues would make it all the more difficult for him to refuse. But the look that held me now was the deepest and most earnest look I had ever had from Arthur Sanes: in its steady contrition, in its dignified, unwavering pleading, it took in everything that his daily bearing had been shutting out for weeks—*Keine Augen,* the moment on the bridge, the unfulfilled promise at the bus stop, the flowers and the note that came with the flowers. If I had rejected that look, if I had explained that I was meaning to go out of town, I would have rejected all these, and I wanted them all.

"Unless, of course, you've made some other plans, Miss Hartmann."

"Oh, no, I haven't any other plans. I'd like to. I'd like to very much," I said.

Chapter 9

BACK IN THE DAYS when I lived in
New York, I had a kind of offhand attitude about concerts:
there were so many of them that I never gave a second
thought to anything I had to miss. But here in town it was
different; aside from the Symphony—and the Symphony
played only twenty-four weeks out of the year—those of us
who were really involved with music had only one thing to
look forward to: the eight recitals brought by the Art
Society and given on the last Monday of the month in
the Music Hall. Each of these concerts presented a top-
ranking artist in a program that made no concession to
popular taste, and the one that promised to be best this
year was the one scheduled for the Monday before Thanksgiving, when Milstein and Artur Balsam were playing the
three violin sonatas of Brahms.

I always went to those concerts with Emily and Julius
Grüenberg. I didn't have dinner with them beforehand because I knew how such arrangements can become traditions
and how traditions can become burdens, but they always
stopped at my apartment to pick me up in their battered
Dodge. In the Music Hall—all creamy white paint and gilt
and deep red plush—I sat with them, and yet I did not

112

sit with them. I occupied Seat One, Row F, and they occupied Seats One and Two, Row G. Under this ingenious arrangement I could turn around and talk to them when I felt they wanted my talk, or I could stare ahead at the gold pipes of the organ ranged across the back of the stage and leave my semi-companions to themselves. Now and again the three of us would go afterwards to the grille of a neighboring hotel, where we would have a sandwich and a cup of coffee together; but more often than not I would ask them to drop me off at my place on the grounds that I was too tired for anything but bed. I was gratified by the ease and plasticity of this arrangement, and I prided myself on knowing how to avoid making a nuisance of myself in my single state.

It was a pity in more ways than one that Emily and Julius had to miss the Milstein concert. They called me—that is, Julius did—at seven-thirty and told me to order a taxi since they would not be able to come for me. Emily had banged a glass coffee maker against the table and broken it and scalded her knee with the boiling coffee; no, she was all right, they didn't want me to come over; I should go and enjoy it and tell them about it later; the only pity was that the tickets would have to go to waste. And it was strangely unnerving to sit in the packed hall with the two empty seats behind me: I missed the Grüenbergs, I ached for Emily, and I felt peculiarly exposed and conspicuous.

The audience, or that part of it at any rate which was on the first floor of the Music Hall, had gone to more trouble than usual to make themselves impressive. Though there were only three or four couples who were in full dress —staid and elderly people who had probably come from formal dinner parties—most of the other women were wearing silks or velvets in dark rich colors and had put on their jewelry so that every here and there prism-like bits of brightness sparkled and flashed. The smell of the place—

113

it was usually redolent of some faint disinfectant and years of settled dust—was lost tonight under a heavy blending of several varieties of perfume. I nodded to people I knew—almost all of the Music faculty was there—and then retreated quickly into myself. Architecture, about which I know next to nothing, is dear to me because the vague contemplation of it has been my sole resort in many periods of embarrassed public solitude: having taken off my coat and smoothed my paisley blouse—it had turned out to be, at best, an inoffensive thing—I looked at the ceiling, a white dome traced over with gilded scrolls and trumpets and flowers, and wondered how long the gilt would last and how much money would have to be spent, once it was worn and scrubbed away, to get it put back on.

I was sitting in what must have been a gawky position, with my head tilted back and my gaze roving over the ceiling, when I felt the chilly shock of his look upon me, coming at me from the middle of the second row. I made myself respectable and nodded to him, and he returned the nod; but I was baffled by the fact that his face was pointedly inexpressive and cold. I wondered whether he could have a "date" in the seat beside him, some pretty youngster or some sophisticated import from New York, and whether he had wished to indicate by his remote stare that he was otherwise engaged; but by this time he had turned round again and was facing rigidly front, and I could see that the seat to his left was occupied by an old gentleman busy with his program and the seat to his right was empty. Plainly—it brought me more relief than I liked to admit—plainly he was alone.

While the late-comers settled into their places and the casual chatter was reduced to a quiet and expectant drone, I stared sternly at my program and asked myself questions: Had his look been as frigid as I had thought? Could the quality of iciness—if indeed it had even been there—be considered a kind of public mask that he automatically put on for occasions like this? Or—the thought came over me like a cold draught—had the things I had said to Michael in my drunkenness a month ago finally gotten around to his ears? A loud burst of applause and the earthy readiness of Milstein, who was presenting himself with the simplicity of a warm and eager workman against the gold pretentiousness of the organ pipes, roused me and made that last conjecture of mine seem far-fetched and neurotic. If he— Arthur Sanes—had heard that tale at all, he had heard it weeks ago and had either forgiven me or dismissed the story as a malicious little lie. If he looked detached, it was no wonder: he was having his troubles lately—so everybody, even the gentle Emily, had said.

Reconsidered against the lyric buoyancy of the first movement of the Sonata in G, those troubles of his seemed petty to the point of sordidness. One of his students—not Cathie, *she* would never have gone above his head to make a complaint—one of his students, a plump and prissy little thing named Lorrie Fawcett, had taken herself in tears from her lesson to Dr. Holland's office and had let it be known in a shrill and breathy fashion that she was not spending her parents' good money to be told that her performance was about as stirring as a cold potato taken out of a refrigerator. Although I had not listened to that particular scene, I knew she had not misquoted her teacher: the remark was characteristic, and Lorrie was too stupid to have invented it herself. According to reports, and God knows there were plenty of them, her interview with Dr. Holland had included a fit of hysterics; a shot of brandy had been offered, and the secretary had been sent out for aromatic spirits of ammonia. Fifteen minutes after the bulgy heroine had been led from the main office by a sympathetic girl friend who had been listening at the door, Mr. Sanes had been summoned, Mr. Sanes had been asked, doubtless in the twangiest and most casual way, for *his* side of this nonsensical business. The rest of the story was vague, since

115

it had been wrested by Jenny from the secretary, who was given to clichés and was naturally torn between the wish to show secretarial discretion and the temptation to be on cozy terms with a member of the faculty. It was generally known that Mr. Sanes had been "pretty high-handed about it," had not shown "the proper spirit of co-operation," had "carried himself in a provoking way," and had ended by "getting himself a first-class talking-to." This incident, reported to me by several of my colleagues with varying degrees of enjoyment, had elucidated the sudden change in the nature of communication on the other side of the wall: ever since Thursday of last week, the criticism there had been confined to technical matters and had been delivered in a lifeless and deflated voice, as if he were breathing out every comment on the end of a sigh. All of which amounted to a sufficient reason for other changes in his behavior. Hurt pride and angry isolation were enough to explain why he had not met my eyes when we ran into each other in the corridor, why he had not yet approached me to arrange for our practice session, and why he had turned such a cold, ungiving look on me tonight.

In the short pause at the end of the first movement—the doors were opened briefly and a dozen people tip-toed down the aisles and sank into their seats with lowered eyelids and self-deprecatory smiles—I had time to reproach myself with the thought that I had not been listening. Milstein was at his best—I had heard enough to know it, and eyes in faces that I did not recognize appealed to me to share the general gratification. Asking myself how many times it is given a person in the course of his life to hear such music in such a performance, I determined to fix my attention; and the slow piano solo that opened the second movement—tender, yearning, addressing the hearer directly with an aching earnestness—partly shut out the sickening scene in Dr. Holland's office, but could not exorcise the thought of Arthur Sanes.

116

He was inextricably intertwined with both the themes, the first yearning one and the questioning one brought in by the violin. The more closely I listened, the more profoundly I thought of him. In fact, held solitary and suspended with no means of escape and stirred by the ardor of the music, I thought of him with more intensity and abandon than ever before. I looked at his proud back, and the slight stoop in it made it all the more painful that his pride should have been exposed to a "first class talking-to." I looked at the nape of his neck with the darkness of his cropped hair in the deep cleft between the two tendons; I wished he might turn a little so that I might see his temple and the hollow line of his cheek; I thought of his hands. I wished—and the longing in the music gave me license to wish it shamelessly—that he was sitting beside me as he had sat in the faculty dining room, close enough for accidental touch and the sweet impropriety of knowing his scent and hearing his breath. Indeed, in that strange mood it seemed very possible that he *would* sit beside me, that during the intermission he would come up to me in the lobby and suggest that the two of us take over the Grüenbergs' seats, that, mute and separate as we had been of late, his pulse was somehow keeping pace with mine. What was in me was somehow authenticated by the longing earnestness of the second movement of the Brahms. What was in me was good and capable of transmitting itself: if we sat together in those empty seats, even if no words passed between us, what was in me would flow over him and salve his wounds and heal his pride and nourish and sustain him in his loneliness.

The feverish restlessness of the last movement of the sonata became in me an almost intolerable agitation: I could not keep my eyes in one place; they kept roving about, they kept following the darts and flashes of light given off by the beads and earrings and bracelets. The theme of that movement sometimes goes on long stretches of melancholy wandering and sometimes falters and seems to fall into a kind of sick nervelessness; and under the music, under my conscious and uneven breathing, I kept feeling the approach of the moment when the doors would be opened and the audience would stream out into the lobby: I desired it, I longed for it, and yet the inexorable advance of it was like the growing symptom of some illness coming on. If the pervading depression of the music unexpectedly gave way to a lyric theme borrowed from the second movement, if light and tenderness flooded the final passages, the change registered on my mind alone and did nothing at all to relieve the obscure confusion that was going on in some dark and hidden part of me. In the burst of applause that followed—there were bravos, there were stampings, there were vigorous attempts to show that Artur Balsam deserved an equal share—I could only wonder how I could sit waiting for the inevitable encounter in the lobby through another whole sonata. Not since my youth, which was more alive in me than I had either known or desired, had I waited in such agitation and distress.

I took a grim, peculiar pleasure out of measuring the inadequacies of that second sonata, the one in A major. Probably because I had never heard it side by side with its authentic predecessor, I had never before realized how synthetic it was; and I wondered whether Milstein was consciously trying to pass off a piece of clever construction as a bona fide creation, or whether he himself had been taken in. I had usually found the second movement candid and touching, but under cold scrutiny what I had taken for candor turned out to be merely facile, and the middle part was silly—it sounded in the pizzicato passages like the chattering of a giddy girl. During the last movement, I did not even try to listen; I resented the fact that I could not take out my mirror and reassure myself about my face; and, with certain vague motions that might have been taken for automatic expressions of physical nervousness, I managed to smooth the top of my hair.

118

Yet, if I was concerned about attracting attention to myself, I was hardly consistent. The applause had scarcely risen to its crest when I was out of my seat, and, once out of my seat, what could I do but walk up the aisle and be the first of the whole excited assembly to pass through the door? I had wanted—I knew it with a sharpness that made me blush—to take possession of a place where none of my friends or colleagues would be likely to see me and come over to chat with me. Through the broad and oppressive emptiness of the lobby—it was an expanse of yellowish marble bigger than the concert hall itself and broken at intervals by greenish pillars that opened at the top into clusters of gilded leaves—I went directly toward a certain little alcove that I had plainly been thinking about, a place where two people could be more or less alone. Once there, I unrolled my crushed program and stared at it assiduously, seeing nevertheless over the edge of it that all the doors were opened now, that the long applause was over, and that others were beginning to come out, small in the marble vastness, by twos and threes. The sound of voices, big and jarring in the hollow reaches of the place, grew and multiplied with the issuing crowd and quickened the irregular beating of my heart.

He came—solitary, assertively separate from the others who walked out around him—into the chilly emptiness that could not be properly peopled even by such a crowd as this. By the lag in his step and the lift of his eyebrows I saw over my program that he had caught sight of me; and I knew that he was weighing two possibilities, both of them so unsatisfactory that they gave a sour twist to his mouth: either he must pretend he had not seen me, or he must step over and talk to me. He settled reluctantly on the latter, nodding and then advancing by a devious route and at a halting pace, and when he stopped in front of me I could see that his face was the cold, repellent face on the record envelope without the benefit of highlights. He looked stooped and confined in his blue serge suit and his tight white collar; and his stance—hunched, with his hands in his pockets and his chin thrust out—was at once ungainly and arrogant. It was as if he were waiting for me to say the first word. It was as if he were implying that he had come because I had beckoned him and that he expected to be informed without delay what the devil he was wanted for.

"It's a beautiful concert," I said, loathing myself for making such a feeble and shopworn effort to appease him.

"Yes. The audience seems to think so, anyhow. But that kind of excessive display always has a negative effect on me. Stampings and bravos—the minute I hear them I start to pick for flaws."

"He's very fortunate in his accompanist, don't you think?"

"Balsam? Oh, yes, Balsam's adequate."

More aggressive than the words and the supercilious tone in which he uttered them was a strange new manifestation—at least it was new to me: I could not get him to look at me, he rejected my eyes, he stared steadily at something above and beyond my head. And he continued to fix his icy look on that remote and unidentified point even while he mechanically offered me a cigarette, which I ill-naturedly refused. Before either of us could make an attempt at further communication, old Mr. and Mrs. Beinhauer—respectable and undistinguished friends of my mother's—came up and delivered themselves of a string of middlebrow obviosities long enough to give him an excuse for taking himself off if he wished. But he did not avail himself of the opportunity; he stood a little to one side instead, staring at the bluish wing on Mrs. Beinhauer's hat as if it had been ripped from some disgusting creature whose existence was an affront to him; and I concluded—without gratification, since he had become almost hateful to me—that he was waiting to tell me when I might expect to have the honor of seeing him again.

That, however, was not the subject he resorted to once

the Beinhauers were gone. "How does it happen you're here by yourself tonight? I thought you took this series with the Grüenbergs," he said.

"The Grüenbergs couldn't come." I blushed, remembering how I had thought of the two of us sitting together in the Grüenbergs' seats. But the blush was nothing for me to worry about. He would not see it; his hazel eyes, more strained than usual and streaked with veinings of pinkish red, resolutely refused to have anything to do with me.

"They're neither of them sick, I hope?" he asked in a tone that suggested he wouldn't give a damn if they were.

"Emily is, in a way. She broke one of those glass coffee-makers and scalded her knee."

He winced, and I triumphantly chalked up another vulnerability against him. Two things at least distressed him: he could not tolerate weakness—I had learned that when I had admitted my dizziness on the bridge—and he could not tolerate the thought of pain. His face, once the brief spasm had passed over it, was even more rigid and impassive than it had been from the beginning. "I come to these things alone. I always like to sit by myself at concerts," he said.

"So do I."

"I thought you sat with the Grüenbergs."

"I sit in front of the Grüenbergs." I cursed the quaver that had come into my voice. "I've lived long enough to have mastered the gentle art of letting people alone. I think I'll walk over to the fountain, if you'll excuse me. They're lining up over there, and I want to get a drink."

Now, too, he might have detached himself—I gave him a curt nod to release him to his precious privacy—but he walked along a step behind me, his hands out of his pockets at last and dangling at his sides with a singularly uncharacteristic helplessness. Hughie was in the long queue at the fountain, and so were the Boyds. It taxed and rattled me to exchange the required comments with them—I knew

121

that I was talking in clichés, that my voice was unnaturally high and vivacious, and that my smile was a stretched, dry kind of smile. My face was so hot that I wished I could spatter my cheeks and my forehead with the water that rose from the ancient brass fixture. In that brief time while I was bending over, safe and hidden, tears of affront and disappointment came stinging into the corners of my eyes; and, without waiting for him to get his drink and come along with me, I started back across the blocks of yellow marble for the door.

"Wait a minute, Miss Hartmann," he said, catching up with me near the cold bulk of one of the efflorescent granite pillars.

I stopped without turning more than my shoulder in his direction. If he could look above my head, *I* could always stare imperturbably at the floor.

"About that—that tentative engagement to run through the Mozart in Thanksgiving vacation—"

The bell was jangling to announce the end of the intermission, and people I knew well and people I knew vaguely were milling past us, waving and nodding. I gave them all the same stiff smile. "Oh, yes. What about it?" I said.

"I'm sorry—I'm very sorry—but I just can't make it."

"Don't give it a thought. There isn't any hurry. Any time you get around to it will do."

"I can't make it because I've got to go up to New York."

"You don't have to explain why you can't make it. It isn't of the slightest consequence to me."

"But your attitude would seem to suggest that I don't want to—"

I remembered the note in the flowers and the flowers themselves. I remembered them in hate: the flowers were gone, but I still had the note, and tonight I would tear it to bits. "Why should you want to?" I said, wheeling round

122

at him, forcing him to look at me, feeling the cold and cruel clash of our looks. "Naturally, it's a bother. What could it be but an obligation, something the school expects of us, something we're forced to do? That's the way *I* look at it, anyway."

"Of course."

"Intermission's over. Everybody's going in. Good night."

Chapter 10

ALL DAY TUESDAY there was an ominous silence on the other side of the wall. He was not there, I did not have to go into the hall and read the note on his door to know it; but go and read I did, though I might have saved myself the trouble: for exhibiting my curiosity in the corridor, I got nothing but the information that he would be absent all day and would probably meet his students on schedule tomorrow. My own day was a slack one because two of my people had taken double lessons in the preceding week so that they might start their Thanksgiving break early. Fred Wade—I was glad to be rid of him, the fact that he was on terms of loud-mouthed intimacy with Cathie Dugan did not exactly recommend him to me—was on his way with his mother to his grandmother's place in Boston; and Liz Stoddard was getting herself engaged in Philadelphia—the number of formalities lined up for the event seemed to me more than her plain, tremulous little person would be able to bear. So I had two hours on my hands, and I spent them in my office, with the view of the campus, bare and half sunken under brown mud, forever being called to my attention by icy rain which kept being driven in nasty, unexpected gusts against my window pane. The hate that had nerved my hands to tear up the letter was still in me, but it was not strong enough to deliver me from a tendency to worry and examine and accuse myself: if he was absent, he was probably ill, and if he was ill today, he might very well have been ill last night. The hateful way he had carried himself, his wounding words, the arrogant unconcern with which he had broken his twice-made promise, these *could* have been the result of incipient fever; he *could* have been talking to me out of a nightmare state. But, fortunately, I was still too galled to allow myself to brood over his possible discomfort or danger: if he needed hot soup and had nobody to bring it to him, if he got the wrong sort of doctor, non-interference was plainly what he wanted, he had nobody to blame for his isolation but himself.

Of course, he was back at school again on Wednesday morning. He couldn't have been more than mildly ill or he would have stayed at home, since the day was a short one, the holiday, such as it was, beginning at noon. I could hear no symptomatic hoarseness in his voice, either—he offered the same flat comment that he had been specializing in for days, and, if there was any sort of change, it was in the direction of a slight increase in vitality. Yesterday's temptation to excuse him doubled the force of today's resurgence of resentment against him; I had probably also been nursing a hope that he would not be making his New York trip, and was all the more bitter at the emptiness of my own four vacation days because that hope was gone; and when I heard him passing my office—by now I could distinguish his walk from any other—I vented my fury by hurling a crumpled sheet of memorandum pad against the closed door.

The weather—I had an ugly bout with it on my way home from school—was designed to encourage a snarling state of mind. When I came into the glaring greyness of my apartment I was disordered by wind, affronted by sleet,

125

and chilled to the bone. For months I had been thirsting after a few hours of leisure, and now that I was free for the better part of a week I found that there was nothing I wanted to do. The day was too miserable for a shopping trip; I could not even occupy myself with bathing since I had taken a shower in the morning; to begin to read a new book called for more effort than I was willing to make, and when I paged through the collected novels of Jane Austen, which I had been re-reading for years with continually deepening pleasure, they seemed for the first time in my life trivial and thin. I sat on the sofa in the ring of light cast by the standing lamp—it looked feeble, competing with the glare—and turned the pages, stopping here and there, not absorbing anything I read, wondering instead whether it was only those who were in desperate straits who took to drink—it seemed to me I would be more likely to finish off the first bottle on a flaccid, empty afternoon like this.

Yet when the insistent ringing of my buzzer told me that somebody had come to fill up the vacuum, I felt nothing but exasperation. It couldn't be Emily—she and Julius had gone to Akron to visit her sister—and there was no other member of the human race that I would care to see. I answered the buzzer on a self-destructive impulse, in order to make my afternoon even worse than it promised to be; and I was eminently successful since it was Jenny Willis' voice that came up to me through the house phone. She had been shopping in the neighborhood and the weather was unspeakable and she was like a drowned rat, she said—and what could I do but ask her in?

Perhaps because she presented me with a kind of crisis, thereby furnishing me with something to do with myself, she was more appealing in her drenched, chilled state than she had been at any other time in the year. Her hat was ruined, her bangs were plastered flat against her forehead, and her Harlequin glasses were spattered; when

126

she took them off to wipe them, I saw the vulnerability and the innocence in her dark, short-sighted eyes. She smiled helplessly at me when I took her bundles to put them on the kitchen table to dry, and she refused to sit on anything upholstered for fear she might ruin it, which showed an amiable consideration for my property. I pulled one of my ladderback chairs close to the radiator and made her take off her shoes and got her a pair of slippers, and, by the time I had her settled, some of my sluggishness was gone. "What would you say to a hot toddy?" I said.

"Oh, honey, I wouldn't put you to that much trouble for anything in the world."

"Don't you like them? Say so if you don't."

"I'm crazy about them, only they're a bother to make, I know."

"They're easy to make. It won't take more than a couple of minutes. Anyway, I'd like one myself."

"Well, far be it from me to stop you in a case like that. Can't I help, though? Isn't there anything I can do?"

I told her to stay where she was and warm herself through, and I went into the kitchen to make the hot toddy. The fumes of it rose, pungent and sustaining, from the bowl into which I poured the boiling water from the kettle— rum, sugar, whiskey, the sharpness of lemon juice, the rough tang of the rind. I bent over the bowl and breathed up the blended fragrance: it was like invoking the ghosts of other such concoctions that had been simmered for me long ago, when I was a croupy child. And the remembrance of those old remedies, if it could not cure me, at least was soothing to me. I decked the cups with thin slices of lemon and little floating boats of cinnamon bark, and carried them, with a more authentically celebratory air than I had imagined I could muster, into the living room.

I found her sitting on the floor with her back pressed against the radiator and her very creditable legs stretched out in front of her, their well-advertised female attractive-

127

ness only enhanced by my green velvet slippers and the residue of moisture that made a darkish line along the straight bone of her shin. I put our cups of toddy down on the carpet and sat on the floor beside her, stretching out my own legs only long enough to assure myself they did not suffer by comparison before I pulled them back and sat on my feet. The heat behind me was comforting, and the toddy was delicious, and she did not introduce either of her favorite subjects—not Hughie and not Arthur Sanes. "Well, it looks as if Emily and Michael are all lined up behind Boyd. As for me, I'm trying to keep out of it as much as I can," she said.

She had chosen a legitimate and obvious subject: any two Music faculty members meeting during the Thanksgiving break would hardly have discussed anything else. Dr. Boyd, whose touchy self-esteem had been painfully pricked by a wretched student performance of the Beethoven Seventh under his baton a week ago, had sent a long memorandum of complaint to Dr. Holland and had circulated a carbon copy of it among the rest of us, pointing out that the orchestral material given to him to work with had been steadily declining, that the standards for admission were slipping, that the grading system was growing appallingly lax, and that there had better be a tightening up of requirements all the way along the line. Emily and Michael, who still harbored the remembrance of European conservatories, had sent a memorandum of their own to buttress Dr. Boyd's contentions; others, realizing that any rise in the admission standards would probably mean a decrease in their class enrollments, were engaged in composing a counter-memorandum; and I, though I was generally in agreement with "the Europeans," had hung back a little because it seemed to me that Dr. Boyd was less concerned with the condition of the orchestra than with his reputation and had not always done as much as he could to get the maximum out of the mediocre student material on hand. I sipped my toddy and chewed my cinnamon bark and talked as freely as a person dares when he knows that whatever he says is going to be repeated; and—since Jenny's classes were elementary ones and her future raises would probably depend on a large influx of freshmen every year—I urged her to sign her name to the counter-memorandum. "After all, Boyd's looking out for himself, and I don't see why you shouldn't look out for yourself," I said.

"It's just that I'm deathly sick of all this drama, all these arguments."

She wasn't, of course. Like most people whose lives are limited, she dearly loved a row; but at the moment I felt too kindly disposed, too well warmed within and without, to imply as much. "We'll have to take a stand eventually," I said. "Dr. Holland told me yesterday he was going to call a faculty meeting and put the business to a vote. And if everybody's going to have to commit himself in the end, there doesn't seem much point in holding off at the start."

The thought of that future meeting—it was taking shape before her, charged and contentious—cheered her more than the radiator and the whiskey; and we spent an involved and vigorous twenty minutes trying to figure out how each of the votes would be cast. Hughie, she said with a grand sweep of her hand, would do whatever *she* told him to: Hughie was aware of his lack of experience and trusted her implicitly. She was certain—far more certain than I was—where most of the others would stand; she tallied them off on her carefully manicured fingers, all but one of them: something—it might have been forgetfulness, or it might have been hesitation to introduce a matter I had been disinclined to hear about in the past—something kept her from mentioning Arthur Sanes.

"And the piano people—how do you think they're going to vote?" I said, wondering whether I wasn't making myself more obvious than I would have been if I had named him outright.

129

"Mr. Sanes, do you mean? Oh, he'll vote with the Europeans, naturally. He'd vote with the Europeans because that'd be the smart thing, the classy thing to do. Not that he'd have any convictions of his own—how could he?—I doubt he ever gives the place a thought outside of working hours. In at nine, out at four, never a word to anybody—that's Mr. Sanes."

"That's about it. He was sick or something yesterday, wasn't he?"

"He didn't look very sick to me—that's not exactly fair, of course—a person can never really tell. But if you want to know what *I* think, *I* think he took the day off to pack up all the paraphernalia he's going to need while he's staying at Mrs. McIvor's. In *that* kind of a set-up, he'll probably have to change his outfit two or three times a day."

"How do you know he's staying at Mrs. McIvor's?" I set my cup and saucer on the strip of wood between the radiator and the rug. I did not want to be holding them if my hand was going to shake.

"Oh, didn't you know about that? I thought everybody in the department knew about that. Three times last week she phoned him at school—Jeannie got the calls in Dr. Holland's office and had to come down and drag him away from his lessons. Not that he seemed to mind it in the least—they went on and on, just as if it hadn't been long distance. Jeannie said she never heard him give out like that, he was so mush-mouthed and sweet."

"Really?" I said, wiping a trace of lipstick from the rim of my cup and floundering among half a dozen questions, every one of them clamoring avidly for an answer. I would have to wait, I would have to word them properly and introduce them with strategy if I did not want to betray myself: she was giving me a hard, bright look through her cleaned spectacles, she was raising her cup to her mouth to cover a knowing smile.

"Hughie tells me—"

"What's that?" I said. An uncertain knock, so light

130

and feeble that it could have been taken for a child's knock, had sounded on my door.

"It seems you've got a visitor, Frieda." She sagged a little. As pleasant as it would be to keep me in suspense, it would have been even more delightful to hand me the sordid details one by one.

"Who's out there?" My voice was loud and unnatural and had in it the uncontrollable quaver which had warned me off the concert stage.

"It's just me, Miss Hartmann—Cathie."

"Oh, hello, Cathie," I said despondently, without moving.

"Are you busy? Can I come in?"

"Certainly. Wait a minute. I'm coming."

But I had left the door unlocked. Before I could get across the room to open it and before Jenny could pull herself into the necessary academic order, Cathie had pushed it back and stood on the threshold, hatless, in a sodden trenchcoat, rain running in trickles over her forehead and down her cheeks and chin. Her face, swollen with crying and reddened by the raw weather, was a simplified and coarsened incarnation of the face of Dirk Bouts' Weeping Madonna—a fact which only added frustration to my rage. What did she mean by coming to the door instead of ringing the buzzer and giving me the chance to pretend I wasn't there? What did she mean, after behaving for weeks as if I didn't exist, by bringing me whatever desperation was eating at her, without so much as a telephone call? She looked only at me—she seemed oblivious of Jenny's presence. There was stark exigency in her big green eyes, and whatever tag-end of sanity had been left in me made me afraid she was going to say something she would afterwards regret. "How nice to see you," I said with utter falseness. "Here's Miss Willis."

"Good afternoon, Miss Willis." She turned her head in Jenny's direction, but her eyes did not leave my face.

131

"You're soaked," said Jenny, with more censure than concern. It would have been hard to think of two people on the campus who had less use for each other. To Jenny, Cathie was a self-assertive brat who held up class procedure and deliberately exposed the instructor by raising objections and irrelevant questions; and Cathie considered Jenny ill-grounded in her own subject and totally ignorant about everything else.

"You certainly are," I said, crossing the room and thinking that I ought to take her wet, hanging hand. She was here, it would be impossible to turn her out at once, there was nothing to do but offer her some show of hospitality and hope she would take herself off in half an hour. And maybe her needs, whatever they were, could be disposed of in the briefest of private conversations; maybe all she wanted was a few minutes alone with me. "Come on out into the kitchen and take off your coat," I said with the same false ring in my voice. "We're having hot toddies, Miss Willis and I, and I'll take a little time off and make another one for you."

She did not answer or even acknowledge with a nod my implication that her visit was to be brief; but when I had her near the stove, helping her out of her coat, I was forced to admit to myself that there was no wilfulness in her—she was simply numb. Her drenched ringlets and the nape of her neck, white under beads and trickles of rain, were exasperatingly pathetic. Her arms were stiff and heavy coming out of her coat sleeves, and she gave me a desperate slant-wise glance over her shoulder and looked away again almost at once. The under layer—a gray woolen dress with self-covered buttons down the front—turned out to be almost as wet as the upper one. "How did you ever get yourself soaked through like that?" I said in a voice almost as censorious as Jenny's.

"I don't know. I guess it was silly of me." The meekness in her tone was uncharacteristic enough to be a reason

132

for alarm. "I should have gone into the Museum or some place where it was dry. I was just walking around in the rain."

"Just walking around, in a downpour like this?" It was the feel of the dress that put the anger into my voice. No matter where he was staying tonight, no matter what was between him and Mrs. McIvor, no matter how many gnawing questions kept breeding litters of other questions to gnaw in their turn, I could not let her walk out of my place in this damp and clinging thing. She was exhausted, she was icy to the touch, she could come down with pneumonia, and whatever she came down with would be on my head. "We'll have to take this off, that's for sure," I said, coming around and beginning to work at the stubborn covered buttons. "We can let it dry over a radiator. It won't take more than half an hour. I'll get you a heavy bathrobe—that and a toddy'll warm you up in no time at all."

"Thanks, Miss Hartmann. I didn't notice it before, but I guess I'm pretty cold."

She stood helpless as a four-year old, letting me undo the long line of buttons. "All right, get out of it," I said, and she shrugged and jerked, and the damp grey dress came down to the floor and lay around her stockingless feet. When I saw her meager haunches under the cheap petticoat and her underdeveloped breasts slung up in the cotton brassiere, I felt the first pang for her forcing itself through my anger: it struck me with a sickening stab that she did not know what to do with her mind or her body, that she was pathetically vulnerable, tragically ignorant. No matter what sordid business *I* had blundered into, if I had the facts I would know where I was going. But Cathie—God help her!—Cathie was a child.

"I've got to talk to you, Miss Hartmann."

If it had not been for the pitiful bare strip of her between the brassiere and the petticoat, I would have told her outright that she would have to do her talking another time.

133

As it was, I could only temporize. "But Miss Willis is visiting me," I said.

"Is she staying for dinner?"

"I don't know, I haven't asked her."

"Don't ask her! Maybe she'll go." She said it in a whisper, fixing her green look full upon my face, her eyes suddenly brilliant with tears.

"We'll see, Cathie. Let me go into the bedroom and get you a bathrobe before you freeze to death."

I found my white terrycloth robe and a couple of big turkish towels and brought them out into the kitchen. She had pushed the kettle back a little, and her poor powerful hands were spread over the burner, her fingers stretched above the bluish circle of flame. I laid the robe over her shoulders, and she got into it and said it was very nice, very warm and comforting; though, even after she had rubbed her hair and dried her face and neck and arms, she didn't look in the least comforted.

"We could talk a little while I'm making your toddy," I told her, going at the ingredients with every possible suggestion of haste.

"It's terribly complicated. And it's private, too—I wouldn't want anybody else to hear."

"Nobody can hear all the way out here. What's the matter? Did you have another run-in with Mr. Sanes?"

"Oh, no, nothing like that." She put the kettle back on the burner. There was a melancholy humility in the gesture: it was as if any doings of hers were necessarily suspect and ought to be undone. "Mr. Sanes doesn't seem in any shape to have a run-in with anybody—not the way he was today."

"Why, how was he?" I measured out the sugar and squeezed the lemon. "Is he sick or something?"

"No, I don't think he's sick—not actually. He just seemed terribly upset to me. All the time I was in there this morning, his hands were shaking. It made me feel miserable to look at them—I was glad when he put them in his pockets.

134

I've seen them shake a couple of times before, but never anything like this."

A spurt of steam coming out of the mouth of the kettle reminded me that I was scarcely making the most of my time. "If it's not Mr. Sanes, then what is it?" I said.

"I can't talk to you—not now—not like this."

Tears—and they only antagonized and exasperated me—were sliding down her cheeks, one after another. "No," I said without charity, "I don't suppose you can. Here's your toddy. Take it into the living room, and we'll talk to Miss Willis while you drink it. After that, we'll just have to wait and see."

Jenny was seated primly in the corner of the sofa, her tight skirt pulled down over her knees. When I asked her if she wanted another toddy, she did not cooperate; in fact, she said rather brusquely that she always found *one* more than enough, thereby giving me to understand how unwise it would be to suggest to a student that either of us could down more than that. Cathie sat down stiffly on the ladderback chair that Jenny had abandoned, and I spread the soaked dress over the radiator behind her, thinking that every now and again I might call attention to the fact that it was drying out nicely. But my hopes of holding Jenny were slighter than I liked to admit: she had the ready, impermanent air of having alighted on her way out, and was monosyllabic when I brought up a recipe for making Madeira sauce, and would not take a piece of hard candy, and did not want a cigarette.

"Say," she said, flashing her spectacles in Cathie's direction, "what was the matter with your teacher yesterday? Was he sick, or did he just decide to sleep in?"

"I don't know. I didn't ask him."

I had to remind myself that the curtness of the answer could be attributed only in part to intentional rudeness: it was true that she hated Jenny Willis, but it was also true that she had just managed to put down a fit of crying and could not trust herself to say too much.

135

"Naturally, you didn't ask him," said Jenny. "He doesn't exactly encourage personal conversation, does he?"

"No, I don't suppose he does. We talk a good deal, but we always talk about music."

There was a charged pause, in which Cathie drank her toddy and Jenny walked over to the radiator and looked down at the damp grey dress. "It'll take that thing an hour to dry. I'd better get along about my business," she said.

"But Jenny, it's pouring—"

She turned around in time to catch the desperate, beseeching look that Cathie was sending at me. "Oh, I'm on my way, I can probably pick up a taxi," she assured me with a tight little smile. She was vengeful now: there was *one* person in the room, at any rate, who had reason to want her to stay, one person who would be left hung-up for an unsettled number of days and nights, open to the nagging bite of unanswered questions. She walked about, her chin thrust out, her trim legs jerking in something of a strut, stopping here and there while she picked up her wilted coat and her ruined hat and her indestructible leather bag.

"Your packages are out in the kitchen, Jenny."

"That's right, I almost forgot them. I'd be in a pickle tonight without them—Hughie's coming to dinner, and you know how *he* eats." She stood where she was, uncooperative and pleased with herself, in the middle of the room.

"I'll get them for you," I said, losing my last hope of a hurried private exchange in the kitchen, and sick of her, sick of Cathie, sick of myself.

When I came back with the moist brown paper bags, she was standing near the door, all the way across the room from Cathie, but looking at her still. Her lips were pursed to control her shrewd smile, and there was an ugly glitter in her eyes. "By the way, Miss Dugan, how's your boy friend?" she said.

"What boy friend do you mean, Miss Willis?"

"Oh, now, why be coy about it? You're among friends.

136

Everybody on campus has you paired up with Frederick Wade."

Cathie's face went a startling pink against the standing collar of the white bathrobe. She opened her mouth twice, the way a fish does coming up to the surface, gasping for air. Then she turned grey-white, so that the bluish veins showed up in her forehead, veins I had never noticed there before. "Fred Wade is perfectly all right," she said in a weak voice. "I think he's gone to visit his grandmother in Boston—anyway, that's what Lorrie Fawcett tells me. Personally, I haven't seen him for several days."

"Really?" She took her bundles and winked at me. The conspiratorial wink, used to the disparagement of a third party, always infuriates me—I refused to take cognizance of it, I could scarcely manage to show her a friendly face. "Drop over some time, any time you want to," she said. And I wondered if she knew I could never bring myself to come to her for information, to sit in her room and lead up to the subject while she watched me, her eyes gleaming with satisfaction behind the shining lenses. No matter how many nights I might lie awake, I would never ask her—so I swore as I let her out and closed the door.

Now that she was gone, I must somehow drum up in myself a sense of duty. I could not cry, I could not fly at the disorder that had gathered in the room, I could not put on old clothes and crepe-soled shoes and beat myself into dullness by walking through the rain. I turned back to the sad, rigid girl and to the wrinkled dress hanging over the radiator. I came and laid a pack of cigarettes and a folder of matches in her lap, and she did not help me: she simply stared at her own open hands while the tears coursed over her bony cheeks and dribbled onto the terrycloth. I went away and sat down in the corner of the sofa, diagonally across from her, so that I could look or not look at her as the occasion might require. If I was waiting for her to begin, I could wait forever: all that she could manage was a long, wavering sigh. Thinking with some bitterness how little I knew about her anymore, how long it had been since she had confided in me, I asked, without being able to keep a note of injury out of my voice, what on earth had been going on between her and Fred Wade.

"Nothing. No, that's not true. Everything. But actually it was nothing, if you know what I mean."

"No," I said, seeing an unacceptable image: that crass, self-satisfied operator, and this crazy child. "No, Cathie. I'm not sure I do know exactly what you mean."

"I mean we were together. I mean I slept with him."

"My God, what for? Whatever made you do such a thing?" I turned aside, I made a blank mask of incredulity out of my face, I did not want her to guess at my disgust.

"Well, Miss Hartmann, a person can't put it off forever. A person has to do it *some*time. If you build a jail around yourself, the way I did, you can't live in it forever. You've got to break out of it, you've got to get yourself free."

"You can't make yourself over like that. Nobody changes himself by making insane gestures—I told you so. You must have been crazy to try a thing like that. That's no way to get yourself free."

"I guess you're right." The mournful humility was there again: she hung her head so that her chin and mouth were lost behind the standing collar. "Anyway, in this case, I guess it wasn't. But it seems to work for other people—at least they say it does—and it might have worked for me— I mean, it might have worked if I'd been different."

"Or if *he'd* been different?"

"Oh, I don't think it was any fault of his. If it went all wrong, I'm sure it was my doing. He's had a lot of experience, and I—I wasn't good for anything. He said so afterwards to one of the boys, and the boy repeated it to a girl I know, and she repeated it to me: he said I wasn't good for anything, I was stiff as a board and scared to death."

It was not affronted femininity rising in defense of a

138

virgin that made me detest him, made me think for a moment it would be easier for me to resign than to listen henceforth while he brayed out Mozart and Schumann and Schubert in his blatant baritone. If he had taken her, no doubt she had come flying at him in her violent, reckless way, offering her services; she had been offering her services—I knew it now—when she talked to him with loud-mouthed intimacy in the corridor and waited for him outside while he finished off his lesson: I could remember her face, vulgarized by orange lipstick and a smirk, pressed against the glass pane in my door. I loathed him because I knew in my bones that he was taking a collector's pride in being the first to bring her to whatever tawdry bed he had found for her. "He makes me sick. He always did make me sick. I'm damned if I know how I'll ever be able to put up with the sight of him," I said.

"Don't say that. Please don't say that, Miss Hartmann." Alarm had cut off her crying; she dashed the sleeve of the bathrobe across her cheeks and looked at me with reddened, begging eyes. "I wouldn't want to make any trouble between him and you—after all, you're his teacher—and really he wasn't a bit to blame. It was my doing, I brought it on myself, I swear to God."

"Whether it was your doing or not, he had a responsibility in the business—"

"Oh, he was responsible—I should have told you that. He took precautions and everything, and I'm perfectly all right."

"I'm glad you're all right. It would be a pretty mess if you were pregnant into the bargain. But that isn't what I was talking about. What I mean is: if he couldn't get you over being afraid, if he couldn't make it good for you, then he just had no business—he ought to have let you alone."

"I'm sure he did whatever he could. I don't know much about all that, but I think he went to a great deal of trouble. Whatever was the matter, it was the matter with me. I'm no good—I was always afraid I wasn't. And if you're no good, you're just no good, I guess."

I felt an urgent need for a cigarette, but I did not move from my place on the sofa. To come closer to her now, to bend over her and take anything out of her lap was unthinkable: it would be like walking up to get a good look at a bloody accident or an incurable sore. That she should be convinced of her own insufficiency—this was shameful and might even prove to be fatal. Frightening symptoms were already showing themselves: the childishness, the new humility, the inert assumption of utter helplessness. With the able assistance of Fred Wade, she had probably done some annihilating thing to the core of her whole being. And Mr. Arthur Sanes, whose extraordinary pedagogical methods had put her up to it—what was *he* doing at the moment? Doubtless he was taking his ease in a parlor car, sipping a four-o'clock Manhattan and looking forward to his weekend at Mrs. McIvor's.

"Anyway, it was nothing—absolutely nothing," said Cathie.

"For God's sake, Cathie, what did you expect? It's never good the first time. What do you think you are? A light switch or something that'll turn on no matter who touches you? It's bound to be a miserable business if you go at it like that. A person has to learn—" Because of the grateful recollection of how fortunate that learning had been for me, my own eyes were suddenly flooded with warm tears. "And how could you expect to learn anything from a big blow-bag like that? He isn't even interested in his own pleasure—the only thing he cares about is his pride."

"I *wish* he hadn't gone and talked about it," she said, and her face wrinkled up like the face of an afflicted monkey.

"Do you want me to tell him to keep his mouth shut? Believe me, I'd be very glad to do it."

"Oh, no, what's the use? Vincent knows. I know he knows by the way he looked at me when I ran into him in

140

the library this morning. Oh, poor Vincent, that's the worst of it!" She covered her quivering, simian face with her hands, and shook, and cried so copiously that tears ran between her fingers. "You should have seen him, Miss Hartmann—you just should have seen his face."

I could conjure it up too readily: the milky paleness of the skin, the childish, almost colorless mouth, the evasive eyes. When—where had I seen it like that? Yes, in my office, late in the afternoon on Halloween; I had turned my back on it, I had shut my purse with a click at it, I had dismissed it; and, while I was calling other people's pedagogical proceedings into question, I had better look to my own—the remembrance of that face arraigned me and made a watery thing of my heart. "What happened between you and Vincent?" I said.

"We broke up." She took her hands from her face and dragged the cuff of the bathrobe across her cheeks. "We went with each other all last summer, while you were away. But now we don't even speak to each other anymore."

"When did you break up with him, Cathie?"

"Sometime the end of last month—I can't remember exactly—everything's been all mixed up for me ever since. But it couldn't have been too long after that terrible run-in I had with Mr. Sanes."

"Did that run-in have anything to do with it?"

"Yes, it did. Not that it was any fault of Mr. Sanes'. Nobody's to blame for this—not Mr. Sanes and not Vincent either—only myself."

With the last word she clenched her fist and struck herself on the thigh, hard, with her knuckles; and I realized with a shock that the self-loathing in her—self-loathing which would have been alien to me a few months back— was by no means strange to me now. I could imagine my hand coming down against myself like that; I had wanted to strike myself when I had turned back to her after saying good-bye to Jenny: I could see myself, gnawed by questions

141

and mocked with remembrances of *Keine Augen* and semi-promises and flowers, striking myself in my solitary bed tonight. "Everybody's got something to reproach himself with," I said.

"Not the way I have." Her hands lay open in her lap around the untouched pack of cigarettes. The apathy, the sorrowful humility were upon her again. "Nobody should have anything to do with me—I ruin everything," she said. "He was fond of me, somehow I was always sure he was fond of me, even if we never got very far—we talked a lot and we played sonatas together, but we didn't do much, we only necked and kissed. Other people went further, and that bothered me. Especially after Mr. Sanes let me have it about what sort of a person I was, that bothered me. I got to thinking that maybe the way Vincent and I were together—always stopping at the beginning, never doing what the rest of them did—I thought *that* might be the reason for the mess I was in inside, and I told him so."

"You told him so?"

"Yes, and at first he was very nice about it, he said he was sorry. He said it wasn't exactly that he didn't want to—when he was home by himself he thought about it a lot so that sometimes he couldn't sleep. Only, he said that when we were alone together it just didn't seem to him like a thing that the two of us would do—it seemed sort of violent and crazy—it didn't seem to come naturally out of anything else."

"It isn't exactly a thing that you can force yourself into."

"I know it isn't, Miss Hartmann, and maybe I would have just waited to see what would happen if he hadn't said that probably it would be different with him now that he knew I wanted to—"

"How about that, Cathie? Did you really want to?"

"Yes. No, not exactly. I don't know, but I certainly thought I ought to, considering the way I was inside. And he said he'd get his father's car and we'd go out in the

142

country to some woods he knew, and then he kept putting it off and putting it off, and I fought with him—I said he needn't if he didn't want to, I said I wasn't so bad that I couldn't get somebody else. And the day after that he said to me in the hall, 'Get your practising done this afternoon because we're going up there this evening', and I was afraid because he was so cold and hateful when he said it, and I told him I thought it was going to rain, and he said since I was in such a god-damned hurry he didn't see why I was worrying about a little rain. But it didn't rain, it was only cold and foggy, so that we had to drive very slow, and all the way up he didn't say a word to me, he just sat there with his mouth pulled in as if he was biting the insides of it, acting as though he was going up there to have some terrible operation or something. And when he stopped the car I didn't move, I asked him who could have an affair with anybody who acted the way he was acting—all frozen up and sick-looking and tied in knots, as if he was going to a funeral. And he said I'd given him orders to make love to me, and there he was, doing exactly what I ordered him to do, and what the hell did I expect—did he have to cheer about it too? And I said he didn't want me, he'd only pretended he wanted me, and he turned around and looked as if he was going to hit me in the face, and he said nobody would ever want me the way I acted about it, and actually I guess he was right about that, when you consider the way it turned out with Fred Wade. Anyway, he started the car, and he didn't say a word to me all the way home, he didn't even get out to take me to the door. And after that he wouldn't as much as look at me at school, and the two times I tried to talk to him it wasn't any good—all he said both times was: hadn't I had enough, couldn't I just let him alone."

"You shouldn't have done it, Cathie. You can't grab onto another person and order him around like that. That isn't love, that hasn't anything to do with love."

"Oh, I know it, I know it, Miss Hartmann, and I'm terribly sorry. I haven't got anybody else, and I was really

143

awfully fond of him all last summer, and I miss him so much!"

She had begun to cry again, but not in the cold, stricken way she had been crying before. Her tears were coming so easily that she did not trouble to hide her face; her chest heaved up in the easing sort of sigh that children breathe out when they have decided to be finished with crying, and her hands stroked the folds of terrycloth gathered in her lap as if she were stroking his cheek or his hair. Something in her crying—perhaps it was the spectacle of sane tenderness breaking through the crazy shell she had built around herself—something softened me so that I felt my own eyes filling up with tears. "Don't cry," I said in a voice which sounded wet and foolish. "If you keep on like that, I'll catch it from you. When anybody cries, especially if it's a student, I can't help it, I start to cry myself."

She came to me across the room, and I stood up to meet her, saying that her situation wasn't as bad as she made it out to be, that the two of them weren't necessarily finished, even if they had gotten off to such a bad start. And, having said that much, having offered her hope of something beyond her present wretchedness, I was weak and shaken enough to wonder what there could possibly be for me. That question broke in my mind just as she put her arms around me and clung to me in her gratefulness; and her warmth against me—nobody had held me like that for God knows how long—only gave me a measure for my loneliness. "You'd better go and get your dress off the radiator. It's wool and it'll shrink," I said; and, when she had obediently taken herself to the other side of the room, I began to empty the ashtrays and stack the cups and saucers. The room was disorderly, I would clean it up and take her to an Italian restaurant for dinner; and then I would go to the movies, and then I might take a walk, since the sky seemed to be clearing; and if I did all that between now and midnight, I ought to be very tired, I ought to be ready to go to bed.

144

Chapter 11

Possibly it was the spectacle of Cathie's frontal attack on life that shocked me into self-criticism. During Thanksgiving vacation and for a couple of weeks thereafter, I spent my leisure—and I had plenty of leisure—talking reason to myself. I did not have to grapple with the temptation to wring information out of Jenny or Hughie or anybody else who might be collecting tag-ends of gossip; I settled my questions thoroughly, if somewhat violently, simply by answering them in the manner that was most damaging to my own untenable cause.

Mrs. McIvor had the strongest imaginable hold on Arthur Sanes—so I told myself while I did the mending, the cleaning, the book and file arranging which filled my vacant days. The tone that Dr. Holland's secretary described as "mush-mouthed" had doubtless been authentic tenderness frozen by the fact that somebody else was listening. I would be foolish if I consoled myself with the fact that she was fifty: one of the eighteenth century mistresses—I could not remember now whether it had been DuBarry or Pompadour —had been fascinating enough at seventy to hold a young lover; there were men—and Arthur Sanes' peculiarities suggested that he might very well be one of them—who found love a possibility only with the well matured, the thoroughly self-contained, those whom experience had made exquisite and knowledge had made all-accepting and resigned. Arthur Sanes and Mrs. McIvor were doubtless lovers, and it was probably jealousy or a distaste for scandal on the part of a Mr. McIvor whose name I had never heard mentioned which had necessitated the departure from the studio with the oyster white grillework that curled and swished; he must have left New York an unwilling exile—certainly his detachment from all of us, his scorn for the school, his furious outbursts against his students were proof enough of his unwillingness; and anybody who thought otherwise, anybody who hoped to be more in his estimation than a tolerable associate in his bafflement and his loneliness was destined to come to grief.

And the seekings out, the long looks, the walk on the bridge, the flowers and the note in the flowers? Now that I had taken a steadying hold on myself, they seemed of no more significance than the little attentions Dr. Laurent had been in the habit of showing me in the old days when we fed pigeons at his window: hadn't *he* brought me two hand-embroidered Swiss handkerchiefs for my birthday, hadn't he taken me out to dinner every month or so, hadn't he sometimes slipped his frail old arm through mine on the way up the stairs or down the hall, hadn't he stopped behind me once when I was examining a score and lightly stroked my hair? It was a matter of manners—Dr. Laurent and Arthur Sanes were metropolitan and continental; it was a matter of manners—and I had been provincial enough in Mr. Sanes' case to make too much of mere elaborate courtliness. In such circles as he and Mrs. McIvor inhabited—circles far more complex and sophisticated than any I had moved in during my own inglorious stay in New York—every man doubtless showed such courtesies to every woman with whom he meant to keep up any sort of connection. I had once heard it said—and I remembered agreeing vigorously at the time—that no real friendship can exist between a man and a woman unless it involves at least the possibility of love: what is downright undesirable is somehow not worth cultivating at all. I had no claims on him, then, other than such minor claims as exist at the beginnings of a friendship. There was nothing which required him to keep a tentative engagement with me, to forego a trip to New York in order to have a practise session in my company, to sit with me in a pair of empty seats at a concert—nothing but my own solitary and unruly heart.

It was for me to choose, of course, whether I wished to be friends with him; and for a few days it seemed to me that I didn't: when I thought with my new, chastened mind of running through Mozart songs with him or eating an occasional lunch with him in the faculty dining room or exchanging a few lively sentences with him at such parties and meetings as he considered himself called upon to attend, I felt something which was not so much disinterest as heavy-hearted weariness. He was not, by common consent, exactly easy to get on with; whoever was his friend was bound to incur some unpopularity with others; his hateful way with his students and his high-handed comportment in academic affairs would make him, under certain forseeable circumstances, an embarrassing and even a dangerous connection. Yet by the time I was back at school it seemed to me that I could only be the loser if I crossed him off my list: a cold greeting in the corridor, a noticeable attempt to avoid him in the library would only show him plainly that I had been entertaining dreams which shamed me and left me exposed. We were to do the Mozart songs together, there would be no getting out of that; and the decent way to carry it off, the civilized way to carry it off was to accept his third invitation to dinner—*this* time he set the day and the hour—with casual amity.

And after I had said I would come, possibly because his courtliness during our little exchange had been made the more acceptable by his distinctly shamefaced smile, I was not sorry. Entering the apointment in my relatively empty daybook, I said to myself I was not so surrounded by clamoring acquaintances, so pressed by fascinating engagements that I could afford, on the basis of a groundless pique, to dismiss a possible friend. I liked him: unpredictable and supercilious and venomous as he sometimes was, I liked him better than anybody but Emily and Dr. Holland; and the fact that he had singled me out, had shown me uncalled-for attentions, and had gathered the courage to hurdle our former dilemma and start again was solid proof that he was somehow attached to me. Circumspection and inclination combined, then, to bring me to accept what he offered for whatever it was; and I made the same preparations, no more and no less, for my evening with him as I would have made for dinner at the Grüenbergs': I dressed myself in my new brown sweaters and my old tan skirt, but I did not paint my nails or buy a fresh bright lipstick or do anything in particular about my hair.

I got downtown to the twelve-story building in which he lived at five o'clock on the first real day of winter. I was not in the least nervous—I thought of that building as a haven from the biting cold and from the crowd of workers and late shoppers through which I had come. But it was scarcely the sort of place a person could relax in: it was assertively new—so new that the smell of its mortar and paint had not yet left it—and meretriciously elegant. The lobby was almost as crowded as the street: I was put out by the number of people in uniform unnecessarily darting about, by the thick mustard-colored carpet, and by the back show-windows of expensive shops where every article from a traveling case to a lace brassiere was displayed as if it were priceless and had just issued from a master's hand. The soundless elevator—I was alone in it and could examine the pearly pushbuttons and the fake paneling—carried me to the eleventh floor, where I stepped out onto more deep carpeting into a shadowy hall with an imitation marble bench, a face-freezing mirror, and two tall tripods bearing some kind of slick-leaved tropical vine. The stillness was a humming stillness, and I could not tell whether the muted sound was the gathering of voices coming up from the street or the mindless mutter of machines. He lived in 1117. I pushed the pearl button in the door frame without delaying to powder my nose, and heard the small, bursting, discreet little gong sound off inside.

He let me in—strange in his bulky grey sweater and dark flannel trousers. He got his hands into his pockets at once, and I wondered whether that was because he did not want to offer the right one to me or was afraid they were going to tremble. The big room behind him—I said immediately and foolishly that it was beautiful—had a bleakness and a rawness that was almost shocking after the ornate condition of the hall. The far bank of windows, an entire wall of them, opened on a metropolitan stretch of lighted skyscraper windows and somber roofs and towers against a sky that was washed in watery gold, and it seemed possible that he had consciously subordinated the interior to the drama of that view. But if such was the case, it seemed to me that he had overdone it: each piece of furniture stood in total isolation from any of the others, and the general effect was one of vacant space—space on the white walls that demanded pictures, space in the corners that wanted tables and occasional chairs, space between the little Persian rugs scattered over a vast floor that had plainly been intended for carpeting to the walls. Even the seven-foot Steinway near the windows seemed small and alone.

"Bleak, isn't it?" he said, smirking.

"You've got something to cope with here. I can't imagine anything in the way of furniture that wouldn't be dwarfed by your view."

"*I* can." He took me lightly by the elbow and directed me through emptiness to the low black sofa, where I settled

149

myself. "I had some stuff up in New York," he said, standing in front of me, "some carved chairs almost as tall as you are, and a really massive coffee table with a ton of yellow marble on top of it, and a tremendous Portuguese chest. I thought of bringing them down with me, but I didn't. It costs a fortune to ship them, and any old things like that are always the worse for a trip, and, anyway, I don't have the slightest idea how long I'm going to be here."

I nodded a reasonably enthusiastic assent to all of that, telling myself that I had no cause to feel a pang. He had come and he would go, as many had come and gone before him; if the silence that followed was mournful with the melancholy of the evening and a semi-furnished room, I would be cheerful enough as soon as we got down to the Mozart, which stood open on the piano; if he took himself off, a year from now I would barely remember that he had given me pain. That first time in the faculty dining room he had said he didn't know how long he would be able to put up with his current situation; and, considering the reputation he had earned with his colleagues and his students in the interim, it might be well for him to leave of his own accord at the end of the year. There was a vulnerability about him as he stood slouching there, spare in his loose and threadbare sweater—I noticed it without allowing myself to wince for it—there was a vulnerability which suggested that a dismissal in his case might turn out to be ruinous.

"Nobody'd miss me."

It was a strange thing to say, and the grin and the jerk of the shoulders that accompanied it did not lessen its strangeness. I made an unconvincing gesture of protest with my hand.

"Oh, come on, now, you know nobody'd miss me. I'd have a very special place in their memories, of course—I'd always be the Number One Son-of-a-Bitch. Do you want a drink? I've mixed some whiskey sours. But you don't have to have that if you don't want to. I can make up anything you like, anything with bourbon or whiskey or gin."

150

"A whiskey sour will be perfect."

"Good. Have a couple. You could use it—" I felt that his yellow look, sharp and malicious, was focusing on the tip of my nose—"you look cold."

"Is my nose red?"

"Pinkish." He started with a kind of swagger toward a door that probably led into a kitchenette; but on the way he stopped and said humbly, without turning, "Believe it or not, for once I'm keeping my promise—we're having a magnificent steak with bordelaise sauce."

While he was gone I became aware that certain unquestionably beautiful and valuable things were to be seen here and there in the emptiness: a small portrait of a handsome boy in puffed sleeves and pearl-studded jerkin stared from the white wall opposite me with brooding eyes; the passionate and emaciated head of a male saint, carved out of wood in the thirteenth or fourteenth century and still bearing traces of gilt and rose and yellowish green, stood on a small onyx slab on the windowsill; and a puzzling piece of tapestry—it showed itself later to be Actaeon turning into a stag—was vaguely and somberly shadowed forth by the twisted tapers that stood on either side of it in heavy brass candlesticks. I could imagine him packing these things among his clothes and keeping a wary eye on the suitcases in which they were being transported on the train, but I did not want to project myself into his packings or his journeys. I occupied myself instead with his current coffee table—a very makeshift thing—small, with black wrought iron legs without the faintest suggestion of a swirl, the top made out of tiles which bore a poor facsimile of an incorrect concept of the classic lyre. It was on this—bending over awkwardly, because it was a very low table—that he put our drinks and a small silver tray of spread crackers.

We talked while we consumed most of the crackers and a couple of whiskey sours, but our talk was halting and uncertain at best. I could not fix my eyes on his face or my attention on Cathie Dugan's troubles with the Chopin

151

Scherzo she was to play next week at a public recital. My eyes kept wandering in spite of me to the cuff of his sweater—the ribbing at his wrist was sadly raveled—and I kept wondering how a man could have such a thing repaired and thinking that, if somebody didn't take a needle to it soon, the whole sleeve was likely to go. But I was not here to worry about the drawbacks of his solitary state; I was here to rehearse some Mozart songs that we were to do together at Dr. Holland's request. And when he got up from the sofa, saying that the room was getting gloomy now and he had better turn on some lamps, I also rose and walked over to the piano. "How about the songs? Did you get a chance to look at the ones I checked?" I said.

"Oh, yes, I looked them over," he told me from the other side of the room. The lamps, whitish in their colorless parchment shades and glaringly bright after the semi-darkness, made the place uglier still by sharpening the edges of the furniture and casting big areas of light onto the walls. "There *is* one thing, though: as a group, I think they're a little monotonous. Maybe you ought to drop one or two of them and add something else to spice it up a bit."

"What would you suggest I add?" I had realized that the group might be tedious in its uniformity; but, my voice being what it was, I had chosen only such songs as I knew I could sing with the poise of security.

"There's *Der Zauberer*—it's got a little more bite to it."

"I know, but it won't do. I can't sing it. I haven't got the voice for it—not anymore."

He had come over to the piano and was preparing to turn on the last of the lamps, a tall torchiere close to the music rack. I looked at him, and he looked away, looked intently and consciously at the switch of the lamp. His face in the sudden flood of light was even more pained and uneasy than it had been when I told him on the bridge that I was given to attacks of dizziness. But if he was embarrassed

152

by the fact that my voice had its limitations, I did not mean to help him out of his embarrassment: I continued to stare at him, keeping my face merely neutral and serious, not indulging him so much as to offer him the faintest smile. And, having fiddled with the lamp, having dragged it nearer and then pushed it farther away, he subsided onto the piano bench without a word, turned the pages of the music until he came to *The Violet,* laid his fingers on the keys, and began to play the introduction.

I had somehow expected him to be nervous—I suppose I was remembering Cathie's description of his shaking hands; but his attitude was one of complete relaxation—he played casually and easily, though part of the self-confidence in his playing seemed to arise from the fact that he was doing everything he could to give the impression that he wasn't really playing at all. He did not commit himself to a performance: he played a few bars, and stopped, and played another phrase or two. His eyes sometimes peered quizzically at the notes on the rack and sometimes gazed at the dying gold and the black buildings beyond the window; he nodded now and again as if he wished to indicate approval to Mozart; his self-possession had so fully returned to him that at one point he lifted his chin and looked me straight in the face. I could see he expected me to sing, and I began to sing when he moved, with a stronger sense of sequence, from the introduction of *Abendempfindung* into the body of the song. It was I—little as I had expected it—it was I, not he, who was embarrassed: the difference between my flat, dry speaking voice and the ardent outward flow of my singing voice somehow made me ashamed of myself. The very words of the song—speaking as they did of the brevity of life, the certainty of death, and tears dropped on a grave—the very words of the song seemed excessive and incongruous in his barren room and his unbending presence. I was glad to go on to other ones less passionate, less profound, and less tender; but even in the relatively superficial ones I was by no means

153

at my best, since my tone was constricted and roughened by the quick, uneven beating of my heart.

We must have been at it for something close to an hour when he took his hands from the keyboard, rubbed them together with a dry and silky sound between his knees, and said we'd better stop, because he'd have to put the asparagus on and see to the final stages of the bordelaise. He asked me to come into the kitchen with him, and the atmosphere there turned out to be more authentic and less depressing than in the sitting room: the place was small and pleasantly crowded with copper pans and heavy crockery dishes, some of them heaped, as if they were meant to be painted in a French still life, with chopped and shredded vegetables. He offered me a high stool near the stove, and I climbed up onto the little round seat, feeling myself put at a disadvantage: any attitude except a completely relaxed and friendly one was bound to look priggish and spinsterly if it were assumed on such a seat. He stood at the workboard some six or seven feet away, with his back to me, examining each spear of asparagus before he dropped it into a copper cooking pot. "You know, you have a pleasant voice—no, I really mean it," he said. "Also, it seems to me I heard you some time back. Weren't you one of the soloists with Shaw when he did the Saint Matthew Passion—how far back was that—six or seven years?"

"That was me. That was almost my last performance."

"How does it come you aren't doing that sort of thing anymore?"

If it upset him to hear the truth about people's frailties, he would have to learn not to ask them embarrassing questions. I told him, leaning forward with my elbows on my knees and my chin in my hands, that my voice wasn't at all what it had been when he heard me in New York.

A couple of spears of asparagus went together, unexamined, into the pot of water. He did not turn his head.

"My voice got undependable," I told him with shrill

154

emphasis, exasperated by his stubborn silence. "My range was never much to begin with, and it was on the downgrade."

"But maybe it wasn't as bad as you thought it was," he said without turning around, after a long and stressful pause. "What I mean to say is: maybe it was only a temporary thing. You might have been upset, you might have been on some kind of nervous strain or something the time it happened."

"I wasn't on any particular strain, not so far as I can remember. Anyway, I stopped trying to put myself across as a concert performer—it just didn't seem to make much sense to me. I mean, there didn't seem to be much point in keeping up a desperate effort to get myself and everybody else convinced I was better than I really was. I'd never let myself in for it again—it isn't worth it—anyway, it doesn't seem worth it to me."

"You know," he said in a strangely subdued voice, "you puzzle me, the way you talk about it. You sound as if you didn't mind much about giving it up. Didn't you really?"

I felt that he was asking for total honesty, and what he demanded of me I demanded of myself. "I don't know what I might have felt about it if I'd had the time or the peace of mind to feel anything," I said. "I suppose I was just too busy—the way it worked out I didn't have time to think. My mother—she died last spring, that was why I didn't meet you when you came down here for your interview—my mother had a stroke not long after I began to notice the trouble with my voice, and I had to come back here and look after her, and what I had on my hands at home drove everything else pretty much out of my head, as you can well imagine. There was so much to do at home and at school that, before I had a chance to notice what I was doing, I was used to the set-up, I had worked myself in. Whenever I looked back on it—the life I used to have up there—it seemed strange and far away and I didn't want to think

155

about it much. And by now—maybe it sounds peculiar, but I'm telling you the truth—I hardly ever *do* think about it anymore."

He did not answer. It seemed to me he was making himself very busy around the sink in order to escape the intimacy that would be inherent in any kind of answering. He turned the faucet on full force, he noisily scraped some shredded vegetables into a pan, he slammed the refrigerator door with his elbow; and during all these maneuvers he kept his spare, stooped back to me. So far as I could recall, my words had been unemotional enough, but I wondered whether my tone had been colored by the images that had come and gone while I talked behind him—images of stripped rooms and long watches and a changed face—and I was disturbed by his persistent and ungiving silence. A change of tone seemed called for. "Did you have a good time in New York?" I said.

"Do you mean when I went up there over Thanksgiving?" He came across the room to the stove and stood, not a foot away from where I was sitting, with a saucepan in his hand. "Oh, yes, I guess so. That is, not particularly." He lighted the burner, set the pan on it, and suddenly turned around and looked me straight in the eyes. "Not that I'd want you to quote me—according to my colleagues, I'm supposed to have such a wonderful time up there, and I wouldn't want to disillusion them for anything in the world. *You* know what it's like, Frieda—the usual rat-race—too much food, too much drink, not enough sleep. A person has to go—a person goes to mend his fences—"

He was so close to me that I had to keep a stern watch on my face, I had to down a flicker of surprise and a self-betraying smile.

"You know, I've been thinking," he said in a voice that startled me with its candor and its gentleness, "I made a mistake about the dinner, I should have had potatoes tonight. Not that I need them for myself, God knows, but I

156

should have had them for you." Unbelievably, unaccountably, he reached out and touched me, lightly, tenderly, running his fingers over the round of my shoulder. "You should eat starches, you're sort of thin, you could do with a little more flesh on your bones."

The touch, the look, the concern in his voice—utterly unexpected, no longer hoped for—worked upon me with a sudden and incomprehensible power. I glanced down at the fingers that touched me and at the raveled ribbing around the dark wrist. I was sorry for the shabby sweater, so sorry for it that I put up my hand and touched the pulled threads. "And this could do with a little mending," I said.

And knew at once that I should never have moved or spoken, should have sat on my perch motionless and voiceless as a statue. Whatever living, melting thing had been between us for an instant died and hardened as his face became the icy face in the photograph. "Yes, it's in bad shape, I'm afraid it's beyond mending. I guess I ought to throw it away," he said. His hands went into his pockets as he moved away from me, back to the workboard, and I wondered whether the one that had been upon me was pressing against a handkerchief, trying to wipe away the lingering sensation of touch.

It was an impossible situation, and I could sustain it only by telling myself that it was *his* situation. *He* had gotten into it, and it was for him to invent the means of extrication: I would not say a word, not if the sick, charged stillness hung over us for hours. He opened a package wrapped in bloody butcher's paper, and I was shaken and bitter enough to enjoy the embarrassment that drove him to put on an exaggerated pantomime of the chef at work, wiping the meat with a damp cloth, swishing it through olive oil on a platter, grinding fresh pepper onto it with a pepper mill. How long we remained suspended, how many minutes passed before he came toward me again—carrying the steak on the oily platter, holding it out with a totally false en-

157

thusiasm for my inspection and praise—I do not know. But I am sure my face was unexceptionable: I smiled and nodded and said it was certainly a prime piece of beef, you could tell that by the streaks of fat and the color of the chunk of marrow in the bone.

"Tremendous, isn't it?"

"Much too big for the two of us. You'd better cut it in half if you don't want to be eating cold steak for the rest of the week."

"I've got a better idea than that." He tried to give the illusion of an exchange of looks by staring steadily at the middle of my forehead. His mouth curved up in a tight and unconvincing smile, and he kept rocking the platter back and forth, perhaps to distribute the olive oil and perhaps to hide the shaking of his hands. "What about your friends the Grüenbergs—do you think they're doing anything in particular this evening?"

"I wouldn't know. Did you want to ask them to dinner?"

"If you don't think they'd be put out by a last-minute invitation. It seems a pity to waste a steak like this."

"They don't stand on ceremony. They'd probably be delighted. Why don't you call them up and see? The number's Freemont 1-3707."

He telephoned them, and they accepted, as I knew they would, even if Emily had already put on their dinner. They felt called upon to respond with cordiality to the first advance of this solitary stranger, no matter how sudden and peculiar the nature of it was; and, once they arrived, they did everything imaginable to establish ease and *Gemutlichkeit*. Two or three times in the course of the evening I found myself thinking how contented I would have been a month ago with the terms on which we were functioning: there was good talk, there were no signs of snobbishness or hostility, and before we got up from the excellent dinner all of us were calling each other by our first names. But under the discussion and the jokes and the minor intimacies, I felt an ache in my chest, persistent and unnerving, as if I had been crying so long that I had bruised myself inside. And my response to the repeated suggestion that we should do this sort of thing often was less enthusiastic than the Grüenbergs': for me it was dangerous, I had better keep clear of it, I could not trust myself.

Chapter 12

THAT RECITAL BY six of the senior instrumentalists, in which Cathie Dugan's performance of the Chopin B minor Scherzo was, or was supposed to be, the high spot, mobilized me on the side of Dr. Boyd and "the Europeans": there was no question about it, the standards had come down appallingly. I tried to tell myself that the concert might have been less disheartening if I hadn't had Harrison Frye at my elbow—he had slipped, ponderous and apprehensive, into the empty seat on my right just before the student ushers closed the doors of the recital room; and throughout the twelve pieces on the program he had made his feelings obvious by frequent shiftings of his impressive body and by emphatic sighs. But even if he had not been there I could not have blinded myself to the shabbiness of the whole event: the audience was nine-tenths made up of teachers and relatives of the performers; there were whole rows and half rows of empty seats; and almost everybody in the meager crowd of listeners had the sad, glazed look of waiting for the business to be over and wishing to be somewhere else.

Cathie came at the end of the program and should have profited by the lack of distinction in those who came before her. The best that could be said of her predecessors was that nobody broke down, nobody had to start over, nobody made any glaring mistakes. I winced when I thought of Arthur sitting in the audience—just where he was sitting I didn't know, since I hadn't been able to locate him before Harrison's arrival and I certainly didn't want to be looking around for him in Harrison's presence; I knew that his opinions about the mediocrity of the department could only be confirmed by what he heard tonight. There was nothing to recommend any of the performers on the grounds of appearance, either: the boys were for the most part childish and ineffectual, and the girls lacked taste and self-confidence —every one of them was over-dressed. Aside from Cathie, there was not a real musician in the line-up; by the way they walked across the stage and bowed, as well as by the total lack of distinction in their playing, they showed themselves foredoomed to teach chorus and direct orchestras in the public high schools. I contemplated their accumulated futures with discouragement, and I had to warn myself not to sigh, with Harrison, over the dreary prospect of their days.

"The Dugan girl's supposed to be good, isn't she?" he said in a loud whisper as the spattering applause for the spindly flutist who had come before her began to die out.

"She's excellent. She's a real musician," I said defensively.

"Where's her teacher?" He turned around from the hips and made an exhaustive survey of the wretched little audience. "I don't see anything of her teacher."

I believe I paled a little. It was unthinkable that he would not turn up at a performance given by one of his own senior students. Dr. Holland was standing against the wall at the back of the recital room, noting everything with his lively blue glance; and not only the teachers of the performers but every other member of the Music department had made an appearance, bleak and rainy as the evening was,

161

out of courtesy. "He's probably backstage," I said, knowing that backstage was the last place on earth he was likely to be: he was nobody to pat sagging backs, nobody to hold moist and shaking hands.

Any other questions that he might have been pondering were forestalled by the appearance of Cathie. She was dressed with propriety: she wore a simple shirt-waist kind of thing made of olive-green velvet, with a small bunch of yellow artificial flowers stuck into the belt. She was scrubbed and brushed, and the color of the dress was good for her hair and eyes. Her looks, especially in contrast with the dullness and tawdriness of the others, were dashing enough to stir the sodden audience; she was the star performer, and most of them knew it and gave her a vigorous round of applause. But I was not at my ease about her—perhaps because of the uncharacteristically calm and matter-of-fact manner in which she entered, bowed, and seated herself, perhaps because I kept thinking how hollow her heart must be if her teacher had not felt called upon to come—and I reproached myself with the thought that somebody, myself if there was nobody else to do it, should have sent her a corsage.

The main body of the B minor Scherzo has a tense and relentless swiftness, and I was convinced that her nervous drive and her hammering attack would stand her, for once, in good stead. But there was no drive, and she did not hammer. Her present teacher had taught her at least to take things easily: she was taking her Chopin so easily tonight that the effect was smooth, controlled, capable—and curiously spiritless. I knew what she was feeling as she sat there with her bony and expressionless face exposed to the audience. I had felt it myself on two or three occasions: a detachment from the moment and the music, a sense of proceeding mechanically step by step from the beginning to the end, a conviction that one is watching oneself from a vantage point many feet away—efficiency without involvement.

162

She played with perfect clarity and sureness: in such a state of mind, a skilled performer seldom makes a mistake. Considered phrase by phrase, what came out from under her strong, effective fingers was unexceptionable; but there was no passion in it; and, with the passion, the overall form— the build, the sense of large stress and temporary lull and ultimate climax—was completely gone. After what should have been a stunning conclusion, there was a disturbing second in which nobody made a sound, and I wondered whether the rest of them were feeling what I was feeling: that nothing had happened, that she had not actually played, that, when she got up from the piano bench, she was issuing surprised out of a dream. Then there was a loud burst of clapping, much louder than any that had come before it, so loud and so prolonged that it judged her more severely than if it had been a lukewarm response: either they were determined to approve her work since they had committed themselves by the enthusiasm with which they had greeted her appearance on stage, or they had somehow sensed her failure and did not want it there, and had made up their minds in pity to applaud it out of sight.

I did not see her walk backstage because Harrison laid his pudgy fingers on my arm. "Say, Frieda, what's up with her?" he said.

"What do you mean: What's up with her? It was a very smooth performance. She used to hammer dreadfully, and now she's not hammering at all. She's made considerable progress—"

"Really? That's peculiar. *I* would have said she'd deteriorated since I heard her last."

"She's expert—not showy."

"To me, she sounded dull. I kept saying to myself: Suppose this girl didn't happen to be in our department here—would any of us give her playing a second thought?"

"I'd keep my voice down. The place is full of relatives."

"Her relatives are in the second row—I've met them."

163

They were, and I knew as much. Her mother and father—thin, ingrown, self-effacing people—were sitting shoulder to shoulder, as if they were trying to sustain each other by touch; and I hoped that the enthusiasm of the clapping was helping them to deceive themselves. "Actually, Harrison, she's made great strides. It's a technical matter, and hard for anybody from the outside to understand."

He gave me a look of reproach and affront: after all, he was *not* from the outside—he read their weekly themes, he knew their hearts. "Oh, doubtless, anything the great Mr. Sanes does is sure to be for the best," he said, and his large face puckered in an infantile pout. "But my limited mind refuses to be impressed. I still think she sounded better last year."

My anger showed in my face, showed so definitely that it warned him off from asking what he usually asked on such occasions: whether I wouldn't like to come over to the grille at the hotel and have a cup of coffee with him. When I said shortly that I was going backstage to congratulate the performers, he said with melancholy self-righteousness that he couldn't put in an appearance back there without being obviously hypocritical: he'd just slip out without seeing anybody—anyway, he ought to get home to Corinne. I shrugged and walked through the thinned crowd to the front of the house, up the three steps that led onto the stage, across the worn planks, and into the cork-lined, wire-strung, crowded place that was called backstage.

The greater part of the sorry little audience—I had been right in thinking that almost everybody at the recital was closely connected with one of the participants—was jammed into the relatively meager space, which smelled of their damp umbrellas and furs. Although there was no reason for muting the conversation, their talk was as low and decorous as talk in a funeral parlor, and all of it was of a kind: Selma and George and Theodore had played beautifully, just beautifully; Joan's dress had looked stunning; the

164

audience had been very warm and enthusiastic, and the great wonder was that so many people had come out on such a night. Through knots of performers and their friends and parents—most of the parents looked as if the academic atmosphere put them at a disadvantage against which they bridled—I made my way to the corner where Cathie was standing with her mother and father and two or three of her classmates, getting toward her by slow stages, peering all the way between the clustered heads, looking for Arthur, not yet willing to face the preposterous conclusion that he had not come. Anna Webb, the secondary piano teacher— a sandy-haired and inoffensive young woman with a flat figure and a colorless mole on the lid of her eye—plucked me tentatively by the sleeve. "Where's Mr. Sanes? Didn't he turn up?" she asked without acrimony. And I told her with more sharpness than she deserved I was sure *I* didn't know.

As I drew closer to it, the group around Cathie grew a little, increased by people who had finished congratulating those they were particularly concerned with and who felt called upon to pay their respects to the star of the evening; and I was delighted to see them coming over, not only because the swell would be heartening to Mr. and Mrs. Dugan but also because I felt I could carry off my false little function more gracefully if the atmosphere was superficially celebratory. Cathie saw me at a distance and gave me a sick smile and a nod, and the others, with exaggerated respect for my professorial status, made way for me. I kissed her— her cheek was cold against my mouth—and I shook the spare dry hand of her mother and the hard moist hand of her father. "You people can be proud of her—she's a real musician. You did beautifully, Cathie," I said.

"Thanks, Miss Hartmann. Anyway I got through it." The uncertain laugh which came at the end of that told me she was doing what she could to put a good face on it for her parents' sake. I fitted myself in and put my arm around her waist and added what I could to the routine compliments by pointing out specific things: her relaxation, the firmness of her tempos, the clarity of her passage work. And, even if she looked at me in a way that showed she understood what I was doing, I was glad I had been maneuvered into standing beside her while she greeted her line. Every other performer had his own teacher hovering at his elbow. It was unbelievable, it was shameful, it was so bad that I could not even try to mitigate it by mentioning it in an offhand manner—the fact that Arthur hadn't come.

There was an instant when I thought he *had* come—she flushed and her arm tightened against my side; but when I looked up I saw that it was only Vincent. I had forgotten him, I had not looked for him in the audience, and he was the sort of person one does not see without intention. I realized at once that he had not exchanged a word with her since he had told her to let him alone: I knew it by the tight way he carried himself in his clean shirt and his newly pressed suit, by the awkward vigor with which he thrust out his hand to her, and by the uncertain and apologetic wording of his congratulatory formula, into which he did not insert her name.

"Thank you. It was nice of you to come backstage," she said.

"Well, I wanted you to know I liked the way you did it." His eyes—until now they had fixed themselves on a button under her chin—began to wander about, and I knew he was looking for Arthur Sanes.

By the red spots that burned suddenly into her bony cheeks, I could tell that she knew it, too. She stared sternly at the thatch of hair that slanted down over his forehead. "Nobody could possibly like the way I did it," she said.

"Don't be silly, darling, you were fine," I said. I tightened my hand hard at her waist, near her ribs, and sent a significant look in the direction of her mother, whose peaked, tired face was twitching with controlled distress.

"It's certainly nice to see *you* Vincent," Mrs. Dugan
166

said. "It's months since you've been over. Where have you been keeping yourself?"

"I haven't been going anywhere very much, I guess," he told her lamely. "School's been keeping me pretty busy."

"We're having a little affair over at the house tonight. Just us and Sarah Friedman and her parents and my brother and sister and a couple of Cathie's cousins." She did not see the sick, exasperated look her daughter turned upon her. "It won't be much—just a bite to eat—but maybe you'd like to come."

"Thanks, Mrs. Dugan, but—"

"He's *busy,* Mother. Didn't you hear him say he was busy?"

"Thanks just the same, Mrs. Dugan. Maybe some other time." He shook hands all around, unnecessarily and miserably, and took himself off.

"How about you, Miss Hartmann? Maybe you'd like to join us," Cathie's father said.

"Oh, for God's sake, Pa," said Cathie, "what do you want to drag poor Miss Hartmann into it for? It's bad enough she had to take a whole evening off to hear a rotten recital. It's a weekday anyway, she's got to be in at nine-thirty tomorrow. She probably wants to go home and go to bed."

But I did not go home. I walked only as far as the lobby of the building—teachers, parents, and performers, some of the latter with their instruments laid away in cases, kept crossing the stony bigness in isolated groups; and I sat down on one of the marble benches, tired because I had been standing so long. I had meant to rest there only a few minutes, but I fell to wondering why he had not come— whether perhaps a long distance telephone call, coming in just as he was about to leave his apartment, had held him in mush-mouthed conversation until it was too late for him to make an appearance without drawing undue attention. Almost everybody who was left had walked past me, the

167

tawdry dresses flouncing out ridiculously from under the hems of trenchcoats and raincoats, and the big center lights had gone out and had left the lobby as dim as a hospital after visiting hours are over—quiet except for an occasional echoing "Good night" or the heavy steps of a janitor, shadowy except where the night lights burned, as ineffectual as stars, high up on the walls. I could not sit there forever. The rain had stopped: no drops broke up the black sheen of the puddles visible through the plate glass door. I opened my purse to take out my comb, but I did not comb my hair: Vincent Booth had come up and was standing in front of me, much as he had stood on that afternoon when he had come into my office; and I closed my purse softly, without a click, looking up at him eagerly, hoping that my contrition and my readiness showed in my face.

"Have you got a minute, Miss Hartmann?"

"Any number of minutes." I patted the empty half of the bench beside me.

"They're closing up, I guess." He looked dubiously around at the dimness and the emptiness.

"Don't worry. I've been here a lot later than this. They won't throw us out, and they won't lock us in."

He sighed and sat down beside me, with his topcoat laid neatly over his knees. "What did *you* think of Cathie—the way she played tonight?" he said.

I was glad for the semi-darkness: I felt, rather than saw, that he was watching my face. "It certainly wasn't bad, it wasn't anything nearly as bad as she was making it out to be backstage," I told him, rousing up a reproachful series of echoes in the hollow lobby. "There's one big improvement —she's relaxed—she isn't hammering the way she used to. I guess Mr. Sanes ought to get the credit for that—"

"Oh, sure, give him the credit for that—and for a lot of other things," he said, with a bitter little snort of laughter. "Like that tailspin she went into after he told her she'd never be any good. Like the deadgone way she's playing

168

now, and the way she broke up with me, and that rotten business with Fred Wade. I wouldn't mention it, not even to you, if everybody on campus wasn't talking about it—"

"Nobody ever mentioned it to me, Vincent. I'd never have heard a word about it if she hadn't come and told me herself."

He closed his hands into fists under his folded topcoat, and I knew that in the last few weeks he had covered the recollection under routine labor, that he had almost managed to forget it, and that the thought of Cathie and me speaking of it together had given it a terrible immediacy for him, had torn away the swathings and shown it to him again, alive and raw. "She never would have done such an insane thing if *he* hadn't gone at her about how she was all tied up in herself. And who's he, I'd like to know, to tell anybody that? I don't know how he plays—he wouldn't lower himself to play for any of us—but if there's anybody all tied up in knots, *he* is."

He broke off at the sound of footsteps. Far down the hall, Anna Webb had walked out of her office, carrying books and an umbrella; and while she advanced on us in her flapping black denim raincoat, with the hood over her head so that she looked like a penitential medieval monk, I was given the leisure to consider his last outburst. "All tied up in knots" was a description I could not take exception to—it was apt, and it was just. I was forced almost immediately to dismiss the recollection of his casual tossing off of the accompaniment to my Mozart songs: I remembered the spare face turning one way and another against the view of the skyscrapers through the big window, and knew that there had been some trick involved. Even then it had struck me that his apparent relaxation and poise had come from an unspoken understanding between us that he was not responsible for a performance, was only playing at playing; on a more formal occasion it was possible he would conduct himself quite otherwise. . . .

169

"You won't need your hood, Anna," I said. "It's stopped raining."

"Oh, has it? That's good." She paused in front of the two of us, and her unwillingness to conclude her lonely and unsatisfactory evening was palpable there in the dimness and the stillness. I was sorry that I could give her no encouragement, could only wait until she said, "Well, I'd better get to my bus stop while I can, between showers. See you tomorrow. Good night."

Vincent had risen, discommoded by his topcoat, at her approach. Now, as she retreated toward the door with the voluminous denim rustling around her, he subsided onto the bench, robbed of the vitality of his bitterness by the interruption, unable to start off at the same pitch, willing to consign the next stage of the discussion to me.

"He *is* tied up in knots," I said, touching the fold of the coat where it lay over his hand, "and it *was* a questionable thing for him to do, lighting into Cathie like that, though I doubt very much whether *that* was as bad as she made it out to be either—she has very strong feelings, and she's inclined to exaggerate. Anyway, I can imagine him talking to any number of people like that without causing a major blowup. He didn't know Cathie—not the way you and I know her—"

"He doesn't know anybody, if you ask me. He doesn't even know his own student well enough to turn up and hear her in a recital. What's the matter with him? Didn't he want to take the responsibility for what he's done to her?"

I had been thinking with a surprising surge of pride that he did know me—at least he knew me a little—though I did not mention that to Vincent. "You can't put all the responsibility on him," I said. "You've got to take Cathie's personality into consideration, too. And besides—" I hurried on, taking advantage of his silence—"Fred Wade had something to do with it. I wouldn't say—and I'm sure you wouldn't either—that he was exactly innocent."

170

"He's a—I don't have to tell you what I think he is, Miss Hartmann." He made a sudden jerky movement, turning his head away from me, pulling his hand from under my masked touch. "I'd like to bash in his face, I'd like to kill him—"

"Of course you would. I don't blame you at all. But what would be the good?"

"No good. No good at all, I guess," he said, letting his knobby forehead sink down on his fists. "Actually, I'd like to bash my own face in. I don't suppose I'm altogether innocent myself."

"Do you mean because of that business when you and Cathie went up to the woods together?"

"Did she tell you about that?" he said without lifting his head. "She must be pretty fond of you to tell you a thing like that. I don't know what you think of me—I guess I must look like a terrible fool."

"No, you don't look at all like a fool," I said, sitting stiffly, afraid to touch him. "But, if you really want to know what I think, I think you were pretty nasty to her about that. You *do* know her, and you must have seen she was upset, and it seems to me you might have watched your temper—"

"Don't you know why I lost my temper?"

"Because she was so insistent and demanding?"

"Well, yes, partly. But the main thing was, I'd never had a girl before, and I wanted to until she laid it on the line like that, and then I just didn't feel the way I was supposed to feel, if you know what I mean. To tell you the truth, Miss Hartmann—" he took his hands away from his face and looked me briefly in the eyes—"she thought I was a lot sorer than I was. I wasn't up to it—fact is, I was afraid."

A janitor came by with a long-handled brush and a bucket of that ground-up corky stuff they strew on the floors to settle the dust. He slowed down in front of us and looked as if he meant to empty the bucket around our feet,

171

but I eyed him, and he thought better of it and went away whistling—his tuneless whistle came back to us, far and thin, while he scattered his dreary confetti on the main stairs. "Anybody with any sensitivity wouldn't have felt like himself under the circumstances, and it's no sin to be sensitive," I said.

"Well, all I wanted to tell you was: I was partly to blame."

The quiet conviction that the years of my life had left me a minor deposit of wisdom—it is a conviction that comes upon me most frequently, and most blessedly, when I am at my weariest—made me willing to direct him. "Listen, Vincent," I said, daring to touch him again, putting my hand over his hand, which lay limp on the bench beside me, "it seems to me we're going to get nowhere if we sit around trying to figure out who's to blame. Really, everybody who had a hand in it is to blame for it: Mr. Sanes and Cathie and Fred Wade and you—yes, and I am, too, for that matter, because I heard Mr. Sanes lecturing her on the other side of the wall, I heard it all; and it wasn't as bad as she said it was, and I should have admitted I'd listened, I should have gone over it with her and got her to realize what he really said. After this sort of smash-up, everybody feels so guilty he spends a lot of valuable time chewing on his guilt and wondering whether he should have done this or that—and, actually, standing around immobilized like that is the worst thing a person can do. The only sensible way to make anything out of it is to bestir yourself and pick up the pieces— provided you want to pick up the pieces—"

"Of course I do."

"Are you sure? She's a very difficult girl, Vincent. Fond as I am of her, I've got to admit she isn't likely to give anybody much peace."

"I guess I've had more peace than I can use lately. I guess I miss her. And honestly, Miss Hartmann—" his voice quavered for the first time, and he blinked and set his teeth in

172

his lower lip—"you'll never know how I felt when I watched her up there—I was so sorry for her, sitting up there dead-gone like that and all by herself."

I told him he'd better find an occasion for talking things over with her. I added, laughing, that I thought he'd better find it soon—there was no knowing what she might think up next if he left her to herself. He said he couldn't figure out right now how he'd go about it, but he supposed he'd find a way, and he offered to drive me home in his father's car, an offer which I accepted. As we went toward the plate glass door, the shrill unmelodious whistle of the janitor kept sounding behind us; the atmosphere was heavy with dampness and the smell of strewn cork and the recollection of the dreary recital, and I was more depressed than I should have been, considering my affection for these young lovers. As I stepped out into the night, holding onto his arm, I wondered whether the arms of students were the only arms I could hope to hold in the long succession of oncoming years, and I was more than a little sorry for myself.

Chapter 13

THERE WAS ANOTHER note to dismiss his students on his door next morning. Dr. Holland's secretary went out of her way to tell me he had reported himself sick: she dragged it into the conversation in a way I did not like—she seemed to be implying that I would be particularly interested. It was easier to assume a casual and detached air for her benefit since I did not believe in his illness, possibly because the small twitching smile on her full face suggested she did not believe in it herself. I was too busy all day to worry much about the effect these one-day absences of his must be having on his superior and his students, though how much they were annoying his colleagues I was forced to realize at the lunch table, where his sudden seizures and miraculous recoveries were the subject of much feeble and far-fetched joking, indulged in not only by Jenny and Hughie but also by Michael and the good Anna Webb, who had formerly shown herself completely free of guile. My Israeli student's throat had reacted to the climate in an alarming manner—for five days the city had been drenched with intermittent drizzles, and now it was beginning to snow in big wet flakes—and I was spending every minute between lessons with him, getting him an

174

appointment with a throat specialist, locating the means for paying the doctor bill through an emergency student fund, assuring him that his laryngitis was minor and temporary, that he would be singing as well as ever in a week or so, and that nobody had the slightest intention of packing him up and sending him home. By the end of the day, my own voice was husky, perhaps with the strain of talking too much vehement common sense and perhaps with an oncoming cold. Eating my dinner alone in a little Hungarian restaurant where the smell of the food was always better than the food itself, I decided to take a hot bath and spend the evening reading in bed.

While I was unlocking the door of my apartment, I heard the telephone ringing inside. A telephone bell repeating itself insistently in an empty room has for me an urgency which is almost ominous, and I lost the chance to answer it by becoming so nervous that I dropped my key out of my wet and slippery hands. Just as I got inside, chilled and soaked with the residue of the big melted flakes, the ringing stopped, and I was unaccountably disturbed over the fact that I might never know who had called. As a precaution against any further speculation, I made myself busy: I undressed, put on a newly pressed housecoat, started the water into the tub, opened a box of pine bath soap which I had intended as a Christmas gift; and I was ready to step into the tub when the phone rang again. My curiosity was enough to send me out to it without my bathrobe; I took off the receiver without speaking into it and wrapped myself in an old afghan that was hanging over a lounging chair. "Hello," I said, and got no immediate answer. I was about to repeat the "Hello" when a voice—Arthur's voice, so unexpected as to be almost unrecognizable—came over the wire. "Hello, Frieda. This is Arthur—Arthur Sanes. Are you there by yourself? Could I talk to you for a minute?" he said.

"Yes, I'm here alone, I just got back from dinner. Did you call me a few minutes ago?"

"To tell the truth, I've been calling you every fifteen minutes for the last two hours."

"I'm sorry. I usually don't come back here until after I've had my dinner. Is anything the matter?"

"No—yes—what I wanted to ask you was: Are you busy tonight?"

"No. Why? Are you sick in bed? Did you want me to bring you anything? I'd be glad to."

There was a long pause before he said, "The fact is, I haven't been sick at all—not today and not last night. But I'd like very much to have a talk with you, if it wouldn't be putting you out, and I thought maybe if you weren't busy you'd let me come over and see you tonight."

The antagonism which had flamed up in me when he announced he had simply malingered his way out of the recital was immediately quenched by the humility of his request. A scared student could not have asked more humbly. There was a shy, beseeching quality in his voice that made it impossible for me to say anything but, "Certainly, come ahead."

"When can I come, Frieda?"

"I was just about to get into the tub—" I broke off awkwardly, stiffened by the notion that he could somehow see me standing at the phone with the afghan half covering my nakedness. "I was just about to get into the tub," I said again with ridiculous firmness, "and I'd like to have enough time to take a bath and get dressed. I'd be ready in three quarters of an hour, if that's all right with you."

"That's perfect with me. I've got to shave—I haven't shaved for a couple of days."

"Do you know where I live?"

"Yes, I've passed it."

"I'm on the fourth floor. You have to ring the buzzer."

"All right. Thanks very much. It's really very good of you to let me come like this. I'll see you then in three-quarters of an hour."

Once in the tub, I found myself so tense that even the
176

warmth of the water and the soporific scent of the soap could not soothe me. I asked myself what in God's name could be nagging at me so, and got around to seeing—just about the time I was drying myself—that I was worrying about what he was going to think of my living room. Even if a person discounted the marble top table and the Portuguese chest and the wrought iron that he had left behind him in his New York studio, such possessions as he had in that bare, somber downtown place of his made my belongings a batch of shoddy, ill-assorted things. My sofa was dented and faded; my armchairs had been bought singly and had little to do with each other; the big brass jug on my coffee table with its embossed ornamentation of feasting peasants—I had always known I should have never bought it, I had suspected it from the beginning of gross Bavarian sentimentality. I owned no single precious and distinguished thing—no saint's head, no brooding boy in puffed sleeves, no horned Actaeon; and I wished, as I dressed myself in my moss-green jersey, that I had one picture on the wall that wasn't a reproduction, one strange box or shell-shaped dish on my coffee table that would make such a visitor wish he owned it himself.

When I was dressed, I went into the living room and surveyed the depressing situation. My worry over the lack of distinction was overlaid by a more distressing contingency: the steamy scent of my bath had apparently drifted all over the place—the room was filled with the pungent and private odor of essence of pine. I thought of opening the windows, even on the thick dance of wet snowflakes, but I did not do it: not for anybody was I going to get a cold by standing in a draft after a bath. I took out a bottle of whiskey and a bottle of cordial and a couple of unimpressive glasses and set them on the coffee table. I had thought I had some nuts, but there were only a few broken halves and a smattering of crumbles, and I had just time enough to throw the oily box away before the buzzer rang.

In the few minutes it took him to come upstairs, I was

177

at once oppressed and exhilarated by a strange excitement. It was as if there were no Mrs. McIvor, it was if he had never pulled his hand away from my touch; it was as if I were still in my twenties, waiting, with the force of my heart pounding up into my throat, for the arrival of a lover. I walked to the window, unable to stand still in my agitation, and saw my reflection in the dark glass, with the dizzy flurry dancing vaguely behind it. There was a smile on the mouth, knowing and subtly joyous. The smile grew, the lips parted and asked to be kissed. I shocked them into desirelessness by letting them come up against the coldness of the pane, and turned away from the whirling flakes and pulled myself together just as he knocked at the door.

To see him was to take again my predetermined position in regard to him. If I had been harboring any notion that he would come to me in a baggy grey sweater, with unshaven cheeks and a hangdog air, I was disappointed: he looked as he usually looked when I ran into him in the corridor at school—poised and scrupulously well-dressed in his greenish-grey worsted and his immaculate white shirt, with an onyx tie-clasp setting off his amber tie. If there was trouble in his face—and I thought as we exchanged the senseless amenities that there was a hint of trouble—he did not mean to come out with it like a breathless boy as soon as he stepped into the room. He was self-possessed enough at any rate to take a long look at everything I did not particularly want him to look at: the dent in my sofa, the obvious cheapness of my prints, the battered, third-hand look of my Baldwin—all these were stored now, for as long as he might trouble himself to think anything about me, in the recesses of his enigmatic brain.

I was exasperated at myself, too, for wanting so much to look at him. I wished I had had a piece of embroidery— Emily had been trying to get me involved in embroidery— to fix my attention on for the remainder of the evening. No matter how much I willed it otherwise, my eyes kept coming

178

back to him, kept noting with unbecoming and foresworn eagerness the stoop of his shoulders, the shape of his head, the tense, closed line of his lips. Perhaps it was annoyance with myself that prodded me to say, in a teacherly tone, as soon as we were settled at opposite ends of the sofa, that, if he wasn't sick yesterday, he should have dreamed up some more convincing excuse. I gave him an account of the conversation at the lunch table without removing any of the sting; I even quoted Hughie Saunders verbatim, possibly because at the moment he was gazing—intently, if blankly—at my foolish piece of Bavarian brass. "The fact is, I don't think there was a single one of them that believed you were sick," I said. "Not that you care in the least."

"Do you think," he asked me, gravely and candidly, "they'd be more likely to believe it if I stayed home tomorrow too?"

"Lord, Arthur, I don't know. Did you stay in all day?"

"Yes, of course."

"Still, somebody might have seen you on your way over here tonight."

"That's right. I guess I'd better go in tomorrow then."

"Unless you don't give a damn—which I took to be the case."

"Is everybody of that opinion?" There was not the slightest hint of the sardonic in the question: it was a simple bid for information, put to me with a straight and mild and melancholy look.

"I suppose so. I don't know about Dr. Holland. He's never said a word about your cuts to me."

"If he ever does—" he leaned forward and reached out with his left hand, as if he wished to indicate he would have touched me if I had been nearer—"if he ever does, and you could do it without getting yourself into an embarrassing spot, I'd be grateful if you'd let him know I'm not exactly itching to get fired."

"Would you rather leave under your own steam?" I

said, half out of uncontrollable curiosity and half out of some inexplicable devilishness.

He looked first at me and then at his hands—he had brought them into composure, like the hands of a carved pharaoh, on his knees. "So everybody's concluded I want to get out," he said.

"Don't you?"

"Not exactly. Not for certain. To tell the truth, Frieda—" he pronounced my name with conscious friendliness—"I'm confused at the moment, I don't know what I'm going to do."

For an instant I let my exhilaration whirl about with the white flurry churning on the far side of the window. Then I told myself that Mrs. McIvor must have had a temporary setback in her attempt to appease or hoodwink Mr. McIvor, that tomorrow or day after tomorrow she would make more headway and would relay that information in another long-distance call, that, whatever happened in the end, I would be less vulnerable in the interim if I took it for granted he would go away in spring. "You'd better make up your mind by the end of February," I said with a fine off-handedness, "That's when our contracts come out."

"If you get a chance, will you tell him?"

I stared stupidly for a second before I realized he had harked back to Dr. Holland. "Tell him you're not trying to be utterly hateful, just more or less objectionable?" I said.

He was not amused. His face hardened, and his yellow eyes narrowed at me before he assumed a smile. "Yes, something on that order. Provided, of course, as I said before, it wouldn't put you out too much."

"It wouldn't put me out at all, if the occasion presented itself. If it didn't come up naturally, though, I don't imagine it would do you any good for me to drag it in."

"Of course not. I know that."

A long and uneasy silence settled upon us, in which the assumed smile and the anger underlying it died from his face.

180

The fingers of his right hand, laid over the sharp crease in his trousers, made a fluttering beat as if he were practicing trills. I bent toward the coffee table and touched the tray that held the bottles and the glasses. If his purpose in coming had been to ask me to intercede for him with Dr. Holland, then his business was finished, and an offer of hospitality would provide him with a way to get out: he could tell me he had to keep a clear head, had to hurry back home on some pretext or other. "Would you like a drink, Arthur?" I said.

"Yes, I'd take a little of that cherry cordial."

"It isn't very good—it's not the Danish stuff—"

"I'm sure it's fine. Don't you want some, too?"

"Yes, I'll have a little."

"Here, let me do it." He came close to me, bent over, and poured the appropriate amount of cordial into the inappropriate glasses. He turned around and handed mine to me, so carefully that I could not think it was an accident—the fact that his fingers brushed against mine. Neither of us looked at the other, and for me the instant was sick with the recollection of his pulling away from me and thrusting his hands into his pockets. Also, I was disturbed by the piney smell of my bath soap, and it seemed to me when he took a deep breath that he was acutely aware of it too. "That business with Holland—that was a side issue. That wasn't what I wanted to talk to you about," he said.

"Sit down—I'm listening—make yourself comfortable."

But there was nothing comfortable about him as he got himself back into his corner of the sofa. With his head turned front, his shoulders forcibly straightened, his way of lifting the glass with a kind of practised elegance, his whole body was the incarnation of rigidity. "I take it you went to that recital last night, Frieda."

"I certainly did. Every other member of the department was there—those who didn't have students in it as well as

181

those who did. You just don't stay away from a senior recital—"

"Unless you're a dirty dog. Did you see anything of Miss Dugan? Afterwards, backstage, I mean."

"Yes, I did. I went and stood in line with her—she had quite a lot of people to congratulate her. It's a good thing I thought of it—all the other performers had their teachers with them—she was the only one that didn't have anybody."

"She had you," he said with a tight and aggravating smile.

"I'm not her teacher."

"No, of course you're not. I was only joking. Was she very much upset because I didn't turn up? Did she say anything about me?"

"No, she didn't." I resented the relief that allowed him to sag a little. "To state it exactly: your not being there was so painfully noticeable that nobody could bring himself to mention it—it was one of those awful things nobody can talk about."

He turned his face toward me—furious at first and then immediately icy and mocking. "Look," he said, "aren't you dramatizing it a bit? It wasn't Oistrakh making his first appearance in America—it was Miss Dugan playing for a collection of duds in the recital room."

"It was your student, and she needed your moral support."

"My moral support!" He said it loudly, setting his glass down on the cherry wood so hard and inexpertly that the cordial sloshed around in the bottom of it. "I'm all out of moral support. If she wants moral support, she'd better go look for it from somebody else!"

"You don't have to shout at me about it. I didn't bring up the subject—"

"No, you're right, you didn't."

"You asked me, and I told you—"

"All right, Frieda, and there's one more thing I'd like

182

to ask you: Do you think, like everybody else, I stayed away because I just didn't give a good goddamn?"

I was tempted to tell him I hadn't given the matter any consideration. I would have told him so if the shameful need to look at him hadn't forced me to see his eyes. The yellow glint that animated them when they moved was completely gone when they were fixed; the whites were streaked with red, the irises were faded, the lids above them were discolored and netted with fine wrinkles—they spoke of tormented sleeplessness. "I don't know, Arthur. I just don't know what to think about you—I never did," I said.

"Well, don't make me out to be worse than I am— I'm bad enough as it is. It wasn't because I didn't care that I stayed away last night. The fact is, I care very much. I can't stand the way she plays, that's all—I just can't stand to watch her. That crazy stiffness of hers—that jerky tenseness—it drives me half out of my mind even when we're only having a lesson. I started to get dressed to come, I meant to come, and then I couldn't. I just couldn't see myself watching her go through it in front of an audience. I couldn't pull it off—not even with two phenobarbitals and a couple of Scotches—it was just too much for me."

Through the whole speech he had not relinquished my glance; his eyes, naked and hounded, had kept demanding my look. Only by telling myself that Mrs. McIvor must have seen him often like this and had a better right to comfort him than I, could I keep the pity and the tenderness out of my face. "Have you talked to anybody about the recital, Arthur?" I said.

"No. Don't you know you're the only person here I'd talk to?"

"Well, then, maybe you'll be glad to hear she wasn't a bit rigid. She wasn't good, she was *too* relaxed, as if she was deadgone or something—but she certainly wasn't jerky or nervous or any of the things you were afraid she was going to be."

He sighed, picked up his glass, finished off his residue

183

of cordial, and held it out, with an unthinking readiness that was strangely touching, to be filled by me—I suppose he reminded me of a child asking for more. "So it wasn't so bad—she didn't break up—or—forget or anything?" he asked as I filled his glass.

"No, of course not, it was as smooth as butter. It was *too* smooth, it was as if she wasn't there."

He sighed and set himself again to beating out the fluttering trills on his knees. "That's good. That's better, anyhow, than the feeling that you've committed yourself to something horrible and there's no way of getting out of it," he said.

"I suppose it is, from her point of view. But she's not going to get anywhere playing the way she did last night."

"Where do you think she'll get playing any other way she can? She's got a pretty good technique, but she's—well, hell, why should we go into that? What I want to know is: Now that I've cut the thing, what'll I tell her when I see her tomorrow? Shall I say I was sick? What do you think?"

"You don't look sick, Arthur. You haven't even got a cold."

"I could say I had a blinding migraine. I do get migraines." A dull flush came up in his dry, dark cheeks as he said it; he could not have looked more ashamed of himself if he had been confessing himself a kleptomaniac or an incurable liar.

"I suppose you could tell her that. The only question is: Would she believe you? Maybe she'd feel better if you told her something more like the truth."

He flashed me one hard yellow stare and looked away again, stiff with resentment. "Surely you can't expect me to tell a student I'm the sort of person who works himself into a minor nervous breakdown over a performance," he said. "Anyhow, what good would *that* do—aside, of course, from living up to some boy-scout slogan like Honesty Is the Best Policy?"

184

"It might give her some indication that you're not what she thinks you are—totally unconcerned about her."

"If she thinks that, she must be pretty stupid. I'm more concerned about her than I am about anybody else around here—" he said it hatefully, he said it sneering—"anybody except yourself. But I'm not so concerned about her that I'm going to run out and get myself and my screaming meemies talked about all over campus. From the going over they gave me at lunch today, I'd think you could see why I wouldn't want to hand them any more ammunition than they've got."

"Yes, I can see that. Tell her you had a migraine, and I'll do what I can to back you up. I'll tell her I expected to see you at the recital and telephoned you afterwards when you didn't turn up, and you were so sick you could scarcely talk to me."

"You aren't used to lying, are you?"

"Oh, like anybody else, I lie when there seems to be some good reason for it. My morals aren't exactly built on boy-scout slogans," I said.

Another long silence followed, eerie with the creak of my neighbor's footsteps overhead, and heavy with the smell of essence of pine. I finished my cordial and got up, out of intolerable restlessness, and walked to the window. The dizzy whirl of snowflakes had not lessened in the least: they seemed to be flying toward me like threats out of the night, they danced crazily around the street lamp, they almost hid the houses on the other side of the avenue. Some childhood remembrance of a dream of being "snowed in," wrapped in great swaths of whiteness with a beloved teacher or a friend, came at me, magical, out of the past; and I watched an approaching bus intently, trying not to see the reflection of my face.

Yet I did see the reflections. After I had stared a while, they asserted themselves over the realities beyond them. I saw his blurred image get up from the far corner of the sofa,

185

move toward me, and define itself against the white whirling just as I heard the sound of his breath. I thought I saw his hand go up in a futile gesture: I could have sworn that his fingers were about to settle on my hair. Everything I saw, or dreamed I saw, was indefinite, shot through with spinning flakes, blanked out every here and there by passing headlights or the veiled square of a yellow window; yet my flesh tingled and my hair seemed to take on a life of its own, seemed to stir and rise at the roots to meet his touch.

"Still snowing," he said at last.

"Yes, harder than ever."

"Would you like to run through a couple of the Mozarts?"

"I'd like to, but I wouldn't dare to—my voice is husky. Somehow all day I've been talking at the top of my lungs, and I think I'm getting a cold into the bargain. I can't afford to risk it—my voice is a very undependable sort of thing."

"You harp on that a lot."

"I harp on it because it's the sad truth."

The silence came again, and I turned around to him. The two of us here in the room were less charged, more manageable than our shattered likenesses floating on the agitated dark. I gave him a workaday smile and saw, or imagined I saw, a kind of falling away in his look, as if a bonfire had died. "I guess I'd better go home. You're tired, and so am I," he said.

"You do look tired, Arthur."

"That's nothing new with me. I seem to have been tired since the day I was born. By the way, the things I said to you tonight—I wouldn't have said them to anybody else."

"You can be sure I won't repeat them."

"I didn't mean you shouldn't repeat them. It never occurred to me you would. I just wanted you to know I wouldn't say them to anybody else."

Every possible answer to that, even a simple "Thank you," seemed either too casual or too ceremonial. I nodded and walked with him halfway across the room, as far as

186

the near end of the sofa, where he stopped, inexplicably, and looked down at the faded green arm with the dent in it. "You must lead a pretty complicated social life. An awful lot of people must have stuck their elbows into that arm," he said.

"You mean that dent? That's not from people's elbows," I told him, noticing for the first time that there was a patch where the hairy, matted upholstery was showing through. I wasn't really as poor as all that—I thought I had better buy a new sofa one of these days.

"What's it from, then?"

"My head—I used to sleep out here when my mother was with me—I made it with my head."

"Did you?" He bent over and stared at it. He went further—he touched it, his spare fingers carefully exploring the concavity. Then, laughing unconvincingly, like an embarrassed schoolboy, he did touch me: he cupped the back of my head in his hand. "Yes, it'd just about fit in there, wouldn't it?" he said, and dropped his hand, and started for the door.

As I followed him and waited for him to get into his scarf and his overcoat, the sense of urgency seized me again. I reproached myself with all I wildly wanted to know and had not even tried to ask: Were his mother and father alive? Where were they? With what brothers and sisters, in what rooms, had he been playing and struggling thirty years ago?

"You were pretty fond of your mother, weren't you?" he said, buttoning up his fine English overcoat.

"Yes, we struck a good bargain. She was good to me when I was little, and I was good to her later. There weren't any odds, if you know what I mean. We were able to be fond of each other. And your mother—is she alive?"

"Oh, yes, she's alive. This tie-clasp"—he pushed aside his scarf and put his thumb under his tie and thrust the clasp out for me to see—"she gave it to me for my birthday a couple of years ago."

"It's very handsome. That's a strange spot in the corner of the stone. I was noticing it earlier in the evening."

"It's an onyx. Do you like onyx?"

"Yes, but I'm scarcely an expert. I haven't a precious stone to my name."

"Oh, this isn't precious—it's only semi-precious." He put it back under the folds of his scarf, straightened the lapel of his overcoat, and laid his hand on the doorknob. "Let's get some rehearsing in next week, Frieda, if you're not too busy. Thanks for the drink. And the suggestions. Yes, and the patience." He gave me a short, self-disparaging smile.

"I'm glad you came. It was good talking to you."

"Let's do it again. Take care of your cold. Good night."

I went to the window to see whether I could make him out on his way to the bus stop. It was, or seemed to be, a long time before he appeared on the walk—I wondered whether he had lost his way coming down, had taken the rear staircase and found himself in the basement among the clothes lines and the wash machines. He was only dimly visible, going away at a slow, steady pace; but the prints of his soles showed black and sharp against the thinly whitened pavement, and I watched them for a long time, while they turned grey and lost their edges and were transformed into faint, shadowy hollows and then disappeared altogether under the white level of the snow. He had not smoked while he was with me—possibly because he was afraid of getting a migraine. There were no ashes to be cleared up—there was, in fact, no sign that he had been here except his empty glass. I turned my back on it: I would not touch it now, I would wash it tomorrow. But I dreamed in the night that I came out here in the darkness, and carried the glass to the snow-blinded window, and put it to my lips.

Chapter 14

THAT FACULTY MEETING on raising the standards—it was held in a big empty classroom late in the afternoon a couple of days before Christmas vacation —that faculty meeting was, for the members of our department, the academic event of the year. It promised to be something of a disappointment at first. We had discussed the business so much before in twos and threes that, when it was officially brought to the floor, it had the effect of a warmed-over dinner; and Dr. Holland further robbed it of its drama by wandering back and forth in front of the room and propping his shoulder against the blackboard and presenting the problem in his twangy fisherman's voice. Some of us found ourselves staring at the harmony exercises scrawled on the slate, and some of us watched the windows over sills that were heaped with porous snow; but, since attendance was mandatory and everybody, even Arthur, was there, somebody was bound to say something that would stir up somebody else, and Hughie said it in his brash, un-self-conscious youth, and in no time at all we were warring factions, though the fighting was conducted strictly according to the complicated and confining rules of academic chivalry.

Beforehand it had been taken more or less for granted that the victory would go to the stand-patters, with certain minor concessions about entrance exams that would allow Dr. Boyd and "the Europeans" to save face. A mere counting of noses would have suggested such an outcome, and the weight of Dr. Holland's authority had been scrupulously held out of the ranks: nobody knew how he wanted it to come out—it was part of his conscientious practice of democracy to keep his views on major issues suppressed at first, even at the risk of giving his faculty the temporary impression that he didn't much care.

But about twenty minutes into the meeting, after the casual presentation and the preliminary skirmishes, Emily spoke at length on the decline that had taken place in the twelve years she had been teaching at the College: her warm, brusque delivery called up the ghosts of better terms and more distinguished graduates, and she stirred in some of us recollections of what it had been like to teach those with the gift to learn and the passion to know. Before the other side put the label of sentimentality on her arguments, Michael followed her up by quoting from a collection of student boners he had been writing down in a little black notebook, a procedure that was bound to involve most of us, since there was scarcely any of us who hadn't contributed at one time or another some choice item of his own. By the time he was finished, the cause was so solid that the faintly oratorical rendering of Dr. Boyd's grievances had a borrowed authenticity. I myself did not appear in single combat that day: I reserved my strength for re-stating in hard colloquial English what might have been blurred by the difficulties Michael and Emily had with the language, and for answering embarrassing questions put by the other side.

Anna Webb was the first on the opposition to come over to us, and a couple of others came with her, whereupon Dr. Holland made his position known in plain words—he had first given a pantomimic indication of it by wincing

190

as if he had a jumping toothache while Michael was reading to us from his little black book. And after that there was a fine resurgence of good will and high intent—Hughie was willing to listen, Jenny was willing to sacrifice herself—and a motion to raise the standards generally and to appoint a committee to make specific recommendations was presented by Matt Cusick and seconded by Anna Webb. It was late, and the classroom was growing very cold: since the tense nature of the discussion had necessitated an unusual amount of smoking, the windows had been opened, and some of us were shivering, and all of us were thinking of going home high-hearted to our suppers. "Anything anybody wants to bring up before we put it to a vote? Any remarks? Any questions?" Dr. Holland said.

I was sitting toward the front of the classroom and could not, without turning, see the lefthand corner at the rear, where Arthur had been lounging in silence during the entire meeting. But I knew by the universal uneasiness that he must have put up his hand.

"Yes, Mr. Sanes?" said the head of the department, with cheerful alacrity. If it was late in the day for complications, if he had been hoping we would vote and get out while the euphoria was at its crest, he was glad, nevertheless, that this standoffish new member, who had cut two meetings and had never offered to open his mouth in one before, should show some willingness to participate.

"One question, Dr. Holland. It may be a little upsetting, but I believe we ought to clear it up."

"By all means. We're glad to hear from you. Go ahead."

"In this business about the professional level of the students, we've been going on as if all we have to do is tighten up the entrance requirements. And maybe you can't raise the standards, not if you want to have any students left."

"I don't quite understand what you're driving at. Wouldn't you like to clarify a bit?"

"Well, it's pretty obvious that most people in this country are in better shape financially than they used to be—finding money for a musical education isn't exactly the problem it was when Mrs. Grüenberg came twelve years ago. I don't pretend to be an expert on the subject, but I imagine if one of your mill-working families in the district came up with a gifted youngster, they could probably find the means to send him to Curtis or Juilliard or some place like that, and if they couldn't lay their hands on the money they could probably find a scholarship—there are plenty of those around these days, too. If I'm figuring it right, that leaves us with this situation on our hands: no matter what we do about entrance requirements and the rest of it, the good ones will go to the better schools and all we can do is take our pick out of the ones that are left."

I did not turn, I kept my eyes on the head of the department. Whatever was coming up at him from the faces of my colleagues—amazement, affront, wounded sensibilities —Dr. Holland was able to deal with it consummately. He put up his strong hand and flicked his ear; he managed a smile that was neither condescending to the speaker nor a conspiratorial signal to the others, but was, most masterfully, simply a good-natured smile. "Well, there *is* something to that," he said in a perfectly even voice. "None of us delude ourselves with the idea that this is a top-ranking school, and, if the more promising students have the means to go elsewhere, we ought to keep that fact in mind. What shall we do, ladies and gentlemen? Adjourn and meet again after Christmas and attack the whole business from another angle, or permit ourselves to hope to a certain degree and put it to a vote?"

"Let's put it to a vote," I said.

The "Ayes" were more assertive than they would have been if Arthur hadn't expressed himself. There were no "No's"—I could not tell whether the new member, sprawling as he doubtless was with his hands in his pockets in the rear corner of the room, had added his languid "Aye" with a shrug, or had merely abstained. I thought I would give him a piece of my mind the next time we got together to rehearse, but not at the moment. If I waited at the door, it was only to walk out with him so that he needn't go down the corridor, like a pariah, by himself. But I could not go out with him because Dr. Holland asked if I could stay a minute or two; and I stood on the threshold and watched him leave in isolation, though the isolation didn't seem to ruffle him in the least: there was a glint in his yellow eyes as he passed me, and his mouth was tight with his supercilious smile.

Instead of wondering, as I normally would have, what my superior could want with me, I spent the time while he closed the windows and gathered up his notes in thinking how unlucky it was that he should ask to see me at this particular moment: I had not had a minute's private conversation with him since the charged, strange exchange between Arthur and me on the snowy evening, and the present occasion was scarcely propitious for letting it be known that Arthur "wasn't exactly itching to get fired." I stepped back to the door, ostensibly to say goodnight to Matt and Emily, but really to see whether his fellow teachers would let him walk the length of the hall by himself. They did —Anna and a couple of the others merely nodded toward him over their shoulders as they passed him in some noisy and cozy colloquy; and the sight of his stooped back and his slow, self-conscious walk was disturbing to me, so disturbing that I had to force my face into cheerful attentiveness when I turned back into the room, where Dr. Holland still stood behind the desk, brushing a streak of chalk from the sleeve of his dark blue coat. "Are you in an awful hurry, Frieda?" he asked me.

"No, not at all." To show that I was at his service, I made for one of the seats in the front row.

"No—wait a minute—how about making it in my office?" he said.

193

I turned around with a start: to be asked into his office, especially so late in the day, was to be warned that whatever was coming would be weighty and might even be grim.

There was nothing in his look to brush away that suspicion: it seemed to me that his bright blue gaze had never been trained on me so sharply before. "I wanted to talk to you about something that's got me a little worried," he said, and added, with his usual consideration, that the matter on his mind certainly had nothing to do directly with me.

We walked in silence up the hall and into his relatively spacious office, where a reflection of the pale orange sunset still shone in the glass doors of his bookcases. Nobody else was there, and nobody was loitering nearby in the corridor; but, after he had turned on his goose-neck lamp and taken out a manila folder and laid it on the top of his fine new metal desk, he closed the door. The name on the tab of the folder was "Sanes"—I read it while his back was turned. I sat down in a hurry, because my heart had begun to pound, partly out of indefinable fear and partly out of avid curiosity—his history, at least his academic history, was lying there within my reach—and I fumbled around in my purse and got a cigarette.

He lighted it for me, pushed an ashtray in my direction, and sat down in his swivel chair on the other side of the desk, his hands clasped behind his head, his left ankle resting on his right knee, in an attitude which was none the less soothing because a person knew it had been taken consciously to lessen the tension of dozens of such stressful incidents. "It's about this gentleman," he said, nodding in the direction of the folder and thereby indicating he assumed I had taken a look. "I wanted to talk to you sometime before vacation, though I didn't intend to haul you in at this hour of the day. He's been on my mind for weeks— I'd say since the day he came—and the show he put on at the meeting touched it all off again, and I thought I'd feel better if I could go into it a bit with you. I'm not a man to

194

get easily upset over the way a faculty member conducts himself, but this one's different. He worries me, Frieda, he certainly worries me."

For the last five years at least I had been in the habit of saying whatever came into my mind to Dr. Holland. It was strange—and the strangeness added to my agitation—that I should merely nod and stare at the streaks of orange and gold in the glass behind him: I did not look at him, and I did not tell him that Arthur was a worry to me too.

"That little speech of his, now—that was peculiar, that made for a decidedly uncomfortable situation."

"Yes, I can see how some of them might have been disturbed—he does have a rather forthright way of expressing himself. And yet—" there was a defensive edge to my voice, and I knew I was sitting too erectly in my chair— "there's probably more than a grain of truth in what he said."

"Oh, certainly, the meat of it was true enough, nobody'd deny it." He bent forward a little and clasped his leathery hands around his knee. He rocked in his creaking swivel chair and smiled at me as if, by a more emphatic show of ease on his own part, he could loosen my unaccustomed rigidity. "But it was a bit ill-timed, or so it seemed to me, and the others thought so too, from the looks on their faces. He needn't have waited until we'd all arrived at a point of agreement."

"Oh, but you know how those things are, Dr. Holland. It was all planned out, the way it was supposed to go—first Emily and then Michael and then Dr. Boyd—and it went like clockwork, according to schedule, and in the early part of it he wouldn't have had much opportunity."

A faint smile—rising, I am sure, in good-natured mockery of the notion of his faculty engaging in devilish backstage machinations—flitted across his weathered face and lighted up his eyes. For the first time, I found it impossible to sustain his look. I raised my glance to the top

195

of his shadowy bookcase and saw certain things I had never been aware of before—a bust of Bach and a set of six or seven little wooden angels playing medieval instruments, though the dust on them indicated that they had been there for a long time.

"All right," he said, "let's take it for granted he couldn't have timed it better. The way he put it—the way he worded it—don't you think that was a little extreme?"

"I suppose it was, though we don't know how they talked at other schools where he taught—it does take a while to pick up the tone of a place, I guess."

"To me it sounded as if he were going out of his way —" he laughed as if he were on the point of sharing a joke with me—"to put it in the worst tone he possibly could."

"Maybe it was worse than I thought it was—I wasn't listening too carefully at the moment." It was a transparent excuse, and I felt him looking through it keenly.

"I'd say it had a kind of nasty sharpness—as if he were trying to put us all in our places."

"Oh, he can be sharp. Everybody says so. But everybody expects him to be sharp, and maybe he feels that he's got to live up to their expectations."

"Maybe so, Frieda. But the thing I keep wondering about is: What came first—the expectations or the sharpness? When he came, he was in something of a spot, I know. If you hire anybody at the professorial level, there's bound to be a certain amount of jealousy, and it could have been particularly bitter in his case—he *is* young for a full professorship, and his reputation is on the minor side, and we haven't promoted anybody to a full professorship for a good number of years. If they were all pretty hateful to him, I ought to know it. Was that the case? Were you the only one who showed him a decent amount of friendliness?"

His face came far forward into the yellow area of light from the goose-neck lamp, and I could not entirely reject his look. "Oh, no, that wouldn't be a fair way to put it. Some of them did try to be friendly with him," I said.

"I know your status with him is pretty special." He swung backward with another creak and raised his eyes, to relieve me of the embarrassment of his gaze, to the window beyond my head. "The three or four times I've talked to him, you're the only person he's ever mentioned, and he mentions you with real respect. If I thought he had it in him to feel such a thing, I'd say he mentions you with affection. But I'm in trouble, I'm really in trouble where he's concerned, and the fact is I expected it." His hand moved into the circle of brightness in the middle of the desk and came down on the manila folder. "These references here—they're from the heads of departments at the other two places where he's taught, and they say only the best things about him, but still they're peculiar—whatever they're saying, they're curiously cold. And his own correspondence with me before he came—you can look at it if you like—"

My very avidity to lay my fingers on it made me stiffen and shake my head.

"It didn't reassure me any. My tone was friendly, or at least I thought it was. And his answers were so formal I really blushed for everything I wrote him—I made a few feeble attempts at humor, and I've been sorry ever since: I'm writing like a nineteenth century schoolmaster now."

"Oh, I'm sure it's no fault of yours, Warren," I said, driven to admit it by the defenseless candor in his voice and the recollection of the years of his frank and honorable dealings with me. "He lets everybody have it, and don't think for an instant he hasn't let me have it, too."

"I've tried, Frieda. I've done everything I could think of. That business with Lorrie Fawcett—that fit of hysterics she threw over whatever it was he said to her—I *didn't* light into him about that—"

"But everybody on the faculty wants to think you did," I said in fright, knowing I had better keep our exchange

197

limited to the difficulties between him and his colleagues, seeing that if we waded out into the dark morass of his equivocal dealings with his students, I would be utterly lost.

"But actually I didn't. I used it—and rather neatly, too, I thought—to let him know that Dr. Laurent had been pretty soft with the lot of them and even a perfectly justifiable amount of strictness might blow up in his face. I never said a word about the way he kept cutting the meetings, though God knows I was tempted to tell him off for that. And just a few weeks back, when the President's office let me know I could have the money to bring somebody for a lecture to the department, I asked him if he wouldn't like to invite that critic friend who thinks so much of him— Hansford Lindsay—I thought it might give him the feeling he was right on the inside of things. And Lindsay's coming —he'll be down here right after Christmas—and Sanes *did* seem pleased about it, and there was a sort of thaw or something right after that: Emily told me she and Julius'd had a very pleasant evening at his apartment, and he stuck his head in here to say hello a couple of times, and the piano majors weren't griping quite so much. But now—who knows what comes over him?—he goes and puts on that extraordinary performance this afternoon, and everybody, even Emily, is rubbed the wrong way. To tell the truth, Frieda, I've been asking myself whether he does these things on purpose. I know it sounds crazy for me to say so, but do you suppose for a minute he could be deliberately trying to get himself fired?"

I laughed and shook my head with my first real show of conviction. "That's one thing we can check off from the beginning," I said. "I don't really know him very well at all, we haven't talked too much, but the one time we did talk, he went into all that in detail, and what you think just isn't the case. He wants to stay—I'm sure he wants very much to stay—he told me so in so many words."

But as soon as I had delivered myself of that statement

198

I doubted its authenticity: wanting very much to stay is not synonymous with "not exactly itching to get fired." I knew that the just authority on the other side of the desk had complete confidence in my evidence and would proceed upon it without further thought; and as I occupied myself with the business of putting out my cigarette, I felt dishonest and exposed: without stretching my imagination in the least, I could envision Arthur Sanes walking into this office next week and saying that he asked for nothing better than to be released, without remembering what he had requested of me on the snowy evening, without a thought as to what the consequences could be for me.

"Well, anyhow, *that's* cleared up," he said. "It would be a damned sight more comfortable for me if he did stay—we *are* second-rate, as he's been going to such lengths to point out, and it's hard to find a good man at a salary we can manage—I was using the fine-toothed comb when I picked him up last spring. I'm reasonable, I'd put up with a lot—I already *have* put up with a lot. The one danger is that he'll carry it to such extremes I'll be forced to let him go."

A melancholy darkness had come down upon his office: the circle of light between us was the only remaining glow—the window behind me had darkened, and the streaks of orange and yellow light in the glass front of his bookcase were gone. "He might—I certainly wouldn't want to guarantee that he wouldn't," I said.

"I've been thinking, Frieda—" it was tentative, it was uneasy—"I've been thinking maybe you could talk to him, steer him a little—"

"I? Honestly, Warren, I've only talked to him once at any length. I really don't know him very well."

"Yet you might be talking to him sometime again—mightn't you?"

"Yes," I said, and my mind was a gusty agitation with remembered snowflakes. "I hope I will, I suppose I will."

199

"If you do, maybe you could tell him it just isn't protocol for a teacher to cut a senior recital. Any senior recital, to say nothing of a recital one of his own students happens to be playing in."

I was glad now for the shadow: I knew I was red in the face, I could not have colored up more intensely if the dereliction had been my own. "He had a migraine—he had a terrible migraine that night—I know because he was so sick he could scarcely talk to me on the phone," I said; and a blank coldness followed the surge of heat: for the first time in seven years, I had told him an outright lie.

"Migraines—they're supposed to come from nervous tension, aren't they? He's tense all right—people have noticed that he gets himself into a froth over next to nothing. Michael was telling me about walking in on him one night—he was practising at the moment, and Michael just looked in to listen. It seems there was a real do about it, a regular crisis—it seems he actually got the shakes. That's pretty queer, now—don't you think?"

"Yes, he's very jumpy," I said, hardly aware of what I was saying: I was preoccupied with the remembrance of that first run-in between Arthur and Harrison Frye.

"How's he doing with the Mozart?"

"Oh, beautifully. It falls off his fingers like so much water."

"He might have played for us when I asked him—"

"Maybe he'll ease up—maybe if you ask him again he will."

"He might have played for us, and he might turn up at recitals and the few little parties we have around here. He might put himself out once or twice a week to eat lunch with the others. When he sees John Boyd in a restaurant downtown, he might ask him to his table instead of pretending he didn't see him. If Miss Webb consults him about the fingering for a certain passage, he might really go into it with her, instead of giving her the impression that the

200

way she plays, he doesn't think it worth his time. He might stop getting himself up like the Duke of Windsor for an ordinary day in what he thinks is a second-class institution—though I wouldn't expect anybody to mention *that* to him—that's his own affair, I guess."

If I had not felt myself in such an equivocal position, I would probably have asked him pertly whether he expected me to cover the whole list of grievances in one sitting. As it was, I was appalled at the very notion of laying such matters before the cold image that had been summoned up for me; and I felt the pressure of authority from the other side of the desk as an unreasonable, even a cruel thing. "Yes, sir. It's a fairly large order, considering I scarcely know the man. But at least I'll make a try at it," I said.

"Since when have you taken to calling me 'sir', Frieda?"

I had no answer to that, and I recognized the feebleness and the evasiveness of the little laugh I offered in place of a reply. He pushed himself back in his chair to indicate that I need not stay any longer. As I got up, I forced myself to look at his face and saw worry in it, worry which he immediately obliterated with one of his quick, stiff, flashing smiles. "Well, tackle what you can of it, my dear—I know, of course, you couldn't cover half of it," he said. "I only thought, since you're tactful and a general peacemaker and closer to being a friend of his than anybody else, maybe it wouldn't be too much to ask you to give me a hand in this."

"You know I'll be glad to. You know I'll do whatever I can," I said, turning from his sharp blue look to the door.

With his unvarying and somehow old-fashioned courtesy, he came and opened the door for me and did not close it, but stood on the threshold smiling and nodding good night to me until I was halfway down the hall. I was glad to be delivered from him, glad to hear the little click of the lock amplified in the emptiness. My concept of Arthur—my image of Arthur, for I saw it in front of me with a startling immediacy—underwent a complete metamorphosis

201

as I walked between the rows of closed lockers: he was no longer the frozen enigma I had conjured up in Dr. Holland's office; he was my fellow plotter, with whom I had talked intimately only a few days ago; he was the one colleague with whom I had ever desired to conspire—and I desired it until the blood prickled in my fingertips. I saw myself closed up in the first available telephone booth, ringing his number. I heard myself telling him to come over right away because I had done that little thing he had asked me to and had gotten such a complete survey of his situation as nobody else could have wrested from the seat of authority. I saw the two of us at the table in my kitchen, munching fried chicken—the market was still open, I could get a couple of chicken breasts—while I told him how I had said this and Dr. Holland had said that, thereby making myself inestimably valuable, possibly even dear.

But it was a dream I held by the bridle, a crazy, charging, spirited dream, and I did not mount it, I did not ride it into actuality. When I came out onto the still, white campus, the very impact of the icy air on my face and in my lungs was a sobering shock. I would not manufacture an opportunity to talk to him today, since day after tomorrow I would have one as a matter of course: only yesterday we had planned another long practise session, this time at my place; and it would be more circumspect to work up to the matter subtly and casually. I would take the bus straight home without stopping off at the market, and I would spend the evening at the local movie—even if the picture was nothing special, I would have the walk there and back in the invigorating cold. And I did what my reason told me to do, though what it was that buttressed my reason—whether it was fear that the yellow eyes would be focused scornfully upon me or a lingering need to be honorable still in my dealings with Dr. Holland—to this day I do not know.

202

Chapter 15

THE JUDICIAL STEERING to which I had committed myself did not interfere in the least with my enjoyment of the Christmas vacation. Those eighteen days, brisk and crusted over with layer after layer of new snow—except, of course, for Christmas itself, which was as mild and unseasonable as a person should have learned to expect—those eighteen days were the happiest days I had known in the months of bereavement and agitation since my mother's death. Arthur said at the beginning of them that we could rehearse whenever we wanted to, since he was staying in town and catching up on his practising; and my sense of triumph over his decision was only faintly tainted by a chance chat with Hughie in the supermarket: Hughie asked me if I'd been seeing much of him, and I said I had, and Hughie said there wouldn't really have been much point in his spending the train fare to New York this time, because Mrs. McIvor usually flew over to England to her sister's, and his friend Hansford Lindsay would be coming down to see *him* in a week or so. But if the afternoons and the evenings we spent together in the cheerful interim were available to me only because neither Mrs. McIvor nor Mr. Lindsay happened to want them, still they had a solid value, and they offered me a timely series of opportunities to lead him in the way that Dr. Holland thought he ought to go.

Twice when people telephoned to ask me over and found that he was at my apartment practising with me, they had me summon him to the phone and talked him into joining their projected parties. Not that much talking was necessary—he was in an entirely sociable and available state. We had Christmas dinner at the Grüenbergs', with turkey and the usual trimmings. We had a midnight supper on New Year's Eve at Michael's bachelor quarters—spaghetti made according to the recipe of his old Italian landlady, and a really professional Caesar salad, and garlic bread to sop up the drinks. We had Saturday afternoon cocktails at Anna Webb's, and her hors d'oevres were so pepped up with horseradish that we couldn't fill up on them and had to eat a late supper afterwards—he and I by ourselves—in a Chinese restaurant downtown. He came in and helped me to put together *my* dinner party, which was the last of the string of events: lobster tails—he insisted that I buy them in a very smelly butcher shop in an out-of-the-way district—duchess potatoes in the shell, spinach loaf, and a caramel cake.

I remember the details of the menus so well because he made such a point of getting food into me. When the service was buffet, he insisted on going back to get me a little more of this or that; and when things were passed around the table—none of us were in a position to have a regular maid—he kept adding choice bits to my plate when I wasn't looking, and what he had filched for me I couldn't refuse. The affability and the solicitousness did not stop short with me, either: he extended himself in some measure for several of the others, too. He drew Julius, who is usually lost at our musical parties, into a discussion of the philosophical implications of recent nuclear research; he made an appropriate comment on Anna Webb's white-

and-silver Christmas tree; he examined the score of the first movement of Michael's current sonata and even went so far as to play bits of it for us, stopping whenever he liked and bending close to peer at the illegible manuscript.

All through that vacation he gave the impression that he was dating me without really dating me. If we arrived at dinner parties together, it was only because we had been rehearsing at my place beforehand; if he took me home, it was only because, without rudeness—and I had been teasing him about his reputation for rudeness—he could do no less. In the snatches of solitude I had, I forced myself to draw sharp lines through the accumulating obscurities: I dismissed as fantasy the notion that he kept staring at me whenever my head was turned; I told myself that nothing but simple friendliness had made him put my hand into his big pocket and hold it there to warm it in his dry, close grasp on a cold walk home. That he himself wished such demarcations to be laid out, I knew: I knew it when he gave me a Christmas present without exactly giving me a Christmas present—he brought me, two days after Christmas and still in grey paper wrappings from the shop, a beautiful book of reproductions from the St. Ursula frescoes of Carpaccio. Those pure and airy fragments of late medieval Venice—the particolored crowds in the square, the boughs of olive or ailanthus fanned out in green precision against the watery blue of the sky, the spare masts going up between the rosy blocks of the towers—somehow lent their innocent light-heartedness to the whole vacation. I kept seeing them in my mind's eye while we rehearsed and at the parties and on our long walks or our little shopping trips; and when the day with him was over it was never quite over, since I could look at my book—I took it to bed with me and turned the pages until I was ready to sleep. If people were putting the two of us together in talk, if Emily told me once that he looked at me as if he were in love with me, if Michael acted out an extravagant pantomime of a possible lover cruelly rejected and replaced, it did not matter: I knew how things stood; I was making gratifying progress in easing up the stress between him and his colleagues; and in the interim I was happy—the long rehearsals in the winter dusks, the walks over the crunching snow, the little intimacies, marked though they were with the stamp of "purely temporary," were nevertheless a little heady and sometimes almost sweet.

I had taken it for granted that the happy time, since it had begun with the holiday, would come to an end with it. I was even prepared for a marked recoil: I would not have been suprised if he had taken to turning off again at the bulletin board or hiding his face over the fountain when he caught sight of me in the hall. So I was not prepared for his walking into my office the second day classes were back in session—friendly, a little embarrassed, his head on one side and his hands in his pockets. Since he'd accumulated such a list of social obligations over Christmas time, what did I think of his giving a little party? he said. His friend Hansford Lindsay would be coming in late tomorrow afternoon; and, though Dr. Holland had issued invitations to a general reception at his house on the following evening, after Hansford's lecture, it seemed that something a bit more intimate wouldn't be amiss. If I were free—he wouldn't think of tackling such a business without me—he'd like to have drinks and late supper over at his apartment—just me and Hansford and Michael and Emily and Julius. Was I fond of duckling? He could do six duck- lings in his new electric roaster all at once, and he had a terrific recipe for orange and grapefruit sauce.

I had a tentative engagement, though I didn't say so. I was more or less signed up to have dinner and go to the theater that evening with Jenny, and I would not dare lie myself out of it, since she was an efficient detective and would be bound, eventually, to nose out the truth. I told him I was free, but I did not offer to help him, partly because I knew I was, in comparison with him, a mediocre cook

206

and partly because I did not want to find myself sitting again on the high stool in his kitchen, where I had indiscreetly touched him. He looked genuinely pleased, and sauntered down the hall to look for Michael and Emily, whistling to himself; and, in order to take the cloud of conscience away from my anticipation, I phoned Jenny in her office right away and told her that our date would have to be cancelled because something had come up that I just didn't want to miss.

For the rest of that day and all of the next I stayed out of my office as much as I could. It was, I suppose, an effort to practise magic: I wanted him to be on the night of his party what he had been during the holidays, and whatever I would hear through the wall if I stayed at my desk for more than a couple of minutes was likely to turn him back into his former self. It was an attempt at magic again when I looked into my cupboard on the evening of the party and decided what I would wear: the dark brown velvet dress was the obvious choice—he had never seen it and it seemed right for the occasion—but I could not bring myself to put it on, since I had worn it at my Halloween party, to which he had not come; and I settled on my much less appropriate moss-green jersey, trying to convince myself that the pair of crystal crescents I had gotten for Christmas gave its simple lines a rich formality. Julius and Emily came to pick me up in their Dodge—I was glad they had offered to, I had a superstitious distaste for arriving, as I had arrived on the afternoon of our first rehearsal, by myself, and I was undone by a sudden accession of frightened curiosity about the guest. All the way down, in the cutting cold—it had grown somewhat warmer, but much damper, and only the most full-blooded could hope not to be peaked and withered by the chill—I kept telling myself I was about to see the first embodiment of that other life of his, and I was glad to be sitting close to Emily, with the fold of her old grey muskrat coat lapped over my unsteady knees.

There was no sign of the redoubtable Hansford Lindsay

when I came into his living room. Arthur told us that his guest was shaving and would be out in a minute, and meanwhile I looked around me, bewildered and a little embarrassed, because I had mentioned to Michael that the place would be rather bare, and bareness was certainly not the impression it was giving tonight. Not that he had imported any of the massive pieces, the Portuguese chest or the marble-top table. What he had imported—probably for Christmas—were great rough masses of long-needled pine, set everywhere in vases: on the piano, on the coffee table, on empty areas of the floor, from which they rose in brushy masses against the stark whiteness of the walls. It was as if he had hacked it down and dragged it in from some raw forest, with its dark shadows still webbed in it and its rank and sappy odor scarce begun to dry away. The horned Actaeon rose naked and tormented out of a vast mound of it; projecting chunks of it caught at our skirts as we crossed the room; every here and there tapers burned dangerously near the green-black, overhanging clumps of it; and when we had seated ourselves on the flat black sofa it was as if we had retreated to a clearing, in which the tray and the crystal glasses and the bottles and the silver ice-bucket with the chaste Greek border were singularly incongruous things.

"I dolled the place up a bit for the season," he said, pouring our drinks. He himself looked a little dolled up—under his impeccable grey flannel jacket he was wearing a scarlet vest. He caught my eye examining it and flushed up under the diminished sunburn. "It's not exactly my style," he explained, low, out of one side of his mouth. "Hansford brought it for me for Christmas, and I thought I'd better put it on."

"It's beautiful," said Emily. "Men should wear more of these colors. Julius has one just like this, only yellow, but he never wears it." She wet her full, warm lips, conscious of having made some vaguely uncomplimentary implication, and her husband hurried to explain that he loved his vest,

208

only lacked the courage to wear it, and now he wished that he had followed his inclinations and put it on tonight.

I did not carry my fair part of the burden in the small talk that followed. My mind was on Mr. Lindsay; I kept watching for Mr. Lindsay to open a tall white door, which, since I had never seen it open, must lead into the room where Arthur slept. Had he taken some of the pine forest in there, too? I wondered. Did it overshadow his pillow and send its resinous smell into his dreams? Was Mr. Lindsay looking at himself over a bunch of it while he did whatever final thing it was that men do to their ties? I expected him to be tall and portly, maybe because of the size of the room and the decorations, and maybe because of the swelling proportions of my uneasiness. But when he came in through the doorway I had been staring at, my glance had to drop a good eight inches: "natty" was the proper word for Mr. Lindsay, a man in his early fifties, more nimble than his sleek white hair would suggest he ought to be, dwarfed, or rather "gnomed" by the expanse of the room and the masses of long-needled pine.

"Am I late? Is everybody here?" he asked in a ringing kind of tenor.

"Everybody but Michael," said Arthur. "Don't bother with the apologies—you're relatively on time. This is Emily Grüenberg, and here's her husband Julius. There, meek in the corner of the sofa, sits Frieda Hartmann. All of us are one up on you—what can I give you to drink?"

"The usual thing, Arthur—Scotch with just a tiny bit of water." He had nodded affably enough and smiled at each of us, turning his head in jerks as Arthur pointed us out. But something—perhaps it was diffidence—kept him standing at a distance, his small right foot set slightly forward in a navy blue suede moccasin, his left hipbone thrust up and out—it struck me as a curious stance. His face, probably the rosier for the whiteness of his hair and eyebrows, looked naked, as if he had shaved it too closely; his eyes

209

were china-blue and as opaque as china; he had no wrinkles, only deep creases that kept appearing and disappearing in his cheeks and on his straight and not too ample brow. He was dressed in a fine navy blue worsted, cut in the English way, a little too tight for him; and under the jacket—somehow it disturbed me—he wore the scarlet twin to Arthur's vest. He did come up and join us then, putting his small, pink and white, padded hand in Julius's long hairy one; and I noticed that something in him or his manner kept Emily from doing what she always did: offering to shake hands.

It seemed to me fortunate that Michael should arrive just at that moment—the five of us were at an impasse, taking long inward breaths as if we were about to utter weighty matters, smiling quick and empty smiles at each other, making noises against the stressful silence with the ice in our glasses—and we were glad to have somebody new to greet. Michael was continentally at ease and set off a kind of chain reaction of reminiscence in which all of them were eventually involved: he had a behind-the-scenes knowledge of European musical life, and so did Arthur, and so did Mr. Lindsay, and so did Emily and even Julius to a certain degree, so that everybody had something to bring up —everybody but me. I found myself sitting silent through a type of cabalistic conversation which it is supposed to be a privilege for the uninitiate to hear, a conversation that alluded obliquely to Mahler's wife's lover and Strauss's widow's attorney, and Schwartzkopf's mother's maid. It comforted me not at all to tell myself that such talk, if the principals had been different, would have been the shallowest sort of gossip: the fact that I had never been to Europe robbed me of my social authenticity. I sat sipping my drink, which I suddenly did not want, and thinking how poor a showing I was making in front of Arthur's dear friend, a friend so dear that the two of them wore matching vests. The smell of the pine became downright oppressive, and I knew that my moss-green jersey was glaringly inappropriate and that the Christmas crystals did nothing but emphasize its shabbiness.

Yet after half an hour of it I realized that Mr. Lindsay was aware of my isolation. From the low hassock on which he had hunched himself up like an impish and prematurely aged little boy, with his elbows on his knees and his face still further creased and distorted between his small hands, he kept sending china blue glances in my direction, he kept raising his eyebrows and opening his eyes to an almost frightening extent, and I could not disregard the fact that this mugging of his was intended for my benefit. It was probably because of me, too, that he initiated a shift from musical personalities to music: he somehow got them back to Mahler's wife's lover and cut off from there to Mahler's symphonies. But it was an unfortunate choice—neither Arthur nor I cared much for those symphonies, and the Gruenbergs took our indifference in the most personal way, as if we had been insulting a beloved and recently buried relative of theirs: and Hansford—he had insisted twice now that we call him Hansford, a name which it was somehow almost impossible to say aloud—Hansford suddenly lost interest in the whole matter and took to surveying the room, sending appraising glances over the furniture and along the walls.

"But it is *not* sentimental—God forbid! It is spiritual —it is so intimately and tenderly spiritual—you simply do not see. It is spiritual in a German way which only Germans can apparently understand," said Emily with tears in her voice.

"You know, my boy, now that I've lived with it for a while, I've come to the conclusion that you've got too much pine in here—just too damn much pine in here," Mr. Lindsay said.

"Overdone it—have I?" said Arthur, grinning.

"Distinctly—that is, if you ask me."

211

"I wasn't asking you." But his hand—long, with blunt-ended fingers, undid whatever sharpness might have been in the words. It came down, without effort or any sense of stress, on Mr. Lindsay's shoulder, where it lingered with an ease that forced me to remember it had never offered me so casual a touch.

"Oh, but I think it's very nice," said Emily. "It makes the Christmas season longer."

"If you put it up before Christmas," said Julius, reaching out to finger a sprig of it, "I'd advise you to get it out of here pretty soon. It dries—you could have a fire if you leave it around too long."

"Come to think of it, I guess I could."

"But it was on *aesthetic* grounds that I was objecting," said Mr. Lindsay, pressing the palm of his pink hand carefully along the side of his head, over the sleek whiteness of of his hair. "It *drowns* all your beautiful things—simply drowns them."

"Fact is, Hansford, they're all above surface, if only you'd bother to look. I just don't have that many beautiful things around anymore."

The tone was strange, at once mocking and rueful. The statement lay there in front of us, something about which something would have to be done; and Michael, with his usual suavity, got up and walked over as close to the Actæon as the masses of greens would permit and asked whether the tapestry was seventeenth or eighteenth century. The others followed him, all except myself: a weary distaste for motion and change had come over me, and I sat where I had been from the beginning, in the corner of the black sofa, sipping my way slowly to the bottom of my undesired drink. I wanted nothing, neither a lecture on the Actaeon toward which I suddenly felt unaccountably unfriendly, nor anybody to keep me company; and I was less pleased than constrained when the guest of honor bowed himself away from the others, walked round the tawdry little coffee table,

212

and settled himself beside me, so close that his shoulder rested against mine.

"You know, Frieda," he said in a quiet and intimate voice which seemed to imply that we were continuing, rather than initiating, private conversation, "you mustn't take Arthur too seriously when he makes one of those tragic little speeches of his—like that business about not having so many beautiful things around him, I mean. Actually, he's got more stuff stored away up in New York than he'll ever know what to do with. He's better off without it, better off where he is—I don't mind telling you it's *years* since I've seen him looking so well."

"Really?" I said, hoping for clarification, puzzled by his air of telling me something of great significance—his small hand had beat out certain of the words on his knee, and he kept looking me straight in the face. How did he mean that Arthur was better off? Better off away from the distractions of the metropolis? Better off leading the ordered life of a college professor? Better off—I did not think it, I could not afford to think it—better off with me?

"Oh, yes, he looks absolutely wholesome," he said, nodding vigorously and thrusting out his mouth as if he were about to make a puffing sound. "Wholesome and collected and generally at peace with himself."

"Maybe this town agrees with him. From a couple of remarks he's made, I've gathered that he wasn't altogether happy in New York."

"Is that so? He actually said that in so many words—did he?" His pleasure in the information was obvious, permitted him to raise his voice a little and to rub the palms of his hands up and down his small thighs. This also struck me as peculiar: why he should be delighted to hear that Arthur wasn't altogether happy in a place where *he* was permanently settled, I couldn't make out, and no enlightenment was forthcoming from the bright blue opacity of his fixed eyes. "Well, I'm happy to hear it, it's even better

213

than I thought, then. For a while I was convinced it was going to be the ruination of him—living beyond his means and associating with exactly the wrong sort of people— wasting his time, wasting his money, wasting himself. I'll frankly admit I didn't think he had it in him to pick up like that and walk out."

The conversation around the Actaeon had flagged a little, and I thought he would change the subject to cover up what we had been talking about; it seemed strange to me that he should merely fall silent with an air of waiting, though he gave some justification to the wordless interim by making me a second drink. Arthur—or so it seemed to me in my uneasiness—was acutely aware of the two of us conversing so quietly there on the sofa; and Mr. Lindsay must have had the same impression, since it was not until his host had been drawn into a discussion about the relative merits of French and Flemish looms that he began again, talking quickly while the chatter was on the rise and taking long sips from his glass during the intervals when it fell.

"That place is a habit with him—a very bad habit, Frieda," he said. "The longer he stays away from it, the better off he is. If there's anything that can keep him from running up there every time he has a weekend on his hands, it's the best thing in the world for him. To tell you the truth: much as I miss him up there myself, I'd be the last person on earth to regret it if he never turned up from one year's end to the other. He's beginning to put down roots here with you and your friends—that's what I said to myself the minute I saw him at the airport and saw how well he looked: 'He's putting down roots,' I said. And we wouldn't want them pulled up at this stage of the game, they're not deep enough yet—are they? No, I can't put it too strongly, Frieda—" it was my knee that he tapped now, beating it with a curiously impersonal touch, as if it were a piece of wood—"he'd be a different man if he detached himself, just completely detached himself. . . ."

214

"But doesn't he have to go up there every now and again? He can't just stay away from New York, not entirely, not if he's to have a career as a pianist," I said.

"Oh, but that's not the way it is. Not with him. Not the way things stand with his musical reputation at the moment." He waited, never releasing me from his bright, flat stare; he waited with evident satisfaction while Emily led the others still farther away to look at the saint's head among the pine twigs on the window sill. "You see, my dear, you've got to be in New York only if you're building yourself up through *concerts*. And concertizing—believe me, I've given a great deal of thought to it, and I know what I'm talking about—concertizing is exactly what Arthur Sanes *should not* be doing—not this year and probably not next year."

"No?"

In my surprise I had said it so loudly that he turned a warning look on me and then blinked and smiled. When his eyes were open, they were so intensely, so abnormally open that they dominated his whole face. When he closed them, even for an instant, it was disturbing to see how much was lost—how withered he looked and how old. "No." He pushed out his lips and slowly shook his head at me. "For quite some period—for a year at least—Arthur *should not* concertize. His recordings—they're coming out now at the rate of two or three a year—his recordings are what he ought to concentrate and depend on. I don't know whether you follow the record reviews, but you ought to—my dear, for his sake you ought to. It's there that he's going to make a name for himself, it's *there* that he's beginning to get his just due. In my own sheet, in *The Saturday Review,* in *High Fidelity* everything he puts out is listed among the best. A reputation built on records is accumulated slowly, but it's a sound reputation, as solid as a rock. And I want him to have such a reputation to stand on before he ever thinks of walking out on a concert stage again."

I had no answer. My mind was veering in a feverish fashion, stimulated by the drinks, irritated by the loud and rather affected conversation going on over by the window. I remembered Dr. Holland's bewilderment over Arthur's blank refusal to play a Mozart sonata; I saw Arthur playing the songs and Michael's composition as if he weren't performing at all. And meanwhile my present companion had bent forward and edged a little closer, so close that, even through the resinous and aromatic odor of the pine, I could smell the eau de cologne on his clothing blended strangely with the raw whiskey on his breath.

"Of course," he said, "there are other people—old friends of his like Julie McIvor—who simply refuse to see this thing from my point of view. The slow, patient building up of a reputation through recordings—that doesn't appeal to her, she doesn't even begin to understand. You can't give a reception after the release of a record, you don't hear any applause, you can't sit up and swill champagne all night, waiting for the reviews in the morning papers to come out. There isn't any drama in it, and Julie McIvor's a dramatic woman, you can take it from me."

From his place in the group by the window sill, Arthur was watching and trying to listen. Emily was talking at him, but he did not hear her. His face, intent and grim, with the dark eyebrows drawn together, was turned our way, and the saint's head was precariously balanced in his left hand. But Mr. Lindsay was so taken up with his subject now that he either did not notice or did not care.

"When she sets her mind on something, she won't let it go, she holds onto it like a dog with a bone," he said. "She's got a tentative date lined up for him at Town Hall— it's for some time in February, in between your semesters, I think. And she has herself convinced he'll make such a sensation there that she can get him a date with the Philharmonic next year—she's on the board, you know. She's in a hurry, that woman. Not that you can blame her, she's got

216

to be in a hurry—her hold on him isn't what it used to be, and she knows as much."

"And Arthur—what does he think about it?" As I said his name, almost in a whisper, I saw him turn on his heel and stride into the kitchen, from which certain noises began to issue, noises that I knew to be in protest against our private conversation, the clinking of plates and the loud bang of the oven door.

"*He* knows what he ought to do," said Mr. Lindsay, setting down his empty glass and clasping his hands around his kneecap. "Whatever he says, whatever or whoever it is that's pushing him back onto the stage, he *knows*. Arthur is at his best in his recordings—I can't emphasize it too strongly, it's the core of the whole business. Some performers take fire from an audience, some performers get an extra indefinable something when they're on stage, but Arthur. . . ."

I also set my glass down on the cocktail table and wondered if Mr. Lindsay had noticed the unsteadiness of my hand. I was remembering, and something was stifling me—either the remembrance or the closeness of Mr. Lindsay or the heavy resinous smell of the torn boughs—I was remembering how Arthur's cheeks had turned a spotted green under the sunburn when Harrison Frye had talked of listening at his door and how Michael had made "a regular crisis" by sticking in his head to hear. But if a communicable question lay beneath that confusion of recollections, it never got itself formulated. Arthur appeared at the kitchen door, coatless, in his scarlet vest, with a white apron draping him from waist to knees. His face was as distorted and discolored as the face he had shown to Harrison that first time in the faculty dining room. "Frieda!" he said in a peremptory voice that made everybody fall silent and look at him. "Aren't you going to give me a hand out here? It's just too much for me—I can't manage by myself."

The first few minutes I spent with him in the kitchen were some of the sickest in my existence. Neither of us said

217

a word, and while I did the obvious things that lay at hand
—arranged the rolls in the wicker basket and began to
toss the salad—I felt as if I were moving about on a seething
surface, waiting for the fury that stirred it to subside. It
was strange then—strange and somehow disturbing—that
he should come up and stand a little behind me as I bent
over the salad bowl. It was strange that he should say in a
casual voice, with a lying flicker of humor under it, "He's
quite a talker, isn't he? What's he been giving you out
there?"

"Nothing," I said, keeping my eyes on the watercress
and the avocado. "He was talking about your recordings
mostly. He was telling me what good reviews they got."

There was a long stretch of silence in which I could
almost feel him deliberately calming himself, steadying his
stance, evening out his erratic breathing. "What do you
think of the party? How do you think it's going?" he asked.

"Oh, beautifully. Nobody's been quiet for a minute,"
I said, aware that the peculiarly contrived quality in his
voice had somehow gotten into mine.

"Do you really think so? It seems pretty stiff to me."
The words stirred my hair over my ear, and I wondered
why he should be standing so close to me. I could not enjoy
it, I did not want it. I had a crazy but inescapable conviction
that he was forcing himself into proximity.

"That's probably because you're the host," I said.

"I have the feeling it's the wrong size—not big enough
and not small enough." His tone was none the less false
because of the note of intimacy he was striving to bring in.
"When there's only one conversation, it gets too conducted.
And it's not big enough to split up into groups comfortably.
Four would have been better, I guess. For all that matter—"
he took a deep breath, and I turned around and saw him
cock his head to one side in a way that was insincerely
arch, unconvincingly cute—"for all that matter, we do
very well as a twosome—don't we?—just by ourselves."

218

I did not answer. I could not answer because he had laid his arm, as he had plainly planned and forced himself to lay it, around my waist, where it rested in heavy motionlessness. That he should touch me in an attempt to play up to me, that what I had not even allowed myself to hope for should come at me in the shape of a shabby pretense—it was more than I could bear with self-possession. I stiffened and stepped aside, reaching for the oil cruet. "You'd better take a look at your ducklings. They smell as if they might be burning," I said.

I could not bring myself to watch him going. I kept my eyes on the salad, and knew I had tossed it too much—the cress had lost its crispness and the slices of avacado had taken on a spotted and slimy look. I knew I would not be able to eat this salad, or his ducklings either. The whole process of nourishment, the taking in and using up and giving out, seemed to me a loathsome indignity perpetrated upon humanity. In fact, before his voice broke the wretched silence, humanity itself seemed an indignity, with its sordid necessities and its preposterous desires.

"How do you like Hansford?" he asked at last, lifting the first of the ducklings, trussed and horribly intact, out of the new electric roaster.

"He's very nice. I like him very much."

I had said it spontaneously and without reservation, so I took it for granted I had spoken the truth. I did like him and continued to like him through the remainder of that ravaged evening. He was welcome when he came into our unhealthy isolation in the kitchen, offering to help; he was an amiable partner at supper—he chose to sit on the hassock at my feet, making a hunched gnome of himself and sending me knowing little smiles and affectionate blue glances; it was he that started the round of "stories" when the conversation drooped and he that told the most amusing ones over the coffee and the apricot tart. Yet I wondered then, and later in my bed where I could manage nothing

219

better than a broken and churning kind of sleep, whether I would have liked him if we had not had our little chat. Was it—so I asked myself a dozen times, turning my creased pillow, getting my blanket closer around my cold and offending body—was it because we shared common enemies, because he had lined up with me against New York and Mrs. McIvor, that I was willing to accept the eau de cologne and the multiplication of drinks and the dead look of his face when he happened to close his eyes?

put down forty-five for a plum-colored satin shirtwaist dress reduced from seventy-four fifty; I laid out another three for a tight little bunch of velvet moss roses to wear at the waist; and, having gone as far as that, I saw no reason why I shouldn't indulge myself in a pair of crystal drop earrings at five ninety-five plus tax to play up the Christmas crescents that had passed unnoticed last night.

If, while I was dressing, my heart went down like a dropping elevator at the thought of what I had spent, as soon as I walked into Dr. Holland's party I felt justified in my extravagance. The company, in contrast with the rooms —which were long and low and draped with white crisscross curtains and filled up haphazardly with old Victorian pieces inherited from Warren's mother—the company had done everything short of getting into formal evening dress to give the reception for Mr. Lindsay an air of importance and elegance. Nobody would have guessed that Anna Webb was a tired spinster listening out of charity to the bumbling of an old Polish violinist; in her loose black crepe dress, with her hair done up in elaborate coils over her ears, she looked like a completely sophisticated lady who was being completely charmed by a colorful musical personality. Mrs. Boyd was striking, if a little flat, in quantities of mulberry taffeta, and her husband looked even more aristocratic than she. Jenny, set up on a needlepoint sofa, was the showiest member of the assembly: she had invested in a madras cocktail dress striped in bronze, pink, and peacock blue. Hughie, on the other hand, had gone conservative—he was all greys and blacks, and the only brightness about him was the coppery gleam in his newly washed hair and the brand new shine on his shoes. Arthur was wearing exactly what he had worn the evening he had come alone to my apartment, even the same onyx tie-clasp, and I wondered with an unsteady heart whether the sameness could be intentional, whether he could have resorted to my kind of wardrobe necromancy. The guest of honor—if anybody had told me

223

he was going to change, I would have been apprehensive—was in line with perfect propriety: in his charcoal worsted he looked much like the rest of the males in the crowded living room—trim, semi-formal, recently cleaned and pressed.

The Hollands also had outdone themselves in their capacity as hosts: there were bunches of florist's roses and dishes of nuts and candy on the high round tables and under the frosted glass lamps; there was a Jamaican negro in a white coat, handing out long drinks; and two small, pale, plump ladies in starched white uniforms—known to be employees of a moderately expensive Swedish catering establishment often called in for administrative parties—kept coming backwards through the swinging door to the kitchen, carrying large trays of hot hors d'oevres in their puffy little hands.

I am never really lost at these parties, though I'm always afraid I'm going to be. I had not been there for five minutes when there was an influx of secondary members of our department, men from the Symphony who taught a few hours a week at the College; and, seeing me by myself in the archway between the almost empty dining room and the very full parlor, two of them came over to talk to me. They were unmarried men in their forties, and they made themselves agreeable in the assured, irresponsible fashion of confirmed bachelors: one of them bent close to examine the crystal crescents, and the other one stroked the sleek material of my sleeve. Arthur was not watching—he was holding what looked to be a reassuringly pleasant conversation with the sharp-eyed, sharp-faced little Mrs. Holland; but Mr. Lindsay, who was involved with the host, kept jerking his head around in my direction, stretching his eyelids and trying to indicate something—whether it was that he deplored the familiarity of the Symphony members or merely wanted an opportunity to talk to me, I couldn't make out. But I had a sense of stress, of being called upon to be available and in complete possession of myself; and I edged my little group toward the beautifully polished round table with its centerpiece of freesia and roses, and continued to refuse the proffered drinks. Jenny, who was huffed at me for my desertion last night, came in to see to it that I was not admired too much; others followed, suddenly realizing that there was plenty of room in here; and I retired to a flowered chintz window-seat, where I sat down against a sweep of white curtain, found myself a little silver shell of an ashtray, and lit a cigarette.

I was there alone through only one round of hot hors d'oeuvres when Mr. Lindsay made his way in my direction, stopping now and again to shake hands but never taking his bright blue glance from my face for more than a few seconds. He complimented Emily on the transparent grey Indian scarf she was wearing around her shoulders, he addressed some pleasantry to Dr. Boyd who did him the honor to laugh at it, he smelled the freesia at the invitation of a blond young thing smuggled in by one of the Symphony men, and then he emerged, sighing, into the emptiness in front of me. "How *good* it is to find you here by yourself, Frieda," he said, sinking down on the flowered chintz. "I haven't had a word with you since last night—haven't seen you, in fact, except as an attentive face in the audience this afternoon."

I think I flushed, partly because I had failed to present myself after the lecture and partly because I was not at all sure my face had been attentive. I congratulated him on his speech—it is always hard for me to make a creditable showing under such circumstances, and I am afraid I over-emphasized the enthusiasm of the student response. But he plainly expected no cover-up and bore me no malice: he slapped himself on the side of his raw and rosy cheek and puffed out his mouth and shook his head.

"But it was terrible, darling, just terrible," he said in a confiding undertone. "I don't know what came over me—

I'm usually not as bad as that, though I'm never really good. My notes got all mixed up, so I simply abandoned them. I didn't go into half the things I intended to take up, and to tell the truth I think Arthur is a little ashamed of me. Well, he knows what I'm like, he knows I'm a writer, not a lecturer, and it was he that took the risk. He and I have this much in common, anyway: show us an audience and both of us are petrified. But why should we be going on about my silly old lecture? Tomorrow I'll be leaving, and God knows when I'll see you again, and there's so much I ought to tell you before I go that I don't know where to start."

The Jamaican hovered in front of us with a tray of tall and misty glasses. I refused, but Mr. Lindsay took what I concluded to be his third, and my sense of urgency was only increased by the four avid little sips he took before he began again. "This business of Arthur and Julie McIvor, now—it's been a disastrous thing for him," he said.

I took a deep drag on my cigarette and blew out the smoke and watched it spread in a curling cloud between me and the people who were chatting near the table. I could see myself reflected far away in the glass of a tall breakfront, and I trusted I was the image of incurious quietude.

"Yes, in more ways than one I'd say she's had a disastrous influence," he said, and I had a peculiar impression that what he was uttering now had been rehearsed far more thoroughly than the speech he had given us this afternoon. "Did you know how dependent he was on her?"

I knocked my ash delicately, carefully into the ashtray. "I suppose I got the impression somewhere that Arthur is—or used to be—financially dependent on Mrs. McIvor," I said.

"Financially dependent?" He flashed his china blue eyes at the advancing little blonde in a way that warned her off into a corner. "Oh, he was *that* all right—she saw to it that he got used to a way of living miles beyond anything he

226

could ever hope to manage for himself. Those parties, that big studio of his, those clothes and those 'beautiful things' and all the rest of it—she saw to it he needed them the way an addict needs his drugs. But let's face it, Frieda, that wasn't the sum and all of it." He shook his head and laid his hand, curiously unwelcome, considering its lightness and gentleness, over mine. "You realize, of course, that they were living together, darling? Everybody knows—and I took it for granted you did, too—they've been living together for years."

"How many years?"

"Seven—eight—it's been such a long time now I can't remember."

"In that case," I said, pulling my hand away and using it in the business of squashing out my cigarette, "he must have been very much attached to her—at least that's what I would think. Little as I know him—and I assure you, Mr. Lindsay, I don't know him anything as well as you seem to think I do—little as I know him, he doesn't strike me as the sort of person who would be a kept man, pure and simple. There must have been more to it than that—there must have been love or something like love—"

Mrs. Boyd rustled around the table and came straight for us and asked me to introduce her to Mr. Payne's friend. Her perfume—jasmine or something equally enervating— deepened my depression while she stood over us saying how much she had wanted to hear the lecture, how much she regretted that the duties of a mother had kept her downtown at the dentist's all afternoon. I turned my face against the coolness of the curtain, unable to compliment her on her dress, even though she was going on at a great rate about mine. A quaking sickness was in my chest—it was as if my heart were actually shaking; and the best I could do was to wait with dignity for her to depart.

"Oh, he was attracted to her at first—I'd be the last one to deny it," he said as soon as the intruder had turned

227

her back and attached herself to the group near the table. "I'm sure he was attracted to her at first—she's beautiful even now in a ravaged kind of way, and ungodly clever, too, so that anybody else would seem pretty much like a bore. Certainly, there was a time when he couldn't get on for two days straight without her. But that time's past—it's been over for years—however mad he was about her in the beginning, he's deathly sick of her now."

"How can you be certain?"

"Oh, but it's obvious, Frieda—everybody knows it. That's why he left New York—to break it off, to get out of her clutches. He didn't have to move clean out of town to get himself a job—he had an offer up there, an offer that was better in many respects than this one down here. I was in on the final scenes, my dear—not in person, of course, but he kept coming back and telling it all to me. He came down here because he wanted to make a clean break of it, and he even mustered up the courage to tell her so."

"But it didn't turn out to be a clean break—did it?"

"No, not exactly. But that doesn't prove he didn't want it to be. It's *she*, not *he*, who keeps trying to rake up the ashes and start it all over. Her husband's a sick old doddering fool, and she can't stand being alone, she can't get on by herself. Surely you must have guessed what's been going on—how she calls him and asks him to come, how he puts it off and argues with her, how he tries to keep his word to himself and then gives in. And when he gives in, it's poison, rank poison to him. He hates himself for doing it—he goes into one of those black fits of his and I get the most despondent letters. He hates himself, and he gets himself worked up into a state where he hates everybody else."

"Yet he does go back, which certainly would seem to show that he—"

"Don't jump to conclusions about what it shows, Frieda. Actually, all it shows is that he's ambitious. For twenty years he's been seeing himself as a concert artist

228

—in his own eyes he's that or nothing. Either he's a success on the concert stage or he's totally worthless—that's the way he sees it, and I'm not suggesting he should see it in any other light. I've told you how I think he can build himself a reputation—he can come by it slowly and safely if he sticks to his recordings—it's been done by people a lot less gifted than he is. But that takes patience, and he hasn't got it: he knows it's got to be soon or never, he's into his forties now, he's no boy wonder anymore. And there she is, always at him, always dangling the glittering possibility of a quick sensation in front of his eyes. If he gets the all-out critical success she's counting on at Town Hall, then she can use her influence to see that he appears with the Philharmonic, but that's a big 'if,' and personally I can't feel sure he's ready, personally I'd rather—"

He broke off and picked nervously at a loose thread in the chintz padding. I saw that he was looking covertly through the wide doorway that led into the parlor—Arthur was there on the other side of it, close to the door frame, in conversation with the department head. But he was not so absorbed that he didn't see the two of us: his glance —narrow, yellow, and cold—met mine, and I put on a pantomime of innocence, managing a stiff nod and a feeble smile.

Mr. Lindsay took a long gulp from his glass, wiped the corners of his mouth with the tip of his forefinger, and went on in a whisper, his eyes signalling urgency. "What he needs, what he *desperately* needs at this stage of the game is the peace of mind to go quietly about his business. And that's where you can help him, that's where you come in—"

"I doubt it, Mr. Lindsay. He's never talked to me about his playing, he's never so much as mentioned his plans to me. What you're telling me now—I've never heard a word of it before."

He blinked—I could not tell whether it was a mani-

229

festation of surprise or a physical necessity brought on by so much earnest and protracted staring—and for an instant the dead and withered look passed over his face. "If that's the case, if he's never discussed his difficulties with you, it only goes to prove how much he wants your respect. He's a proud man, much too proud to let you see the worries and the doubts that are upsetting him." His hand came down on mine, harder this time, and I did not resist it. "Surely you know how important you are to him—surely you must know it if I do. Every time he and I have talked since I've been down here with him, in every letter he's written to me in the last three months, it's Frieda this and Frieda that—"

He pulled his hand away and resorted to his drink. Arthur and Dr. Holland were making their way through the crowd by the table more quickly than one would have expected. He could manage only a couple of sips before they stood in front of us, Dr. Holland spruce and affable, Arthur rigid and saturnine. If a fierce accession of happiness had swept up in me during Mr. Lindsay's last speech, if that happiness prompted me to look at Arthur with more ardor than I had ever before permitted myself, I knew I had anticipated my cue: I got nothing in answer but a cold and level stare.

"I've been going into all the New York gossip for Frieda's benefit," said Mr. Lindsay.

"Obviously," said Arthur, sneering. "Frieda's a great one for gossip. I knew it was gossip by the way she's been lapping it up for the last half hour."

"Half an hour?" said the guest of honor, jumping up. "Was it, really? It didn't seem anywhere near as long as that. I *am* rude, and I know it—there must be ten people here I haven't said a word to yet. But don't bother to scold me—I'll be about my business."

"And I'll be about mine," I said, seeing to it that I did not encounter the yellow eyes again, staring at my full-length reflection in the glass in the breakfront. The three of them bowed me off, and I made my way into the parlor, where, in the confidence that there would be no more charged encounters, I allowed the Jamaican to give me a drink.

The rounds of drinks had been coming on so fast, the tone of the party had grown so noisy and vivacious, that it was no great feat for me to cover up my agitation. If my cheeks were flushed, so were Mrs. Boyd's. Surrounded as she was by Michael, Matt, and a young violist, she was graciously moved to share her plenty with me, and we covered an assortment of subjects, ranging from a visiting conductor to the difficulties of finding baby sitters, before I wandered off to another little group. If my voice was not quite steady, neither was Julius Grüenberg's. He was deploring, with wide motions and for Mrs. Holland's benefit, the instability of our foreign policy in Palestine, and he called upon me so confidently to support him that I found myself waist-high in a subject about which I knew far too little and Mrs. Holland knew everything. If I was shaken enough to want to sit down, so was Anna Webb, who subsided beside me on the needlepoint sofa and told me at once that she felt like a fool with her new hair-do. The front lock, it was true, had fallen into two divisions, and a straight twig was sticking out of the coil over her right ear, but I told her that it did wonders for her, and Emily and two of the Symphony men came over and agreed. The hot hors d'oeuvres kept coming back, and I ate them shamelessly, partly because each tray offered something new that I did not want to miss, and partly because it seemed better to stuff myself than to drink too much or to signal my nervousness to the assembly by lighting too many cigarettes.

It must have been close to half past ten before I collided with Jenny. I had left my velvet purse in the dining room, and I wanted a handkerchief, and there she was, sitting on the window seat, unluckily by herself. She gave

231

me a reproachful look, summoning up my last night's desertion, which I had forgotten; and there was no steering her away from the subject—she merely waited in ungiving silence while I looked for my purse and admired her madras cocktail dress—nor was she discouraged in the slightest by the fact that I did not sit down. "Well, did you have a good time at the party?" she asked.

"The party? You mean last evening at Arthur's? It really wasn't a party, there were just a few of us, gotten together on short notice. Nobody was there but the Grüenbergs and Michael and me."

"Yes, I got the idea that it was to be very select. Not that I would have wanted to spend an evening listening to the sort of stuff we heard at the lecture this afternoon. But it's a pity Hughie wasn't invited. Hughie was dying to meet him, and now that they've gotten together it looks as if they have plenty to talk about."

Her eyes, dark and angry in her immobile face, flashed behind her Harlequin glasses. I looked in the direction she was looking in and saw, between clumps of people and drifts of cigarette smoke, that Mr. Lindsay was sitting in the parlor in a big maroon plush chair and that Hughie was sitting cross-legged at his feet. Each of them was bending toward the other, straining toward the other from the hips; Mr. Lindsay was making exaggerated gestures with his small pinkish hand; and Hughie was listening with his mouth a little open—in his utter absorption, he was drawing one long lisle-clad foot slowly out of his shoe.

There was nothing in the little scene to arrest my attention; yet it had for me—as it seemed to have for Jenny—a steady fascination. Even when we were joined by Dr. Boyd, who sat down between us and told us everything he thought was wrong with Mr. Lindsay's lecture, we kept craning our necks to watch, though there was nothing for us to see, nothing but an old man talking to a young one, nothing but waving hands and absorbed faces and wide-

232

open eyes. Arthur—near the arch in the doorway again, this time with a bassoonist and the blond young thing—Arthur, or so it seemed to me, kept looking in the same direction. His face had assumed the hateful coldness I had seen on it during his first encounter with Harrison, and I thought that the blonde must be very stupid to merit such a look.

I was delivered from my chat with Dr. Boyd and Jenny—my need to be quiet and to think was so urgent by now that every situation in which I found myself seemed a kind of captivity—by the arrival of the Dean of the College, who had dropped in after a dinner party at the home of one of the Board of Trustees. He was a plump, rosy little man with a white bristle of a moustache, and he made himself pleasant to everybody, working his way from one lively group to another. In the general shift that ensued, Dr. Holland got a word with me: he said he'd been wanting to mention that our little talk seemed to be bearing fruit; he looked at Arthur's back, bent attentively toward Mrs. Boyd, who had taken over one corner of the needlepoint sofa, and added that there was certainly a gratifying change. Other people, including the Dean, wanted a word with me, too. During a series of brief and routine party exchanges, I noticed that a cold draught was moving across my feet and conjectured that in the flutter over the Dean's arrival the front door had been left open—a guess that proved correct when I excused myself to the violist and stepped out into the empty hall. It was a narrow, old-fashioned hall, with a steep white stairway going up to the second floor. It was lighted by a single frosted glass lamp, which cast a chaste kind of light on the white walls and the red carpeting. The door, with thin white curtain stuff arranged in neat gathers over its glass top, stood at a slant and revealed a long segment of wet, black night. I shut out the darkness and, turning with my hand still on the door-knob, saw that Arthur had come up behind me, his shoulders

233

stooped, his hands dangling at his sides, his face grave and uncertain. He looked as if he did not know whether he would be welcome, and I wondered why and then remembered what I had forgotten in the crowded confusion of the evening: the sickly minute when he had played up to me, when he had forced himself to touch me with false tenderness last night in his kitchen.

"I've been trying to see you alone all evening. To say the least, you've been surrounded." His voice was free of any implication of reproach. He was offering an honest explanation, with overtones of regret.

"Nobody ever really sees anybody at these big parties." It seemed unfortunate to me that our conversation should be a continuation of what we had been saying to each other last night before his disturbing approach. "Small groups are better, except for celebrations." Now it was I who was constructing meaningless conversation. I deplored the coolness of my voice, particularly because there was so much exposed earnestness in his eyes.

"Well, small groups can be pretty terrible too. All day I was wishing I could go back to yesterday afternoon and start the whole thing over again and do it in some other way. That's what I wanted to tell you; last night was pretty terrible," he said.

He meant that the encounter in the kitchen had been pretty terrible—I knew it by the slight quaver in his voice and the feeble movement he made with his hanging hands. Perhaps I would have answered him on his own terms if my eyes, in avoiding the vulnerability of his, had not happened to glance through the doorway between the hall and the parlor, made narrow by a pair of crimson velvet drapes. Through the small divide between the heavy panels, I could see only one thing: Hughie and Mr. Lindsay. Hughie was on his knees now, his shoe off, his elbow on the arm of Mr. Lindsay's chair, his face strangely, distressingly close to Mr. Lindsay's face. "Oh, I don't know. The guest of

234

honor seemed to be enjoying himself, and that's all that matters, isn't it?" I said.

He pulled back his head as if I had struck him, and I thought that Mrs. McIvor must have schooled herself never to reject his most tentative advance. Anger flared up in him, and died; his face, lighted up from below by the glowing globe of the frosted glass lamp, revealed by its look of resignation his awareness that a reconciliation could not be achieved as easily as that. "Oh, yes, *he* enjoyed himself all right," he said with a bitterness that was not directed at me. "And if you ask me, he's enjoying himself too much tonight."

"What do you mean?"

He made another gesture, exasperated and helpless, toward the division between the crimson drapes. "He doesn't have to go on like that—I mean, he doesn't have to put on a show like that with Hughie—it's embarrassing—he ought to have some consideration for my position here even if he doesn't give a damn about himself."

I made some crazy movement, as if to try to find my way in the equivocal darkness that was opening up all around me. I could feel my face going ugly with abhorrence, and I covered it with my hands and started in blind darkness for the stairs.

"Frieda—" he said behind me.

I did not turn. I groped for the banister and found it and shook my head.

"Wait a minute, Frieda—"

"No!" I said without stopping, putting one step after another between us. "I've had enough. Go away and let me alone."

A bedroom opened off the shadowy upper hall, a serene and dimly lighted bedroom. I walked into it and closed the door. I had a right to be there, so I told myself in my pain: it was intended for the use of visitors—powder and fresh squares of cotton had been set out on the bulky

235

mahogany dresser, and evening purses and scarves and coats lay on the white candlewick spread. The order and the stillness of the place worked on me like a motherly remonstrance: I did not fling myself across the white tufting and clench my hands and beat against the mattress; I went to the dresser, bent close to the oval mirror lighted on either side by tall hurricane lamps, and started mechanically to do what I could about my ravaged face. It was as if by staring at myself in the mirror I could exorcize the devastating image of Hughie and Mr. Lindsay, and, looming obscurely behind it, the more monstrous implications to which I dared not even give a shape or a name. It was as if, by getting on my lipstick with unwavering accuracy, I could do away with the necessity to consider, at least at the moment, what the blind imbecility of my love had never allowed me to see.

Footsteps—his footsteps—were coming up the stairs. I waited until they started down the hall and were very close before I did what I knew I must do, before I went and locked the door.

"Frieda. Are you in there, Frieda?"

"Go away. I told you I've had enough of it," I said quietly against the white panelled wood. "Just go away. I can't stand it anymore."

Now that he was gone, I walked back to the dresser, where, since I had finished putting on my make-up, there was nothing left for me to do. I touched the comb and the brush with the worn gold handle and the mirror with the tarnished gold backing. Under the lamp there was a gleam of more faded gold—an ornate and unfashionable picture frame. Out of the picture the clear eyes of Warren Holland, as they had been in his youth, looked at me. And suddenly I was shaken, not by disgust and not by terror, but by a vast, enveloping surge of longing and loneliness. This life, this staid and orderly room, this honorable and peaceful bed—why had all such things been denied to me? The

236

manly face, held up by the stiff collar, continued to gaze at me with frank, uncomplicated, untainted goodness, and I wished to God I could be Mrs. Holland, and I took the picture of her husband and pressed the cold glass of it against my breast.

After I had cried a little and wiped off any possible fingermarks with my crumpled handkerchief, I set the photograph back where it had stood. There was a dark spot from one tear on the front of my plum-colored satin, and I waited for it to dry, helping it to dry by blowing on it, before I took my purse and unlocked the door and stepped into the corridor. Others had come into the downstairs hall in my absence; I could hear the host chatting in his twangy voice with Mr. Lindsay about the Hollands' projected trip to Europe next summer. Warren was saying he wasn't entirely happy about that trip—he hated to skip his usual kind of vacation at his place in Penny's Run.

"Lucky *you!*" said Mr. Lindsay, and I stopped on the third step down, struck motionless by his voice, hearing in his voice what any fool could have heard in it long ago. "You're a married man, you've got a ready-made traveling companion to push off with whenever the notion strikes you. With me, it's different—would you believe it: even though my living depends on it, absolutely *depends* on my keeping in touch with what's going on over there, I haven't been across for a couple of years. I *loathe* going by myself and sitting around in hotel rooms like some dreary old monk. All we poor bachelors can do is wait till somebody else is willing to come along with us. Arthur and I have been talking for years about doing France and Italy together, but Arthur can never get himself detached, though it's beginning to look as if we might really make it this time—we've got a tentative date for next June."

I clung to the banister, forcing myself to face it, to see what sort of use Mr. Lindsay had been making of me. He had planned it with all the creative inventiveness of his kind: after I had detached Arthur from Mrs. McIvor, he would only have to sit and wait until I had proved myself the intolerable bore he confidently expected I would be, whereupon he and Arthur could set out on their long-delayed journey, standing side by side at the railing in matching vests.

"Oh, well, you can have it," said Dr. Holland as I started down. "It's for Jane that I'm doing it. I spent a couple of years over there in my early thirties when I was collecting the stuff for my book, and I enjoyed it then. But I guess I'm getting to the age where I want my own rooms and my own trout stream and my own bed."

He nodded to me as I reached the bottom, and I gave him a set smile. As I walked between the two of them—they had stepped back to make way for me—I had the small but burning satisfaction of seeing Mr. Lindsay's face go withered and of glimpsing the fear in his blinking eyes.

The Dean encountered me again in the dining room and engaged me in a discussion about the new admissions policy. He joined the Jamaican in urging a second drink upon me, but I did not really drink it—I only held it and sipped at it, and the cold of it numbed my hand. I had a hard time making sensible answers because I was watching Arthur. He was drinking, quickly, continuously, alone in a corner, and I had the conviction that he had finished off two at least since he had walked away from the door upstairs. Jenny and Hughie were having a charged and muted exchange by a vase on a pedestal in an alcove; Anna Webb was asking for an aspirin; Mrs. Boyd was looking for her husband because she thought they'd better be going now, though when she found him he made it plain that he was of a different mind by saying in a loud and irritated voice, "Oh, for Christ's sake!" As I moved off to give the Dean an opportunity to converse with somebody more attentive and less shattered than I was, I noticed that the carpeting had the weary look which comes upon it at the end of a

238

party: the fine maroon pile was tracked up in every direction, and bits of hors d'oeuvre had been dropped and trampled in.

They would not let me alone—I was not let alone for a single minute. I did manage to get rid of the icy glass—I set it down, three-quarters full, on a dish that had formerly held candy—but I could not even chafe my hands in peace: the plump bassoonist was there at my elbow and insisted on warming my hands for me. He and the blond young thing edged me back into the parlor, where everything was very noisy and then suddenly quiet. In the serene bay, against the sweep of the crisscross curtains, in the light of the frosted lamp, Arthur and Dr. Boyd were all too obviously having a difference. They stood on either side of an inlaid table, with florist's roses showing between them, and glared at each other, and neither one of them seemed very steady on his feet.

"Why don't you give the Jupiter Symphony a rest?" said Arthur in a voice that was crudely, jeeringly familiar. "Day after day, the same damned thing—it's enough to drive a person crazy."

I knew that the inordinate amount of time Dr. Boyd had been spending on the Jupiter with the student orchestra was a raw subject with him. He had gotten into hot water by under-rehearsing the Seventh, and he was determined to redeem himself with the Jupiter, was even hoping that the Dean or Dr. Holland would suggest that it be added to the Mozart Festival. "And where did you get the idea that our aim is to keep the faculty entertained? These people are students, and they need to be drilled on the fine points," he said.

"The fine points! God Almighty, man, don't talk about the fine points—there's not one in twenty that could see a fine point if you stuck it in his face. They'd be a damned sight better off if you gave them a little more repertoire instead of fooling around with fine points."

239

"Are you trying to tell me how to do my job?"

"Do it any way you want—I don't care. But in case you don't know it, the students are sick of the piece—you can hear them complaining about it all over the place. They started to get sick of it a month ago."

"Are they? Well, let me tell you something, Mr. Sanes: you see to it that *your* students get sick of a piece the first week. All they need for that is one lesson from you."

Michael and Emily hurried in from the dining room, Michael grey in the face, Emily with her thick dark brows drawn together. "Give me a cigarette, Arthur," she said. "Julius is gone someplace with my purse, and I cannot find him, and I must be given a cigarette." Mrs. Boyd, white and insistent, came up and tugged on her husband's sleeve. "Either you come now or I get a cab and go without you," she said in an audible whisper; and the gentlemen parted, drawn away from each other, still glaring, and the first moves for departure set in.

I, too, thought of going, thought with all the more longing of the time when I would find myself in the quietness of the Grüenbergs' Dodge since Mr. Lindsay's china blue stare kept darting at me from the window seat in the dining room, where he was talking spiritlessly with Anna Webb. Emily had located Julius—he was in the alcove, listening solemnly to the bassoonist—but I knew she would not go so far as to disengage him, and I had a nauseating suspicion that the guest of honor meant to have another little chat with me. It seemed to me that he had been trying to make out from my behavior whether I had heard him when he told Warren about the trip he was planning with Arthur, and, with the warmth of too many drinks radiating through him, he had probably answered himself in the negative—at least he had enough confidence to hazard a coy and friendly wave at me through the doorway, to which I responded with a non-committal nod of the head. I sat

240

on the arm of the needlepoint sofa and watched the Boyds make their farewells to Dr. Holland and the violist help the blonde into her imitation beaver coat. There were more comfortable places to sit: the big chair where Mr. Lindsay had carried on his conversation with Hughie was unoccupied, but I could not bring myself to go near it, tired though I was. Emily, having walked away from her husband with a shrug, was keeping close to Arthur, taking his empty glass and setting it out of his reach and holding onto his arm as if she was afraid he might waver if she let him go.

The living room was relatively empty when Mr. Lindsay mustered up the courage to come in and try me out. He advanced across the marred carpet and took his strange stance in front of me, and I stood up, not wanting him to bend over me, sick even at the thought of the blend of liquor and eau de cologne on his person, glad that I was the taller of the two and need not look into his eyes. "Well, you're certainly still looking fresh for this hour of the night," he said. "Did I tell you I think that's a perfectly beautiful dress?"

Arthur pulled away from Emily, turned around, and came over to us. He did not weave, but his eyes were bloodshot, and I thought he must be seeing us through a reddish mist. "And what's the subject of the conversation *now*?" he said.

"Why, nothing. I was telling Frieda what a beautiful dress she has on." He put out his hand and laid it on the satin sleeve, and my flesh crept under his touch. "Look at her, Arthur. Doesn't she look perfectly lovely in this dress?"

"Doesn't she look perfectly lovely in this dress?" said Arthur, not loudly, but pitching his voice in a piping and venomous mimicry. He turned his sneering face away from Mr. Lindsay then and brought it close to mine. "She'd look a damned sight better out of it," he said.

It was Michael who stepped in, not because he had heard it—it had come out in scarcely more than a whisper

241

—only because he saw me breaking away from the two of them and making for the hall. I heard him saying sternly behind me that coffee was brewing in the kitchen, that it was getting late, that they should all have a cup and then he would be glad to drive them home.

Nobody but Mrs. Holland was in the narrow hallway. She had just closed the door after some departing visitors, and when she turned I knew how strange my face must look by the amazement in her own. She was making some standard cordial remark about not having seen much of me that evening, but she broke off and came up to me and laid her small, brown-spotted hand on my arm. "What's the matter, Frieda? Aren't you feeling well?" she said.

"I feel shaky—I'm getting a terrible headache."

"Oh, that's a pity. Come on upstairs with me. I'll get you an aspirin and you can lie down—it'll be quiet for you in there if I close the door."

"No—no—thanks very much—" I knew that if I found myself alone again in that hushed and orderly place I would cry so hard that it would be a long time before I could stop. "I'd better go home—I'd better call a taxi and go right home—"

"Oh, don't call a taxi." The honest concern in her bright birdlike eyes brought the tears stinging into mine. "Nobody wants to stay much longer anyway—everybody's going. I'll get Hughie or Michael or somebody else to take you."

"Please don't," I said, trying to stiffen my shaking mouth. "I don't want to break up the party. And anyway I don't feel up to talking, I'd rather just sit in a taxi, I'd rather go by myself."

She would not leave me. She called the Jamaican and had him telephone for a cab and find my coat. She did not look at me: she merely stood by, gentle and attentive, even though she stared only at the carpet, until the glaring spotlight of the cab cut across the gathered stuff over the glass

242

in the door. "Stay in bed tomorrow. Don't think of coming in tomorrow. I'll tell Warren you're under the weather, and he'll take care of everything," she said, walking out onto the damp black porch with me. She looked as if she meant to kiss me good night, but then thought better of it and didn't, which was a good thing: even without the melting influence of her kiss, I was crying uncontrollably before I sat down in the cab, and I had only a shattered voice with which to tell the driver how to get me home.

Chapter 17

I DID NOT GO to school next morning. There was nothing the matter with me, not even the suggestion of an oncoming headache, only a kind of nerveless, bled-out weariness that made the fact that I did not have to put my clothes on seem a dispensation not to be rejected. All night I had slept a thin and shattered sleep in which futile and half-wakeful ruminations had passed imperceptibly into heartsick dreams; and I was so little refreshed that the business of making and eating my breakfast left me tired, so tired that when I lay down on the sofa to read, in order not to think, I went promptly back to sleep.

I am not one to sleep in the daytime, and when I started up into a light that was undeniably the light of late afternoon—cold snow-light reflected on my nightgown and the cup of scummed coffee and the crust of toast on the cherrywood table beside me—I had a feeling of time confounded. To my misery—and I knew how miserable, how bereft I was the instant I wakened—was added the conviction that I had made my suffering sordid by dragging myself and it out of the sustaining normal order of things: I had missed my classes and I had no proper excuse for missing them, even if I had been given absolution beforehand by the wife

244

of the department head; it was four o'clock and I was still in my rumpled nightclothes with the refuse of my breakfast beside me; I had not bathed and I was acrid and sickening to myself with the smell of my wretchedness and my laborious sleep. The pattern of my physical existence seemed to have run amuck, to have gone off from the established course of human behavior: I did not know when I should eat again or whether I should eat any more at all today, or at what time I could sensibly go back to bed. And, to make matters worse, while I walked aimlessly from the living room to the bedroom, not knowing what I ought to put on, it suddenly occurred to me that a certain complicated form which should have been delivered at the Dean's office before five was lying uncompleted on my desk. In a less unwholesome and conscience-stricken frame of mind, I would probably have decided to get it in tomorrow morning—it was of no great importance, it was merely a record of student absences before and after the holidays. But it obsessed me, possibly because I preferred to be obsessed by it than to think naggingly, constantly of Arthur Sanes, and I knew I would not be able to settle down until I had filled it out and handed it in.

I could not have it in before five, that much was certain. Even if I could have pulled myself into presentable shape, gotten down to my office, and completed the form before five, I would not have dared to make an appearance there, since everybody had doubtless taken it for granted that I was sick. Still, if I finished it and put it under the Dean's door sometime before the end of the evening, it would be available for his secretary the first thing in the morning; and I made up my mind to go down to school sometime after nine-thirty, when there would be small chance of running into anybody. I bathed, dressed, cleaned up my apartment, made my bed, and had a glass of milk. I would stop on my way back from school at an Italian restaurant that was open until one, and that prospect and

245

the routine work that waited in my office served as land-marks in my shifting confusion.

It was a raw, harsh night, such a night as few people would care to come out in. The bus was as empty as I hoped the school would be, and the campus was almost deserted—the hedges and the stone pylons were coated with a thick layer of white rime, and the air was painful to breathe and tasted of frost. Only three squares of yellow showed in the stark front of the Music Building; few foot-prints blackened the white sparkle on the steps and across the entrance, and the lobby was vacant and blurred with a frosty mist—nobody in any of the first floor offices and nobody on the stairs. I took those stairs very slowly, at first because I wanted to give a creditable impression of feebleness to anybody who might meet me on the way up, and afterwards because I was genuinely incapable—dizzy with the sudden warmth of the building after the cold, and surprisingly tired. Light falling through the doorway of one faraway office cut across my corridor; I stopped and counted the doors and knew with a contraction of my heart that the lighted office was *his*. But then I noticed that the hall had not been swept and that other rooms were stand-ing open, and I concluded that he had forgotten to turn off his lights before he had gone home this afternoon and that the janitor had not yet made his rounds. I did not feel the usual security when I stepped into my own little cubbyhole: I had a crazy conviction that something ab-horrent—possibly Mr. Lindsay—was sitting in there in the dark. But nothing was there, of course, and I settled myself at once behind my desk and unfolded the form and opened my roll-book and began to record the necessary informa-tion.

I had completed about half of the tedious job when I heard the sound of familiar voices coming from one of the practise rooms at the far end of the floor. I had to listen for a few seconds—they were blurred by the echoes they

246

kept calling up in the resounding emptiness—before I could place them: Cathie and Vincent were in there talking and laughing together, and I took a small measure of comfort out of their ease and high-heartedness, though I could not make out a word of what they said. Their presence somehow lessened the eeriness of my being here in my office at this hour of the evening, and I thought that one or the other of them might step out in a little while and see my light and come down and talk to me. I went to my door—I had closed it in my nervousness—and set it slightly open to make them welcome. I reapplied myself to the form, and found a mistake in my addition, and started to look for a blotter, but I never found it. Somebody had come down the hall to see me. Somebody was standing on my threshold —not Vincent, not Cathie—Arthur Sanes.

This time there was no dignity, no cool reserve for me to draw upon. And even if I had not been too feeble and demoralized to send him away, I would have been put beyond doing so by the way he looked. He was as immaculate, as well tailored and perfectly shaved as usual, but the impeccable condition of his person only served to show how far he was from being himself. His face was greyish and furrowed with the ravages of a migraine, his eyes were red-rimmed and lustreless, his shoulders were more stooped than I had ever seen them; and, if I did not make any movement of protest when he came over and sat down on the corner of my desk, it was because I guessed that he found it difficult to stand. "Were you sick, Frieda? I came down and looked for you in the morning, but you weren't here," he said.

"I had a headache. I suppose I drank too much."

"I've got a terrible headache myself—it was so bad I couldn't face the trip back downtown." He put up his hand and made a dragging, pulling motion across the nape of his neck and down his shoulder. "I think maybe it's going —it seemed to be going a couple of minutes ago. Not—"

247

he smiled weakly without looking at me— "not, of course, that I'd expect you to be interested, considering the way you walked out last night."

"If your headache's letting up," I said, furious that he should take a tone of normal communication with me and even more furious at myself that I should have given a second thought to any affliction of his, "maybe you'd better take the opportunity to get home and go to bed."

"I will—after I've taken the opportunity to say a few things to you."

"That seems pretty useless." I glanced at the uncompleted form in front of me. "I came here because I had to finish this—I would never have come if I'd thought you were in the building. We've said enough—so far as I can see, there isn't anything more for the two of us to talk about."

"No?" His eyes, yellow and narrow, flashed at me for an instant and then went dull and blank again, and he picked up my big red eraser and began to knead it, plainly for the sake of steadying his hand. "Maybe you can leave it like this, but I can't."

I watched the spare, expressive hand squeezing on the eraser, and such a wave of weariness passed over me that I had to keep myself from putting my head down on my desk and hiding it in my arms like a punished child. But when I found the strength to begin again, the voice that came out of me was loud enough to call up multiplying echoes. "I don't think anything—I'm beyond all thinking," I said. "All I want, as I told you last night, is to have you go away and let me alone."

He got up slowly, still working at the eraser. I thought he was going to take me at my word—he walked across the width of my office—but he only closed the door. "Look," he said, standing with his back against the door frame, straightening himself against it with a deliberate and obviously painful effort, "I'll go if you want me to, but only after I've said what I've got to get said."

248

"It makes no difference what you say—"

"No, I don't suppose it does, not really. I guess you'll believe whatever you want to. You're pretty strong-minded, and all the way back, almost from the beginning, you always wanted to believe the worst things you could possibly think about me."

All the way back, almost from the beginning . . . In the sordidness and the hopelessness of the present minute, now that we were at the end of it, shouting at each other under the glaring light in my office, the savor of the beginning, the strange, compelling way it had been in the beginning came back to me. It was like a clump of spring flowers, narcissus or daffodil, thrusting itself up over shards and crumpled paper at the bottom of a dumping ground. *Keine Augen* and the walk across the bridge and the snapdragons in their tissue wrappings—they were powerful with me still, sweet and powerful in spite of all that had come between. I had to stiffen my body and harden my voice against them. "I don't know how you figure *that*," I said.

"I didn't have to figure it—you said so yourself."

"What are you talking about?"

"Did you or didn't you say—and pretty publicly, too —that I was hateful to everybody—you and Matt Cusick and all my students? Did you or didn't you say that I was paranoid and went around tormenting everybody and trying to make everybody look ridiculous?"

"Do you mean on Halloween night?" I asked him, looking at the battered surface of my desk, not daring to look at his face. "Who told you?"

"Hughie told me. What's the difference who told me? You said it—didn't you?"

"I said it because you didn't come and hadn't even bothered to write me a note to say you wouldn't. I said it because I was hurt and angry, and even so I wouldn't have said it if I hadn't had too much to drink. Besides, I said it before I got the flowers—it was only afterwards, after everybody'd gone home, that I got the flowers."

He came forward a couple of steps, holding the eraser in one hand and pressing heavily down on the back of his neck with the other. "It was the way I told you in the note," he said. "It wasn't that I didn't want to come—actually, I guess I stayed away mainly because I wanted to come too much. To be frank about it, I was involved at the time, I was up to my neck in something else, and it didn't look as if I were ever going to get myself clear, and I felt I oughtn't to drag you into it. The way things stood with me around the time you had that party, I wouldn't have had any right—it wouldn't have made any sense for me to have started anything with you."

"Then why did you? Why did you?" I was shouting at him, I was stung into a fury by the matter-of-fact way in which he was handing me an intolerable truth. "God knows, I didn't run after you—*I* wasn't looking for it—"

"No?" In spite of the greyness of his skin, in spite of the jagged lines drawn in it by the migraine, his face took on the scornful look of the photograph on the record envelope. "You weren't running after me, no—you weren't looking for it, as you say—but if I remember correctly, you weren't exactly averse to it either," he said.

The cruelty of that coupled itself strangely with the coarse directness of the last thing he had said to me at the Hollands' party. I caught my breath and closed my eyes against his arrogant person, and did not know whether the fierce force that was tearing through me was exultation or shame. He was right, and I knew it: I had never been averse to it, never, not from the beginning. And if his body had cried out to me in crude exigency through his confusion and his drunkenness last night, it did not go without its answer from mine.

"Tell me the truth, Frieda—were you?"

He should not have pressed it, he had lost the right to press it. No matter how earnestly he appealed to me now, I had seen him and was seeing him still in his scarlet

250

vest, laying his hand companionably on Mr. Lindsay's shoulder. The burning was going cold in me now; if it had been exultation, it was turning into shame. I was sick— sick in my body and sick in my spirit—so sick of him and the whole world that I had to close my hands on the edge of my desk to steady myself. "Whatever I wanted in the beginning, it makes no difference now," I said after a long silence. "I'm through with it, completely through with it —I just don't want it anymore."

"Why?" He came and sat down on the edge of the desk again, closer this time, so close that I felt or imagined I could feel the stirring of his breath in my hair. "What's happened—what's changed since the beginning—how is it different?"

"Oh, nothing's happened, nothing much." I laughed, and the laugh was cheap and incongruous so that I had to hurry on to cover it up. "Nothing much, anyway, according to the way *you* look at things. But after last night, after I'd had a taste of your friend Mr. Lindsay, I somehow lost my appetite."

He hurled the eraser across my desk—it bounced crazily off the corner, and I could not keep down a nervous spurt of laughter—he flung away the eraser and brought his hand, hard and crushing, down over mine. "Are you trying to imply that I—do you think for a moment I could carry on a thing like that and still be trying to hold onto you?" he said.

I could not answer him, and I did not want to look at him either, seized as I was with a fit of shaking. But he forced me to look at him: he caught me by the chin with his free hand and pushed back my head so that I was constrained to look straight into his reddened and affronted eyes. "He is what he is," he said, "and I'll not sit in judgment on him. You can stand around being high-minded— but let me tell you, life being what it is, the wonder is that anybody comes out clean and in one piece—"

He broke off at the sound of music. In the far practise room, Cathie Dugan was warming up, playing arpeggios, and he broke off and let me go. My hand and my neck both ached with the pressure he had put upon them, but I did not dare to touch them—such a gesture would have looked like a refusal to believe what I felt to be utterly true.

"Look," he said in a tone that was controlled and reasonable, even though his mouth was tight with pain, "it was a bad idea to bring him down here—I only did it because Holland asked me to, and I wanted to keep on good terms with Holland—I couldn't think of going away and leaving you then, I knew by that time how I felt and I wanted to stay on. He's jealous—he's tried to ruin any other connection I've ever had in my life. But I owe him a lot, I owe him everything—I owe him more than I could hope to make you understand. He stood up for me in my worst days, he stuck out his neck for me half a dozen times in his magazine, he wore himself out peddling me to the record companies. Whatever he is, I'll not break with him—no, not even for you. I owe him too much."

"Do you owe it to him to take a trip to Europe with him next summer?"

"No! Did he tell you that? That's another one of his lies—he tells himself lies until he gets to the point where he believes them himself. I never told him I'd go away with him—not to Europe and not anywhere else. But I can't stop him from having fantasies, I don't pull the crazy strings in his head. If he told you that, God knows how many other lies he told you—"

"Is it a lie that for years now you've been living with a married woman?"

"No." The music had begun again, a tentative go at the opening bars of the ill-starred and forbidden Schumann Fantasia. He started and looked over his shoulder and then turned back to me with a maddeningly unrepentant face. "No, that's true in the main, though there are married

252

women and married women—this one happens to be married to a man in his seventies, and he was an invalid before he was old. I'll buy that, I'll go along with that—according to your Sunday School way of looking at it, I've been living with a married woman. And if he told you she was keeping me—" spots of red stood out on his forehead under the greyish cast—"I'll buy that, too—she pushed me into living three or four times beyond my means, and then she paid the bills, so Hansford wasn't lying, not exactly, if he told you she was keeping me—"

It was plain that he was forcing himself to repeat the word "keeping" and that every time he uttered it his pain was increased. He was racked, too, by the sound of Cathie's playing: now that he had no eraser to knead on, his hands were clenched into fists, and when he opened them I could see the marks of his nails, red dents in the palms of his hands.

"I was fond of her in the beginning." He stared at the wall behind my head, and my heart withered under an acid inundation of jealousy, knowing that he was evoking lost images of that beginning, feeling its sweetness and its power. "I wouldn't expect anybody to believe it, of course, but I *was* fond of her in the beginning—she was something precious and entirely out of my reach, or so I thought, and I was naturally set up by the notion that she could give a damn about me. But it went to pieces, it was bound to go to pieces—she couldn't believe she really had me, she had to sew everything up to reassure herself. For the last two years, I've been sick of it, worn to a shred with it. That's why I came down here—I wanted to finish it off, I wanted to get myself free."

"Anybody who wants to finish off a thing can finish it. A person can just walk out—it doesn't take a couple of years."

"No? Don't you think so? I suppose you're an expert in such things, though I don't know where you could have got your training. Myself, I'm not as adept as that—I've blundered around, I've had my troubles—possibly my technique for ditching people isn't what it ought to be. I wish Dugan would lay off that Schumann. It's horrible, it's even worse than it was when I told her to give it up a couple of months ago. But as I was saying, it isn't as simple as you think. Quite aside from the fact that I owe a great deal to the lady, too—you see, there are drawbacks to my character, I get myself morally indebted to the most inconvenient people—quite aside from that, I'm sorry for her, she seems pitiable to me. It's true she has more money than she knows what to do with, but she's also fifty and lonely—her husband's not what you'd call communicative, sometimes he sits for days and doesn't say a word. And she's neurotic into the bargain—she's sick or she thinks she is, which amounts to the same thing in the long run, and she uses her sickness the way most women do. A week before Thanksgiving I wrote her a letter and tried to finish off with her in a way you would approve of, sharp and to the point—and what did she do? She called me a couple of days before the holiday—yes, I remember now, she called me just before I went out to the Milstein concert where I had that lovely little chat with you in the lobby—she called me long distance and told me she had pernicious anemia. I had a feeling it wasn't true, but I couldn't take the risk. That Dugan girl is driving me crazy—did you ever hear anything like it? No, I couldn't take the risk, and I haven't been able to do anything more than repeat what I said in my first letter the couple of times I've been in touch with her since. I've got a miserable weakness that keeps cropping up: I just can't bring myself to treat her like a dog."

Everything—the blatant music and his visible suffering under the assault of the music, the details I could not bear to hear and his hateful offhand way of thrusting them into my face—everything converged upon me. "You and your friend Mr. Lindsay have one thing in common," I

254

said in a voice as harsh as his own. "Both of you seem to take me for a fool! If you stick to her when you're looking elsewhere, if you keep running up to New York to her whenever she whistles for you, it's not because you have a sense of duty—don't give me that, I know you too well!" I knew I had better stop, I knew there were certain things that should never be said, but his challenging stare and the wild momentum of the music propelled me on. "I know why you stay with her—you stay with her because it's to your advantage, you stay with her because you know what side your bread is buttered on. Pity—duty—don't give me that stuff. There's not an ounce of pity in your body—you're hard, you're ruthless, you're utterly selfish— you use whatever you can lay your hands on, and I'll see to it that you don't use me—"

His hands went up in a frightening movement. I thought they were about to clutch at his head, but he clapped them over his ears and looked at me between them with terrible eyes, such eyes as I had seen in the head of a dying bird, sightless and dimmed. "If that's the way you see it, tell me what you want. What do you want me to do?" he said.

"What I told you last night, what I've been telling you now, over and over. I was happy before I saw you—I had a life and you spoiled my life. Everything you touch, you spoil and poison. Go away—that's what I want—just go away and let me alone."

"All right, then, if that's the way you want it," he said, letting his hands drop to his sides and getting stiffly off the corner of the desk.

More to keep myself from going back on my word than to show him I could match his arrogance with mine, I picked up my pencil and went back to my report. He stopped on the threshold, and I could feel his look upon me, but I did not raise my head—I kept filling up the blanks with a string of meaningless numbers that I would

255

afterwards have to erase. I heard him go away, then, but not in the direction I had expected, not toward his office. He was walking at a quick pace, probably driven on by rage at my imperviousness, toward the practise rooms at the far end of the hall. Suddenly the sound of Cathie's playing was louder, clearer, and then there was silence, and I knew he had opened the practise room door. His voice came hard and peremptory into the quiet. "What are you doing with that Fantasia, Miss Dugan?" he said.

"Nothing—I was just practising it—I've been working on the first movement—"

Her voice was muffled with fright, and I had to go to my door to hear. I stood listening in the darkness of the hall.

"I hope you understand you're not practising it for any lesson you're going to have on it with me. It's very stubborn and foolish of you to persist in— But what's the use of going into that? We've had that out before, and I think I've said enough."

"You've said enough to her altogether, about everything." It was Vincent's voice, quiet, but with a new tone of authority. "I don't know what you wanted to do to her, but whatever it was, you did it. You spoiled her music for her, you made her do a lot of insane things she never would have done except for you, you broke her down until she had next to nothing to hold on to—it seems to me you ought to be satisfied. You ought to be satisfied with what you've done to all your students—there's not one of them that wouldn't rather be a soda-jerk or a ditch-digger or a garbage-man—anything but a pianist—that's what they're saying all over the place. She was the only one that had a good word for you, and now you've fixed it so that she feels the same as all the rest."

I stood in the shadow, listening for the annihilating answer. When no answer came, when nothing came but the sound of footsteps leaving the practise room and coming in my direction, I knew the extent of his defeat—knew it and was so appalled for him that it did not occur to me to withdraw. I stood on the threshold, watching him walk slowly, with stiff dignity, up the corridor, hoping that with a single gesture of compassion and tenderness I could unsay everything that I had said; but he did not stop, he did not even look at me with his dim, fixed eyes; he passed me and left me standing there behind him—it was as if I did not exist. There was nothing for me to do then but go back into my office, where, in the middle of the floor, I found the big red eraser that he had kneaded in his trouble and his pain. I picked it up and held it against my face and cried in a dry and gasping way—small hiccuping sobs that he might have heard if he had passed my door on the way out of the place. But if he heard them, they did not move him: half an hour later, when I put the finished absence report under the Dean's door, the lights in his office were turned out and I knew that he had gone home. The practise room, too, was dark and closed, and I knew that it was late, much later than the deranged clock of my life had allowed me to think. I would have another glass of milk at home, I would not go anywhere to eat—for the first time in my life, I was afraid of walking along dark and empty streets alone.

Chapter 18

I WAS SURE I was going to be wretchedly nervous at my performance for the Mozart Memorial Concert. I had reason to be nervous; since the arrival of Mr. Lindsay there had been no practise sessions, and my mind had been too confused and too weary even to give any thought to the songs. Arthur and I had run through them exactly once in a couple of weeks, and that had been a hurried business with no time to stop and go back over the spots that had grown weak in the interim, since it was at a dress rehearsal, with the Dean and Dr. Holland and most of the Music faculty standing by. After that, I did not see him again—not even in the halls—until we met backstage among the tangled wires and raw lights behind the recital room, with half the long-prepared-for event over and done with and our own section of it about to go on. If certain tremors of excitement passed through me then, making a faint stir in my dead-heartedness—if I kept wishing we had rehearsed more often and that I had bought a new formal instead of resorting to the old mustard-colored crepe—my agitation subsided almost at once: he was so rigidly correct with me, so elaborately and impersonally polite during what was likely to be the last little time we would ever spend alone, that I went dead cold.

258

Once we were on the stage, with the crowded recital room stretching in front of us and the dusty green curtain behind us, I could think about nothing but how we must look to those who knew us and might wonder and guess. I had put down a tremulous tendency to cry, and I had the feeling that now I looked pretty much as Cathie had looked at her senior recital—remote, uninvolved, getting through one song after another with the spurious ease of an uncommitted automaton. As for Arthur—I scarcely dared to look at him, his face was so icy and so stern. If it had not struck me as horrible, the sternness with which he played the airy little introductions would have seemed ridiculous.

I do not know to this day what sort of applause we got when we found ourselves numbly on the other side of what had been—for me, at least—a ghostly and unreal experience. I did not hear it, and I could not make a graceful bow because I was distracted by a person in the audience whom I had never seen before, a white-skinned, red-haired woman sitting in the fourth row toward the center, with blond mink draped over her shoulders and an empty seat to her left. Her eyes, of that pale and penetrating green that gives the whole face an arresting look of absorbed attention, were occupied, or so I imagined, with appraising me; and as I walked backstage again, with Arthur frigidly opening doors and kicking wires out of the way for me, I was convinced that the pale lady in the mink had left the concerns of the New York Philharmonic to her fellow members of the Board while she mended her fences with Arthur and took a long and careful look at me.

I managed to get back into the audience, into the seat that had been saved for me between Anna and Michael in the second row left, before the quintet filed out to play the last number on the program; but I did not see them come on stage—I could not keep myself from looking around to get another glimpse of the light-eyed woman, which I was able to do without being too obvious since hands reached out of the dimness behind me to place con-

259

gratulatory pats on my shoulders and my arms. I must have been entertaining some hope that I was mistaken, because I felt a faint, pervasive nausea when Arthur slipped into the empty seat beside her, giving her the same sort of icy nod that he had given me backstage. She stopped in the middle of her applause for the members of the quintet, turned her head a little, smiled at him, and laid her arm along his. It was a beautiful arm, at once delicate and full, encased to the wrist in tight black silk and ornamented by a single antique bracelet.

The mind, especially when it has been stupefied by too many assaults, has strange ways of protecting itself. I did not brood on my jealousy, I did not consider my loss—I occupied myself instead with being achingly sorry that the Mozart Memorial Concert, toward which we had looked and worked for months, should be moving irretrievably into the past without my really having savored a single part of it. I was sorry for the concert, and at the same time I was ashamed of it. Sitting there between Michael and Anna in the semidarkness, trying to make myself small, I blushed for my unconvinced and feeble singing, for my old crepe dress with its dated lines and its shabby hem, and for the way the quintet must be striking Arthur's guest. Though Hughie was unquestionably professional and Emily was impressive in a rough and sturdy way, Mr. Kendall and Mr. Kahn, second violinist and violist, were doing a shoddy job; and I felt a burning and personal responsibility for Matt Cusick, who was certainly throwing himself into the music, nodding his head and smiling like a village fiddler and whispering to himself. Anna Webb's gentle hand laid over mine in sympathy or congratulation was an exasperation, a maddening confinement—I could barely keep myself from shaking it off in my distress. It seemed to me that the last number on the program had been arranged by a spiteful fate to expose the weaknesses of the school; and the burst of applause that came at the end—loud, overdone, as if

260

to make up for the tepidness of the response to earlier performances—served only to indicate that musical appreciation in the city was in a hopelessly provincial state.

Fear succeeded shame in me before that applause had risen to its first big swell. I did not want to see anybody—least of all Arthur with Mrs. McIvor on his arm; I wanted only to get out of the recital room, into the safety of the snow-spattered night. I squeezed unceremoniously past Michael, and started up the center aisle, but it was a futile move: students gushed and Mrs. Boyd couldn't understand why I should be running away after such a lovely performance and Jenny wanted to know why I had worn that dress. And, even though I arrived in the lobby before most of the audience—awkwardly getting into my coat on the way, treading twice on the already dilapidated hem of my formal—I was not permitted to make my escape through the big plate glass doors. Dr. Holland—it was the first time I had ever been sorry to see him—came running up behind me and stopped me in the path of a freezing draught. "Now wait a minute—what's the idea—you're not walking out of here before you're properly congratulated and thanked for your services," he said.

"Oh, it wasn't anything to call for much in the way of congratulations." I could not keep my sick-heartedness out of my voice, and I stood helpless, unable even to smile at him, while he straightened out the collar of my coat for me.

"It was as smooth as butter—not a hitch from start to finish. I thought Mr. Sanes was pretty impressive, too, though I must say he was looking a little grim."

"It wasn't nearly as good as it could have been—it's days since we practised." Remembering that all occasion for practising was over now, I could not suppress a shaking sigh. "I thought maybe we'd run through it once this afternoon, but Mr. Sanes didn't call me. I guess he was busy—"

261

"I guess he was." He looked over his shoulder in a way that startled me: it suggested that he had caught sight of the subject of our conversation coming through one of the doors. "He got an unexpected visitor, you know."

"No, I didn't know." Since the whole wretched business was over and done with, I could not understand why it should make any difference to me that she had come without notice.

"Yes, she called him up at school—Jeannie had to haul him into my office to get her call this morning." He lowered his voice, and I could see out of the corner of my eye that the two of them had stopped not ten feet away from us. Arthur was plainly set on making straight for the plate glass doors, and she was lightly but imperiously steering him toward the spot where we stood. "It was obvious he wasn't expecting her—Jeannie said he seemed flustered. I was in the other office, I couldn't quite hear—But here they come."

She led the way, her body inclined a little forward as if in gentle eagerness, her hair falling on either side of her face in large red-gold waves, the face itself less perfect and luminous than it had seemed when I had seen it from the stage. Here and there the smoothness of her skin was broken up by a few small wrinkles, but they did not mar her beauty in the least; they only suggested a greater reserve of withheld expressiveness. "Please don't think of going away until I've had a chance to talk to you," she said in a controlled contralto, taking my hand by the fingers only, and giving it a little squeeze—it was a strange handclasp, the sort that a self-assured adult would offer in an attempt to be kind to a shy child. "You have a lovely voice, and I think you did the songs beautifully. Really, Miss Hartmann, I enjoyed it ever so much."

The sleekness of her blond mink cuff, falling against the rubbed black velvet of my old evening coat, did not make me any more capable of responding to her gracious-

262

ness. "I have no voice to speak of. I chose the songs because they fitted in with my limitations," I said without warmth and without being able to meet her pale, attentive eyes.

"Oh, but I can't believe that. Arthur tells me you've had a concert career."

"Scarcely anything like that—that's an exaggeration. I used to appear sometimes as soloist with choral societies, but that was years ago."

She released my fingers, smiled as if to say she still reserved the right to disbelieve me, and then turned to Warren, giving him her hand, all of it, up to the mink draped wrist. "It was lovely—every minute of it was lovely, Dr. Holland," she said. "I forgot to mention—I'm an old friend of Arthur's, Julia McIvor. Aren't you cold here, Miss Hartmann? Hadn't we better move out of the draught?"

I did not want to move away from the door—I wanted to move out of it. "I don't mind it—it's refreshing after being in the stuffy recital room," I said.

"But it's thoughtless of me to keep you standing here altogether. I'm not far from here—just over at the Morrissey—and I thought we might persuade the two of you to join us. Miss Hartmann probably hasn't had her dinner—most of the singers I know never do before a concert—and maybe a little food and hot coffee and a glass of brandy wouldn't be amiss."

I felt rather than knew—I did not dare to look at him—that Arthur was staring at me with a grim kind of sympathy. "Actually, Julie," he said before either of us could answer, "these people are both probably very tired. Miss Hartmann's just finished singing, and Dr. Holland's had the whole weight of this concert on his shoulders. Very likely they'd rather—"

"Oh, but it wouldn't be anything that would keep them very long." Her voice was so unassertive that it was easy to overlook the interruption. "I'm going tomorrow, you know, and I did so hope. . . ."

263

I kept my stolid, ungiving silence, sure that Warren would make our excuse. He had a creditable one on hand—his wife had missed the concert because she had a touch of grippe, and I waited for him to explain that he couldn't leave her alone at home much longer. But he only looked at his watch and said, "Well, what do you think, Frieda? It's only half past ten," and there was nothing for me to do but take his offered arm and walk with him behind Arthur and Mrs. McIvor through the plate glass door.

We went to the hotel in Dr. Holland's new car, a big pearl-grey Buick, an unsold last year's model, which he boasted of having gotten at a large reduction. But even when I was safely in the front seat with him—there had been a sickening minute when I had been afraid I was going to have to ride in the back with Mrs. McIvor—even when I had rallied enough to commend the elephant-colored upholstery and the handsome dashboard in sentences long and consecutive enough to prove I was not mentally below average, I was so wretched that I was on the point of tears. It was probably the elegance of the car that made me remember I had set up a loose sort of arrangement about meeting Emily and Julius and going with them in their broken-down Dodge to eat at the Italian place; and, while Arthur maintained his icy silence and Mrs. McIvor went on to Dr. Holland about our local Symphony, I could imagine the Grüenbergs standing around in the draughty lobby and hearing from somebody else that I had found myself something better to do. The voice behind me was so mild and pleasant that I could measure my malice by my exasperation: in many respects, she kept assuring Dr. Holland, our Symphony was more interesting to her than the Philharmonic—our Symphony was young, responsive, vigorous, growing, whereas the Philharmonic had such a long history behind it that it was naturally inclined to be a bit blasé, a little tired. . . .

Their lively communication survived the business of

264

parking the car and getting out of it. She walked with Dr. Holland across the chintz-spattered lobby, between the heavy sofas and the big brass cauldrons filled with ferns and palms; she stood beside Dr. Holland, still talking to him in the quiet elevator; and there was nothing for me to do but stand with Arthur, which I did with bad grace, since I was doing it with her implied permission. He did not so much as look at me until we were close to the seventh floor, and then he made a strange, futile motion around the pocket of my evening coat. "What's the matter? Am I losing something?" I asked, looking at him coldly.

"No, you're not losing anything. There was something on your cuff, that's all. Some ashes or something—I brushed them off," he said.

I thought with bitterness that it was a pity I wasn't chic enough to do him credit before his mistress, and my bitterness did not decrease when we walked into the suite. It was furnished with a respectable facsimile of eighteenth century, it was bright with chintz patterned over with blueberries, and it smelled of that powdery fragrance characteristic of rooms in expensive hotels, and also of flowers that were doubtless of his sending—on the neat if slightly battered table, beside the big painted china lamp, was a tremendous bunch of white and lavender chrysanthemums. It was Arthur who helped me out of my coat; he seemed infuriatingly eager to get it out of sight, but I very much doubted he would find my dress more satisfactory. Having shed her mink, she gave it over to him with a little toss, and stood in her unexceptionable, simple, revealing black dress, looking at me, offering me some of her vast reserve of courtesy. "Do sit down, Miss Hartmann," she said, indicating the blueberry-strewn sofa with the sparest motion of her carefully manicured fingers. "That's a very charming dress."

I thought she must be sorely lacking in empathy. She ought to have known—any woman ought to know—how it would feel to be bare-armed and bare-backed in the presence of somebody slickly encased from calf to chin in black silk; with those attentive eyes of hers she should have discovered and probably had discovered that the hem was worn and marked from having been trodden on. I sat down on the edge of the sofa without any grace and without a smile. "I hate formals—I don't live the kind of life where I need them," I said. "The only time I ever use them is to sing in, and I hate to spend the money. This one was cheap to begin with, and it's three years old."

"It doesn't look it, not in the least. Classic lines like that are always good, and the color is particularly becoming. Arthur!" He had walked into the bedroom with our coats, and she was summoning him back with proprietary ease. "Would you take the flowers off that table and set them over on the window sill? That's the table we're going to have our supper on—I just don't like those wheeled-in things. Please sit down, Dr. Holland." She nodded toward a leather chair opposite the sofa. "Arthur can pull up that straight chair." Having arranged the grouping, she settled herself in the remaining corner of the couch, and shook back her hair, and crossed her hands in her lap. Though the veins showed a little and there was some looseness to the skin, her hands were white and beautiful still, especially against the dull black silk.

"Yes," she said, addressing Dr. Holland as if their conversation in the elevator had never been interrupted, "that Mozart quintet is something you never tire of—I love the clarinet—sometimes I think it's my favorite instrument. He was very good, you know, that young clarinetist of yours. Is he one of the students?"

Warren laughed and leaned back in his leather chair with perfect and enviable relaxation, his weather-worn fingers clapsed behind his snow-white head. "Oh, no, Hughie's first clarinetist with the Symphony. I guess you would class him as part-time faculty—he spends five or six hours a week with us, teaching clarinet. We don't have any students of that calibre, do we, Sanes?" Arthur had seated himself upright, like a Cambodian god, on the straight chair, and merely shook his head. "We're not strong on geniuses here, Mrs. McIvor—we take what's left after Curtis and Juilliard have had their pick. Most of our graduates go into teaching—public school music and that sort of thing."

She bent forward ever so slightly—all her movements were so economical in scope that they seemed precious— and fixed her pale, absorbed gaze on Arthur. "Your students, too?" she asked with the faintest inflection of surprise. "Won't any of them go on to be accompanists or anything like that?"

"No, I'm afraid not."

"Really? And yours, Miss Hartmann, won't any of them—"

My interruption was plainly an interruption. "They'll teach in the public schools. They'll sing in local churches and conduct glee-clubs and fill up the town choral societies," I said.

"Well, of course, such people have to be well trained —they keep the musical life of a city alive at the base— and it's reassuring to know their training is in good hands."

"So I always tell myself," said Dr. Holland, stretching out his legs to relieve the stress of the occasion. But it was not entirely relieved: my own voice, hard and sullen, and some faint false overtone of her gracious inflection hung above us in the air.

She was conscious of the tension; she smiled and shifted a little against the blueberries to dispel it. "Now, what shall we have to eat?" she said. "You'll find a pencil and paper over on that desk, Arthur, if you want to take it down. What about some lobster Newburg—that's light enough for this time of the evening, don't you think? And some cold roast beef—Dr. Holland looks like a cold roast beef man— rare?—all right, Arthur, pretty rare. And hot rolls, and a

267

good chef's salad—tell them the salad has to be absolutely fresh—and one of those nice things with raspberry ice inside and a layer of crumbled macaroons. Coffee, of course, and a bottle of brandy—what was that brandy we had this afternoon, Arthur?"

"Courvoisier," he said, getting up and moving in the direction of the bedroom.

"Where are you going?"

"I thought I'd phone in there, so that you can go on with your conversation," he said.

But while he was ordering the food the conversation remained curiously bodiless and desultory in spite of Warren's efforts; and when he returned he did not sit down, he busied himself about clearing the table and bringing in a vanity bench and a couple of small chairs from the bedroom. His journeys into that bedroom—I could see a rosy patch of it in a mirror opposite the sofa—were almost intolerably painful to me. Once his image appeared on the surface of the glass, and I saw him looking at me with a stern, mournful face before I realized that he could see I was staring at him, too. He disappeared then, and was long enough about returning to the living room to permit her a remark on Matt Cusick's enthusiasm and Anna Webb's precision. Dr. Holland said that Anna was a good girl and had held the summer session together practically single-handed last year; and I was gratified by the fact that he did not offer Matt Cusick's wanderings over the face of Europe in the nature of an apology for the whispering and the smiling and the jerking head. I contributed nothing, absolutely nothing. That I could sit attentive and keep my face in a decent condition was enough—no more could be expected of me.

While the grave Italian waiter—it seemed to me that he also deplored my having overdressed for the occasion—was setting the feast on the table under the painted lamp, I was affected in a distressing way by the smell of the food. Though I would not have told her so for anything, I had *not*

268

eaten my dinner that evening, and I knew now that I was weak and sick with hunger, hungry beyond appetite. In fact, the rich smell of the lobster sickened me; and when she got up and went over to the table and commented favorably on each of the dishes as the waiter uncovered them for her appraisal, I felt that the stamp of approval she was putting on the food was making it unacceptable to me. She was— or so it seemed to me—playing the great lady dispensing hospitality; and, though Arthur stood beside her, nodding icily whenever a new wonder was uncovered, and Dr. Holland strolled over to exclaim with her, I did not choose to move. I sat on the edge of the sofa and forced her to issue a summons. "Do come over and sit down, Miss Hartmann," she said. "And please don't feel called upon to eat any more than you want. I know how it is—there are times when food of any sort isn't appetizing, especially after a person has been on a strain."

We sat close to each other—too close to each other— around the table. She and I were opposite, and I noticed that, in the glow of the lamp shade, which was lined with some pinkish stuff, her face had taken on again some of its smooth luminousness. Since the waiter had been dismissed and Dr. Holland was completely taken up with her and Arthur was so frozen and remote he could barely cope with the business of feeding himself, it was she who served me, and I thought it showed some measure of empathy that she did not attempt an easy show of hospitality by heaping my plate. We did relatively well with the talk—she had steered us into musical anecdotes, which she told beautifully, one after the other—until her glance happened to settle on Arthur's barely touched food. "But, really, my dear, you're not eating anything to speak of," she said, reaching past the salad bowl and laying her hand lightly over his. She put her head a little to one side, and an archness—the first thing I had seen in her that was incongruous with her poise and her years—came into her face. "You're supposed to be getting in shape for a concert, and you never will, not if you pick at your food like that."

"Thank you, Julia, I'm very well taken care of."

His tone was so cold that I felt sorry for her for an instant, and Dr. Holland was prompted to leap into the uncomfortable silence in her protection. "Oh, so there *is* going to be a concert, then?" he asked, covering his mouth with his napkin since he was still disposing of a piece of roast beef. "Is the date all set? When is it going to be?"

"Oh, yes, there certainly is going to be a concert. It's all set for Town Hall," she said, channelling her rejected graciousness toward Dr. Holland without disturbance or pause. "We had your convenience in mind when we settled on the date—it's the third of February, in the week that falls between your semesters, or so I understand. The ad's going to be in the New York papers this coming Sunday."

"Isn't that pretty short notice for you?" said Warren, bending across the table toward Arthur.

"No, not exactly." He used the fact that he was being drawn into conversation as an excuse for putting down his fork and shoving aside his scarcely touched plate. "It isn't as if I were going to have to work up anything new. Most of the program will be things I've been getting into shape for a recording session in March—I've been working on them for some months now."

"Nevertheless," she said, turning back to him, still arch, still undaunted, "it does take some practising to keep a program as ambitious as that at your fingertips. That's why I've been telling Arthur he mustn't break training. Whatever time he has—and I gather his teaching schedule isn't a light one by any means—whatever little time he has on weekends and evenings, he'd better keep at it. Between now and the third of February, he'd better see that his social life is at an absolute minimum."

"I don't think he'll have much trouble doing that," I said, surprised that I should actually be uttering the angry
270

words. "Mr. Sanes doesn't find the society around here that irresistible."

In the appalled silence which followed that—I would have despised myself for a coward and an unworthy adversary if I had not been able to raise my eyes—for the first time I met her pale and penetrating glance and saw nothing in it but contempt and surprise: contempt for any shattered pretensions that my bitterness had revealed and surprise, that, at my age, I should expose myself. She did not smile, she was too wellbred to smile, but a kind of gentle indolence came slowly into her face, minimizing the little lines and relaxing the lips. I knew that she could have yawned; I knew that she was thinking how deeply, now that every nagging doubt had been put down by my own avowal, she would sleep in that rose-colored bedroom tonight.

"Tell me something about this recording business—I've never seen it done, and I'm curious," said Dr. Holland, abandoning his food to give his full attention to the crisis. "Now that they're recording on tapes, how do they go about it? Do you play the whole thing through three or four times and take the one that's best?"

"Excuse me," said Arthur. "I didn't quite follow."

"When you're recording on tapes, do they take down several performances and choose the best one?"

"No, they do it pretty much the way they used to in the days of the old short-play records." He got it out wearily, he seemed to be saying it on the end of a sigh. "No, you play it in bits, about four minutes of it at a time. It takes a long while—they make you do whatever little section you're working on over and over until it comes out just right."

"I don't think I'd care for that. I bet it plays the devil with your sense of continuity."

"Well, it has its advantages." I looked at him because he had fallen unaccountably silent. I looked at Mrs. McIvor because she was making a delicate, appealing gesture in the

271

direction of the faraway coffee pot. "What I mean," said Arthur, "is that they collect your best moments and string them all together. That way, you don't stand or fall on a single try—which is a kind of advantage, you'll admit."

"Arthur," she said, "I'm dying for a cup of coffee."

"Certainly. Just a minute." He stood up and took the aluminum coffee pot and poured for her and for the rest of us. When he tilted the spout over my cup, I noticed that the stream was wavering, and I knew with satisfaction that his hand was unsteady. Wherever he was sleeping tonight, I doubted he would sleep as soundly as she.

"It still sounds like one hell of a strain to me," said Dr. Holland. "It's not an easy thing to pick up in the middle like that without a score."

I wondered why Arthur should be so long about replying, should remain silent while he moved a couple of plates and made room for the coffee pot under the lamp. Even after all that was done, he did not answer. He sat down with a peculiar and disturbing smile on his thin lips— a weak, childish smile such as I had never seen on him before—at once apologetic and provocatively insolent, like the smile of a ten-year-old boy caught at some secretive pursuit.

"I suppose most of them *do* keep a score around, just for reassurance—not that Arthur has any occasion to refer to it," said Mrs. McIvor, lightly, as if there had been no protracted stillness and no disturbing smile. "Before I forget it, Arthur, would you remind me that I have to telephone about my reservations? They're made, but it seems I have to call back and confirm them—they're dreadfully fussy about those things."

Just then there was a discreet knock—she smiled as if to welcome it—and the grave Italian waiter came in again behind a table on wheels, bringing our dessert and a fresh pot of coffee and a bottle of Courvoisier, and began, wordless in our silence, to clear the table and to cut and serve

272

the precious thing covered with crumbled macaroons. It was—or so we had called it in our childhood—a porcupine. Her stamp of approval was powerless to discredit this particular dish for me: I had eaten it in my eleventh year at a birthday party given by the wealthiest girl in the neighborhood, and had afterwards pestered my poor mother into buying one for a much less impressive affair of my own. The tartness of the raspberry ice and the bitter almond flavor of the crumbles—I rejected the chocolate sauce that came with it because that was a recent innovation—were so appetizing and so grateful to my queasy stomach that I felt impelled to ask her for a second piece.

"I'm sorry I have to be leaving tomorrow," she said, dispensing the coffee while Arthur poured out the brandy. "I would have liked so much to stay for another day or two. But there are always so many last-minute businesses in connection with a concert. It'll take days just to line up the press and alert the right people, you know."

"Myself," I said with downright rudeness, "I have to be at school tomorrow at eight-thirty, which means I have to get up at half past seven."

"Of course! How careless of me to forget about it!" She bent toward me, inclining her head so that she could see me around the curve of the painted china lamp. I felt sure that, if I had been within reach, she would have given my hand another little squeeze, in lieu of which she offered me her gentlest and most giving smile. "I know how hard all of you work over there—Arthur's told me what a gruelling schedule you have. He works very hard himself, much harder than he ever did when he had his private class in New York. I've been telling him he ought to let up on it a bit—just until he puts his recital behind him, I mean. No matter what his plans for the future turn out to be, whether he goes on just as he is—" her pale, absorbed glance fixed me, made it impossible for me to look aside—"or comes up to New York where he's closer to the center of things, or goes on

273

a little European concert tour next year, the recital is the crucial thing."

Dr. Holland drank off the remainder of his Courvoisier. If he was thrown by the prospect of having to fill up a blank in his faculty, he did not show it. "Yes, it's business as usual with me, too, tomorrow. We'd better be going, Frieda," he said.

Arthur got stiffly up from the table and headed for the bedroom, frozen-faced and without a word. It was good, it was harshly gratifying to see her turn to watch his movements, as plainly upset as any hat-check girl. "You're not going, Arthur—are you?" she called after him. The lines sprang into her face, destroying the smoothness, and a hard, scared brightness changed the shape and color of her eyes.

"No, not just yet. I thought I'd get the coats," he said.

He helped me into mine as frigidly and expertly as if he had been a well-trained butler. It was our hostess who walked down the hall with us to the elevator. He remained behind, merely nodding as we made our exit; and I did not look at him or even direct a "good night" at him—I was glad to be finished with him, glad to leave him there with the ravaged table, detached from me, placed irrevocably in the finished past. She was as gracious in the hall as she had been in the suite, filling the short wait for the elevator by telling us how pleasant it had been to meet us, how kind we had been to be her guests on such short notice, how sorry she was to have kept us so long.

No comments passed between Warren and me in the elevator, which was crowded with young things in formals, the worse for the hour—their dresses crushed, their hair ruffled, the smell of humanity asserting itself above the powder and perfume. We did not talk to each other on the way to the car, either, and I wondered whether his conscience had come at him with the bitter cold, whether he was thinking of his wife waiting in their orderly bed, her

274

small spotted hands folded in enforced patience on the coverlet. It was not until he turned the key in the new dashboard that he came out of his spell of brooding. "Well, now that our brief experience with the glamorous life of the big city is over and done with, all we can do is settle back into our humdrum little lives," he said.

"I guess that's about the size of it." I was incapable of a witty answer. I was so sick-hearted that I wanted only to rest my head against the icy pane of the window—the cold of it seemed to send a numbness into my mind, cutting off the tormenting capacity to think. Nor could I take any consolation from the fact that he was beside me: he had so plainly been taken in by her charm that it would be a long time before I could think of him again as a friend.

During what was left of the ride, we confined ourselves to routine and spiritless talk about the concert. I was startled when he introduced it: I had completely forgotten it and could scarcely believe it belonged to the day we were concluding—it seemed to me a week ago that I had stepped out on the stage with Arthur and gone automatically through the Mozart songs. The real subject—Arthur's position at school, Arthur's intentions for the future—we were too dispirited and raw to tackle. When we had exhausted the concert, we remained silent until we stopped in front of my apartment house and said good night.

If the Mozart Memorial Concert seemed like something that had happened a week ago, what had gone on before it was pushed even further back in time—in fact, it had slipped quite out of my memory. I had no recollection of the state I had left my apartment in; I was surprised to find the bed virtually buried under the clothes I had worn during the day, the top of the dresser covered with the pink powder I had spilled in my haste, the arm chair cluttered with my unopened mail, my scarf, and the coat that I had worn to school. I knew then that, in spite of myself, I had been almost high-hearted when I had left this litter. If,

275

during the last few days, I had made myself strong promises to renounce and forget, some part of me had disregarded them, some part of me had continued to hope: the mere knowledge that I was to see him and stand beside him in the dim space behind the recital room had revived my spirits, and I had left these things lying about behind me when I closed the door because I believed that something would happen in the interim—something so good that I would be able to set about the business of picking up and putting away with a high heart.

But now the ache in my spirit had communicated itself to my body. My arms and shoulders hurt vaguely as I took off my evening coat and laid it over the foot of the bed; getting out of the formal with its complicated closings was a long and exasperating task, and when I finally shook off the weight of the gathered crepe, I flung the thing into the bottom of the cupboard, knowing that I would never wear it again. I blew at the powder and saw that there would be no getting rid of it without a damp cloth and decided to abandon it until morning. The rest of my clothes I could not bring myself to put on hangers—I simply tossed them onto the disorder on the arm chair. My evening coat—I hated it, the dull velvet showed itself to be even more worn than I had remembered in the light of the lamp —would have to go into the closet: it would be hopelessly rubbed and creased unless I hung it up tonight. There were gloves rolled up in the pocket—I had forgotten them, I had not put them on once during the evening—and as I reached in to get them, I felt something sharp-edged, unexpected, and unfamiliar against my hand. It was a small box, held closed with a rubber band. In ink on the lid of it, in a handwriting that I had seen only once before, was my first name.

I dropped the coat onto the floor and sat down on the edge of the cleared bed, not opening the box, only staring at it where it lay in my lap among the folds of my petticoat. Tears blurred my eyes and ran down my cheeks, and I did

276

not bother to wipe them away—whatever it was I was crying about, for once I would let myself cry in peace. When I took off the rubber band, I laid it carefully on the spread beside me, thinking foolishly that I would save it, would put it between the pages of the Saint Ursula book. There was a wad of drugstore cotton, ill-arranged, on top, and under it the gleam of gold—a bracelet, a simple gold band, with a spotted onyx set in it, the onyx that had been in his tie-pin when he had come to see me on the snowy night. The bracelet was lying not on cotton but on a folded piece of thin paper that was plainly a letter, yet before I unfolded it I put the bracelet on and saw that the gold band had been made exactly to fit the rather meager span of my wrist.

"Dear Frieda . . ." I could not see it very well, I had to find my handkerchief and wipe my eyes. "Dear Frieda: I hope you will not reject this little present. I had it made for you out of the tie-pin that was given to me by my mother —I think I told you one evening where I got it; so you see I came by it honestly and you can be sure in taking it you would not be taking anything I received from a source that you or anybody else could not approve. In some crazy superstitious way, the onyx was a harbinger of good luck for me, and I want you to have it and hope you will wear it. Whether I deserve any happiness or not, it would give me great happiness to see it, if only once, on your wrist. I wish there were some mark or sign I could make to stand for all the things I would like to say and cannot say. I suppose I must admit you were right and wise in cutting off whatever there was between you and me. I suppose, too, you know that in losing you I lost what I wanted most. Though I am almost beyond feeling anything, it would be a very bitter thing if you were to send the bracelet back. I had it made for you with only the kindest intentions. Please keep it. Please wear it, even if you only wear it once. Regretfully, and with more affection than you would want from me, Arthur Sanes."

I put the rubber band into the book of Carpaccio

277

prints. I put the box on the night table close to the bed, thinking how he must have been trying to get it into my pocket when he made the strange futile movement in the elevator on the way up to Mrs. McIvor's suite. I undressed and was naked for an instant, except for the bracelet. I put on my nightgown and went to the marbletop dresser and looked in the middle drawer for another little box, a flat druggist's box with blue and orange capsules in it, sleeping pills that the doctor had given me the day my mother died. One capsule was soothing, two were benumbing —I took them both and lay down on the bed, waiting for the darkness to gather in. But before it came on, now that everything was over, I allowed myself to dream as I had allowed myself to cry: I put up my arms and embraced his image; I pressed my face against his face; it was in his arms that I fell asleep.

Chapter 19

ON THE LAST day of the semester I came down to my office in my oldest clothes, with a big pumpkin-colored smock under my arm in brown paper, prepared to get rid of four months' accumulation of school correspondence, useless music, and dust. I had my grade cards to make out, too, though that looked like a minor task: I always knew weeks before grades were due exactly what each of my students was going to get, and I was surprised that the mere business of recording should keep me at my desk for more than half an hour—surprised until I realized I was pondering every case. In general, I was pushing up my grades a bit; and when I paused with my pencil in my mouth and looked up into the brilliance of a ten o'clock winter sun, I knew the reason: I wanted to appease my students, I suspected I had not been the teacher I had intended to be for them this semester.

Mr. Perlstein, my Israeli, for instance, should have had a high B. But the weird mathematics of conscience—I had not been as attentive as I should have been to a stranger transplanted from a far land—brought him up to an A. Liz Stoddard should have had a disciplinary D for missing two lessons in order to make desperate trips to visit her fiancé in Philadelphia; yet, considering that I had been glad to have the spare time to listen through the wall, I could not bring myself to give her less than a C. Fred Wade, who would ordinarily have gotten a C, made himself so objectionable in the Cathie affair that I could not trust my judgment and pushed him over into the category of weak B's. And when the cards were ready to be sent to the registrar, I was appalled at the general impression they would give: my class, weaker than usual this semester, had made as good a showing as the best crowd I had ever had.

It was small wonder then that I set myself to the business of housecleaning my office with energy. I had more to forget than my moral dilemma over the grades, and I did not make forgetting any easier for myself by wearing my onyx bracelet. It flashed at me while I took useless music— some duplications, some with missing pages, some so marked up that they were beyond deciphering—out of the cabinet and threw them into the wastebasket; I fell to staring at the spotted stone, rather than at the dry debris that I wanted to get out of my desk drawers, the dust and the bits of tobacco and the paper clips and the stray pins. I was sitting with one of the smaller drawers across my lap, going at the corners of it with a dust cloth, when Dr. Holland came in. I was apprehensive that he might pick up my grade cards and flip through them, and I felt even more uneasy when he closed my office door.

"Planning to go any place between semesters, Frieda?" he said.

"No, I guess not. I'm tired—I thought I'd just give myself a rest."

"Not going up to hear Sanes' recital?"

I instinctively put the hand with the bracelet down at my side, among the ample folds of the smock. "No," I said, unable to think of anything that might take the edge off the sharp negative.

"Nobody else on the faculty is either." He removed a

280

heap of music from the single available chair and sat down. Except at a general faculty meeting I had not seen him— or Arthur—since the evening of the Mozart Memorial Concert; and I gathered with some disturbance that he intended to take up with me now what we had been too tired or too rattled to discuss in his car that night. "All things considered, I don't blame them if they don't feel inclined to make a trip to New York for the sake of hearing him—not without a special invitation, anyway. Did you get an invitation?"

I pursued a sliding and lustreless paper clip with stern absorption, reminding myself that he must know my involvement was by no means a slight one, since I had taken no trouble in Mrs. McIvor's suite to cover up my anger and my pain. "No, he didn't invite me," I said flushing. "He's never said anything to me about that recital. All I ever heard of it was what we heard together—I haven't seen him since."

"Then you wouldn't know anything about whether he's coming back next year, would you, Frieda? I hate to press you, but in case he isn't, I'll have to start looking around for somebody else, and I'd better get started damned soon."

I abandoned the drawer and set it down on the floor beside me, hoping that a calm attitude—hands crossed in my lap in spite of the bracelet, eyes brought to focus on his face—would obliterate the impression that I felt myself pressed. "Honestly, Warren, I don't know anything about it," I said loudly, with what I hoped was utter candor. "I took it for granted, just the way you did, that he *was* coming back. All that stuff about his teaching in New York to be closer to the center of things or going on a little European concert tour—" in spite of myself, I was mocking her voice, I had gotten an exaggeration of her gracious inflection— "it was all news to me."

"That's what I thought." He put his elbows on my desk, propped his chin on his hands, and gave me, over the

281

neat heap of my grade cards, a somewhat sheepish smile. "I don't mean I'm going to start writing to the agencies this afternoon or anything like that, but I guess I'll just have to proceed on the idea that he's getting out of here next spring. In some ways I'm glad of it—God knows, he's difficult. It seems he just can't miss an opportunity to make himself obnoxious—look at that row he had with John Boyd at my place the other night. Actually, what he said was more or less true, and somebody would have been forced to say it sooner or later—but he wasn't the one to do the saying, and he certainly found the worst possible way of getting it out. If he handed in his resignation, I guess there wouldn't be much moaning at the bar."

"No, I guess there wouldn't," I said.

"And yet—" he edged closer, looking at me earnestly, as if he were begging me beforehand to agree with what he was about to tell me—"you know, Frieda, it isn't so black and white as most of the others seem to think. That piano class of his—much as they gripe and grieve about him, they're in a hell of a lot better shape than they were at the end of last year. Laurent had them all ticking things off like so many music boxes, and it's different now—there isn't one of them that hasn't been forced into a more musical approach, and I'd even say that some of them are beginning to show real understanding. Besides—I'd admit this to you though I wouldn't think of mentioning it to anyone else— for all the drawbacks, all the antics, I find I like him, somehow I like him in spite of myself. There's depth to him, even though he doesn't give us a chance to see it very often. He has a mind of his own, and it makes itself felt, even when he isn't exactly among friends, if you know what I mean. Of course, these are intangibles, but *I* can't bring myself to discount them. If he ever got the knots untied—not that I think he ever will—he'd be a credit to the place. There's a tendency to get provincial in a school like this—there's bound to be—and a man like Sanes has a healthy counter-effect."

282

I agreed with him vigorously enough, though I wondered how anybody in his fifties could be as naive as that. He had apparently been too taken with her to see that neither he nor Arthur would have much to say about Arthur's plans; he had liked her carefully manicured fingers too well to notice how adeptly she was pulling all the strings.

"If somebody up there offered him more money, I'd be in a bad spot," he said. "My budget's terribly tight. I couldn't give him a raise, not until he'd been with us at least another year."

I wondered whether he was implying that I shouldn't hope for a raise either, and for the first time in my life I didn't care much whether I got one. The past was still there, unburied in me, and no matter how energetically I housecleaned my office I could not invoke the future, could not imagine how it would be too see this layer of snow grow porous and reveal the green or to lay away my winter clothes and buy what I would need for spring. "I doubt money would decide the question one way or the other," I told him. "Not that I really know anything about it. He's never talked to me about money—or, for that matter, about much of anything else."

His blue eyes took on a certain keenness that made me think for a second he did not quite believe me. Then he got up and rubbed his leathery cheek with the palm of his weather-worn hand and smiled his usual smile. "Well, I'll let you get on with your cleaning," he said, stepping backward toward the door, leaving my heap of grade cards as I should have known he would leave them, untouched. "Take it easy, Frieda. You look as if you could use the rest."

When he was gone, Emily dropped in for a minute and so did Michael, and there was a long telephone call from the Dean's office, and at half past eleven the two largest and most complicated drawers hadn't yet been touched. The last interruption arrived in the person of Cathie Dugan, smart and well polished up in a burnt orange skirt and sweater; she came and perched on the corner of my desk with her head on one side and a piece of torn newspaper in her right hand. But it was her left one that she thrust at me with the peculiarly smug and triumphant look I had learned to recognize as a signal that I was being called upon to admire an engagement ring. The band on her bony, capable finger was silver with a small pale blue sapphire in it; and while I praised its simplicity and originality I could not help myself, I had to touch my bracelet, "It's lovely, just lovely, Cathie," I said. "When did he give it to you?"

"This morning. He's been carrying it around in his pocket for three weeks, but he only gave it to me about an hour ago. He's very practical about things like that. He wasn't going to get himself engaged—not formally, not with a ring, anyway—until he knew he had a job. And he had an audition this morning at nine o'clock, an audition for the Symphony, and the Maestro said the nicest things about him, and he came right back to school, and we had coffee and muffins in the cafeteria, and that was when he gave it to me."

"I'm very glad for you, Cathie. I think the two of you are going to be happy. It's wonderful about Vincent and the Symphony."

She took a deep breath, and I knew she had a speech to make. I let her make it, paying less attention to the words than to the fact that her hand—it had come to rest on top of mine—was lying warm and flat over my fingers: she had never touched me like that before. What she had to say was mostly in the nature of a testimonial: how she and Vincent would never have made up their quarrel if it hadn't been for me; how the fact that I had understood and forgiven that crazy thing she did had made it possible for Vincent to understand and forgive it too; how when she took over Miss Mitchell's class—Miss Mitchell was moving to Cleveland and had recommended her to all her pupils, and four of them had already called—she only hoped she would be able to teach like me. I cannot say I felt much gratification while

284

she was holding forth, or any temptation to say "I told you so." Praise from a student invariably takes on a formality that robs it of its immediacy and pushes it over into the category of the cliché. And it is not a pleasant thing to stand by and watch while the vast, high-hearted illusions are being cut down to size. Girls dream so extravagantly that any actuality which comes their way is bound to be comparatively minor, and it is no wonder that they obscure the facts by making an undue fuss over their engagement rings.

Not that Cathie Dugan was aware of any shrinkage in her aims. Now that the dreams were buried, some of the fervor that had attended them had been transferred without her even knowing it to the students she would inherit from Miss Mitchell and the furniture she and Vincent would buy with their savings and the wedding trip they would take to Tanglewood a year from next June. She who had hoped to see herself on the concert stage would meet me in the street two or three years from now and tell me with all the pride of significant accomplishment that she had been invited to play on the local educational television station. She would be happy, as happy as most people, happier than I myself could hope to be . . . "Invite me to your wedding, darling," I said, trusting that she would take herself off before any of my sober reflections showed themselves in my face.

But the ragged piece of newspaper was still to be shown to me. It was not what I thought it was—a planted announcement of their engagement on the Society page; it was an item on Arthur's recital torn from yesterday's *New York Times*, and I could see by the green glint in her eyes when she identified it for me that the giant figure of her teacher still hung shadowy at the edge of the mild little landscape she and Vincent were staking out for themselves. "You'll never guess what his chief number is," she said, holding it tantalizingly out of my sight.

"I wouldn't have the least idea."

285

"Believe it or not, it's the Schumann Fantasia."

"Really?" I said, avoiding her eyes by fixing mine on the newspaper item. "I can't imagine how he'd do that. He'd have to take an altogether different approach from the one in those Brahms intermezzi."

"I'll say he would!" There was exuberant malice in her voice and her bony face. "I remember what he had to say about the way *I* did that Fantasia. I didn't have the ardor, I didn't have the passion, it was one of those things I was just too dull and ordinary to tackle—I made a travesty out of Schumann and a fool out of myself. Well, now, *he's* going to play it, and I tell you I just can't wait. Him—all dried up and as cold as a fish—I'd like to see *him* be ardent, I'd like to see *him* be passionate!"

"Oh, I don't think you ought to get yourself all worked up over it again," I said, in an unconvincingly casual way. "You've only got to put up with it a few months more. It'll be no time at all until you graduate. If I were you, I think I'd just try to forget it—"

"Forget it!" Her mouth fell open at the preposterousness of that. "I'll never forget it—it's not the sort of thing a person forgets. I've got to hear what *he* can do before I'm finished with him. And don't think I'm the only one—you'd be surprised how many of the others feel the same way and are going up there too!"

"I don't see what good—"

"Oh, I'm going up there, that's settled. Vincent's driving, and we'll have room for some of the others. George Bauer's riding up with us and so is Liz Stoddard—"

"What's *she* going up for? She's not his student—"

"Partly for the hell of it and partly to see her boyfriend in Philly. We told her we'd drop her off there on the road back, even if it does take us out of our way—" She broke off, plainly struck by a new idea, and put her hand back over mine. "Look, Miss Hartmann, why don't *you* come along, too? You could drive up with us, it wouldn't cost

286

a thing, and it wouldn't take more than a day out of your vacation—we're leaving right after the recital, we aren't even going to stay overnight."

"No," I told her with a sternness and finality that obviously dashed her. "No, I don't want to go anywhere. I'm tired, dead tired, and all I want to do is rest."

She got down off the corner of my desk, and I went back to the things we had talked about at first—her ring, Vincent's audition, Miss Mitchell's students, Tanglewood. But a disquieting change had come upon all of it—it was as if a scene had been slowly obscured by the shadow of a cloud that was passing over it; it was as if a piece of music had slipped weirdly out of key. Even the perfect affability that was established between us before she took herself off did not dispel my sense of profound disturbance, and I was glad to see her go.

But the door was no sooner closed behind her than I wished somebody else would drop in—anybody, even Harrison Frye—anybody to interrupt the troubling succession of questions that kept churning up to the surface of my solitude. Why had he never mentioned to her, in all their charged exchanges, that he was working on that Fantasia? Why had he never, not to my knowledge at any rate, played a single phrase of it to show her how he thought it ought to be done? Why had his nerves, stretched like taut rubber bands over fifteen or twenty different pieces in the course of the last few months, snapped on that particular composition? Frigid and hateful he had been a dozen times within my hearing to a dozen of his students—but why was it that the Schumann Fantasia and nothing else had driven him, and driven him twice, to devastating cruelty?

I could not sit still. I went into the washroom—it was fortunately empty—and contemplated myself in the mirror and knew that the strangeness of my face could not be accounted for merely by weariness and streaks of dust. I took off my bracelet and washed my hands and my arms up

287

to the elbow in cold water. I washed my face until it was raw with the harsh institutional soap and dried it on the unyielding brown paper towel, and still it was strange, in spite of its scrubbed cleanness. The water running out of the sink made a gurgling sound, as if the drain were clotted with hair. I put my hand over my stomach, knowing that I was nauseated and that I was nauseated because I was afraid. Afraid for how it would be with him when he seated himself at a piano in a crowded hall, with Cathie's eyes and Vincent's eyes and how many others' eyes upon him. So afraid that I could not let him do it alone. If he had been playing anything else, I would have stayed in town. But I would have to go by train and find myself a seat in some inconspicuous part of the hall and lose myself afterwards in the crowd. Like Cathie, but for different reasons, I had to see what he would do with the Schumann Fantasia.

Chapter 20

I AM A ROOTED being; tentacles go out from me to attach themselves to street corners and the blank sides of old buildings and the configurations of hills and clustered trees; and I suppose for that reason I should never revisit a place where I have put down roots. When those roots have been cut away, the things they were once attached to—or so it was at any rate with Pennsylvania Station and 43rd Street and Sixth Avenue—have for me a kind of glaring unreality. To find myself putting a coin in the slot of a subway turnstile where I used to pay my fare automatically almost every day is to feel myself moving in a nightmare. To come suddenly upon the artichoke-heaped window of a small French restaurant where I used to eat is to grow bemused with the incapacity for feeling what is called for: I simply reject the window and the artichokes and move on, absorbing nothing, taking none of it to myself. And this continual refusal—the streets through which I walked on my way to Town Hall were particularly familiar to me—seemed actually to affect my vision. Neon signs and lighted window displays shone as they would shine at a person who sees them in a fever, with a bleared and yellow glare, and the rejected shapes were before me and

289

behind me without ever being with me, as elusive and immaterial as shapes in dreams.

It was the same with Town Hall as it was with the city—strange to buy a ticket at the box office in the white lobby, strange to know without being directed by an usher which door I should pass through, strange to have the curved sweep of the seats, with their remembered red upholstery, align itself against the same curve still drawn in memory, and not to care in the least for the occasions when I had been there before, occasions whose savor and significance were lost. The crystal chandelier, hanging from a ceiling that was not quite so far away as I had expected— vacant time, like fever, plays pranks with perspective—the faded Sophonisba tapestries, the white box stage with its brown carpeting and its open brown curtain and white paneling, the balcony railing and the balcony behind it— all these had existed in the past and could not, for that very reason, be absorbed into the present by any effort of will. I found my seat in the fourth row, well over to the left of the stage, and sat down and became a part of the murmuring audience and opened my program as in a dream. My fear that I would run into some of the students was quieted less by my knowledge that they would have come early and found themselves places in the balcony than by the illusion that, since they were part of the present, they could not have forced their way into the past. And the shock of seeing his name—Arthur Sanes, pianist—on the little printed sheet in my hand arose from the same unreasonable source: he did not belong here any more than I and the students did. Arthur Sanes taught at the College of Fine Arts and was of that other life back there; and it was unbelievable that this audience should be expecting him to walk onto that stage.

The audience—my sense of not belonging gave me the courage to turn around and survey it thoroughly—was the living manifestation of Mrs. McIvor's power. The house was

290

three-quarters full, and the quality was even more impressive than the quantity. All around me were people whose very persons exuded a quiet importance—red-faced, white-haired, cosmopolitan men with their unpretentiously dressed women, sleek and lively middle-aged couples, young men with cropped hair and narrow conservative ties, escorting girls who were cool and upright with the confidence of doing the right thing in the proper place. On the other side of the center block of seats, with his legs crossed, I recognized a critic from the *Times,* and somebody—doubtless some other critic whom I did not know—stood conversing with him from the aisle. At the very back of the hall, talking to a little withered lady, was Hansford Lindsay, with his right foot forward and his left hip thrust up in the memorable stance. Having seen him, I began to look around for *her,* and for the first time I was frightened. There was a pair of empty seats in the second row, directly in line with me, and I was afraid she might walk down the aisle and settle there, might turn from there and take me in, knowingly, pityingly, with her pale and attentive eyes. But I was relieved of that fear almost at once: she brought herself and her mink and two other people into the only empty loge left in the front of the balcony—an old gentleman, flaccid and doddering enough to answer to the name of Mr. McIvor, and a dark young man who became, after another queer adjustment in my mind, a well known conductor who had appeared last year with our local Symphony. It was the conductor who helped her out of her coat, and I saw that she was wearing a sheath of greenish blue Italian silk, as unexceptionable in its complication as the little black dress had been in its simplicity. A single yellow orchid was pinned on her shoulder. Seen at a distance, she looked very pale, and there were darkish circles under her eyes.

A lean man came out with strangely incongruous vigor and readiness and propped up the lid of the piano and went away again. The audience settled, the quiet murmur became quieter still, stragglers got themselves out of the aisles, and the middle-aged couple in front of me gave each other a look of expectation. The lights in the central chandelier dimmed a little, or I thought they did—I could not be quite certain because of the troubling condition of my eyes. There was an attenuated minute, a minute that I did not take on any more than I had taken on the corner of Sixth and 43rd or the window with the artichokes. I looked at the program —Bach, Schumann, Chopin, Hindemith—an ambitious program, as she had said. There was what I knew to be the usual restlessness behind me and around me—he should be coming on by now, there must have been some minor delay backstage—but it was over before a new murmur could begin. It was he, it was unbelievably he who came through the opened doorway into our silence and our sight, and my mind cried out to him to go back, go back. I protested the moment, I wanted a reversal of time, I wanted it all undone. His face glistened with a residue of rubbed-away sweat and was the color of clay. His eyes were wide open and fearfully fixed—I could lean forward as far as I liked, he would not see me, he could not see anything. He walked with a graceless stiffness, forcing one step after the other, like a man with the inexorable armed representatives of the law behind him, compelling him on toward his execution.

"He doesn't look like himself—he must be nervous," said the blond woman in front of me, permitting her voice to rise a little under the applause. It was solid applause, but it did not seem to hearten him, and I doubted that he heard it. Stooped, with his shoulders slanted forward and his hands stiff at his sides, he stopped in front of the Steinway and made a bow, a short and scornful bow, not from the waist, only with his cropped head. He let himself down on the big stool with the black leather padding, and I thought irrationally and horribly of metal discs with wires being strapped to the ankles and the wrists. He had to lower the bench, and he went jerkily through the awkward business,

292

staring straight before him. "He's always like that," whispered the gentleman with the blonde. "He'll be all right once he starts." I looked wildly at the program, realizing suddenly that I did not even know what Bach he was about to play. It was the E flat minor Prelude and Fugue from the Well-Tempered Clavichord, slow and not too difficult technically. It was a wise choice: calling for subtlety instead of pyrotechnics, it would show his painstaking musicianship to advantage at the same time as it gave him a chance to get the feel of the keyboard and steady himself—so I tried to believe, staring at the stooped arc of his back and the side view of his livid face, seeing his hands rub against each other and move impulsively toward the keys.

Yet once they were on the keyboard the blunt-ended fingers seemed capable of their work, capable enough to make it possible for me to rest against the back of my chair again with a shaking sigh. That he should be playing the Prelude at all, considering the sickening minute of doubt begotten by his manner and his face, that the dramatic recitatives should move to their climaxes and subside again was wonder enough. If the music was not taking on the fervor and intensity I had always attached to it, there were compensations: not only was he getting through the thing, but he was rendering it with the "architectonic" qualities attributed to him on the back of the record envelope. In fact—and it seemed to me that the experts around me were warming to a similar realization—he was giving the all too familiar piece of music a new effect by treating it as he had treated the Brahms in the recording, as a contrapuntal composition rather than a rhapsodic one; and here and there my darting vision sighted a nod, a pair of attentively raised eyebrows, an appreciative smile. I was not yet able to smile myself—the tension in his stooped back and his taut cheek was too obvious; but a faint effervescence of reassurance, less likely to call up smiling than hysterical laughter, stirred in me as he brought the Prelude to its conclusion. And while

293

he was holding down the final chord I sensed a certain settling, a relaxation around me that seemed to indicate a shift from doubt to tentative confidence.

Well-founded confidence, I thought, as he moved into the Fugue with assurance and quiet impressiveness. A wise choice, an excellent choice—the music was subtle and mystical, it could stand in the earnest simplicity with which he executed it, and he would let it speak for itself. It spoke so well that there was an instant when I almost shrugged off my fears: he should have played for us in the Mozart Festival, he should have played for Cathie or anybody who wanted him to—the voices emerged in lyric spaciousness over our heads, the thematic transformations were brought out clearly but unobtrusively. Except, except—there was something now that did not quite conform with the pattern set for it in memory. Had he gone off, or was my recollection out of joint? The growing conviction that he was floundering drove me forward in my seat again, staring at his back, too frightened to look at his face. He *had* forgotten, and a crazy notion went off like a gong in my head —the notion that this Fugue was the same one which Harrison had heard him trying over and over in the empty building months ago. Now he had gone back to the beginning, but with such complete poise that there had been scarcely a discernible pause. Admirable as his control was, I saw nevertheless that it was purely external: now that I could bring myself to look, I saw the muscles twitching in his cheek, I saw the fixed, glazed white of his eye. Seeing these things, I was not shocked that the hoped-for recall was not given to him when he arrived at the same perilous place. I only sat in numb consternation while he faltered, skipped a good third of the remainder of the piece, and moved lamely into the brief rising sequence that brings it to its close.

"Too bad—he really muffed it, didn't he?" said somebody behind me in a compassionate whisper.

294

There was applause which my ears, as strangely undependable as my sight, could not measure with much accuracy. I saw him drag out a handkerchief and rub it between his stiff, dark hands, and that gesture brought him into the present, transformed him into himself, made his suffering so immediate that I could not tolerate the possibility of failure, I must look for every palliative. Most of the non-musicians here tonight—and no audience, no matter how select, can boast of more than a smattering of experts —most of the non-musicians would not even have realized that he had forgotten and been forced to start over again: he had saved his face with them at least by his masterful recovery. As for the others, they were not likely to take an instance of forgetting too seriously; they would probably not regard it as anything more than a minor hazard of the art. Everybody, including the critic from the *Times,* who was talking behind his lifted program to his companion— everybody with any musical sophistication would know that a Fugue is the easiest thing on earth to forget and that the performer, once he has forgotten, is simply sold out, has no starting place to return to in the intricate body of the piece, can only go back to the beginning and hope to God . . . The applause had thinned out to silence, and a few late comers were still slipping in through the three rear doors that had been opened to admit them. It was cruel that he should be forced to sit in the public eye and wait like that—he was putting his handkerchief back in his pocket and moving restlessly forward on the bench—it was cruel, too, to watch him, and I looked up at *her* loge in the balcony. She was smiling and talking with false animation to the young conductor. The orchid on her shoulder trembled with the forced energy of her gestures, and the luminous whiteness of her skin was gone: a deep flush covered her throat and face from the round neckline of her dress to the roots of her hair.

He flung himself into the first movement of the Schumann Fantasia as a man who is deathly afraid of water

295

might fling himself into a river. The impetuous ardor of the opening was more weirdly marred under his stiff fingers than it had been in Cathie's first rigid performance: where there should have been passionate eloquence there was a savage drive, made the more terrible by the convulsive thrusts from his shoulders and the glassy whiteness of his eye; what Schumann had conceived as a fervent outpouring, he was playing in something close to hate. I thought of Cathie, too, when the seething waves of arpeggios subsided into the lyric second theme: his desperate effort to render the candor and tenderness of that was as much a travesty as hers had been, and he knew his failure; his tight mouth was twisted into the familiar line of contempt—contempt for the ingenuous music and for himself. In the slow middle section that follows, marked "In the manner of a legend," he regained some hold on himself, but, though he played with a subdued quiet that I would not have thought possible after his driving beginning, it was the quietness of nervelessness, the calm of disintegration. Still—or so I told myself, shaken by the fierce beating of my heart as he came out of it into the recapitulation—he had recovered enough to play with a little more control, a little more unity, and was managing something that might have been acceptable if the difference in the tempo of the repeated material had not made it obvious that his nerves were shattered beyond the possibility of his carrying out a coherent concept of the piece. As for the tranquil, sustained conclusion, I could not tell what sort of effect he was getting in that: the serenity of the music was so horribly at variance with the trembling of his hands, uninvolved now with technical exigencies, fearfully exposed in their quaking effort to simulate repose.

The gentleman in front of me gave his blond companion a look of condolence, as if it were she who had been doing the suffering. I jerked around in the charged moment between movements and looked again at Mrs. McIvor's loge, but I did not see her; I was distracted by the sight of Cathie and Vincent, who must have come down earlier from the back of the balcony and taken empty seats within the line of my vision—I had never seen Vincent so hunched and brooding, I had never seen Cathie so ghostly white in the face. Both of them, bending far forward with their chins supported on their clenched hands, had the air of terrified gargoyles. Liz Stoddard and George Bauer also floated out of the ranked anonymity three or four rows behind them, but their faces were vague and blurred to my strained eyes. Before the agonizing business on the stage began again, I could get only a brief glimpse of Mrs. McIvor—somebody had draped her mink around her, possibly because she had shuddered and was trying to pretend that she was cold.

I knew in that instant how much my hopes for him had dwindled, how little I asked. I no longer expected him to give us a performance that could be credited, like his recording of the Brahms intermezzi, with minor distinction. It would be enough if he could drive himself through the next two movements, it would be enough if he could reach the end of the Fantasia without breaking down irreparably, and I took a grim relief in the fact that the steady, crashing chords at the opening of the second movement should be affording him a support for his shaking hands. The tension, the hard strokes with full arm were no drawback to him here; they were actually generating a mounting excitement in the audience; and even in the quieter parts that tension did not fall away—the regular march-like rhythms had channeled his erratic attack and given it a kind of goading steadiness. If the lyric interlude lacked conviction, its impersonal and casual manner was better than the false emotion he had brought to similar passages in the first movement; it was simply another obstacle to be surmounted, and he surmounted it decently, moving with assurance into the restatement of the march theme. If he missed several of the tricky octave leaps in the conclusion, they were a well-known and consciously contrived hazard for any pianist, and he did himself no great discredit. Some members of the audience, caught up as I was in the drama of his triumphant emergence out of what he had seemed doomed to fail in, could not keep from expressing themselves before he raised his hands from the final crashing chord in a small, congratulatory burst of applause.

He did not respond to the clapping, though he started a little at the sound of it. His face was a stern, inexpressive mask, and at first I thought he had been affronted at applause between movements or at what he might have taken for an attempt to encourage him in his time of stress. But in an instant I realized that this was not so: the somber cast of his features, the motionlessness of his body slanted forward toward the keyboard, the dead stillness of his hands on his knees were outward manifestations of an effort at profound concentration. Having beaten his way through twenty minutes of burning hell, having somehow won to the bleak ridge on the other side of it, there was nothing left in him that could concern itself with others. Exposed and vulnerable as he was, he was yet completely removed: he was trying to let his tormented spirit be gathered unto itself and pass into the music utterly.

And when he began the final movement after a prolonged silence, I knew that for the first time this evening he was absorbed in the music, had rendered himself over totally to the murmurous background of arpeggios and to the grave melody of exaltation that beautifully and unobtrusively detached itself. His silent communion was bearing pure and faultless fruit: in the high, fervent, descending melody that followed, there was a flawlessness which was more than the exquisite balance between the singing of the right hand and the muted brooding of the left—he had attained to a perfection of feeling in which every nuance had a rightness that could have issued only from complete identification with the music itself. To hear him rise to that,

298

to know what he had attained to after what he had suffered was to be drawn up with him toward an unhoped-for consummation. Tears coursed over my cheeks, and I did not have the strength to wipe them away. He had passed now to the high-hearted theme, the one whose progress toward its climax is twice withheld by sudden modulations before it moves in its third appearance to its triumphant fulfillment. A soaring theme—confident, buoyant—offered to us with a rare coupling of ardor and purity. . . . But at its second appearance he faltered, and the faltering was like the flutter of a bird shot in the midst of flight. He paused irresolute, he could not remember whether he was playing the theme in its second or its third appearance. An audible sigh, an awed and compassionate murmur rose around me, and I could not believe in the silence, the stricken and noteless quiet that closed in. Yet there he sat, his hands trembling over the keys, fearfully unable to go on. The restless murmur strengthened, took on a questioning tone, and his hands dropped to his sides, hanging over the edge of the bench in weighty helplessness. He got up then, supporting himself on the corner of the piano, and, averting his face from us, walked rigidly across the brown carpeting and off the stage.

Now that he was gone, the subdued hum became much louder and more articulate. Here and there, with the object of compassion departed from the scene, above the embarrassed speculations as to what could have happened, the need of the expert to flourish his knowledge asserted itself in phrases like "pathological forgetting" and "no control." People were getting out of their seats, and I got out of mine and turned and stared at the balcony. *She* was going—I saw nothing of her but a swinging length of mink —and through the empty space where she and her party had been the students were plainly visible, drawn out of their seats by the same impulse of fright and pity that had assailed me, Vincent and Cathie close together, holding onto each other's hands. The noise grew louder, became a babble with a kind of whine of complaint sounding over it. Then the voice of authority, twangy and nasal, made itself heard: "Ladies and gentlemen, just a moment, please, may I have your attention?" Somebody fat in a dark suit had come out and was standing in the middle of the abandoned stage. "We regret to announce that Mr. Sanes is unable to continue with the recital. If you mail in your ticket stubs with a self-addressed envelope, your money will be refunded. Do not stop at the box office. May I repeat: Do not stop at the box office, mail in your ticket stubs with a self-addressed envelope."

Doubtless the audience was reasonably well-conducted, doubtless the amount of chatter and standing in the aisles to conduct the post-mortem was no more than could be expected under the circumstances; yet it seemed to me that I was caught in a riot—every look was an assault, every remark was an affront, and even the slightest brushing against me seemed to cause me pain. I pressed halfway up the aisle with urgency, and then stopped and let myself lag along with the rest of them. Why should I hurry? Where did I imagine I was going? Not backstage—I would not dare to go near him in his exigency and his shame, and furthermore, *she* would be with him now, *she* would be carrying him off from the scene of his disgrace; it was she, not I, who had been appointed to do the offices of consolation . . . "Allow me to repeat once more: Mail in the stubs of your tickets," said the insistent voice behind me. I could not find my scarf in my sleeve, I had left it in the seat behind me, but I did not think of going back. If my mind worked at all, it was only to wonder whether his clothes had been soaked with the sweat of his ordeal and how it would be with him when his body, wet and shaken, was exposed to the bitter cold.

For I was in the lobby now, and icy drafts were moving all around me. I stopped there, unable myself to face the chill and the glaring brightness of the street beyond the

300

opened doors. Small groups had gathered along the white walls and were talking woundingly about his weaknesses and even more woundingly about other unrelated things—it seemed to me that I was the only one in the lobby who was alone. I allowed the turgid tide of people to edge me into an angle between the wall and the ticket office; I had no impulse to hide from the students—whether they saw me or not seemed of small consequence. In fact, my sense of isolation made me long for their fellowship, and I was glad when I saw their known faces moving past the unfamiliar ones and toward me; even George Bauer, whom I scarcely knew, seemed like a friend. The four of them made a semi-circle around me, objectionable because they were blocking an exit, and a target for curious glances because Cathie was crying. Short and soundless sobs shook her shoulders, and her bony face was white and wet with tears. "Oh, Miss Hartmann, wasn't it awful? I'm so sorry for him, I'm so terribly sorry for him," she said.

They were all terribly sorry for him. All I could sense in any of them was the immediately accessible compassion of the young—in Vincent, who had much to forgive him, in gangling, raw-nerved George Bauer who had so often been the whipping boy on whom he had vented his bitterness, in pale little mediocre Liz Stoddard who had come along for the free ride to Philly and the hell of the thing. They were so sorry for him that they quite forgot to ask me how I had happened to turn up when I had said I meant to stay at home for a rest—after the cataclysmic reversal that had taken place on the stage before them, a little matter like my change of mind could scarcely engage their curiosity. But they were as forlorn and as much in need of companionship as I was: they would not hear of my taking the night train back—I must come with them, there was plenty of room, they had blankets too, we would keep each other warm. And the prospect of driving in their company, even the long way home through Philadelphia, seemed better to

301

me than the sleepless, lurching ride in the night train, where I would be solitary and forced into concentrated thought when there was no purpose in thinking and nothing really to think about. My sole protest was a feeble one: "But I've got to get my overnight bag, I left it in one of those lockers in the station."

"Oh, Vincent can pick it up for you," Liz Stoddard said. "He's got to go for the car anyway, and it's only a few blocks from there. He'll pick it up for you, and you can go back with us. Please do."

Cathie, still sobbing, looked at me beseechingly and nodded her head, and I found the locker key and gave it to Vincent. George Bauer was going with him, and the rest of us were to have some coffee in an appointed place on 40th Street and appear in front of the restaurant, ready to be picked up, in exactly half an hour. Cathie came around beside me and put her arm through mine, and I stepped with her into the thinning crowd on the sidewalk. But before we crossed, there was a sickening moment when I felt that I had committed myself to something unthinkable, something monstrous, that to walk away from the building in which he must still be sitting in some little backstage room was against every sane and direct impulse in my body. It was a black moment, a moment shot through with icy pain, in which I felt every one of my ties to him wrenched like a pulled nerve, so that my jaw loosened and my arm began to shake and I stopped on the curb and could not bring myself to step down. "Is anything the matter, Miss Hartmann?" Liz Stoddard asked in her mild, piping voice. I could scarcely tell her that it seemed to me very likely that I would never lay eyes on him, never touch him again, so I told her all I needed was a cup of coffee—I was tired, I was cold.

Chapter 21

UNDER ANY OTHER circumstances, I would have been uncomfortable and constrained in Vincent's car. It was an old car, and the heater was ineffectual against the ten degree weather. Vincent and Cathie sat together in the front seat, as lovers should; and I sat in the middle of the back, between Liz Stoddard, with whom I had always had a relationship so cool and formal that it had seldom included touch, and George Bauer, whom I knew intimately only in the sense that I had listened to some of his most painful humiliations through the wall. All three of us were covered to the chin with an Indian blanket; we generated and shared a communal warmth that would ordinarily have seemed intolerably personal to me; and neither of them gave a thought to sitting properly apart. But my consciousness of the crowding was an afterthought—I was not aware of it spontaneously: I was neither surprised nor put out when Liz Stoddard played with the fingers of my left hand under the rough folds of the blanket or when George Bauer let his big bony knee rest either filially or unconsciously against mine.

For we also—I thought of it when we gained the height and the relative openness of the Pulaski Skyway—we also, though in a lesser way, had been dragged through his hell and left depleted on the empty ridge beyond it. As strangers will talk nakedly on the scene of a disaster or mere acquaintances will embrace at a funeral, so we accepted each other without inhibition or reservation as we moved away from the place where he had suffered and was still suffering shame—I felt the tightening pull of that withdrawal in my nerves with every mile. And out of my fright and my exhaustion, a strange fondness for the two on either side of me took its irrational growth: Liz Stoddard was a nice, poor little thing, bony, like a handful of twigs beside me; and even if George Bauer had not been as attractive as he was in his person—he was one of those long-faced, loose-jointed boys who move like bewildered colts and mean nobody any harm—I would have been drawn to him by his inability to think of anything but Arthur, by his frequent shakings of the head and his repeated sighs.

The passing headlights and the lights of apartment houses and factories showed large and soft on the misted windows. Every now and again, we had to open one of those windows a crack so that the windshield could clear a little, and it was surprisingly untroubling to know that the steam was our accumulated breaths. Cathie was crying—she had left off in the restaurant for propriety's sake but could let herself go again in the safety of our closed, moving community. Every few minutes Vincent would reach out automatically, but none the less tenderly for that, to touch her arm or knee. "Wasn't it awful the way his hands shook?" George Bauer said, as if that particular detail had fastened onto him and he could not bear the grasp of it alone.

"Awful, just awful," said Liz Stoddard. "It was bad in the Fugue, but in the last movement of the Schumann it was terrible. My own start to shake every time I think of it—just feel them."

I felt her hand—it seemed the companionable thing to do—and then closed my fingers on my onyx bracelet. It was something to hold onto, something to relieve a sharper need

304

and blot out a shattering fantasy: if I could take his hands, if I could only take his hands and open them and kiss them, dry palms and blunt fingers over and over until they were quieted, until they and I were at peace. . . .

"I never expected him to break down in the Fugue like that," said Vincent, talking straight into the windshield, against the flying light-beams. "He looked pretty upset when he walked on, but the way he did the Prelude, I thought he had everything under control."

"You were up pretty close, weren't you, Miss Hartmann?" Liz asked me, bending forward to peer uselessly through the blackness into my face. "You could see him better than we could. Didn't you think he looked terrible when he came on stage?"

"Yes, terrible," I said, unable to loose my hold on the imaginary hands, chafing them, parting them, laying them along my cheeks, where, if they trembled, they trembled with longing and tenderness.

"Like he was going to the electric chair," said George Bauer, sighing. "The way he looked—I wouldn't want to wish it on my worst enemy."

I wondered in the brief brightness who *was* George Bauer's worst enemy, if Arthur wasn't. Vari-colored clusters of lights—white, orange, red, yellow—floated beyond us, beside us, below us: the Skyway was passing over one of the string of New Jersey cities, which one I didn't know. And I was more appalled than relieved to realize that time had already begun its work in me: the hands, the rigid walk, the stooped shoulders—these I could remember, these I could still see, but I no longer could evoke a sharp image of the doomed and ghastly face. It was behind me, always farther behind me, in some room I did not know; and to give myself over to the westward push on the Pulaski Skyway, to let myself be borne away from it, over New Brunswick or Elizabeth, was to submit to the caprices of an insane fate or a reasonless God.

"He seemed to be going at the Fugue pretty much the

305

way he did the Brahms things on that record," said Vincent, humanely stubborn about keeping the discussion on a musical plane. "You'd never expect anybody who played like that to run into the sort of trouble he had tonight."

"No!" said Liz, "that's right—he was all right on the record. And those songs—those Mozart songs he played for you, Miss Hartmann—I thought he did them very well, and so did everybody else."

We had left the nameless city behind us, and the long stretch of headlight-chopped darkness which we traveled now was charged with a demand for some sort of clarification. I had it and I should have held it out to them for the sake of our new companionship, but I could not bring myself to speak: I did not want to be the one to anatomize his frailties. It was George Bauer who, after fidgeting against me, took the obligation upon himself. "Well, now, that's pretty obvious to me, Liz, though I can see why you wouldn't get it, because you're a singer and you don't usually have to deal with the long, complicated things. Mr. Sanes —his trouble is that he forgets. When he's playing accompaniments, he doesn't have to worry about that, he's got the music right up there in front of him—that's why the songs came off so well."

His face appeared before me in another guise, almost as annihilating as the one that time had just erased for me. I saw it as I had seen it in Mrs. McIvor's suite, turning childish and secretive while her voice went on about how he always took a score to his recording sessions though he never had to use it—the bitter mouth was softened by the peculiar and shamefaced smile.

Cathie blew her nose, turned around in the front seat, and addressed us in a clouded, throaty voice. "That's it, of course. That's why all those months he never gave us a performance."

"It isn't only forgetting, either," said George Bauer, sighing and subsiding against the plastic-covered back of

306

the seat. "When he forgets, he gets nervous and his whole interpretation goes to pieces. It's a crime to make anybody with that kind of trouble walk out on a stage without a score."

Even if a truck had not somehow gotten in front of us and made further consecutive talk impossible by clankings and chuggings, none of us in the car would have voiced what we were thinking in the noisy darkness: that nobody had forced him to do anything, that he had carried his secret weakness onto a public stage through no will but his own. A wild curiosity banged away at me in crazy time with whatever iron object was clanking in the back of the truck: Why had he done it? What dark urgencies hounding him out of his past had driven him to do this murderous thing to himself?

"Come to think of it," said George Bauer after the truck had pulled into the outside lane and let us pass, "the worst laying out he ever gave me was the time I forgot in the last movement of the Beethoven E minor. I went off on a wrong repeat, and the way he jumped on me you would have thought I broke down in my graduation recital."

The stillness in the car was alive now with recollections of his cruelties. His cold voice, his scornful face, his little snorting laugh were with us, the more painful to remember because they were coupled with what we had seen an hour ago. If the hand that had brought down the lash was a crippled hand, the scars of the wounds it had inflicted were still smarting, nevertheless. As the fluorescent-lighted windows of a factory assailed us through the frosty glass—purplish, blinding—I heard them again one after the other, all the merciless and abusive phrases that had come to me through the wall. "He certainly let Lorrie Fawcett have it," said Liz Stoddard. "Lorrie Fawcett says he told her—"

"Everybody knows what he told Lorrie Fawcett," said Vincent curtly. "I'm sure he told her plenty, even if we count out the hysterics. But the fact remains, she played like

307

some sloppy twelve-year-old and he's got her to a stage where she's bearable, which is quite an accomplishment in her case."

"But why did he do it?" It was driven out of Cathie partly by a sudden stop—we were in a pile-up of traffic at a turn-off to another New Jersey city—and partly by the turmoil of her spirit, dragged from the warm solution of her pity and plunged into that icy past. "Why did he have to be so hard on us? Why did he hate us so?"

"Oh, I don't think he hated you," I said, and immediately wanted to withdraw that piece of spurious consolation. It was not true, and I had no right to offer them anything but truth: only sturdy, indestructible actuality can live on the bleak ridge beyond catastrophe. "Or maybe he did hate you —I don't know—" I broke off, appalled by my awareness that I was speaking in the past, making of whatever bitter involvement there had been between him and them a finished thing, abandoned and miles behind us now. "At least, he hated part of you. It had to be like that—it couldn't have been otherwise, considering what he was like tonight."

Nobody said anything, even when the traffic started to move again. As we resumed speed on an emptier stretch, I knew that they were waiting for me to take on my pedagogical mantle, to annotate and elucidate; and I was at a disadvantage, partly because it was *his* spirit that they were requiring me to strip naked for their benefit and partly because my own understanding was inchoate and still tinged with passion, not ready as yet to be committed to speech— I could not even word it for myself. "It's hard for any of us to imagine the kind of spot he was in," I said at last, regretting for the first time that there had been an unspoken agreement not to fill the closed car with cigarette smoke. "Because he *was* in an awful spot, you know. To stake your whole life on one possibility—to stand or fall on just one thing, the way he did—to have no life outside of that— it's awful, so awful we can't even imagine how it would be.

308

All the time he was at school it must have been that way with him. There it was, staring him in the face—how he'd have everything or nothing after tonight."

"That's right, that's about the size of it," said George Bauer. "We were just an aggravation to him—all we did was fluster the poor son of a bitch. Imagine having Lorrie Fawcett on your ear when you were in a state like that!"

"And if you're not sure of yourself, if you've got suspicions about yourself always gnawing away at you," I said, raising my voice against a bus passing on the left of us, "then you can't let other people alone, either: you've got to be probing all the time for the weaknesses in everybody else. Whatever looks pretty good to you, whatever has the success you're afraid you'll never get—you hate it, it's a threat to you, so you've got to pull it down. If an audience goes wild for anybody else, you've got to pick at him, the best you can say for him is that he's 'adequate.' There's nothing for you to do but sneer at the world."

"But none of us were good enough to give him any worries on *that* score, Miss Hartmann." It was Cathie who had said it, turning front again, moving toward the middle of the seat so that she could rest her shoulder against Vincent's. She had come a long way since the day when she had beaten against the walls of her limitations in my office; but, even so, such a confession of the abandoning of high-hearted dreams would not have been possible anywhere but now and here, after the disaster, in the communal dark.

"Oh, but he had to hate the weak ones as well as the strong ones," I said, closing my eyes against the distraction of streaming lights, knowing that this was the heart of it for my companions. "George hit on it—George knows what I'm driving at—if Mr. Sanes had to carry around in him the horrible notion that he was going to forget sometime in the middle of a performance, it would naturally drive him wild to see another person forget. It was pretty much the same thing with Cathie and the Schumann—somewhere down

309

deep he must have known he didn't have the temperament and the passion for the thing. And when he heard her doing it in a way he didn't like, it was as if *he* was the one that was doing it—he went to pieces, it was more than he could bear. But actually he wasn't lashing out at Cathie—she just happened to get in his way when he was beating himself. I wish you could see it like that, I wish you could believe me—if you did, whatever he said or did to you might hurt you less—it might even be possible for some of you to forgive him. God knows, he paid up enough for it tonight."

I was glad for a transitory stretch of darkness, for my throat was tight and my eyes were flooded. In spite of myself, I turned and stared for the first time through the curved and misty back window at the road behind us. It was a narrowing band of concrete, lightly marked with a smattering of new snow and bordered with small, bare trees, some of them white birches whose trunks showed ghostly in the dark. Liz Stoddard, curious to see what I was seeing, leaned over and looked too. "Oh, it's begun to snow a little," she said.

"It's blowing away, though," said Vincent reassuringly —and I was sorry to hear it. I would have welcomed anything—a heavy snowfall or roads glazed over with ice— anything to stop the crazy westward progress away from reason, away from love.

"But the saddest thing about the whole business," said Cathie, turning her wan and puckered face to us in the red violence of a roadside barbecue, "is the way we're sitting here and talking about him. We keep harping on what was wrong with him, and he did some beautiful things tonight. The beginning of the third movement of the Schumann —the way he played that—I was never so moved in my life. I'm sure he would have played it all like that, if only he'd had the score in front of him."

I knew that, with the score in front of him, he would have done nothing of the kind. The phrase detaching itself

310

exquisitely from the murmur of the arpeggios, the fervent descent of the second theme, the confident singing that had come out over our heads in all its ardor and its purity—he had attained to that high and transitory perfection only because of his earlier suffering, only on finding himself absolved and exalted on the other side of hell. They were talking, she and George Bauer, about how much he knew, how much he could teach them, and I scarcely listened. It was a dream—he could teach them only a little more of what he had taught them in the past, if, shattered as he was, he could teach anybody anything. It was a dream, but I did not stop them, I could not bring myself to gainsay them. If the rest of the world turned its back on him—as it surely would—I wanted him to have at least this much. Our speed was increasing; it was as if their longing to carry him out of his disgrace were propelling us forward; another New Jersey city streamed past us like a multicolored comet with a yellow tail. "Now that we know the way things stand with him, maybe we'll know better how to act with him—maybe we won't get on his nerves so much," George Bauer said.

Liz Stoddard, who had been playing with my fingers, suddenly dropped them. "But do you think he'll come back—do you really think so?" she asked, dragging the blanket forward with her. "I've been taking it for granted that he'd stay away for good—just never turn up at all."

I was glad that my hand was free of hers because I felt it turning clammy and cold. Not because I was shocked—her conjecture was precisely the one that had been floating in my own mind, too large and dark to be confined to words—but because the warmth was driven out of me by a cold wash of desolation. "Just never turn up at all" was an annihilating phrase, even when it was uttered in her piping little voice, and I put my head far back against the seat, out of the light of an oncoming car, hoping that none of my companions would see my face.

311

"Maybe you're right," said Cathie. "I've thought of that, too."

"You're all over-dramatizing it," said Vincent without too much conviction. "He'll probably feel terrible tonight and maybe even worse tomorrow—but he's got a whole week before he has to show up, you know. Ten to one, you'll find him in his practise room when you get back to school next Tuesday. He'll be all right, he'll pull himself together, you'll see."

"I wonder what he's doing now." George Bauer addressed the remark over his shoulder to the road beyond the misted glass. "You don't think he'd be sitting around by himself, do you?"

"Of course not!" I said it so loudly that Vincent's eyes sought mine in the mirror above him. "He has his friends—he's got plenty of friends up there, and they wouldn't think for a minute of leaving him by himself."

And yet—my heart was sluggish, my hands were trembling under the blanket—and yet it had occurred to me for the first time that Mrs. McIvor might not be the one to decide whether she would or would not sit with him or lie beside him while the sick night wore itself away into the bleak dawn. It was possible—I could see it taking place —it was possible that he had sent her away from him, had said ineffaceable words to her in the little room behind the stage, had cut off forever in his shame and his self-loathing whatever connection had been between them, had walked out of that emptied and darkened building alone and free . . . Free—the crazy, uneven rhythm of my heart began to race at that. Alone—my pulse went sluggish again, I was so cold and qualmish that I let myself sag back, without inhibition, against George Bauer's shoulder and knee.

"That's good—I'm glad to hear it," said Vincent. "A lot of people around, a lot of drinks, a lot of noise—"

"I wouldn't want it, I couldn't stand it," said Cathie. "If a thing like that happened to me, I couldn't put up with

312

anybody or anything. After a thing like that, I think I'd have to kill myself."

I felt the car sliding to a stop on the shoulder of the road before I knew that I had shouted to Vincent to stop it. There was thin snow and there were trees—black and whitish trunks, I saw them. But I also saw his bloody, slashed wrists—I knew he would do it violently, in his hate for himself—I also saw his dead, unreachable, mocking face. Love—all the withheld love in my body—surged up against that frozen image; I could not live, I would not live if he were dead.

"Are you sick, Miss Hartmann?" said George Bauer, getting his arm in under my shoulders and holding me gently against him.

"No. But I've got to go back. I've got to go back to New York and look for Mr. Sanes."

There was a long silence and an exchange of glances among them. Everything that I had hidden away from them, they saw and understood: they were looking through me totally, and I did not have the strength even to regret my vulnerability. Cathie kneeled on the seat and turned around and groped through the Indian blanket to give me the solace of her touch. "Do you have any idea where to look for him?" she said.

"No, I don't, but I know the names of some of his friends, and there's always a telephone book."

"Yes, of course," said Vincent. "We can make it back faster than we came. I was taking my time, and the traffic's lighter, too. I guess we could get you back there in about three quarters of an hour."

Nobody protested, not even Liz Stoddard, whose fiancé was sitting up for her in some house in Philadelphia. Cathie lighted a cigarette and put it into my hand, and George opened a crack in the back window. We made a U-turn— it was easy to make, the road *was* emptier now—and were on our way back to the city whose vastness and complexity

313

I did not dare even to contemplate. I saw more on the way back than I had seen on the way out, partly because the windows were clearing now that the car was colder, and partly because I stared at anything, everything, trying to blot out the vision of the dead face.

Chapter 22

THE DRUGSTORE AT which they left me—they were reluctant to leave me, but I made them do it —was on Eighth Avenue somewhere in the Forties. I had probably passed it dozens of times while I was living in New York, and it gave me a nightmare impression to realize that I had never been aware of its existence. It was noisy and glaringly bright, and it had a sweet and steamy smell, which made me a little sick at my stomach as I walked to the back to find the telephone books.

The sight of the solid bank of five directories, lined up on a stand outside the row of booths, unnerved me: how could I look at them without thinking how hard it would be in such a city to find a man who had walked away and slashed his wrists? I found myself totally incapable of swinging out the Manhattan volume; I stood stupidly at the stand for several seconds with a sense of complete helplessness before it broke upon me that my trouble was my inability to use my hands—my overnight bag was in one of them, and my purse was in the other. I set my encumbrances down on the streaked asphalt tiles, took the Manhattan Directory, which frustrated me with its chain, and told myself that my business, no matter how preposterous, was nevertheless simple and well-defined. L for Lindsay—very little between La and Li—and if the columns of Lindsays were appalling at first glance, I could thank God for Hansford, there couldn't be two Lindsays with such a crazy name.

He was there, blessedly there, with an address on East 56th Street. It was not until after I had dialed and could hear the low ring sounding in his apartment that I wondered what I would say to him, and that wondering was brief, stifled almost immediately by the fear that he was not going to answer the phone. It rang three times, and I was already resting my shoulder in the weakness of my fright against the pressed metal lining of the booth when I heard the click of his receiver coming off. He said "Hello" breathlessly twice before I could gather the force to answer him. "Is that Mr. Lindsay?" I said.

"Yes."

"This is Frieda Hartmann—"

"Frieda? Are you calling long distance?"

"No—I'm here—I heard him—I was in the audience—"

"Are you with him now?"

Every affectation had dropped from his voice. It was pitiably naked in its tentative hopefulness, and my heart went hollow inside me when I realized that he knew as little as I. "No, Hansford, I haven't seen him. He didn't even know I came up," I said.

"Oh . . ."

"What about you?" I could not restrain myself, I had to demand what I knew was not forthcoming. "Didn't you see him afterwards—not at all?"

"No, Frieda, I didn't. I saw that she—I saw that Julie McIvor went backstage, so I didn't go back. I figured that with her there I wouldn't be able to do much for him, and there *were* some little things I could try to do if I stayed in the hall. Some of the other fellows from the papers were hanging around, and I went and tried to do what I could

316

with them, to put in a good word for him wherever I could. Maybe it wasn't worth it—it certainly wasn't much. But it was a good while before I got backstage, and she wasn't there, and neither was he. The lights were out and they were locking up back there, and both of them were gone."

I saw an image of Hansford Lindsay standing desolate in the darkness. I knew what he was suffering, and I also knew that I was not a person with whom he could want to share his distress, and yet I could not thank him and hang up and leave him to himself. "Do you think he might—do you think he was so upset that he might do something—" I said, pressing my shoulder against the cold metal that lined the booth.

"Honest to God, Frieda, I don't know. I've thought of that, too. Ever since I got home, I haven't thought of anything else."

"Where is he staying?"

"I don't know that, either, but I imagine he must be at the McIvors'. That's where he stayed the last time he was in town."

"And you haven't called him?"

"No, I can't call him. I'm *persona non grata* over there. Besides, he didn't even get in touch with me this trip—he was furious with me about—about what went on when I saw you last. I figure he must know what I'd be thinking, and if he's all right—if he comes out of it and pulls himself together—maybe he'll telephone here. Meanwhile, all I can do is sit and wait."

There was a protracted pause, loud with conversation at the soda fountain, while I considered whether *I* would have the courage to make that call. I knew I could not do it, could not assail her strong fortress with my feeble voice; yet—strangely, very strangely—I began to think I would have the fortitude to assail it with my person: it would be easier for me to knock at her door and demand to know than to dial her number in this steamy little booth, where I felt

317

as if I were smothering, as if my ribs had sunken in and could not be lifted by the diminishing force of my breath. "Do you know where she lives?" I said at last. "If you tell me where she lives, I'll go there and see what I can find out."

"Would you?"

"Yes. I'm afraid to, but I will. Have you got her address?"

"No, but it's on the corner of 74th and Park—the big apartment on the west corner. I know it—I used to go there a long time ago."

"All right, Hansford. I'm sure I can find it. But suppose—" I broke off for an instant, unable to look the prospect in the face— "suppose they aren't there, or *he* isn't there, or I can't get in—then what do I do?"

"I don't know, Frieda. I simply don't know."

"Doesn't he have anybody else? Doesn't he have a family?"

"Oh, yes, he's got a mother and a sister here, but he never goes to see them—I doubt they'll do you much good. I don't even know where they live—I have some vague recollection it's somewhere up in Washington Heights. . . ."

"Well, thanks. Thanks a million."

"If you find anything out—"

"If I find anything out, I'll certainly call you. You can't call me—I'm nowhere—I meant to go back by the night train. But if I know anything, I'll call you. You want me to call you—don't you?—even if it's very late."

"Anytime. All night. All day tomorrow, too—I'll be here until noon and down at the office after that—you can find me there, it's the *Twentieth Century Review*. Call me anyway before you go back home—just in case I should hear something. Thank you ever so much. Good night."

I came out of the booth, picked up my bag and purse, and walked from the warmth of the drugstore into the freezing outdoors. It had a bleak, peculiar look—most of

318

the windows of the shops were darkened, the bars were isolated areas of brash light set far apart, and the Avenue itself was not as it used to be, now that it was changed to a one-way street and the cars and taxis were all streaming north, streaming past me at such a speed that it was hard for me to make one stop since my gestures were confined by the burdens in my hands. I must have been standing there for close to five minutes with a low, wet wind beating at my legs and biting at my gloveless fingers, and the long line of traffic lights had flashed into red for the second time before a taxi pulled up and let me get in.

I told the driver, a jocular big-faced man with thick and shining glasses, that I wanted to go to the corner of Park and 74th. I would have thought that my voice and my manner would discourage conversation, but he turned out to be singularly undiscerning: I had no sooner settled myself in the draughty warmth and the smell of worn leather and stale smoke than he began to talk at a rate that made it impossible for me to collect myself. My overnight bag prompted him to begin a lecture on the sights of the city; and when I let him know I had lived in New York for years, he did not lapse into silence, he merely switched over to another category of entertainment. While we tore recklessly along the avenue, weaving in and out in front of other cars, while we crept along with maddening slowness in the accumulated crosstown traffic of the fifties, while we stopped with jolting suddenness and started with a jerk and a grinding of gears, he told me a series of stories that were the worse for the fact that all of them had to be clean, since I was a woman sitting in the back of his cab alone.

One of the stories was about a little boy who was a financial genius. He had a broken-down dog, and he told his friend on the way to school one morning that he was going to sell this dog for fifty thousand dollars, and his friend said, "How could you get fifty thousand dollars for a mutt like that?" and he said to wait and see. And the

319

next day—at that point we were edging toward the west corner of 74th street at a pace slowed down to suit the requirements of the story—the next day he met his friend again on the way to school, and he said, "Well, I sold my dog," and his friend said, "How much did you get for him?" and he said, casual-like and nonchalant, "Fifty thousand dollars." And his friend said to him, "Now, how could you get fifty thousand dollars for that broken-down dog?" And he said—the pale front of the big apartment house on the west corner of 74th was there over my shoulder as the story came to its conclusion—he said, "I traded him in for two twenty-five-thousand-dollar cats."

I paid the driver and tipped him too much in my unwillingness to wait for change. Probably it was not as late as I had thought—there were lighted windows, plenty of them, showing yellow in the sheer upward sweep of the sandstone wall. All this I saw as I crossed the pavement; I did not dare to stop and look for fear my courage would collapse. Still rattled, with the preposterous lines of the story about the fifty-thousand dollar dog sounding in my ears, I swung open the weighty glass and bronze of the door and stepped over black and white marble tiles and onto thick grey carpeting. The door had come shut behind me, closing out the whir of traffic and every other noise in the street, before I dared to raise my eyes. The lobby was vast, empty, and luxurious with long narrow tables and large bunches of salmon colored gladioli and small mirrors with ornate gilt frames. There was a deep, comfortable chair not twenty steps away from me, and I longed to walk over and sink down into it. The radiators, covered by gilded lattices, were making a gurgling and clinking sound, and the place was dry with abundant heat, and I was suddenly dull and almost unbearably tired.

I walked around aimlessly, away from the chair and toward a long table, and stopped there, overcome by a wave of hopelessness. Since nobody was in sight and there

320

was no visible row of mailboxes to tell me even whether I was in the right building, I had a senseless conviction that I might stand here for hours or wander fruitlessly about in this aged and hostile luxury until dawn. Now and again certain interior sounds—a laugh, the boom of a closing door, a few detached and incomprehensible sentences— came to me, probably through the shaft of an unseen elevator, from one of the floors above; and a new conjecture unnerved me. Suppose, when her door was opened to me, I would see a falsely hilarious party going on inside; suppose that they—and he—were chatting and drinking as if nothing had happened; suppose her pale, absorbed eyes could outstare anything, even such a thing as they had seen on the stage tonight. What would I say in a case like that? How could I explain what I was doing on her threshold, with blown hair and a stricken face?

I walked toward a shadowy hallway, thinking that the mailboxes might be in it. Some of the muted light of the lobby seeped into the darkness as I came closer, showing a tall, carved chair. On this chair, heavy and erect, with his hands laid with inert propriety along the curved arms, was a stately, benignant, sleeping doorman in a wine-colored uniform. His white hair was brushed back in a wave from his large, lineless, and ruddy face, and his soft mouth was emitting regular snores in little puffs.

He woke out of his sleep like one of the just, serenely and without a start, and fixed me with a pair of blue and stupid eyes. I guess it was the realization that I did not belong there—I was the worse for the ride and inappropriately dressed—that made him so slow about getting the weight of his ponderous body out of the chair.

"Yes, Madam? Can I do anything for you?" His feelings apparently had been wounded by the fact that I had caught him off his dignity, and I doubted he would do anything for me willingly, even if he could.

"I'd like to go up to the McIvor apartment," I said.

"Are they expecting you?" It was a formula calculated to baffle all intruders, and, having said it hundreds of times, he said it with conviction and a kind of cold, assumed gentility.

"No—that is, not exactly. But I understand they're entertaining for a friend of mine, and I just got in from out of town, and I thought—"

He did not offer to fill in the pause. He waited, with his big hands laid lightly together in front of him and his soft mouth and forehead puckering a little, to hear what it was that I had thought; and it was difficult for me to keep my look fastened unwaveringly on his vacant eyes. "I think there's been some sort of a mistake," he said at last, shifting his weight from one large foot to the other. "The McIvors haven't got anybody up there tonight."

"No? Isn't there somebody staying with them? A Mr. Sanes? I was told—"

"There was a gentleman staying with them. He went out with them right after I came on—I'd say half past seven or thereabouts. But they came back some time ago, a little after ten, I guess, and there was just the two of them then. I know that because I took them up myself."

"You're sure?"

"Perfectly sure, Madam." He was safe again in the jargon of his calling—he lifted his chin and squared his big sloping shoulders.

"I want very much to get in touch with Mr. Sanes, the gentleman who was staying with them, and—"

"Well, all I can say is: He didn't come in with them and he hasn't come in since. I've been on duty all the time. I could ring them on the house phone, but I don't like to do that. Ten to one, I'd just be getting them out of bed."

"No, don't bother," I told him, my face and my voice growing disorderly under the impact of two weirdly divergent emotions—fierce joy to know that he was no longer with her, and fright at the realization that another way to

322

reach him—the only likely way left—was gone. "Don't bother, there's been some kind of misunderstanding. Thanks for your trouble. Good night."

As I hurried along the darkened stretch of 74th toward the relative brightness of Lexington, I told myself there was nothing to be gained from weighing conjectures and considering eventualities. One move at a time was all I could sensibly think about, and the next move was to find another telephone book, a task that turned out to be more difficult and time-consuming than anybody would have imagined. It was ten after twelve according to the large clock in the window of a Western Union office, and most of the places that would have had telephone books were shut and dark, with nobody inside: I walked three blocks in the biting wind and crossed the avenue twice, drawn on by lighted windows, only to find that the doors were locked. There was one bar in sight, with a neon dolphin in red and yellow leaping erratically up and down in the window. I had not frequented enough bars in New York to be sure that there would be a telephone book, but I went in nevertheless. It was a sad bar, in spite of the energetic dolphin: two somber men and a solitary woman, sitting far apart at the long counter, were the only visible customers. I had to ask the bartender whether there was a telephone, and he did not answer me—he merely pointed to the shadowy back of the narrow stretch with a discouraged sigh.

I had to open the booth and use the dull, bleary light in it in order to page through the battered Manhattan Directory. Sanes—I was sure it must be a common name— I expected to find half a column at least, and I was irrationally heartened by the fact that there were only two, one on Columbus Avenue and one of West 163rd. The latter gave some color to Hansford Lindsay's guess that Arthur's family lived in Washington Heights, and I put in the dime and dialed the number quickly so that I would not have time to think about what I would say or the fright I would

323

let loose on the other end of the line if I did get hold of some member of his family and he was not there. While the phone was ringing, my suppressed nervousness broke out: the shivering that I had controlled during my long walk in the cold took hold on me. The voice that answered was a female voice, high and light, and it said "Hello" strangely, in two distinct and separate syllables. "Is this Sanes' residence?" I asked as well as I could. My jaw was shaking, and it was hard for me to articulate.

"What? What? Speak louder, please, I cannot hear you."

"Is this Arthur Sanes' residence?"

The woman was not listening. She was making, plainly not to me, a swift, light, eerie series of remarks in Czech or Slovak or Hungarian, some soft and sibilant language that I did not understand. This call was futile—I had uselessly disturbed the sleep of some immigrant family that could not possibly be connected with Arthur—

The voice addressed me again, courteously, in stilted English. "If you will please wait a minute. My son cannot speak to you. My daughter—"

"No, never mind, I'm terribly sorry, I have the wrong number, I beg your pardon," I said, and hung up the phone.

It seemed foolish to bother with the other number since it was nowhere near Washington Heights, but there was no other place for me to call. I was so sure it would lead to nothing that I was not disappointed when the bell kept ringing and ringing; and my disheartenment increased not because nobody came to the phone but because the repeated, answerless ring was foreboding in itself. My fit of shivering had given way to a dead numbness. I hung the phone back on the hook and started toward the counter, wondering whether my dull brain would be stirred into activity if I bought myself a drink. But the faces of those who sat at the counter were too sober—so sullen-sober that to look at them would only increase my ominous gloom, and I

324

hurried down the length of the bar and into the street. I stood in front of the place, staring at the jerking dolphin. My mind was purposeless, empty, and the last voice it had heard echoed automatically in the emptiness. The dolphin leaped and the light female voice went on in Hungarian or Slovak and moved into strange English: "If you will please wait a minute . . . my son . . . my daughter . . . my son cannot speak to you now—" A wild notion that I could not even formulate tore through me, and I turned and walked back into the bar to memorize the address in the battered telephone book.

Chapter 23

IT WAS ALMOST one when I got out of the taxi at the apartment on 163rd Street—a big building grown old in its tawdry youth, its yellow bricks grimy in the light of the street lamps, its cement walk out of repair. In the lobby, beyond the creaking door, there were white plaster walls and some massive fake antiques—chests and benches and chairs—carved with people's initials; some of the smaller tiles in the floor were missing; and everything looked as if it would be greasy to the touch.

There was no doorman to contend with here. The mailboxes were easy to find, and the soiled little cards in them were easy to read in the painful light that streamed through the cheap glass fixtures in the ceiling: "Sanes, Mrs. Martha and Miss Anna, 1-E"—they were on the first floor. It occurred to me that, once I had located 1-E inside, I could go out again and walk along the side of the building and see whether any rooms in the 1-E area were lighted up, but I abandoned the idea. I would ring their bell whether they were awake or asleep, and if I got them out of bed, what could they do but shout at me? I took the passageway to the right of the lobby—it smelled of fried onions, pork chops, and some sort of disinfectant—found the door I was looking for, and pushed the button with all the violence of my assumed courage, knowing perfectly well that I might not dare to push it again.

The door knob startled me by turning almost at once, and the brightly lighted entrance way gave me a silhouette of a person rather than a person—a woman so small and slight that I knew she was the possessor of the light voice that had spoken to me over the telephone. Obviously she had not been in bed: she was fully dressed, trimly belted in at the waistline, and her hair, done up in two neat wings, showed a pale, greyed brown in the light behind her. "Good evening," she said, without surprise.

"Mrs. Sanes?" My heart was going at such a crazy rate that I could not manage more.

"Yes. Are you the lady that called on the telephone to ask for Arthur? He is here."

"Is he all right?"

"He is here. He is in bed. He has a terrible headache." She clapped her hands flat against her cheeks and her temples and rocked her head from side to side. "Such a headache! He had to go to bed with pills," she said.

My purse and my bag slipped out of my hands and I allowed myself to sag against the doorway. The room beyond the entrance—brightly lighted by two fringed lamps and crowded with bulbous green furniture—began to go up and down like a see-saw. I took a deep breath, and it righted itself.

"Excuse me, please, are you Miss Frieda Hartmann?"

"Yes—" It came out of me on a gasp, and she put her small dry hand out of the dark and laid it on mine.

"Come in then, please. Anna! This is Miss Hartmann out here, and she is cold like an icicle. You must please come in now, Miss Hartmann, and sit down in a chair."

Before I could bend over, she had darted in front of me and taken up my purse and bag. Holding them both in one hand and grasping me firmly by the arm with the other, she led me across the entrance and into the room, and steered me toward a large, worn green chair.

Once I was deposited there, she stood in front of me and looked at me with a curiosity too frank to be anything but welcome, especially since it invited me to stare as much as I wished. Everything about her was sharp—sharp blue-grey eyes, sharp narrow nose, small, sharply demarcated lips that would have been beautiful if it had not been for the gap behind them where a tooth was missing. She was dressed in a heavy black skirt and a tan blouse with tucks running crosswise on it; the material was so thin that her arms were visible through the long sleeves—childishly meager arms with sharp elbows and little brittle wrists. "Rest a minute, rest a minute," she said in the thin light voice, rocking her head from side to side to the rhythm of it. "Anna will come and make you coffee. In a second she will come, she is putting on her clothes, she is angry with him because he will not talk, she is sick of the whole business, and so she got undressed and went to bed. Anna! God in heaven, you do not have to dress yourself for a party. Wait—whiskey is better even than coffee, I will give you whiskey. I have it always in the house for my heart—I have such a heart!"

I let my head rest against the back of the chair and watched her as she darted around the room, skimming past the arms of the bulbous overstuffed pieces, getting a glass from a painted tray on a small table, opening something that might have been either a china cupboard or a bookcase and was plainly, by its haphazard display of books and odd dishes, used for both, coming back with glass and whiskey bottle, pouring me a drink. "Drink it down fast, please. That way it works better," she said.

"Are you sure he's all right, Mrs. Sanes?"

"Who knows how he is, Miss Hartmann? He does not say. He comes in and he goes to bed with a terrible headache and he doesn't say a word."

328

"Were you at the concert?"

"Me? At the concert?" She shook her head in a wildly merry negative, swept her hand down half the length of her person in cheerful self-disparagement, and winked in a way that could mean only that I should know better.

"I was at the concert, and—"

"And it was terrible!" She clapped the hand that was free of the whiskey bottle against her cheek, and groaned and rocked her head. "Sure, I can imagine, this time it was really terrible—I could see from his face. I know something is the matter, because he never comes here—but he says nothing. Like he is deaf and dumb, he goes to Anna's room and takes off his coat and takes off his tie and lays down on Anna's bed. Like this—" She stepped a few paces back from me and executed another dramatic gesture, crooking her arm and laying it over her eyes. "Not a word. Only like this. So he has been for three hours."

"Hasn't he said anything at all to you?" I asked, assailed by a nameless fright.

"All he says is 'Get out of here and leave me alone!'" She laughed her light little laugh. "He is all right—you must not worry for him. When the telephone rang, he came out in the hall, and he said it must be you, making a call to him long distance—"

"Did he say anything else?"

"No, not anything else, he went back again to bed. But he did not close the door—he left it open this much—" she raised two fingers—"to listen if it will ring again. Excuse me, please, but you should drink the whiskey. You look worse than him—you are cold like a piece of ice and white like somebody dead."

I drank, but not very fast: the whiskey burned raw in my throat and choked me, and the water stood in my eyes. Through the blur, I saw Anna coming into the room, dressed not for a party but austerely and decently, in navy blue woolen with a white triangular piece of handkerchief coming

329

out of the pocket over her bony hip. She was tall and angular and looked startingly like her brother: thin mouth, dusky skin, narrow aquiline nose, thick black hair cut off at the ears and brushed down in a slanting forelock that shadowed one of her yellow eyes. But there was no charm in her—what was arrestingly somber in him was in her only workaday and sullen. She wished me good evening without grace: her face was stiff with resentment; and, though she could not have been much more than thirty, a permanent frown-mark showed between her straight brows. She waited near the heavy green sofa, with forced forbearance, until I had finished coughing, and then sat down on the edge of it, smoothing her skirt over her knees. "How did you come to look for Arthur here?" she said.

For the first time since I had come into the crowded room, I felt the preposterousness of the whole affair: what the mother had taken for granted in her darting and her skimming, the daughter meant to stand firm in front of and inquire about; and I knew with an exhaustion that was not lessened by the enervating warmth of the whiskey that I would be called upon to explain a number of things I did not understand. "After the concert I called Mr. Lindsay— you know Mr. Lindsay—Arthur's friend, the critic—" I broke off in bafflement because she refused to look at me: she kept staring down at her own thin, clasped hands.

"No," she said flatly, forced into speaking by the silence, "I don't know Mr. Lindsay. I don't know any of Arthur's friends, and neither does Mother. None of them have ever been here, and we're not invited any place where we'd be likely to meet them—Arthur sees to it that his friends and his Slovak family are kept pretty well apart. I'm surprised this Mr. Lindsay knows where we live—I always thought Arthur kept it under cover. I don't think he's exactly proud of this address."

I did not look at her—I watched the mother, who had gone into a corner and was edging a battered white hassock

330

out of it with her foot, pushing it over the grass-green rug into the middle of the room. It seemed to me that it would be useless and cruel to remark on Hansford Lindsay's vagueness about their address; and it occurred to me too that the sister might suspect me of a closer acquaintance with that gentleman than I possessed. "I don't know Mr. Lindsay very well myself. I only met him once—a few weeks ago when he came down to the College to give a lecture. I called him only because he was the one person I knew to call," I said.

"Oh, so you're from his college?" said Mrs. Sanes, who had gotten the hassock where she wanted it, directly in front of and some four feet away from me. "You are not up here then?" She sat down, very erect, on the cracked white leather, with the light of the two fringed lamps converging on her hair and the heavy folds of her skirt trailing around her on the floor. "You are back there in his college? You teach with him there, and that is why he thinks you are calling him long distance on the telephone?"

"Yes, I teach singing."

"Then you came up here to be at his concert? He asked you to come?"

I felt the hard yellow eyes, so much like his, regarding me resentfully at an angle from the corner of the sofa. "No," I said, "he didn't ask me. In fact, I'm perfectly sure he would never have wanted me there. He doesn't know I came, and I don't know how he'll take it when he finds out."

"Well, one thing's sure," said Anna, staring balefully at her clasped hands, "he didn't want *us* around, he made *that* clear enough. He let us know that the first time he ever played in public, and he didn't have to hit us with a ton of bricks, either: neither Mother nor I have ever gone to any of his concerts since. The fact is, we didn't even know that there was going to be a concert this time—I wouldn't have known a thing about it if one of our neighbors here hadn't seen it in the paper and showed it to me."

331

"Look, Anna, why don't you go make some coffee?" said Mrs. Sanes, turning the whole upper part of her body toward her daughter with a lively jerk. "There's plenty time to talk, we don't have to be in such a hurry—"

"The coffee's on the stove, Mother. I put it on before I came in. No, we wouldn't have known a thing about this concert, not if we'd been depending on *him* to tell us anything—"

"Well, in a way you can be thankful you weren't there," I said. "It was a terrible thing to see—"

"So? You see, Anna, I told you it was no good. I told you it was worse than before even," said Mrs. Sanes.

If I expected the announcement of his failure to have a softening influence on his sister, I was mistaken. She brought up her angular shoulders in an ugly shrug and continued to stare at her hands. "I thought so," she said in a voice that was the more merciless because it was quieter. "I thought it was all up with him when he walked in here instead of going where he usually goes. I figured the big party must have been called off tonight."

"He broke down completely—just went to pieces in front of everybody," I said.

She did not answer. Her thin lips contracted at the corners, and I could not tell whether what she was suppressing was a wince or a malicious smile.

"I came here because I was afraid for him. It was so awful I thought—I thought he might do violence to himself."

The mother clapped her hand against her cheek and heaved up a heavy sigh, but the daughter did not move. "Oh, if he was going to do that, he would have done it long ago. It's happened to him before," she said.

"I doubt it, Miss Sanes. I don't think it could ever have been as bad as it was this time, or he wouldn't have tried it again. He broke off in the middle of the Schumann—he

332

couldn't finish—he just got up from the piano and walked off the stage."

"Oh, God, if you think of it!" said the mother. "In front of all those people! Oh, it is such a terrible thing!"

"Well, I don't know why he has to turn up here when he's in trouble," said Anna in a louder voice, tremulous and husky. "Why doesn't he go to his friends?" It was obvious that she was trying to talk down a sudden and almost uncontrollable surge of sympathy. "When he lived up here, weeks would go by without as much as a telephone call, and after he left there was nothing—not a letter, not a postcard. We didn't even know he was in town over Thanksgiving until he dropped in one afternoon, and then he only stayed a couple of hours—by the time I got back from work he was ready to leave—he had better places to go, I guess. And then tonight he just walks in, holding his head and looking like something out of a graveyard, so that a person can't even talk to him—he just walks in and goes to bed. Don't shush me, Mother—that's as much as we see of him, and Miss Hartmann might just as well know it. The only time he turns up around here is when he's ashamed to show his face in front of anybody else."

Mrs. Sanes spread her hands and raised her face as if she were appealing to some remote seat of justice. "Is it nice that you should be mad at him because he comes to his own home when he has trouble?" she said.

"Do I have to be nice to him? I don't remember that he was ever very nice to me."

"But maybe he will be different now. Maybe he is finished with all those people—"

"Maybe they're finished with him—that's more likely, if you ask me."

"It amounts to the same thing one way or the other," I said. "I don't know what he'll do—I don't even know whether he'll want to go back to the College after what's

333

happened. But one thing I'm sure of: I can't imagine him ever trying to give a recital again."

"It's about time," said Anna hoarsely. "The best part of his life he's thrown away on that—and look what it's come to! If you only knew, Miss Hartmann—"

"Ah!" said the mother, slapping herself on the cheek again, "poor Miss Hartmann, she is still sitting here with her coat on! Take off the coat—with the whiskey, it will make you sick from the heat."

I had quite forgotten that I was still wearing it, and I struggled out of it awkwardly, afraid to stand up, and bunched it down between me and the back of the chair.

"If you only knew, Miss Hartmann," said Anna, "how *he's* lived and how *we've* lived, if you knew the way he's never settled down to a decent job and spent every cent he's laid his hands on here and got himself into debt with people—"

"All right, now, Anna, this is enough. Go get the coffee. Also, go into the room now and say to him that Miss Hartmann is here—I think he will want to know—"

She got off the sofa and drew herself up to all her angular height, glaring at her mother, with the dark forelock shadowing her eye. "I'll get the coffee, but I'll be damned if I'm going to tell him anything," she said. "The last time I was in there, he told me to get out and let him alone. All right, I'm letting him alone, he can lie around like that till next Christmas, for all I care." And she darted between me and her mother and disappeared into some dark passageway that led to the back of the place.

Now that she was gone, and in a direction that must have brought her close to the room where *he* was lying, I had an acute and sudden realization of his presence there in the apartment, of the fact that he was somewhere within a few steps of me, awake and suffering or asleep after the exhaustion of his struggle, his bent arm laid across his shamed face. Something in my own face must have conveyed my thoughts to the little woman who sat in front of me on the hassock: she bent forward and spoke to me in a voice so light and low that it frequently dropped to a whisper; and her eyes, faded but still keen with perception, fixed themselves on mine. "In a minute *I* will go in there and tell him you are here," she said, "but first I must say something to you—it is about my daughter. She is not a mean girl, you must not think she is mean like she makes herself out. She is angry with him, yes, but she does not hate him. She would not be angry with him, not like that, if she did not love him so much. It is my fault—if there are two children, between both of them it should be divided equal, and in our family this was not so. Everything was for him—he had the big teachers, he went to the Conservatory, he went to Europe. And her—she gets a job right away when she is out of high school, and all day she sits with a typewriter in an office, and this is hard, this is not a good life, not for a woman, as I am sure you will know. She is thirty-two, my Anna, and twice now she wanted to get married and could not do it—her friends are not rich like his friends, maybe they can keep her, but they cannot keep her mother. And me—what can I do, what am I good for? A little cooking, a little baking, a little cleaning—this is all I can do because I have this heart. So she does not get married, she keeps on working on account of me, and I cannot help her with the money, I cannot get a job that is any good. And she is mad at him because he wears fancy clothes and lives in fancy places and runs around with such rich people—she does not understand that he has to do this if he plays in concerts. She is mad because he does not write to her or come to see her or send her even a little bit of money—and how can you blame her? Her life is sad, and she is not very pretty anymore. I tell you this, Miss Hartmann, because I do not want you should think she is a mean girl, without any feelings. She is only sad and all worn out, and all her life she has been very good

335

to me. And now I will go and tell him you are sitting in the parlor." She got up from the hassock in one brisk movement. "I think he will want to know you are here."

"No, don't—please don't do it, Mrs. Sanes," I said, terrified at what I had taken for granted only a few minutes ago. All the rage and hopelessness of my last real encounter with him came back upon me; I remembered what things I had said to him that night in the empty building, and I knew that I was the last person on earth he would want to see in his disgrace.

"No?" she said, coming a few steps closer and peering at me.

"No—don't disturb him—I think I'll go now and try to get a train back home."

"In the middle of the night?"

"It doesn't matter. I just wanted to know whether he was all right, and now I know, and I might as well go back. In the morning you can tell him I was here, if you want to. Only, now I think it would be better for me to go."

"But you are his friend! You are a very good friend to him—I know because you came a long way to hear his concert, and you came to us to be sure he didn't do something to himself. Then why should you go?"

"Because I doubt that Arthur would want to see me. We had a quarrel—we never really knew each other very well, and then we had a quarrel—we—"

She came closer still and moved a little to the left, as if by blocking my way to my purse and overnight bag on the table behind her she could hold me there. Her face, grave until now, suddenly broke into a network of merry wrinkles. Her lips parted and displayed the gap, and her eyes narrowed with a witching kind of knowingness. "So he had a fight with you—yes? You were friends, and then he had a fight with you? Forget it. I tell you it is nothing. He will be sorry. Maybe he is already sorry in his heart."

There was a clink of dishes in the dark passageway,

336

and she let herself back down onto the hassock, actually winking at me and laying her forefinger across her lips. When her daughter entered with the tray, she was sitting exactly as she had been sitting earlier, with the light of the lamps converging on her faded hair and the outline of her meager arms showing through the thin tan cloth.

But I was not as I had been before the coffee had been poured into the old cups with their Czechoslovakian patterns of yellow scrolls and crowing roosters. I was weaker: my hand trembled as I took my cup of coffee from the young woman's thin dark fingers—the trustful openness of his mother, the bare bones of sorrow and anger she had revealed to me in her story, my sudden fright and her eerie assumption of something I could not let myself believe had all left me so shaken that I could not enjoy the warmth of the coffee, could not smile convincingly, could not even keep back my tears. Possibly his sister had seen that my eyes were blurred when she had leaned over me with the cream and sugar; when she took her old place on the sofa and turned her body toward me, there was less resentment in her face, and when she spoke to me it was at least without hostility. "One thing I've been wondering," she said. "What's going to become of him after this? How about his job at the College? Do you think they'll take him back, I mean."

"Oh, they wouldn't *fire* him, he's got a contract," I assured her with an incongruous little laugh. "They'll take him back, all right—but will he want to come?"

"I don't see that he's got any choice," his sister said.

"But it's going to be awfully hard for him, after what happened. It would have been bad enough if he hadn't acted from the beginning as if the school wasn't good enough for him and he was doing us a favor to teach in it. The way it is, he'll have to face a lot of enemies. Our faculty's pretty much like any other faculty, Miss Sanes—we're good teachers, but there's nobody there that's really outstanding

337

—and he went out of his way sometimes to show us he was used to better things."

"I can imagine."

His mother, having drained her cup to the bottom in four or five avid draughts, set it down on the carpet, got up restlessly, and began to trot around the room. "Maybe," she said somewhere behind me, "*you* could fix up these things for him, Miss Hartmann. We would be very sorry if he loses this job. A hundred times we said, Anna and me, for him this job is the best thing in the world."

"Maybe Miss Hartmann doesn't feel like fixing it up for him," said Anna, coming toward me with the aluminum coffee pot. As she held the spout over my cup she looked at me briefly from under the slanting black forelock; she looked at me with something of the directness of a fellow-sufferer, and I managed to smile. "Maybe he hasn't made *her* life exactly easy, either, Mother." She put the pot on the table beside my purse and bag and sat down again, avoiding further contact with my look, staring sternly at the wall.

"I don't think anybody would *say* anything to him about his recital," I said. "But some people won't be sorry, and that'll be hard for him to put up with, considering his pride."

"He'll just have to put his pride in his pocket and—"

She broke off, startled, because the quick step had come up close behind me and the small brittle fingers grasped my wrist and held it in the air. "You see?" she said in the high, light voice, witching and triumphant. "She has his onyx! He gave it to her! He had it made into a bracelet!"

"Mother, for heaven's sake—" said Anna.

"He did, he did! Didn't he, Miss Hartmann?"

"Yes, but—"

"Ach!" It was a strange and comical sound, a vocal shrug. "Now you will be telling me he has spoiled it, he had a fight with you or something. Him—he always tries

338

to spoil it, he has these fights with everybody. But if he gave you his onyx, with you he will make up—you wait, you will see!"

Her daughter recovered her poise quickly: I knew by the strained calm with which she went back to the original subject that she was used to these wild and whimsical sallies of her mother's, had probably learned over a period of years that the less attention she paid to them, the less they were likely to be remembered by anybody else. "If he isn't going to be a concert artist, what's he going to do with the rest of his life? Is all of it wasted—all that time, all that money?" she said.

I found it hard to answer because I was assailed by a hysterical need to laugh: I had suddenly remembered the taxi driver's story about the fifty-thousand dollar dog that was traded in for two twenty-five-thousand-dollar cats, and it struck me that Arthur had been dealing most of his life in just that sort of moral and financial wizardry. "It isn't all wasted—you mustn't think that," I said, downing my tendency to laugh with what was left of my second cup of coffee. "He can always use what he's learned in his teaching —he'd be an excellent teacher if he didn't despise what he was doing. His students say—" I broke off, remembering the talk in Vincent's car and wondering why it should seem to me that we had driven past the lighted cities of New Jersey weeks ago.

"He'd make a better living teaching than *I'll* ever make in an office—"

"He'd make a decent living teaching—not much more. I've taught for seven years, and my mother was with me until she died last spring—"

"God rest her soul!" said the light, high voice behind me.

"And there was just enough for her and me—I couldn't save a cent," I said.

Anna set down her coffee cup, wiped her thin lips

339

with her paper napkin, and turned with a kind of tentative resumption of hostility in my direction. "Of course, I don't know why I should give a damn what becomes of him or what he does with himself," she said. "Any money he makes has always been his—that's understood—we never see a penny of it around here. Suppose he *does* settle down— what do you think'll come of that? He'll probably get married—" her yellow look darted automatically toward my onyx bracelet, and she flushed—"he'll probably marry somebody down there, and it'll be the same old business— all of it'll still be on *my* back, no matter how he works it out."

"Wouldn't that depend on the sort of woman he married?"

"How do you mean?"

"Don't you think there are some women who might not agree to his washing his hands of it?"

She got up and brushed the wrinkles out of the front of her skirt. "I don't know," she said. "Maybe so."

In the silence that settled on the three of us while she collected the coffee cups and put them back on the tray, I allowed myself the irresponsible indulgence of adding the probable figure of his salary to the established figure of mine. A decent apartment with a second bedroom—a person ought to be able to get that for less than half of what either of us made; a working couple could make good use of a little cleaning, a little cooking, a little baking; there would have to be a maid, maybe twice a week, to look after the heavier things—nobody would want her to lift or scrub, not with that sort of heart . . . And, having fallen into such forbidden dreaming, I let myself enjoy it—I was too tired to extricate myself. My head dropped back against the chair, and my eyelids came down between my sight and the two fringed lamps and the bulbous furniture, and I did not know whether I was asleep or only allowing them to think I was asleep. . . .

340

"Miss Hartmann—"

"Yes, Miss Sanes?" I started out of a vague situation in which I was buying cloth for curtains, and saw that she was standing, with the loaded tray in her hands, at the entrance to the passageway.

"I thought maybe I'd tell Arthur you were here, if you wanted me to."

"That's kind of you. I guess there wouldn't be any harm in it. If he didn't want to see me, I suppose he'd tell you so."

"Provided," she said, "that he's speaking to me." And she disappeared into the dark hall with her clinking burden, followed by her mother, who said, "Excuse me, please," and trotted out behind her with the coffee pot.

Now that I was alone, with the instant of rejection or acceptance at hand, I was wide awake again, too wide awake to permit myself the luxury of any further speculation. I had dreamed—in spite of the hard actuality of the bracelet on my arm, I had simply dreamed; but if nobody except these two women ever knew what I had dreamed about, it would make no difference. If he came furious out of his room—I was too weary to be afraid of him—or if he refused to come and dismissed me by proxy, I would not blush in front of them, since I knew that they would wish it to be otherwise. A kind of dull quietness was on me now, and I did not try too hard to hear what was being said in the passageway or later and farther away between the mother and daughter in the kitchen. Delay is never a good sign; and this delay, broken by their unintelligible words, was long; and I was not surprised when Anna came back, her mouth wry and her shoulders up again in the ugly shrug. "Well, I told him—for anything it's worth," she said.

"Does he want me to go?" I reached back for my coat, and thought stupidly that I would never get the wrinkles out of it.

"Honest to God, Miss Hartmann, I don't know *what* he

341

wants. He was awake—I know he was—and I know he heard me. But he didn't say a word, he just turned over on his face."

"Then I guess I'd better—"

"We wouldn't think of letting you walk out of here at this time of the night, Miss Hartmann. He's in my bed, and Mother and I can sleep in Mother's, and we'll make something up for you here on the sofa, if you don't mind—"

"No, honestly, thanks just the same, but I think I'd better—" I broke off suddenly, because a forgotten obligation thrust itself into the black emptiness of my spirit. "I'd better go—I wouldn't want him to find me here in the morning— but before I go, I wonder if I could use your telephone. I forgot all about poor Mr. Lindsay—he was worried to death about Arthur, and I promised to call him the first thing, if I got any news."

"Certainly. Go ahead. It's right out there in the hall."

She switched on the light for me, and I walked, stiff with weariness and with my long, strained sitting, down the bleak hallway to the little round table at the end of it, where the telephone stood. In getting to that table, I passed two doors, one of them closed and the other open a handsbreadth. Beyond it I saw, and tried not to see, his form stretched out, face down, on the bed. I do not think I paused as I passed him: if he did not want me, he did not want me, and to linger in futile hope was only to give him still more pain and to compromise whatever was left of my shabby pride. I did not have to look for Hansford Lindsay's telephone number again: it would probably always be in my mind, burnt into it like a brand.

The phone rang only once before he answered. He must have been sitting there, the poor devil, waiting for it to ring for the last couple of hours—I saw him in my mind's eye, perched on some kind of high stool like the one in Arthur's kitchen, probably wearing a scarlet vest. His "Hello" was scarcely audible—he sounded old, old and shaken. "Hansford, this is Frieda. Arthur's all right," I said.

"Are you sure? Have you seen him?"

"I haven't seen him, but I'm perfectly sure. I'm here now with his family. He's pretty shaken up, and he's gone to bed, but he's all right. I'm leaving here now—I'm sorry it took me so long to call you, I'm sorry it's so late, but I knew you'd want to know."

"God bless you, Frieda."

"He's here with his family on 163rd Street. If I were you, I'd call him some time around noon tomorrow. I'm just going—"

I stopped because somebody was standing behind me. I was sure his mother had come out to comfort me, and I had a crazy conviction that my own mother had sent her, that—since she had said "God rest her soul!"—my mother had asked her to come and give me a little pity, a little indulgence, had somehow communicated with her out of the grave. "Good night, Hansford. I've got to go. I'm phoning here close to his room, and I don't want to wake him up. Take care of yourself. Good-bye," I said.

I hung up the receiver and turned around. But it was not his mother—it was he. He stood—silent, supplicating—with his arms held out, strange in the dark trousers and the stiff white shirt crumpled and still drenched with the sweat of his suffering. Tears stood in his eyes, and his mouth trembled. He caught me and held me and drew me forever into the compass of his pleasure and his pain—he destroyed and renewed me with his hard and shaking kiss. And when his mother called to me from the kitchen, it was he who answered—I did not have the strength to answer. "She's coming, I'm coming with her, we'll both come in a minute," he said, scarcely lifting his mouth from mine. That was as much as he ever said in testimony of our oneness either before or after our marriage, but it was enough.

343